Nina Singh lives just o... husband, children, and a very ... After several years in the corporate world she finally followed the advice of family and friends to 'give the writing a go, already'. She's oh-so-happy she did. When not at her keyboard she likes to spend time on the tennis court or golf course. Or immersed in a good read.

Maureen Child is the author of more than one hundred and thirty romance novels and novellas that routinely appear on bestseller lists and have won numerous awards, including the National Reader's Choice Award. A seven-time nominee for the prestigious *RITA®* award from Romance Writers of America, one of her books was made into a CBS-TV movie called *The Soul Collecter*. Maureen recently moved from California to the mountains of Utah and is trying to get used to snow.

A former job-hopper, **Jessica Lemmon** resides in Ohio with her husband and rescue dog. When she's not writing super-sexy heroes, she can be found cooking, drawing, drinking coffee (okay, wine), and eating crisps. She firmly believes God gifts us with talents for a purpose, and with His help, you can create the life you want. Learn more about her books at jessicalemmon.com

About the Authors

A Christmas
Affair

NINA SINGH

MAUREEN CHILD

JESSICA LEMMON

MILLS & BOON

First Published in Great Britain 2022
By Mills & Boon, an imprint of HarperCollins*Publishers*
1 London Bridge Street, London, SE1 9GF

www.harpercollins.co.uk

HarperCollins*Publishers*
1st Floor, Watermarque Building,
Ringsend Road, Dublin 4, Ireland

A CHRISTMAS AFFAIR © 2022 Harlequin Enterprises ULC

Their Festive Island Escape © 2019 Nilay Nina Singh
Temptation at Christmas © 2020 Maureen Child
A Christmas Proposition © 2018 Jessica Lemmon

ISBN: 978-0-263-31783-1

MIX
Paper | Supporting
responsible forestry
FSC™ C007454

This book is produced from independently certified FSC™ paper
to ensure responsible forest management.

For more information visit: www.harpercollins.co.uk/green

Printed and Bound in Spain using 100% Renewable electricity at
CPI Black Print, Barcelona

THEIR FESTIVE
ISLAND ESCAPE

NINA SINGH

To my children,

you make every vacation and holiday
nothing less than a gift.

CHAPTER ONE

HER SISTER JUST didn't get it. But then again, Celeste had never really been able to get through to her when it came to the holidays. Or through to her mother, for that matter. Her family would never understand. Not that she really understood them in return.

"I can't believe you haven't moved on yet," Tara declared, throwing her hands up in the air. "Your wedding was three years ago. Get over it already."

Tara wasn't often accused of being overly sensitive. For the wedding her sister had so callously just referred to had never actually happened. Celeste bit down on a frustrated groan. She really was in no mood to talk about this. She didn't even want to think about the day she'd been so humiliatingly left at the altar, waiting for a groom who had never bothered to show up.

The humiliation still haunted her nightmares—dozens of pitying eyes staring at her as the minutes ticked by.

She was supposed to have been a Christmas bride. Instead she'd been a jilted one.

How did Tara not understand that she wanted nothing to do with the holiday now? How did she not see that the best thing to do for her mental health was just to get away from the city until the whole season was over?

Her sister's next question only proved that she didn't understand Celeste at all.

"How can you leave your family and just take off to the islands every year? Christmas just isn't the same without you here."

Celeste couldn't help the pang of guilt that landed in her gut. Perhaps one day she'd be able to put all of it behind her. Maybe she'd even enjoy the holidays again at some future point in time. She just wasn't there yet. Nowhere near, in fact. Every street decoration, every holiday jingle, every sidewalk corner Santa only reminded her of Jack and the days leading up to her abject humiliation.

Not to mention, her sister's seeming disappointment held a secondary layer. On the surface, Tara sounded like a caring, loving sibling who just wanted to spend the holidays with her older sister. But there was more to it than that. At the age of twenty-six, Tara was much too dependent on her older sister financially. And so was their mother, for that matter.

Celeste knew she should have curbed that dependence long before. Especially given all that it had cost her three years ago. But her sense of duty and responsibility as the only financially stable member of her family often overrode her good sense. Something had broken in her mother when their father had abandoned them over a decade ago, leaving nothing behind but his debts. Wendy had never fully recovered. And Tara had taken it just as hard. It had been left to Celeste as the older sibling to try to pick up the pieces.

She was still doing so. By now it was second nature. Which wasn't exactly a sound reason to keep doing it, but she couldn't exactly turn her back on either of them. Especially considering Tara was a mother herself now. Besides, wasn't one of the reasons Celeste had worked so hard to be able to help out her always cash-strapped family members?

"I thought for sure you'd stay around this year, sis." Tara's voice was petulant and whiny.

"Why would you think that?"

"Because your usual resort is nothing but a pile of damaged debris."

She spoke the truth. The last hurricane season had nearly destroyed the island that housed Celeste's yearly destination spot. After her devastating non-wedding, Celeste had chosen to continue on and attend her already-paid-for Caribbean honeymoon on a luxe tropical resort. She'd been going back to the same location every December since. This year, that island was sadly not an option.

Celeste had been heartbroken thinking of the usual staff and how they'd lost their livelihoods. She'd been regularly donating to various charities in charge of rebuilding, wished she could do more. In the meantime, she'd had to choose an unfamiliar resort on a different island. Apparently, her family had been counting on her canceling the trip altogether.

Never mind that she'd called weeks ago to tell both her sister and her mother of her exact plans.

Honestly, it was as if they didn't know her at all.

It would take more than a natural disaster to keep her in Manhattan over the holidays. She wanted nothing to do with Christmas, would skip the entire month of December if she possibly could. The non-stop carols, the sparkling decorations all over the city, the hustling and bustling crowds within a mile of any shopping center. It all overwhelmed and irritated her to no end. Even the usually quiet and cozy café they sat in was now a crowded mess of harried shoppers carrying all manner of bags and parcels.

And none of that even had anything to do with the bad memories of her broken engagement. That only added a whole other layer of distaste.

Bah humbug and all that.

Across the square wooden table, Tara's lower lip actually did a little quiver. For the briefest moment, Celeste couldn't help but feel touched. Tara had her faults, but Celeste knew deep down that her little sister really did miss her over the holidays. Tara just wasn't one to show much emotion. No wonder, given the way they'd had to grow up. Though that quality had seemed to be slowly softening since she'd become a mother.

"I was hoping we could go in on Mom's gift together," Tara continued. "You know, split the cost." She glanced downward toward the floor. "Money's a little tight for me right now, and you just got that promotion…"

The usual hint of guilt tugged within her chest.

Celeste wasn't going to bother to point out that "going in together" most often meant she would be footing the whole cost of their mother's gift and the holiday dinner. But what was there to do? The truth was, Celeste really was much better off than her sister. As was usually the case. Still, it was a fact that couldn't exactly be ignored.

Besides, Celeste didn't have it in her to discuss it much further. She had to get home and start packing. She reached for her purse and pulled out her checkbook, started scribbling after deciding on an amount, then handed it to her only sibling.

"Here, this should cover the cost of Mom's gift and a nice dinner out for the two of you. As well as a little extra so that you can pick up something for yourself," she added, despite the fact that she'd already handed Tara the holiday gift she'd purchased for her as soon as they'd sat down—a pair of fourteen-karat gold teardrop earrings she'd meticulously wrapped herself in bright, colorful paper and ribbons. Looked like Tara's guilt trip about her leaving to go on holiday was indeed working.

Tara's lips quivered ever so slightly and her eyes grew shiny as she reached for the check. "Thanks, sis. I'm going to find a way to pay you back one of these days. Once I figure out how to get on my own two feet."

Celeste gave her hand a squeeze. "I know you will," she reassured, despite her own doubt.

Tara smiled. "Hope you have a good trip. See you when you get back."

Even under the bulky, stuffed red flannel suit, it was clear the man who wore it was no regular Santa. No, this man was definitely not old, rotund or particularly jolly. Though Celeste could tell he was trying hard to fit the part. Couldn't the resort have found a better-fitting actor to play the role? Even from this distance where she sat on her lounge chair, she could tell Santa was tall and fit. His piercing dark eyes held no jolly old twinkle, though they did seem to catch the sunlight as he shifted his gaze from one child to the next as he handed out presents from his burly, oversize sack. An odd sensation of déjà vu nagged at her. Something about the pretend Santa seemed oddly familiar. Probably just her imagination.

The kids didn't seem to notice how ill-suited he was for the role, they were all laughing loudly and scurrying to open the gifts they'd just been handed.

Celeste flipped the page of the paperback she'd picked up at the airport and returned her attention to the story. Or she tried to, anyway. The kids were pretty noisy. The scene before her was charming and sweet—Santa sent to the beach to entertain and bestow gifts upon the youngest guests. It reminded her of everything she'd once so foolishly longed for. Exactly the kind of scene she was trying to get away from when she jetted out to the Caribbean every December. She was here for warm and tropical. Not stark reminders of all she'd lost three years ago when the man she'd loved, the man she'd dreamed of having children with like the ones currently in front of her, had so callously deserted her at the worst possible moment.

This resort was definitely geared more toward families than the one she was used to. She might have to find a more remote section of beach in order to avoid such scenes for the rest of her stay. Her heart couldn't take it.

A shadow suddenly fell over the pages of her book.

"Ho-ho-ho."

Santa appeared to be strolling the beach closer and closer to where she sat, the children following close behind him. Now they all stood just a couple of feet from her chair. She watched as St. Nicholas leaned down to tousle the hair of one particularly excited young boy who'd clearly just received some type of toy car based on the wrapped shape.

It was futile. There was no way to even try to concentrate on her romantic suspense novel now. As charming as the children were, and they really were adorable, she couldn't take much more Christmas cheer. Glancing down the expanse of sand, she searched in vain for another empty beach chair farther away from this main part of the resort. They all appeared taken. With a resigned sigh, Celeste dropped the book and stood, wrapping her silky sarong around her midsection. Might as well get another cup of coffee or perhaps a latte until all the commotion quieted.

A squealing toddler darted past her to get to the faux Santa and she nearly toppled over in her effort to avoid the collision. This was so far from the relaxing morning she'd envisioned. Not that the kids weren't cute. They really were, with all their excitement and near tangible anticipation to receive a present. They were just so... loud. Loud, boisterous reminders of all she'd be missing out on in life. Look at how her one attempt to start a family had turned out; nothing more than an abject lesson in humiliation and hurt.

No, she wouldn't be having children. Or her own family. The one she'd been born into took up more than enough of her time and emotional energy.

She leaned down to retrieve her flip-flops from beneath the lounge chair and stopped short when she straightened. A wall of bright red topped by a cotton white beard suddenly filled her view.

"Ho-ho-ho. Well, hello there, young lady." Santa smiled at her.

"Um...hi."

"We appear to have disturbed your morning, miss. A big jolly apology for the nuisance."

His words were cordial enough. But Celeste had the clear impression that he was somehow mocking her.

"No apology necessary, St. Nick," she said with a slight salute, then tried to step around him, only to have him block her path. Of all the nerve.

The smile grew wider under the thick fake beard. "Really? I mean, you practically have a circular thought bubble above your head that screams 'bah humbug.'"

The same strange sensation of familiarity nagged at her yet again. He was clearly deepening his voice for the role but something about the tone and inflection rang a bell. And the eyes. As she studied their golden depths she couldn't help but sense that she'd somehow gazed upon those eyes before.

Had she met him before in a professional capacity?

Her position as VP of marketing for a luxury goods firm had her regularly working on advertising campaigns with various agencies. Maybe Santa had done work previously as a character actor for a project she'd worked on in the past.

What were the chances?

Not that it mattered. Right now all that mattered was that she find some peace and quiet.

But St. Nick seemed to have other plans.

"Excuse me."

Reid knew he should have stepped away the first time she'd said it. But he couldn't seem to help himself. He'd recognized her immediately. She clearly didn't remember Reid in return. He wondered if her cutting look of utter disdain would change at all if she did recall who he was. No doubt it would intensify. They hadn't exactly been on the best of terms the last time they'd seen each other.

Well, the feeling was mutual.

The children scattered all at once, clearly bored with the conversation the adults were having above their heads.

"I didn't realize they'd hired someone to play the part of Scrooge this morning," he goaded her, not even sure why he was doing so. There really was no reason to try to get a rise out of her. Other than for his pure entertainment.

She sucked in a breath. "I'm sorry. I somehow missed the part where my holiday spirit was any of your business."

He shrugged. "We just aim to please every guest, is all."

She folded her arms across her chest. "And this is how you go about doing so? Aren't you overstepping your

responsibility just a bit? You're here simply to hand out
some presents to the children." She pointed to the empty
fleece sack he held. "Clearly your task is over."

Wow, she really was something else. She may as well
have flicked him away like a royal princess dismissing
a lowly jester. Not that he didn't look the part in this ridiculous suit.

"Furthermore, I fail to see how my satisfaction is the
responsibility of the resort Santa." She studied him up
and down. Clearly, he came up lacking in her summa-
tion. He should have walked away long before. Or never
approached her in the first place. Life was too short to
deal with the likes of Miss Frajedi. He had too much on
his plate trying to get this place in order.

Still, Reid found himself studying her closely. The past
three years had been extremely kind to her, she was still
strikingly attractive. Dark, wavy hair framed a strong
face with high cheekbones and hazel eyes the color of a
Caribbean sunset. No wonder Jack had fallen for her so
hard, the poor man. Luckily, he'd come to his senses in
time. Though Reid had never approved of the way his
friend had ultimately ended things. So last-minute. So
hurtful. It was never right to leave a lady at the altar. Not
even one like Celeste Frajedi. He'd made sure to share
that sentiment with his friend, resulting in a now strained
relationship between the men.

Her eyes suddenly narrowed on his face. "Do I know
you?" she demanded.

Reid hesitated. For the briefest moment, he debated
telling her exactly who he was. The look on her face when
she found out would be a sight to see.

Ultimately, he decided against it. What would be the
point? She was a paying guest after all. She was entitled
to the tropical vacation she had paid for. The resort was

large and expansive. The beach alone covered over a mile. If he played his cards right, they would never have to run into each other again for the duration of her stay. In fact, he vowed to make sure of it.

He shrugged. "Everyone knows me. I'm Santa Claus."

She studied him some more. Part of him wanted her to figure it out. Finally, she blew out a deep breath. "Right. Well, Santa. I'd like to go get a cup of coffee." With that, she brushed against his arm in her haste to get past him. An enticing scent of coconut and sun-kissed skin tickled his nose. Some kind of static electricity shot through his elbow and clear down his side.

"Merry Christmas, princess."

He spoke to her back as she stormed off. Her gait hastened as she walked past the breakfast cabana and instead veered toward the residential suite area. Apparently, she'd lost her appetite for the cup of coffee. That thought sent a tingle of guilt through his center.

Reid rubbed a hand down his face as he watched her walk away. Damn it. What had he just done? He thought about going after her to apologize. Now that he thought about it, he had to admit he'd been less than professional just now. As the newly minted co-owner of the Baja Majestic Resort on the beautiful island of Jamaica, he owed it to all of his guests to treat them well, regardless of any past history. He had no excuse. He'd just been so surprised to see her lying there, the recognition had thrown him off.

But he had to make sure not to slip up like that again. He couldn't forget how important his role was here. No one else was going to get this place up to the standards that the Evanson clientele expected. His father certainly wasn't up to the task. In fact, his father seemed to be doing everything possible to run the family hospitality business into the ground. A gambler through and through, his fraternal parent took way too many chances, risked too many valuables. The cleanup always fell to Reid. This current project being no exception.

He couldn't allow himself to forget how much responsibility he bore. An entire conglomerate of employees, contract workers, and their dependents relied on Evanson Hotels and Resorts for their livelihoods and their future. Not to mention his own parents.

And he'd just gone and insulted a valuable, paying guest.

As much as he hated to admit it, he would have to make up for his behavior. He had to somehow atone for the way he'd just treated Celeste Frajedi.

Merry Christmas, princess.

The derisive words repeatedly echoed through her head as Celeste fled to her deluxe suite and slammed the door behind her. Walking over to the glass screen door leading to the third-floor balcony, she pulled aside the curtains to let the bright sunshine in. He hands were shaking, she realized with no small amount of dismay. He'd rattled her. When was the last time she'd actually felt thrown by a man? Or anyone else, for that matter? Her mother notwithstanding.

Perhaps a better question was why had she let the likes of a pretend Santa Claus in an ill-fitting suit and a side-skewed beard get to her so badly?

There was something about the way he'd looked at her. He clearly hadn't liked what he'd seen. Had her feelings regarding the noisy children been so obvious? She hadn't realized she'd shown any outward signs that she'd been bothered by them but clearly the man had picked up something. He'd called her a scrooge!

Never mind that his labeling of her as such was perilously close to the truth. Still, her attitude to Christmas was none of his business. How dare he treat her the way he had? Her ire and irritation shot up even further as she thought of the derision in his eyes as he'd studied her.

His negative view of her seemed way out of proportion to whatever imagined slight he'd witnessed. It was as if he'd disliked her on sight. Which brought back the question: Why had he seemed so familiar to her?

Celeste shook off the query. The answer hardly mattered. She had no doubt the upper-level management in charge of the resort would be appalled if they knew of the actions of their character actor employee. She was in the very business of appealing to consumers as a professional marketer. The faux Santa's behavior would be considered a nightmare to any business leader. That was no way to treat any customer.

Still, the encounter shouldn't have shaken her up as much as it had. She was a professional, after all. And she'd certainly suffered through worse humiliation. The best thing to do would be to try to just forget about the whole incident and put it completely behind her. She would chalk it up to yet one more instance of a negative holiday memory. As if she needed any more of those.

With a calming inhalation of breath, she sank to the carpeted floor. She would meditate until the whole interaction with the wayward St. Nick was nothing more than a mere ghost of a thought in her head. Relaxing all her muscles, she began to count down from ten. Then she did nothing but clear her mind.

It wasn't easy.

Knock. Knock. Knock.

Celeste had no idea how much time had passed before the annoying knocking roused her out of her deep state of meditative trance. Was it too much to ask for just some calming time after the morning she'd had? Apparently, this day was just going to be one irritation after another.

"Room service," came a soft, feminine voice from the other side of her door.

It took a moment to reorient as Celeste forced herself to stand from her cross-legged sitting position on the floor. Her leg muscles screamed in protest at the abrupt movement as she walked to the door.

"There's been some kind of mistake," she said to the petite uniformed woman standing outside with a cart. "I haven't ordered any room service."

The woman smiled as she shook her head. "This is on the house, madam." Without waiting for acknowledgment, she wheeled the cart toward the center of the room.

"I don't understand?"

The woman's smile didn't falter as she answered. "No charge, madam. Compliments of the resort." She handed her an envelope that had sat in the middle of the tray. With that, she pivoted on her heel and left the room.

Celeste blinked in confusion at the shut door before understanding dawned. Sure enough, when she read the note, her suspicion was confirmed.

Please accept this complimentary gesture as a token of appreciation and regret that you may have been inconvenienced in any way this morning.
Sincerely, The Baja Majestic Resort.

Someone in upper management must have witnessed the unpleasantness between her and Santa earlier this morning. She studied the goodies before her on the food service cart. They'd certainly made an effort to appease her. A silver carafe of steaming hot coffee sat in the center of the tray. A chilled bottle of champagne sent a curl of frost into the air. Orange juice and a variety of pastries rounded out the offerings. Not bad at all as a conciliatory gesture. Someone was trying hard to make things up to her. A foolish part of her felt guilty that perhaps bad Santa might have been chastised harshly by his superiors. Or even worse, that he'd been fired.

He may have been an overbearing clod, but he didn't deserve to have his livelihood jeopardized. She would have to look into that. The desk attendant in the concierge lounge would surely know exactly what had transpired and the ultimate outcome that had led to the enticing cart she'd just had delivered. A visit later this afternoon wouldn't hurt. If he had been let go, it was probably not too late for her to intervene. Not that he deserved her good will. Still, she would be the bigger person if needed.

It was a role she'd been well groomed for her whole life, after all.

CHAPTER TWO

"ONE OF THE guests would like to see you, *mi paadie*."

Reid looked up from the spreadsheet he'd been studying to the man who had just entered his office without knocking. Alex was co-owner of the property and Reid felt grateful every day for that fact. He wasn't sure what he would have done without the other man's intimate knowledge of the island and its customs. Not to mention his sharp head for business.

Though Alex definitely had one flaw: a clear aversion to knocking before entering a closed door. Not that Reid had been doing much in the way of concentrating just now. A set of light hazel eyes and tumbling dark hair had interrupted his thoughts unwanted and unbidden throughout the morning. He wondered if she'd liked the tray of goodies he'd had sent to her room. Would she find it all an adequate apology? Or had she huffed in disgust and pushed the tray aside. He suspected the latter. Not that he could really blame her if she had.

"And hello to you too, Alex," he answered his partner without looking away from the screen he hadn't really been focusing on.

"Did you hear what I said, man?"

He nodded. "It appears I'm being summoned by one of the guests, is that it?"

Alex smiled at him. "You wanted to be hands-on, did you not? She's asking for you specifically."

Wasn't it enough that he'd been commandeered into playing Santa this morning when the actor originally hired to play the part had called in sick? The entertainment manager had run to him in a panic. No one else was available to do it. And the resort had announced the event weeks in advance. In the end it was easier just to don the suit and get the whole fiasco over with.

Only he'd come face-to-face with a woman he hadn't ever expected to see again.

Now he apparently had to go smooth the ruffles of a guest who no doubt felt slighted somehow or was trying to finagle a room upgrade.

"I tried to take care of it myself. Explained to her that I was co-owner of the resort. But like I said, the guest insists on seeing you specifically."

Reid sighed and stood. The guest in question had to be one of those checking in this morning who he'd greeted. Apparently, they'd taken it to heart when he'd said that he'd personally see to any detail regarding their stay that they weren't completely happy with. Though why Alex hadn't just taken care of it by partially crediting the guest or explaining that they were at full capacity and had no upgrade to give out was lost on him.

Again, it was probably best to simply go get it over with. It was just clearly going to be one of those days.

Celeste shook her head and tried to blink away the image she was sure she had to be imagining. But when she opened her eyes again, the unwanted vision stood clear as day in front of her still.

This couldn't be happening. "You're the nasty Santa?"

Her words came out harsher and louder than she'd

intended. Every eye currently in the concierge lounge turned to stare at her. She distinctly heard a giggle of feminine laughter from behind her somewhere.

To his credit, Reid Evanson looked as shocked as she was at the unexpected turn. Suddenly, the events of the morning seemed to make much more sense. She definitely hadn't been imagining the waves of dislike emanating from the man playing jolly ol' St. Nick.

Well, the feeling went both ways.

"What are you doing here?" she demanded.

He thrust his hands into his pockets before answering. "You're the one who asked for me."

He was being deliberately obtuse. Celeste tried to summon some semblance of calm. It didn't help that the gentleman she'd spoken to earlier was shifting his amused gaze from one of them to the other. None of this was the least bit amusing.

"I mean, what are you doing here on this resort?"

"You two know each other?" the other man wanted to know.

"We were acquainted once," Reid answered briefly.

Despite herself, she found herself studying him. He'd aged well. Clean shaven before, he currently sported a close-cropped beard slightly darker than the sandy blond hair on his head. He wore said hair longer, nearly touching his shoulders. Instead of the Santa suit from earlier, he now wore a formfitting T-shirt tucked into pleated khaki pants. It all showed off the physique of a man who clearly took care of himself. Had he always been so muscular?

"Why did you ask for me?" Reid wanted to know.

"I didn't. I asked to see Santa Claus." This time, the person behind her didn't even bother to try to hide her laughter. Heaven help her, she knew how ridiculous she sounded. She had half a mind to let out a giggle herself.

Without another word, he stepped around the long, highly polished counter and gently took her by the elbow.

"Let's discuss all this in my office."

His office? The room he led her to, if it held human emotions, would have no doubt been insulted to be referred to as such. Floor-to-ceiling glass walls overlooked a scenic beach with a majestic view of the crystal-blue ocean into the horizon. Plush carpeting had her feet sinking in her flip-flops. A grand desk with three large monitors sat in the center of it all.

"You run the resort," she commented as he shut the door behind him.

"I own it. Along with my partner, Alex Wiliston. "He was the gentleman you were speaking with earlier."

The pieces started to fall into place. She remembered now that Reid came from a wealthy family of hoteliers. Though the family business had suffered some losses recently, Reid had taken the helm from his father and turned things around. Last she'd heard, Evanson Properties had not only returned to a profitable enterprise, the company had expanded, all thanks to the prodigal son.

"You decided to expand into the resort business, I take it," Celeste said.

Something flickered behind his eyes. He gave a small nod before answering. "The Caribbean specifically."

"I see. But earlier this morning…when I saw you…" Now she was just rambling.

"Just filling in for an employee who couldn't make it at the last minute."

"I see," she repeated uselessly.

Suddenly, it was all too much. Far from fleeing her unpleasant associations with the holiday as it related to her failed relationship, she'd somehow ended up face-to-face with someone who'd played a major role in the whole fiasco.

Reid had been her ex-fiancé's best man. And she knew he'd never thought her good enough for his buddy.

"Can I get you something to drink?" Reid asked, for lack of anything better to say. How exactly did one proceed with this conversation? The scenario was so completely unexpected in so many myriad ways.

She shook her head. "No. Thank you. I just had some coffee and a mimosa to wash down several pastries." She took in a shaky breath. "But I'm guessing you already know that. Seeing as you were probably behind the delivery to my room."

"I was. Did you enjoy them?"

Her eyes grew wide. "Are we really doing this?"

"Doing what?"

"Pretending I'm just another one of your regular guests?"

The feeling of guilt from earlier blossomed once again in Reid's chest. Celeste was indeed his guest. A paying customer. He hadn't meant to come off as boorish as he had out on the beach. But he'd just been so thoroughly disconcerted at seeing her again after all this time. If he was being honest with himself, he'd imagined encountering Celeste Frajedi more than a few times over the years. Not that he'd ever been able to explain to himself exactly why that was so. He had no reason to be thinking of her at all.

"But that's exactly what you are," he answered. "An appreciated guest. Hence, my desire to apologize for my behavior earlier. I hope the gesture served as an adequate apology. I should never have let…our history, so to speak…affect in any way how I treat a guest at my establishment. There's no excuse for my having done so," he added with complete sincerity. He really didn't have any kind of excuse. Not even considering the morning he'd had. On top of the missing Santa and the shock of seeing Celeste again, he'd started the day with another aggravating, infuriating phone call with his father, who was once again trying to take over the company he'd almost single-handedly destroyed.

Celeste looked far from convinced by his words.

"I can assure you such behavior on my part won't happen again," he told her. "In fact, you can forget I'm even here."

The skeptical look she speared him with clearly said he hadn't done much to convince her any further.

You can forget I'm even here.

Hah! As if she could forget his presence for even a moment. What a mistake it had been to come here. Of all the resorts she could have chosen as a substitute for her regular vacation spot, how in the world had she landed on this one? The cruel fates were clearly laughing at her.

Celeste flopped herself down on the wide king bed back in her suite and draped an arm across her face. No, she couldn't so easily forget that Reid Evanson was right here on this very island. Nor could she forget the way he'd made her feel three years ago. As if she could never be enough for the likes of his best friend. Never mind that Jack had turned out to be a reckless, disloyal excuse for a fiancé who had eventually left her stranded at the very altar where they were to have made their vows. Sure, now she realized just how much of a favor he'd done her. Aside from saving her from what could have been years of betrayal and heartbreak, he'd helped her come to a conclusion about herself. She clearly wasn't the type of woman who was meant for a family or a steady relationship. He'd enabled her to avoid the mistake of a lifetime.

A mistake that could have led her straight down the same path her mother had traveled.

But that knowledge hadn't stopped the sting of rejection, nor the burn of embarrassment as she'd faced down a whole church full of wedding guests to tell them that the ceremony had been suddenly called off.

Reid had been there every step of the way. He'd witnessed her humiliation in its entirety. And she'd received the distinct impression that he felt she'd only gotten what she'd deserved.

An incoming message on her phone pulled her out of her thoughts. The screen lit up with the profile picture of her sister smiling as she held her toddler niece. Celeste groaned and debated whether to answer. On the one hand, she felt drained and conversations with her sister could often be one-sided; Tara's side. On the other hand, Celeste could really use someone to talk to right about now.

With no small amount of doubt, she pressed her thumb on the icon to answer.

"Hey, Tara."

"Hey, sis." The sound of a musical children's show could be heard playing loudly in the background.

"What's up?"

"Just calling to see how things are in paradise. Still can't believe you're there and not here." Ah, so this was the routine guilt-trip call. Cynical as it sounded, Celeste couldn't help the thought given past experience.

Celeste sighed deeply as she shifted to a seated position on the edge of the bed. "Well, it just so happens, I'm beginning to doubt my decision to come."

Tara's sudden exhalation came through loud and clear across the tiny speaker. "What's happened? Spill!"

"Let's just say there's someone here I didn't expect to see. Ever."

"Details, please. Is it a man?"

"Yes, as a matter of fact. But that's not the import—"

But Tara cut her off. "Ooh, this is getting interesting. Is it someone you had a previous fling with? Can you have another one? Hot and heavy with no strings attached! You could so use that, you know."

Celeste rubbed a hand across her tense forehead. Honestly, Tara didn't know her in the least. "I don't do flings."

"Well, maybe you should start. Heaven knows your serious relationships don't turn out so great." She grunted a laugh. "They don't turn out at all."

Ouch. So much for a sisterly conversation to make her feel better. Foolish of her to even entertain the notion. Celeste found herself wondering if she should have answered the phone after all.

"So, who is it?" her sister asked after a heavy pause.

"Never mind. It's not important. Forget I brought it up. How's Mom? And little Nat?"

It wasn't often any of them referred to her niece by her full given name, Natalie.

"They're all fine," Tara answered. But she wasn't having it with the attempted change in topic. "And no way you're going to try to drop the matter of this mystery man. Tell me who you ran into. And tell me what he means to you."

Celeste opened her mouth to respond with a resounding and emphatic denial that Reid Evanson meant absolutely anything to her whatsoever. That she'd hardly thought about him over the past three years.

But the lie wouldn't form on her tongue.

CHAPTER THREE

ALEX STILL STOOD in the middle of Reid's office studying him like a lab specimen. "Is there something I can do for you?" Reid finally asked, ultimately losing the game of visual chicken.

"Yeah. Neither you nor the young lady really answered me earlier when I asked if you two knew each other. It appears you do."

Reid pretended to type on his keyboard. "Then you seem to have answered your own question."

"I have more."

Reid gave up all pretense of trying to get any work done. Leaning back in his leather desk chair, he tried to stretch out some of the tension that seemed to have tied a knot in the back of his neck right at the base of his skull. "Somehow, I knew you would."

"I do. One of them being, exactly how do you know our esteemed guest? I couldn't help but notice she's traveling alone."

"So?"

Alex grinned. "So does that fact have anything to do with you?"

"What? No! Of course not." *Not directly, anyway.*

He hadn't realized he'd mumbled the last part under his breath until Alex questioned him.

"What does that mean, Reid? Not directly?"

Alex sighed, the tension in his neck traveling farther down his spine. He might have to hit the spa later for some kind of back treatment massage. Though he'd been meaning to do that for weeks, ever since he'd arrived at the start of the season.

"It's not what you're thinking, partner."

"Then what is it? You two obviously have some kind of history and not all of it is positive.

Reid almost laughed at that. Less than positive would be an understatement.

"Celeste was almost the wife of a friend of mine. Let's just say he hasn't been the same ever since their relationship ended."

Alex nodded slowly. "Oh. So she dumped him."

Reid rubbed his jaw. "Not exactly."

"Then I don't understand."

Reid ran a hand down his face. He hadn't been sleeping well. There was always something that needed to be done, some detail to attend to. He also had his father's ill-formed takeover attempt to contend with. Now he'd been thrown another curveball in the form of Celeste Frajedi and he wasn't sure how to explain to his partner exactly what had gone down three years ago. It hadn't really had anything to do with him. So it was hard to explain why he'd taken it all so personally back then. Even when it came to explaining it to himself.

"Well, on the surface, Jack was the one who actually did the dumping."

His friend gave him a blank look. "On the surface?"

"She wasn't in the relationship for the right reasons. He told me all about it."

Alex raised an eyebrow.

Reid felt a sensation of discomfort meander down his

spine. As if he was betraying a confidence somehow. Though he'd be hard-pressed to identify whose privacy he was uneasy about. Celeste's or Jack's?

"Celeste is a shrewd businesswoman. She's very well known in the industry as one of the most successful marketing executives in New York. The business sites have regular profiles on her. She can be ruthless when she doesn't get what she wants."

"You said your friend hasn't been the same ever since the disastrous wedding that didn't happen."

Reid nodded. "That's right. He's still traipsing all over Europe, partying in different cities. Living with various women." Some of those women being wealthy, married socialites looking for a good time on the side.

"Huh. And he didn't behave like that before he met Celeste?" Alex wanted to know.

The uneasy feeling grew from tingling sensation to an all-out burning down his back as Reid sought for a truthful way to answer. If he was being completely honest, Jack had always had a propensity to be a bit of a partier, something of a Lothario. If anything, his relationship with Celeste had seemed to temper that side of him.

"It's just different. Trust me. I heard all about it before he called off the wedding. Celeste worked long hours, was never around for him. He said he felt single most of the time."

"Sounds like she's just ambitious."

"I agree that's a commendable trait. But for people like her, it's never enough," Reid answered quickly, though the uneasiness was now sitting like a boulder at the base of his spine. Damn it, why hadn't he scheduled that massage? Maybe they could fit him in between clients.

Alex went on, "She also happens to have booked our

most exclusive and pricey deluxe suite for an extended stay. So clearly her ambitions have served her well."

Reid shrugged. "I guess. Again, some people can't seem to have enough." He couldn't even tell anymore if he was talking from personal experience about his father or if he was still referring wholly to Celeste.

"You sound like a man who's only considered one side of a story."

"What's that supposed to mean?"

"You sure you're not confusing cause and effect, partner?"

But his friend didn't give him a chance to answer, just turned and left the office. Apparently, the question was a rhetorical one. Good thing, too. Reid would be hard-pressed to come up with an answer.

Had he been completely unfair in his assessment of Celeste three years ago? Of course, it had occurred to him more than once over the years that he'd only heard one side of the story. But Jack had been his friend since they'd been roommates at university. He was a loyal friend and he'd come through for Reid more than a few times over the years. Reid's father's recklessness and wandering eye had started right around that time, too.

Jack had genuinely seemed shaken when he'd confided in Reid as his nuptials had fast approached. He'd talked about how cold and critical Celeste had suddenly gotten when a couple of Jack's business ventures hadn't panned out. How demanding she'd been that he get back on his feet in all haste.

Reid slammed his laptop shut in frustration.

What did any of it matter now anyhow? It was all past history. Jack had moved on, even if some of his current behavior bordered on self-destructive. He was a grown-up who could make his own choices. Even if everything

Jack had told him about her was the absolute truth, Celeste couldn't be faulted for her ex-groom's behavior three years after the fact.

That thought had him feeling like a heel again for the way he'd behaved earlier when he'd first seen her. And also for the assumptions he'd made about her judging him.

In all fairness, Reid had been nothing less than judgmental himself.

Bouncy reggae music greeted her as Celeste made her way down the beach to the seaside cabana she planned to visit for her first dinner here. Her paperback tucked under her arm, she was looking forward to a relaxing evening with a nice glass of wine and a tasty meal of local seafood. Her morning plans had gone woefully astray. The least she deserved right now was a satisfying meal followed by a peaceful stroll on the beach. Then she'd spend the rest of the evening tucked in under her bedcovers, enjoying some further reading. To most women her age, such plans might sound boring and flat. To her, it all sounded like heaven. Exactly what she was looking for during her evening hours on this vacation.

Her step faltered as she approached the cabana. It was already packed and hopping. Every table appeared full. She approached the hostess manning the front entrance.

"Hi, it's just me. Table for one please."

The young lady gave her a sympathetic look before motioning toward the bar area where couples sat sharing various appetizers. Several bartenders stepped around each other mixing drinks and taking orders.

"I'm afraid all we have available right now is bar seating, miss. And those spots are going fast."

Celeste released a sigh of disappointment and made

her way to one of the few open bar stools. Squeezing herself in between a burly older man in a Hawaiian shirt and a bikinied brunette, she reached for the drinks menu.

One of the bartenders appeared in front of her within moments. His gold name tag said Phillipe in black lettering. "What can I get for the lovely lady?" He asked her with a wide grin. "And I do mean lovely."

Celeste tried to smile back. He wasn't doing any harm but she really wasn't in any kind of mood for a flirtation. And she had no doubt the young man was flirting. The way he was looking at her left no question about it.

She almost wanted to tell him his efforts were hardly necessary. She always tipped well and if this was sympathy flirting simply because she was sitting at a bar alone in a popular resort, she had no need for it. She placed her order for a glass of sparkling wine and a plate of fish tacos without acknowledging the compliment.

She'd gotten through several pages of her book before her meal arrived.

Phillipe winked at her as he placed the plate in front of her on the bar.

Maybe she should have ordered room service. Now she would have to spend the entire time eating trying to avoid his gaze. And a quick cursory glance in his direction confirmed he was indeed staring at her. Oh, yeah, she couldn't wait to submit an online review about this place after her stay. She'd normally go straight to the owner with her complaints, but he'd been a part of the problem.

Phillipe appeared as soon as she'd taken her last bite. "So, I have a break coming up in a couple of hours. Can I treat you to another drink then?"

She didn't get a chance to answer as a thick baritone

voice suddenly sounded from behind her. "Miss Frajedi, I hope you enjoyed your meal."

She didn't need to turn around, recognized the voice immediately as belonging to Reid. Unlike earlier, he wasn't speaking in the low husky voice of a makeshift Santa.

Phillipe immediately took a step back. "Oh. Hey, boss."

Celeste darted a glance over her shoulder. Reid stood only an inch behind her. Arms crossed in front of his chest, his chin tight. He didn't look happy. He merely nodded in a curt acknowledgment of Phillipe's greeting.

Then, to her surprise, he held her hand out to help her up off her stool.

"I haven't settled my bill," she protested.

Reid didn't take his eyes off Phillipe when he answered. "It's on the house."

"Yes, boss," Phillipe immediately responded. She could have sworn he clicked his heels behind the bar.

For lack of anything else to do, Celeste wiped her mouth with her cloth napkin and took Reid's hand before standing. He gently led her away from the crowded bar toward the sand.

"I take it there's a rule about the workers fraternizing with the guests," she ventured after they'd made their way to the beach. The sun was slowly setting across the horizon, throwing brilliant shades of red and orange across the evening sky.

"Not yet, there isn't. Though I've made a mental note to get one drafted ASAP."

His voice sounded strained and tight. If there wasn't any such policy, why did he seem so bothered by Phillipe's behavior? Could it possibly have anything to do with her?

And how many times in one day could she wonder

about whether her behavior was going to affect someone else's livelihood, for heaven's sake?

"I'm sorry if you were made to feel uncomfortable during your dinner. We strive to make everyone feel completely at ease at all times. I'll have a word with the staffing manager to make sure it doesn't happen again."

So that was it. She'd been foolish to even feel tempted to look further into it than what lay on the surface.

"Another apology from the top man," she commented, kicking off her sandals to feel the silky soft sand underneath her feet. Reid paused while she nudged them off to the side.

He exhaled. "It appears we are off to a bad start."

She knew he meant the resort, but she took the opportunity to address the proverbial elephant in the room. "Or we're simply continuing along the same path as we were three years ago."

His step didn't falter but she could have sworn she felt him stiffening ever so slightly beside her. "I thought your intention on this trip was to forget all about it."

"Believe me, I see the irony in all of this." An exotic-looking bird flew past them at eye level, a myriad of colors along its wing.

"Tell me something," Celeste began. "You never did appear to be on board with my and Jack's wedding." Or with her, for that matter.

"You didn't seem right for each other," he answered simply.

She couldn't be offended. For he was completely right. Still, his words held enough of a sting that she wondered if she should have even started this conversation.

She could guess what he meant. She and her ex-fiancé were from two different worlds. Celeste had grown up struggling to merely survive while Jack was a trust fund baby who'd always known wealth and privilege.

Much like the man beside her now. Though she'd have to admit, if one were to look closely, the two men didn't really have all that much in common besides factors visible on the surface.

While Reid had worked incredibly hard to make a name for himself in the hospitality business, Jack was a mere figurehead for the yachting company his family owned and operated. Reid had taken all that had been handed to him and then grown and expanded it, becoming an industry titan in the process.

Celeste gave a shake of her head. What good did it do to compare the two men? There was no reason for it. In fact, there was no reason to give Jack another thought. Why had she even brought up his name?

Still, something tugged at her to get to the bottom of Reid's statement, she couldn't seem to help herself. "What do you mean? That we didn't seem right for each other?"

He gave a small shrug. "You're very different personalities. He's not as…ambitious, I guess. You're much more driven. Yet, there's a side of you—" He stopped abruptly. "You know what? Never mind. None of this is my place."

Celeste halted in her tracks and gently nudged him to stop walking. His gaze dropped to where she'd touched him on the elbow. She ignored the way his eyes darkened and quickly dropped her hand. "Please finish what you were going to say. There's a side of me that's what?"

Reid released a deep sigh and looked off into the distance at the horizon. "Just that there's a side of you which must have overwhelmed a man like him. An untamed, stormy quality just underneath your surface. A side a man like Jack wouldn't be able to handle." His eyes seemed to add the words *unlike me*.

Celeste's gasp was audible over the crashing waves behind them. She wouldn't challenge his words, couldn't. For he spoke the very truth. Celeste did everything she could to hide the wild inner-city kid she'd grown up as behind a highly polished professional veneer. She'd made certain to bury the hardscrabble teen who'd bartered, begged and stole simply to survive when the three of them had found themselves homeless on the streets for close to a year.

Then there was her ancestry. She'd fully studied her absent father's Persian roots, intrigued by all she'd learned about the culture. But she'd never explored that part of herself, hadn't so much as looked into visiting that area of the world. Though she'd had plenty of opportunity.

Somehow Reid had seen through all those layers three years ago when they were barely more than strangers.

"I'm not sure how to take what you've just said, Reid," she said once she found her voice again. "That I was somehow too much for Jack to handle."

He turned to fully face her then. "You should take it as a compliment."

Reid had no intention of stopping by the bar when he left his office behind the concierge lounge. He wanted nothing more after a long frustrating day than to head to his suite in the main quarters and pop open a bottle of cabernet and order a thick juicy burger.

But then he'd seen Celeste sitting at the bar by herself. He didn't even want to examine what had made him stop and just watch her for a while. She was alone, but she'd made it clear solitude was what she was after.

She'd seemed perfectly content with her book and sea-food plate. He'd been ready to move on, get going with the rest of his evening, but then he'd seen the way the bartender had been watching her. He'd found himself moving toward her then. So much for having her forget he was here.

Some strange emotion lodged in his chest when he heard the other man ask to buy her a drink. He didn't even know his intention until he reached her side. And what had possessed him to ask her to walk with him? He probably should have bidden her good-night right after intervening then went about his business. For now, they seemed to be awkwardly strolling along the beach, neither one managing to say anything much by way of conversation after the awkward words about their past.

He shouldn't have told her all the things he'd just shared, didn't even realize he was going to until the words were leaving his mouth.

Celeste cleared her throat. "So, you mentioned you'd recently acquired this place?" She was clearly looking to change the subject.

"Yeah. Last summer. I'd been looking to expand into the Caribbean resort business for a while. Luckily, it was one of the few islands that came through the hurricane season unscathed."

She humphed out a small laugh.

"What?"

"That happens to be the only reason I'm here. My usual spot is in shambles." The faraway look in her eyes told him she missed it. "This was one of the few places left to book."

Reid clapped his hand to his chest in mock offense. "You wound me. You mean to tell me the only reason you chose my resort was for lack of other options?"

She smiled just as a slight breeze blew a dark tendril of hair along her cheek. How silly that his fingers itched to gently tuck it back behind her ear for her.

"I'm afraid so. I rather miss the other place. No offense."

"I'm not so much offended as I am concerned as a business owner. What does it say about this place that you only booked it as a backup?" How many other potential clients were doing the same? The resort could face losing all sorts of business further down the line once the other resorts were back up and running.

"Would you like my professional opinion?"

"Can I afford it?" he teased. "You do have a reputation for being the best."

"Consider this a freebie."

He tilted his head for her to continue. "Well, to put it plainly, your marketing and advertising is somewhat subpar. Frankly, it's garbage. Rubbish."

Double ouch. "Hey, don't get technical now."

She laughed out loud. "Seriously. There's nothing on the website to compel me to click Book Now. Aside from a few pretty pictures of the beach, you don't really say anything very enticing about attractions, nearby landmarks, activities for the guests…"

"Yet you booked it anyway."

"Like I said, I was running out of options and grew concerned everything would sell out. It's competitive enough around Christmas under the best of circumstances. And it's really important to me to get away from the city around the holidays."

He could guess why. It was hard to forget that she and Jack had planned their nuptials around the holiday season. A wedding during Christmas in Manhattan. It was supposed to have been so romantic. Until it had all come crumbling down.

He'd been so quick to take Jack's word for everything and toss the full brunt of responsibility for the mess on her shoulders. Alex's words echoed through his mind. *Are you sure you're not confusing cause and effect, partner?*

Perhaps he had been. All this time.

She continued, bringing his focus back to the matter at hand—his resort's lack of a real media presence that would draw more potential guests. "And I have to be honest, now that I'm here, nothing really compels me to consider returning. Our mutual history aside."

Sighing, he answered her. "You're actually not telling me anything I don't already know. But you have awakened me to the urgency of it all. It's just one more thing on the list. We've been interviewing various marketing firms. None seem to fit the bill."

"If I were you, I would make a decision fairly quick."

She wasn't wrong. The implications of the failure to do so weren't lost on him. This was all so new. Not for the first time, Reid wondered if he'd bitten off more than he could chew. The differences between running a high-rise hotel in a metropolitan city and running a tropical resort were surprisingly vast.

He'd be even more lost if he didn't have Alex by his side. But clearly it wasn't enough.

"Any suggestions?"

"Are you asking for me to work on my vacation?" she asked, a teasing whimsical tone in her voice.

He couldn't help but laugh. "I'm shameless."

They'd reached the pier that moored the excursion boats. A couple of them were still out, it seemed. He was due to participate in a few of the outings himself, to get a feel for the experiences as the owner. He rested his arms over the steel railing and let his hands dangle over the side. Several blue-gold fish could be seen swimming right under the surface of the water.

"You're absolutely right," he told her. "About communicating better regarding all that we have to offer." The excursions were a prime example. Sure, there were chalkboards and newsletters written up daily detailing the outings available to their guests. But they were only that, mere announcements. Nothing describing the thrilling adventures waiting for those looking for extra experiences, more than just beach volleyball or swim aerobics.

A glimmer of an idea began to form in his head. Reid knew he was too tired and too distracted—a fact that had everything to do with the woman standing next to him—to voice the notion aloud just yet.

But he certainly had some thinking to do. And when he did think it all through, he could only hope Celeste would be on board with his suggestion.

CHAPTER FOUR

CELESTE AWOKE TO the sound of a piece of paper being shuffled under her door.

What the…?

It couldn't be the bill. She wasn't due to check out for several days still. Honestly, if they had confused her with another guest, Reid was going to get an earful about the way his resort was run. A glance at the clock told her it was past nine thirty. That was surprising. She never usually slept this late. But she'd had a restless night. Every time she'd closed her eyes, she'd been met with a set of bright golden ones. Visions of Reid's smile as they walked along the beach. The way he'd glowered at the flirty bartender when he'd approached her after her dinner.

When was the last time she'd taken a walk with a man? She couldn't recall. Had she and Jack visited any beaches? She didn't think so. Probably the reason she preferred to be on a tropical island this time of year.

For that matter, when was the last time she'd simply been with a man? Out on a date? Or in a capacity that wasn't strictly professional? Too long. With groggily heavy limbs, she climbed out of bed, suppressing a groan of frustration. Such thoughts were only going to make her miserable, thinking about all she didn't have in her life.

There's a side of you a man like Jack can't handle.

Celeste shook her head to push thoughts of yesterday's conversation aside.

The item slid under her door turned out to be an envelope with a card inside. Curiouser and curiouser. Her heart thumped in her chest as she removed the card and read its contents.

Please join me for breakfast if you haven't eaten already. I have a few matters I'd like to discuss. It will be worth your time. I'll be in my office until you're ready.
Reid

What in the world could he have in mind? A cry of warning screamed in her head. His cell number was printed on the top half of the card. She should just call him and tell him she had indeed eaten already. Or that she wasn't available. Or just outright tell him she wasn't interested in seeing him or in anything he may have to say. Though that would be a lie. She was more than intrigued. And more than a little excited at the prospect of seeing him again today. She could hardly get him out of her mind last night. And all the things he'd told her.

As if that wasn't reason enough right there to turn him down.

The man was her ex-fiancé's good friend for heaven's sake. Two short days ago, he practically cornered her on the beach and accused her of being a scrooge. No doubt he still harbored suspicions that she'd ruined her ex's life. After all, what else could he have meant when he'd said she was too much for someone like Jack to handle? Most likely that he thought her too uncultured, too unpolished to sully someone like Jack. Or Reid Evanson, for that matter. Somehow, Reid must have seen straight through her three years ago.

No. There was no reason to go see him.

So why had she walked over to the closet and taken out her prettiest sundress? The red one she knew brought out the hue of her olive skin. With thread-thin straps and a flowy skirt that accented her curves.

The warning cry sounded again, telling her to put the dress back and crawl back into bed if she knew what was good for her.

She lay the dress out on the bureau instead and walked to the shower stall.

It wouldn't hurt to just ask her, Reid thought as he waited impatiently in his office for Celeste's response to his written invite. He'd long ago given up any pretense of trying to get work done and now just stood staring at the tropical scene before him. A line had formed at the main dining hut for breakfast. He made a mental note to address the wait time in the mornings for food. But his thoughts immediately returned to the woman he'd spent the evening with. He couldn't remember the last time he'd simply walked with a lady along a sandy beach, just talking and enjoying the sunset. He had to admit he'd enjoyed it.

Celeste was already sporting the beginnings of a golden tan, her hair had lightened since the first day she'd arrived. She'd looked like a tempting goddess standing next to him as they stood on the marina pier.

He'd been thinking about her all night.

But none of that had anything to do with his invite asking her to join him for breakfast. That was strictly professional.

The door suddenly flung open and Reid didn't need to

look up to know it was Alex. He was the only one who never knocked. "Morning, partner."

Reid merely nodded.

"Your father keeps calling the main office," Alex informed him. "Says you're not returning his calls when he phones you directly."

Reid tried to bridle the surge of irritation that shot through his core. His father. The man was determined to ruin himself at this golden stage of his life. And he'd nearly driven Evanson Properties to the brink of ruin as well until Reid had stepped in and taken over as CEO. All because of a woman. A much younger woman.

Reid rubbed his forehead. "I missed one call from him last night. Not that there's a real need to call him back, in any case. I have no interest in what he has to say."

"Maybe he just wants to talk about his upcoming nuptials."

Reid threw his pen onto his desk. "Ha. If anything, I should be calling my mother about that wedding. Make sure she's all right." His mother had not deserved the way she'd been treated after three decades of marriage to the same man.

"I'll be sure to call him," Reid assured his partner. "Tell him to stop bothering the staff." He made a mental note to reach out to his mother first, however.

Alex gave him a mini salute and turned to leave.

Reid knew exactly why his father was trying to contact him. Now that the company was finally out of the red, Dale Reid was trying desperately to regain the power he'd initially handed over to his only son once the trouble had started.

Which was why he could use Celeste's help. He needed his latest acquisition to be a resounding success. There could be no questioning of his competence or abilities from the board, or anyone else, for that matter. Her marketing expertise could go a long way to establishing this place as a prime vacation spot.

Nope, nothing to do with wanting to see her again. His slight reflection in the glass mocked him even as his brain formed the denial. The truth was, the lines were becoming a bit blurred. Yes, he really was interested in her professional feedback, had no qualms about asking her for it and trying to make some sort of business deal to benefit both of them.

But he couldn't deny he'd been sorely tempted to seek her out this morning even without the business incentive. Something about her called to him, intrigued him like no other woman he'd ever met. The brief time they'd spent together had familiarized him with a woman far different from the one Jack had so often described. "Complained about" would be a more accurate description, though.

He wanted to learn more.

Half an hour after Alex left, a sharp knock on the door had him turning around so swiftly that he sloshed some of the now lukewarm coffee he held onto his desk behind him.

"Come in."

Biting out a curse, he wiped away the spill with the palm of his hand, leaving an unseemly streak of liquid across his highly polished desk. But it was just his office assistant with the latest island tax and duty figures.

He repeated the curse after she'd walked out again. Maybe his invitation had been a mistake. After all, almost an hour had passed.

Looked like Celeste was going to ignore him.

Celeste didn't get a chance to knock on Reid's door before it flung open. In the next moment, she found herself face-to-face with the man himself.

Oomph!

Reid had clearly been in the process of rushing out of the room. He couldn't stop his momentum in time. The crash was unavoidable. She wasn't sure which one of them appeared more taken aback by the collision. A set of strong arms suddenly gripped her around the middle and steadied her back onto her feet before she could topple backward.

"Are you all right?" he asked above her head.

She wasn't sure. Physically she was fine. But a curl of heat seemed to be simmering in the pit of her stomach. The scent of his skin surrounded her, a heady mix of mint, spicy aftershave and pure male. "I'm fine."

"I'm sorry. I wasn't expecting you."

She blinked up at him in confusion. He was the one who had asked her to come see him. But it was hard to think. Her hands itched to reach up and run her fingers through his wavy hair, then move lower and feel the silkiness of his beard. His nearness coupled with her confusion at his words made speaking difficult. "I…uh…got your card."

He had yet to let her go. Heaven help her, she couldn't bring herself to make a move to step out of his embrace. Their faces were inches apart, his breath felt hot against her cheek and lips.

"That was quite a while ago, princess. I wouldn't have pegged you for a late sleeper. Like to linger in bed, do you?"

It wasn't her imagination, his voice had definitely lowered to a huskier, deeper baritone as he uttered the last phrase. But her imagination did rev upward in response. A slew of images flooded her brain. She was in bed in all of them, all right. Only she wasn't alone. And she certainly wasn't sleeping.

His knowing smirk of a smile told her his words had had the intended effect. She shook off the oh-so-dangerous thoughts. What in the world was wrong with her? Two days ago, she would have named Reid Evanson as one the few people on earth she'd be content to never run into again throughout her lifetime. Now, here she was fantasizing about him as he held her in a viselike grip.

"I didn't notice the envelope right away," she lied. What was one small fib in an attempt at saving face? His eyes narrowed on her before traveling down the length of the dress she wore. He wasn't convinced. The truth was she'd agonized over whether to come or not. She'd stood so long in the shower trying to decide, her skin would probably stay pruned into next week.

"I can come back," she managed to say. With some reluctance, she moved out of his arms. He hesitated for the briefest moment before letting her go. "You were obviously on your way out."

"No. Come in," he said then stepped aside, motioning her into the room. "My errand can wait."

Celeste had to take a steadying breath as she moved past him into the spacious office.

"Have you eaten?" he asked as he followed her in. "The offer was to treat you to breakfast, after all."

The answer was no. She hadn't had a bite to eat this morning, just some coffee brewed in the room. But she didn't think she'd be able to summon an appetite right now. Her heart was still stammering in her chest. Her pulse hadn't slowed yet. And she certainly didn't need any more of the strong island coffee in the state she was in.

"Maybe just some tea."

He nodded then fired off a text. Before she'd even had

a chance to sit down, a young woman appeared carrying a tray with a steaming carafe and various tea bags.

"Help yourself."

"What did you want to see me about, Reid?" she asked as she poured herself a cup of steaming water and dunked two bags of English breakfast in.

He sat down in the large leather desk chair across from her. The massive mahogany desk between them served as a makeshift barrier and calmed her somewhat. But not completely. Why was she finding herself so affected by this man? She remembered there had always been a strange kind of awareness between them when she'd been engaged to Jack. But she'd chalked it up to conflicting personalities. She certainly hadn't realized all he'd observed about her, the things he'd shared last night.

Reid began to speak. "You mentioned last night that we don't call enough attention to the various activities and attractions that the resort has to offer."

"That's right."

"I know you have no reason to, but I wanted to ask if you'd help me with that."

The successful businesswoman in her suddenly stood at attention. Celeste couldn't deny she was intrigued. "Help you how?"

He shrugged. "It's what you're known for professionally. Developing and running marketing campaigns that appeal to as large a target audience as possible. Tell me how to appeal to potential vacationers about all we have to offer. I'm prepared to pay you for your time. Or, since I'm guessing you don't need the money, I'm willing to offer you a lifetime of free stays with us. As long as we have space, you can come spend a week here completely complimentary."

"I can afford vacations, Reid. Like you said, I don't need the money and I don't need freebie getaways."

"But you have to admit, it would be a nice option to have at your disposal."

His statement reminded her just how far she'd come in life. The girl she'd been, the one who'd grown up with hardly enough to get by let alone the means to travel, would never have believed the opportunity before her now. Hard to believe that girl had grown into the woman who was about to turn such an offer down.

"I'm on vacation. I really wasn't expecting to do any kind of work."

He smiled and tapped a finger against his temple. Had she found that smile so dazzling three years ago when he'd been a member of her wedding party? No wonder she'd done her best to avoid the man. That smile was dangerous. Perhaps she should be avoiding him now, too.

"That's the best part," Reid continued. "What I'm proposing will only enhance your vacation experience."

Now her curiosity was definitely piqued.

"Hear me out," Reid prodded further.

Despite herself, she tilted her head in agreement. What did she have to lose to just listen for a few minutes? Celeste took a sip of the hot, soothing tea then settled in her chair and waited for Reid to begin.

He was perilously close to the verge of babbling nonsensically. Reid knew he wasn't explaining his proposal as well as he could. But it was hard to focus. He still felt Celeste's warmth down the length of his body. The smell of her shampoo lingered in his nose. Her hair was slightly damp, hanging in loose freshly washed waves down her sun-kissed shoulders. She must have come down to see him right after a shower. The sudden, unbidden image of her naked under a stream of steamy water led immediately to yet another much more vivid one. In this next vision, he was under the water with her, running his hands down her skin. Rubbing soapy bubbles over her shoulders and moving his hands lower… That image had him tripping over his words again.

Get a grip.

She was here at his request so that he could run a business proposition by her. He had no business fantasizing about joining her in a steamy shower.

For heaven's sake, he was an accomplished businessman. He had given talks and presentations to world leaders and titans of industry. There was no reason to act so flustered now.

But then again, he had never before imagined anyone in his audiences naked in the shower.

Luckily, Celeste seemed to be getting the gist of what he was trying to say.

She cleared her throat. "Let me get this straight," she began. "You want me to go on the resort's offered excursions, with you. So that I can offer you some suggestions on how to market them to potential guests?"

"Exactly. What do you say? I'd planned to go by myself. But I could use another set of eyes."

"With you?" she repeated, seemingly hung up on that variable. Would she prefer to go by herself? He felt his fists clench at his sides.

"Yes," he answered simply.

"I thought you said you had a business partner?"

"Alex needs to stay here and run things while I'm gone all day. And besides, as someone who lives and grew up on the island, his isn't exactly the vantage point I'm after."

"What kind of excursions are we talking about, ex-

NINA SINGH   53

actly?" she asked cautiously. He wasn't surprised that she was trying to ascertain all the details.

"The best Jamaica has to offer. We'd be climbing up a rushing waterfall, visiting a beautiful botanical garden, driving ATV's over some rugged terrain."

Celeste bit her lip. "I'd really intended to just lie on the beach and read for the next several days."

"You're here for what? Over a week? You'll have plenty of opportunity to do so in the coming days."

"How many days exactly are you asking me for?"

"Three, max. We should be able to cover all the excursions in that amount of time. I've already booked for myself, I'll just add your name."

She held her hands up. "Hold on. I haven't said yes yet."

"But you haven't said no." He paused for effect. "Come on, there are worse ways to spend three days on an island like Jamaica."

It occurred to him that he was trying too hard. With anyone else, he would have laid his offer on the table then walked away. He'd always been known as a tough negotiator, not willing to budge or cajole. For some reason, with Celeste, he was intent on making his case. Not like him at all.

He would have to think about why that was so. After all, this was nothing more than another smart business decision.

Everything he said made perfect sense, Celeste had to admit as she took in exactly what Reid was suggesting. In fact, his proposal was so logical that a small part of her felt a slight tickle of disappointment. Reid was strictly all business at the moment. He was dressed in black slacks this morning, a white button-down shirt accenting the contours of his hardened chest and torso. The shiny gold watch on his wrist caught the sunlight as he gestured with his hands occasionally while speaking.

An appealing, successful, handsome man was asking to spend time with her on various island adventures but his only objective was her business acumen.

That shouldn't have bothered her as much as it did. But that was a silly notion, it wasn't like she and Reid were friends or anything. In fact, a few short days ago, she would have listed him as one of the few people on earth who actually may not even like her.

"Why me?" she asked. There had to be other individuals he could ask. A man like Reid was unlikely to be lacking in female companionship. No doubt he had a girlfriend. Hadn't she just recently stumbled upon a social media posting of Reid accompanying a famous international pop star to some Hollywood gala event? In the photo, he'd had his arm wrapped around her waist as she looked up at him adoringly, clearly smitten. What would *she* think about another woman spending the whole day traipsing around a beautiful island with her man? If their roles were reversed, Celeste didn't think she'd appreciate the circumstances one bit.

Then again, any woman lucky enough to snare Reid was probably more than secure with herself and her status as his girlfriend.

That wayward thought led her to other unwanted ones. She imagined what it would be like to date a man like him. What it would mean if he was sitting here asking her to do these things with her simply because he wanted to spend time with her.

What his lips would feel against hers if he ever were to kiss her.

Dear saints! What in the world was wrong with her?

Was it simply because she'd been without a man for so long? Perhaps it was the romantic, exotic location. Something had to be causing such uncharacteristic behavior on her part.

Why hadn't she just said no already? Was she really even entertaining the idea?

She wasn't exactly the outdoors type. Or much of an athlete, for that matter. Sure, she'd scaled countless fences during her youth trying to outrun the latest neighborhood bully after defending her younger sister. And she'd developed some really quick reflexes averting touchy men in city shelters. But that was about the extent of it.

Reid answered her, breaking into the dangerous thoughts. "Think about it. Between your professional credentials and the fact that you take frequent tropical vacations, you're actually the perfect person to accompany me."

Again, nothing but logic behind his reasoning. On the surface, she'd be a fool to turn down such an exciting opportunity; the chance to experience so much more of what the island had to offer and, in the process, acquire a host of memories she'd hold for a lifetime. It was as if he really was Santa and he had just handed her a gift most women would jump at.

Still, she couldn't bring herself to say yes. Not right away.

"I'll need to, Reid. Think about it, that is."

His eyes clouded with disappointment but he gave her a small nod. "As you wish."

She could think of nothing else.

Celeste vowed she would take her time and weigh all the pros and cons before getting back to Reid with her decision. So why did she now find herself in the resort's retail surf shop? Why was she eyeing water shoes that

someone would need if she were to go waterfall climbing? And why was there a one-piece swimsuit draped
over her arm? She'd only packed two-pieces or tankinis
and those wouldn't be terribly conducive to water sports
or rock climbing.

So many questions. Like had she imagined it, or had
Reid indeed held her just a smidge longer than necessary when they'd collided in his office? That lingering
uncertainty was what had her debating the merits of accepting his offer.

Her unexpected attraction to him was throwing her
off balance. Reid represented everything in her life that
she'd vowed to move on from. He and her ex weren't terribly similar below the surface but they were cut from
the same cloth; wealthy, privileged, carefree. They'd been
lifelong friends, for heaven's sake.

Reid may be a successful hospitality industry tycoon
but men like him didn't understand women like her. They
didn't get what it took to succeed in life when you'd literally started with nothing. Or what it was like to try
to hold a near full-time job during high school and still
maintain your grades well enough. Or when your single
parent couldn't earn enough to make ends meet, which
meant that you and your younger sister often went hungry. Or without adequate shelter.

None of that however had anything to do with the
matter at hand currently. She couldn't keep Reid waiting for long.

A sales clerk approached her from across the aisle.
The young woman had a dazzling smile and long, tight
braids cascading down her back.

"Can I be of assistance, miss?"

Celeste returned her smile. "I'm just being indecisive,
that's all." In so many ways.

She pointed to the water shoes Celeste held. "Well, if you're going on the tour tomorrow to climb Dunn's River, you'll need sturdier protection than those for your feet."

That was indeed one of the excursions Reid had asked her to attend.

"Follow me," the clerk said, then turned to lead her to a different shelf. "These are a bit thicker in the sole. Better to grip the slippery rocks."

Just how slippery were those rocks? Maybe this was a sign. The universe had sent this pretty sales clerk to warn her not to try to do anything so perilous as climbing up a waterfall. She liked to think she was fit. But her exercise regimen mainly consisted of meditation and yoga. Though the latter could be strenuous and muscle straining, Celeste was no rock climber.

The sales clerk suddenly laughed. "You look very concerned."

"I am a bit," Celeste admitted. "I've never climbed up a waterfall before."

"Trust me, you will love it. It's an experience of a lifetime. There are professional, knowledgeable guides to help you every step of the way. You'll do fine."

"I'm not so sure. Sounds like it could be very dangerous." Part of her was referring to so much more than the climb. She'd be opening herself up to danger on so many other fronts. She could no longer deny her attraction to her ex-fiancé's best man. An attraction which was wrong on so many levels.

The more Jack had learned about her background, the more distant he'd grown. Ultimately, he'd walked away.

What made her think Reid would be any different?

"This isn't an opportunity you want to miss. What if you never get the chance again?" the smiling clerk asked, breaking into her thoughts.

That was certainly something to consider.

"It's just not an activity I would normally do," Celeste admitted.

The woman's smile grew. "What better time than on vacation to take a chance and try something new?"

Celeste didn't bother to explain. She wasn't usually the type to take chances. Too many things could go wrong. Life ran so much smoother when every detail was attended to and risky endeavors were steadfastly avoided. The only time she'd been remiss in that regard had resulted in humiliation and heartbreak.

Climbing up some slippery rocks as a waterfall cascaded over your body certainly wasn't on the same scale as agreeing to marry a man you had many reservations about. But still, risk was risk. What would happen to her mother if anything were to happen to Celeste? Or to her sister and young niece, for that matter? She knew they'd be taken care of financially, she'd seen to that years ago. But they needed her so much more than just monetarily.

Then again, maybe she was just flattering herself. Maybe Tara and her mom would figure out how to move forward without her, especially as long as the checks kept on coming.

Plus, how dangerous could these excursions really be? It wasn't like she was putting her life in danger. From what Reid had explained, dozens of tourists a day participated in this particular activity. Even young children.

She'd spent countless days on vacation lying on lounge chairs with her nose in the pages of a book. Maybe it was time to try something different.

"Also," the clerk continued, "your man is going to love the way you look in that." She pointed to the swimsuit Celeste held. "That shade of blue will look great with your skin tone and dark hair."

"Oh! I'm not— I mean, we don't—"

The other woman quirked an eyebrow at her. "Are you going alone? That's all right, too. Many people do."

"No. I won't be alone. I am going with a man. It's just that—well, he isn't *my* man. Just a man, you see. And we're not even going as friends. Not really. It's more a business thing."

For Pete's sake. Now she was just a rambling, incoherent mess. Hard to believe she made her living the way she did.

Not surprisingly, the clerk stood staring at her with a look of utter confusion on her face.

"You'll be climbing the falls for business?" she asked.

Celeste nodded. "Something like that. It's hard to explain."

"I see."

She lifted the items in her arms and gestured to the shoes the clerk held. "I'd like to charge these to the room, please."

There it was. Somehow, without even realizing, it appeared she'd come to a decision after all.

She could only hope she wouldn't regret it.

CHAPTER FIVE

HER PHONE VIBRATED in her dress pocket just as Celeste slid her keycard into the door lock slot. So much for giving her time to get back to him. Assuming it had to be Reid, she fished it out of her pocket and clicked before checking to be sure.

She was mistaken. It was her mother's voice that greeted her on the other end.

"Are you on the beach, enjoying some fruity frou-frou drink with a paper umbrella?" The question was asked in a mean-spirited and mocking tone.

Celeste took a fortifying breath. The way her mother's words slurred and rolled into one another gave all the indications that she was the one indulging in drink at the moment. And Wendy's choice of beverage would never be described as frou-frou. Conversations with her mother were always beyond draining under the best of circumstances. When she was drinking, they bordered on traumatic.

Though she could be a caring and nurturing parent when sober, Wendy Frajedi was a mean drunk.

"Hello, Mother. I just walked into my room after picking up some things from the resort shop, as a matter of fact."

"Huh. Must be nice. Do you know how much I need

around the house? If only I had a daughter who was willing to help out with some shopping for me." Wendy put extra emphasis on the last word.

Celeste pinched the bridge of her nose and kicked the door shut behind her. "I left a sizable amount of cash in the jar last time I was there, Mom."

"That doesn't mean you're around to help me shop and put the stuff away now, does it?"

She wanted to tell her parent that she was perfectly capable of getting her own groceries or whatever else might be needed. But opposing her mother in any way when she was like this only led to long, drawn-out arguments that merely served to frustrate and demoralize her, sometimes to the brink of tears. As much as she hated to admit it, Wendy Frajedi was the one person on the planet who could make her feel like she hadn't done anything right in her life, even when she knew it was 99 percent the vodka talking. It was just that the 1 percent delivered a mountain of hurt.

Celeste had long ago given up trying push back when her mother was in her cups. The tension only escalated if she did so. No. Her mom would have to get off her chest all that she felt compelled to say. Then she would sleep off the bender until a pounding hangover headache woke her up. At which point a different kind of misery would befall her. The woman refused treatment as she insisted she didn't have a problem, that she only drank once in a while.

"How come you never invite me or your sister on some fancy-schmancy vacation?" Wendy now demanded to know.

Like déjà vu. The two of them went through this every year. More accurately, they went through it every time Celeste traveled. "You know you don't like airplanes,

Mom. Tara can hardly be expected to travel with the baby. And last year she was pregnant."

Her mother grunted in disgust at her response. "There are plenty of places we can drive to together, aren't there?"

Celeste couldn't think of anything less relaxing than driving long-distance with her sibling and parent in order to spend several days together. Of course, she didn't bother to say so.

"I needed to get away, Mom. I'll make it up to you."

Her mother's peal of laughter screeched loudly into the phone. "Yeah, right. Like I'd believe that."

"Is there somewhere specific you'd like to visit?" Celeste threw out the question, just to play devil's advocate. Her mother had no real desire to travel. Right now, she just wanted to chastise her daughter for doing so.

"How should I know? You're the smarty pants in the family."

And her mother would never forgive her for being smart. Or driven. Or successful. She would never understand her older child's fierce desire to escape the cloud of destitution their family had been born under. Celeste sighed. Her mother usually took longer to get to this point in the conversation. Next would come the tirade; the outlining of all the things that were wrong with Wendy's life and how impossible it was to better any of it.

"I'm a little too old to be watching that baby, you know," her mother began, describing Tara's nine-month-old daughter. Her only grandchild. "Since you're not around, I've had to do it more times than I'd like to think."

Celeste didn't bother to remind her mother that she'd only been gone for about three days. Wendy couldn't have babysat more than once or twice since then.

But logic wasn't the point of these conversations. "Sorry, Mother. How is little Nat?" she asked in an attempt to change the subject.

"Loud. Cries a lot. Must be teething or somethin'. I tell ya, I couldn't wait to get outta there."

Celeste bit back the surge of anger that suddenly rose to the surface. Tara's daughter was the sweetest, most loving baby, despite the lineage of women she came from. Celeste uttered a prayer to heaven at least once a day that the pleasant nature the child had been born with somehow carried through as she grew up. She'd do everything she could to ensure that happened.

One thing was for certain, Celeste would have to arrange for a professional babysitter for the child the next time she traveled. She might even have to look into hiring one now long-distance. She didn't want Wendy around the child if she was growing resentful of the responsibility. Celeste was completely confident that Wendy wouldn't drink around the baby. She preferred to drink alone in the privacy of her own apartment, without judging eyes advising her to slow down or stop.

But it simply wasn't worth the risk.

Celeste made a mental note to look into a sitter first thing tomorrow morning and tell Tara.

But Wendy's next words made the issue a moot one. "Thank goodness I won't have to watch her anymore. Not anytime soon. Looks like your sister was let go again."

Celeste didn't even know why she was surprised. It was a wonder her sister ever got hired at all. She tended to arrive late to work and then slacked off once she got there. No doubt Tara's latest setback had something of a hand in her mother's afternoon of binge drinking.

"That was her third job this year, wasn't it?"

Her mother pounced. "Well, I guess we can't all be as

perfect as you." Bingo. Her mother had now hit all the usual notes. Celeste hoped she felt some semblance of relief now that it was out of her system. For the moment and until next time.

Celeste resisted the urge to ask her outright. *Feel better now, Mom?*

Sadly enough, the answer was still no. And Wendy would feel awful once she woke up and remembered how she'd spoken to her eldest daughter. Then the barrage of apologies would start.

Until it all happened again.

By the time he'd walked the entirety of the resort for the third time, Reid had to admit that he was trying to seek Celeste out. It galled him that she hadn't responded yet to his proposal.

He also had to admit that he'd be profoundly disappointed if she ultimately turned him down. Which was sort of funny if one thought about it. Before he'd laid eyes on her, he had a determined set plan in place to attend the excursions by himself and then meet with a marketing team to see how best to advertise them. Now, the thought of going by himself held absolutely zero appeal.

He was doing this for the sake of expanding resort bookings. He wanted this place to be the first resort people thought of when they decided to vacation in Jamaica. Celeste could really help him toward that goal. That was the only purpose behind him asking her to accompany him.

So why did a surge of pleasure shoot through his chest when he finally did spot her? Until he approached, that is. The closer he got to where she sat, the more he could see something was wrong.

She sat alone at a tall table at the outdoor pub by the

stage. A plate of French fries sat untouched in front of her. She was staring at the glass she held which must have once been a frozen drink but now appeared to be a mixture of icy slush and dark rum.

An unfamiliar sensation of concern settled in his gut.

"Something wrong with the fries? Do I have to speak to the chefs?"

She blinked up at him in confusion, holding her hand to her forehead to block the sun in her eyes. "Reid." She gave him a smile that didn't seem quite genuine enough to reach her eyes.

"Were the fries not done to your liking?"

She looked down at her plate in surprise, as if she'd forgotten it was there. Maybe she had. She'd certainly been deep in thought when he'd approached her.

"I guess I wasn't all that hungry."

"May I?" he gestured to the other empty stool at her high top table.

"By all means."

She began to speak as soon as he sat down. "I know I still owe you an answer."

It surprised him that her failure to respond to his proposal was the furthest thing from his mind at the moment. His first concern was why she appeared so, well, sad.

"This is going to sound like the worst kind of pickup line, but…" he hesitated. Maybe probing would be overstepping his bounds.

"Yes?"

"It really is such a shame to look so down on such a beautiful day in paradise."

She let out a small laugh. "You're right. That does sound like a bad pickup line. And here I thought you would have a better game. Given your reputation as such a player and all."

He laughed in return, ducked his head in mock embarrassment. "I might be out of practice. I've been a little busy with this place."

"Fair enough."

What little there was of the smile on her face faltered then disappeared completely.

"Is everything all right?" he asked, now downright worried for her.

"Just fine." He definitely didn't believe her. Was debating whether to push when she spoke again. "And I'd like to say yes, by the way."

For the briefest moment, he wasn't sure what she was referring to. Then understanding dawned. She was agreeing to help him with the marketing ideas.

But right now, all he felt was concern. Celeste looked far from a woman on vacation. Rather, she looked forlorn and melancholy.

Not that it was any of his business.

"Did you hear me?" she asked.

He summoned a pleased grin. "Glad to hear it. You won't regret this. Let's shake on it," he suggested, holding out his hand.

Her hand felt small and dainty in his large palm. He could probably wrap his thumb and forefinger around her tiny wrist. It occurred to him just how vulnerable she looked. Formidable businesswoman or not, Celeste Frajedi had a softness about her that set his protective instincts at high guard status. As backward and downright Neanderthal as that sounded.

He wondered if a man was behind her current state of sadness. That thought had him reeling with an unreasonable degree of anger. She'd been hurt enough romantically for one lifetime.

Celeste had so much going for her. Any man would

be a fool to treat her poorly in any way. How shameful that he hadn't seen that three years ago. Something had blinded him then to Jack's faults.

He'd been told more than once that he could be loyal to a fault. Next time he and Jack crossed paths, he would have a few words he'd like to share with the other man.

Not that it would be any time soon. The two of them had certainly grown apart since the ill-fated wedding. Reid couldn't even recall the last time the two of them had spoken to each other live. For all he knew, Celeste and Jack were still in touch. Maybe Jack was the reason for her current state of sorrow. He felt his neck muscles tighten at the thought. After all, the last time he'd witnessed such sorrow on her face, Jack had been the precise cause.

Without thinking, he blurted out the pesky question that had been lurking in his brain. "So, what exactly went down that day?"

Celeste didn't even pretend to not know what he was referring to.

Her lips tightened into an ironic smile. "You'd like to ask me about my failed wedding. Now of all times."

He wasn't sure what that last part meant, decided to push on anyway. "Only if you'd like to talk about it." She certainly appeared as if she could use the excuse to get something off her mind.

"You said yourself that he and I seemed to be incompatible. Turns out you were right. As I'm sure you heard from the man himself."

"I'd like to hear your take on it," he prompted.

She shrugged ever so slightly, trailed a finger over the condensation down the side of her glass before she finally spoke. "Jack gave me a final ultimatum as a test. And I failed miserably."

* * *

Celeste couldn't bring herself to look up away from her glass. But she could feel Reid's questioning eyes on her nevertheless. He remained silent at her cryptic remark, simply waited for her to continue. But she'd be hard pressed to decide exactly where to begin. The troublesome signs that her engagement was doomed had grown more and more frequent as the wedding day had approached. She'd just chosen to ignore them.

"What kind of test?" Reid wanted to know.

This was all so difficult to talk about, Celeste thought. She'd done her best to try to put it all behind her. To try to forget. What kind of woman was left behind at the altar? How could she ever trust in her feelings again when she'd fallen for a man who had been cruel enough to do such a thing?

Visions of that nightmarish day flooded her brain. Her coworkers seated in the pews, her friends from school, various other invitees. All of them giving her looks of unmitigated pity. The disappointment flooding her mother's face. She'd never felt such a strong desire to sink into the floor and disappear. There'd been no father to walk her down the aisle. Celeste had asked a former mentor to do her the honor. The look on the man's face as they'd waited and waited for a groom who'd never appeared had nearly crushed her soul. Bless him, he'd been the one to finally make the announcement as she'd fled, trying to squelch the flood of tears before she could get away. She'd vowed never to give her heart to another man unless she was absolutely sure of his love and commitment.

"Celeste? What kind of test?" Reid repeated.

She forced herself to shake off the thoughts. "A week before the wedding, Jack decided he wanted to elope."

Reid's eyebrows lifted in surprise. She'd always wondered if Reid had been in on the idea as best man. His reaction just now made it clear he hadn't been.

"I see," Reid answered, clearly confused.

He didn't really. And there was no way to explain it to him, Celeste thought. Jack's sudden decision to forgo a traditional ceremony had had nothing to do with wanting a private event between the two of them.

It had everything to do with being embarrassed in front of his friends and loved ones about the kind of family she came from. Eloping would keep Tara and her mother out of sight. The love Jack supposedly felt for her wasn't enough to overcome the shame he felt about her family.

She'd called his bluff. And he'd walked away.

"I take it you weren't keen on the idea," Reid said.

She shrugged. "I wanted a traditional wedding," she answered simply, leaving out the more relevant part—mainly that her fiancé had been too much of a snob to accept her for who she was and where she came from. In hindsight, Jack's strategy was all too clear. He'd wanted a cowardly way out of marrying her. So he'd given her a choice that wasn't really a choice. How could she have turned her back on the two most important people in her life on the biggest day of her life?

Reid's expression held every indication that he suspected there was far more to the story than she was telling. Well, this was as much as she was willing to divulge. As much as her heart could take to reveal.

"I've known Jack for most of my life," Reid finally spoke after a long bout of silence, one where she couldn't quite meet his questioning gaze. "I've seen him act downright reckless all too often." He paused to take a deep breath and looked away off to the side. "But losing you has to be the most foolish thing he's ever done."

His words hung heavy and loaded in the air. Reid watched as Celeste's eyes grew wide. He didn't regret what he'd just said, but decided not to push the conversation any further. Celeste also appeared to have said all she was willing to say. For now.

She slowly pushed her glass away before standing. "Now that that's all out of the way, I should go back to my room and try to get an early night. I'm guessing we have quite the day ahead of us tomorrow. It won't do for me to be tired and sluggish."

Reid gently grasped her arm. "I have a better idea."

Her gaze dropped to where he touched her. For the briefest moment, neither one of them moved. Electricity seemed to crackle through the early evening air.

Finally, Celeste slowly sat back down and broke the silence. "What would that be?"

He motioned to her full plate. "Well, you clearly haven't eaten. We'll have to remedy that. Aside from not being tired tomorrow, we can't have you malnourished."

"Hardly a danger, but what did you have in mind?"

"Dinner to start with?"

Her eyebrows lifted in question. "Just to start? What then?"

He couldn't help but grin. "It happens to be Thursday."

"So?"

"Don't you read the daily newsletter? Thursdays are karaoke nights on the beach. Tonight's theme is Christmas carols."

Celeste's spine stiffened. "I don't think that's really—"

But he stopped her. "Karaoke happens to be one of the activities we'd like to highlight when advertising. We had a deal that you just agreed to, remember?"

Her look of horror told him she wanted badly to forget.

She really needed to head this development off at the pass. The steely set of determination in Reid's eyes only upped her panic. He couldn't possibly see her as a karaoke kind of gal in any way, shape, or form.

"Uh. I don't do public singing. And I certainly don't do Christmas carols."

He shook his head real slow. "This is all about you experiencing everything the Baja Majestic has to offer. That includes karaoke."

Celeste rubbed a weary hand across her forehead. What had she gotten herself into here? "Listen, I don't so much as sing in the shower."

Something darkened behind his gaze at her words. "I'm certainly not going to do it in front of a beach full of strangers," she added.

Reid glanced at his shiny, expensive watch. She'd been speculating that it was a Rolex. "There's plenty of time to discuss it. Let's go get some real food." He picked up a fry and popped it in his mouth even as he declared her discarded snack fake.

"There's nothing to discuss, Reid."

He stood and took her by the elbow, nudging her to join him. "Sure there is. First, we figure out dinner. Hibachi's always good. My favorite chef's on tonight. Or we could do the Mediterranean restaurant. The kebabs melt in your mouth. Something to do with the marinade."

She wanted to deny that she was hungry, but her stomach had other plans. An audible rumble sounded from her midsection when he mentioned the word kebab.

Reid let out a short but hearty laugh. "Mediterranean it is. Let's go."

He didn't give her a chance to argue. A few minutes later, they were climbing a spiral cement staircase to a building fashioned to appear like an ancient Greek cathedral complete with Ionic columns and goddess statues. The petite blonde maître d' approached them as soon as they entered. Her eyes lit up as she greeted Reid. Her crush was nearly visible. Not that she could be blamed for it.

"Hey, boss. You haven't been in for a while."

Reid returned her smile with a much more platonic one.

"My friend here would like to try the kebab, Michelle. Table for two please."

Michelle spared a glance in her direction, clearly appraising. She wondered if she passed some sort of Reidworthy test as far as the other woman was concerned. Probably not.

"Of course, right this way."

They were seated at an elegant table with ivory-white table settings, a crisply laundered tablecloth, and tall lit candles. All in all, the atmosphere in the dining area could only be described as highly romantic. That notion frayed her nerves a bit further. She absolutely could not be having any thoughts of romance whatsoever. Despite how much she'd shared of herself with Reid earlier. He'd simply caught her at a vulnerable moment. Phone calls with her mother when she was drunk tended to bring out that vulnerability.

She forced herself to focus on the menu. Every entrée and salad description made her mouth water. To think, she'd been convinced she wasn't hungry at first. But the aroma of spices in the air combined with what she read on the menu had her stomach grumbling once more. How very ladylike. Good heavens, it hadn't been that long since she'd enjoyed male companionship. Why was she coming off as such an awkward neophyte?

A white-jacketed waiter took their order within minutes. Clearly, every worker in the restaurant had been made aware that the co-owner was in attendance. Another waiter soon appeared and placed a small glass jug with clear liquid in the center of the table.

Celeste stared at it in confusion. "Is that all the water we're getting?"

Reid looked up from his menu. "Darling, that's not water. And if you're not familiar with it, I would definitely not drink it as if it were."

It was hard not to react internally to the endearment. Reid hadn't really meant anything with the affectionate word, but something curled deep in her belly nonetheless.

She figured out what he was getting at as far as the small pitcher was concerned. Greek architecture, Mediterranean cuisine. "It's ouzo, isn't it?"

"That it is. I'm guessing you've never had it?"

"Never," she answered. "And I probably shouldn't start today."

He nodded. "It's potent stuff. If you change your mind, start with a really small sip. Or we could have it watered down for you."

She shook her head. The last thing she needed in his presence was anything else throwing her off balance in any way. She felt enough out of her element as it was.

"I'll stick to the simple white wine, thanks."

He ordered her a chardonnay then poured himself a small amount of the ouzo into a shot glass that the waiter returned with. By the time their food arrived, the crisp, fruity wine had done a great deal to smooth her frazzled nerves. Between the disastrous phone call with her mother and the sheer magnitude of Reid's presence, she found it rather surprising that she was finally starting to relax.

Until Reid brought up the matter of karaoke again.

"I just thought you were a woman open to trying new things." He was clearly goading her. Unfortunately, she fell for the trap. In a way she was too tipsy to realize she'd quickly regret.

"I am about certain things. See, look."

Reaching for the remaining sliver of ouzo that sat in the mini pitcher. It was barely more than half a tablespoon. How strong could it be? She downed it in one swift gulp. Then gasped in shock as liquid fire shot through her midsection.

Reid sat staring at her wide-eyed. What had possessed her to do something so reckless? Suddenly, he threw his head back and barked out in laughter. He then gave a mini seated salute.

"I'm gonna need some more water."

Her belly felt like she'd swallowed a lit match. A rush of heat shot through to her cheeks. The room seemed to have tilted slightly. None of that was particularly funny.

So she wasn't quite sure why she returned Reid's laugh with a hearty one of her own.

Reid had stopped speculating what might have led to the scene he'd come across earlier this evening when he'd found Celeste so forlorn and defeated at the outside pub. But there was no question she seemed to be enjoying herself now. If her wide smile was any indication.

A trove of pleasure blossomed in his chest at the

thought that he'd helped put that smile on her face. As they left the restaurant and headed toward the beach, he took the opportunity to study her, the way he had through most of dinner.

She was unlike anyone he'd ever met. How could Jack have ever described her as standoffish and guarded? No doubt she'd tried to present herself that way in response to Jack's stilted demeanor.

He wished he'd bothered to ask three years ago. Maybe he could have talked some sense into his friend. Then again, he wouldn't be sitting with her here now if he'd done so. Selfish or not, he didn't feel sorry that the turn of events had led to this current moment.

"How do you feel?" he asked as they reached the sand.

"Surprisingly all right. But I don't think I'll be looking to do any more shots of ouzo this evening. Or ever again," she added after the slightest pause.

"Probably a wise decision."

A speaker suddenly sounded from near the water with a bouncy rendition of "Holly Jolly Christmas."

"We're headed to the karaoke event, aren't we?" she asked, a note of resignation laced in her voice.

"Trust me, you don't want to miss it."

She sighed and continued walking. "I suppose it can't hurt to watch for a bit. There are worse ways to spend the evening."

Reid hung his head low in mock offense. "Wow, not the most enthusiastic response I've gotten to the prospect of spending time with me, but I guess I'll take it."

"Trust me, it's nothing less than a compliment. I can't think of one other person who could convince me to go near an event featuring amateur singing of Christmas carols."

There was no reason for her comment to cause the rush of pleasure in him that it did.

"You sure it's me? It might be the ouzo," he teased.

She groaned out loud. "I can't believe I did that."

They'd reached the area by the wooden stage, the music growing louder by the second. The slow crashing of the waves behind them grew more and more muted. An impressive crowd had gathered. Two staffers sat at a table, surrounded by laptops and sound equipment. They each had Santa hats on. Another staffer dressed as an elf walked around passing out the same hats to guests.

Reid realized he was taking it all in more as a participant rather than the co-owner of the resort. He couldn't recall when that had ever happened before on one of his properties. He risked a glance at the woman next to him. She had to be the reason he was suddenly viewing things through different eyes. Though for the life of him he wouldn't be able to explain why. What manner of effect did she have on him?

"Mr. Evanson," the hat deliverer had reached them. Without asking, she reached up and placed one atop his head. Then she turned and did the same to Celeste.

Reid noticed her hat was different. It had a floral design instead of plain white at the base. The lettering said You've Been Chosen.

The hat elf clapped her hands. "You've been chosen, madam!"

Celeste blinked at her in confusion. She looked at him for some clarity. Damned if he knew what was going on.

"Chosen?"

"You have one of the special hats," the elf answered.

"Special how?"

"It's our version of mistletoe. But you have a choice. You can perform a song onstage."

Celeste's hand flew to her mouth in horror. "What's the other option?"

The elf laughed in response. "You kiss someone, silly. That's how mistletoe works, right?"

The staffer looked pointedly at Reid as she explained. Her coworkers had all turned their focus on the three of them. Several of the revelers turned to watch, as well. So, his employees were taking the opportunity to have a little fun at their boss's expense. Nothing malicious, he knew. Harmless fun.

But Celeste looked as if she'd swallowed a raw conch.

He discreetly drew the staffer's attention and gave a slight, almost imperceptible shake of his head. *Drop it.*

The elf immediately nodded in agreement. But it was too late. The crowd had now gotten involved. Chants of encouragement had begun.

"I'm not up for either of those options," Celeste said in a low voice. Enough of the crowd heard her that the encouraging cheers started to switch to long, exaggerated boos.

This was his fault, Reid thought as he tried to find the quickest path out of the crowd. He'd never forgive himself if she was humiliated.

"Come on," a man urged her to their left. "Pick one."

Reid clenched his hand by his side. His fingers itched to shove the man aside and away from her but it wouldn't do to accost one of his guests.

He grabbed Celeste by the wrist and began to lead her away. The boos grew louder.

She surprised him by halting them both to a stop. When he turned in question, she'd gone pale.

"It's okay. I'll do it," she declared, breathless, her voice aquiver.

He pivoted to face her fully. "You don't have to, Celeste. I'll get you out of here," he said on a low whisper against her ear so that only she could hear.

She nodded slowly. "I'm sure. I don't run from things," she offered with a shaky smile. "Then again, that might just be the ouzo talking."

Without waiting for his response, she turned toward the stage and stepped toward it. Reid shook off his shock and quickly followed her up the steps onto the platform.

The crowd erupted in cheers and applause once more. Reid placed his hand gently on her waist at the base of her spine. Bowing slightly to the crowd, he took the mike.

"What are you doing?" Celeste asked him.

He shrugged. "Can't let you have all the fun, can I? What are we singing?"

CHAPTER SIX

IF SHE HAD somehow managed to sing in front of a throng of beach partygoers last night, the task before her should be a piece of cake.

Celeste took Reid's hand as he helped her off the charter boat onto the smooth beach they'd spent half an hour sailing to after leaving the Baja Majestic earlier this morning.

She could do this. Besides, part of her was looking forward to it maybe just a little. The waterfall they were to climb up couldn't be that tall, could it? She got her answer soon enough.

The falls was tall, all right. But it didn't seem terribly steep. She took a steadying breath, reminding herself that she'd signed up for this. There would be no backing out now. Just like last night onstage.

Hard to believe but she felt a quiver of a smile tug her lips at the memory. She and Reid had butchered "Jingle Bells" so badly, it was a wonder they hadn't been escorted off stage. To think she could laugh about it now, when at the time she'd thought she might faint with nervousness. What choice had she had? She wasn't going to hightail it and run away in front of all those people. And what was the other option? To kiss Reid.

She'd thought about it, she really had. In fact, she'd found herself oh-so-tempted to just lean into him, even in front of all those people, and find out once and for all what his lips would taste like, how they would feel up against her own.

Singing in front of strangers had absolutely been the safer choice.

Though *singing* might be too generous a word. Reid had stayed onstage with her and "sung" too.

"You ready?" he asked her now.

"I suppose." She followed him to the base where two guides were waiting for them. After a brief summary of safety measures and what to expect, they began the climb by stepping on the first big boulder.

So far so good.

Granted, it was literally the first step. But she'd take any encouragement where she could get it. They were both absolutely soaked in no time. Reid seemed unfazed by the sheer physicality required. Lithe and agile, she got the feeling he'd be bounding upward boulder to boulder if he wasn't hampered by her. Despite the early-morning heat, there was enough of a breeze and shaded areas that she found herself shivering with cold.

In response, Reid rubbed his palms absent-mindedly over her arms when they came to a brief stop before scaling the next large boulder. More than once, she lost her footing on the slippery rocks and he was there to catch and steady her. She'd always prided herself on her independence. Even after her broken engagement, Celeste defined herself by her own successes, for being her own person. But something about the way Reid kept rescuing her from slips and falls awakened a side of her she didn't recognize. It was nice for once to literally have someone to fall back on.

The noise of the gushing water made conversation impossible. Not that she would have known what to say. His touch sent electricity over her skin.

Forty-five minutes later, they'd finally reached the top. Her muscles quivered with exhaustion. But that wasn't all she felt. She was elated. She'd done it. She'd conquered the phenomenal task—to her, anyway—of climbing up a one-hundred-and-fifty-foot waterfall.

Their guides congratulated them with a round of high fives. Reid reached for his waterproof wallet and handed several wilted bills to the two men.

He turned to her with a wide grin. "You did it!"

She didn't get a chance to respond as he lifted her by the waist and twirled her around in a tight embrace.

Celeste didn't even bother to try to suppress her squeal of laughter. She *had* done it! She'd successfully conquered a feat she wouldn't have even attempted a week ago. All because Reid was by her side throughout it all.

She would have to examine at some point what that meant for her going forward. But right now, she was due a bit of a celebration.

When he sat her back on her feet, an unknown heaviness hung in the air between them. She could have sworn he was going to touch her again. Instead, he clenched his hands into tight fists and squeezed his eyes shut.

Heavens. Maybe she should have asked for that kiss last night when she'd had an excuse.

"Reid?" she wasn't even sure what she was asking of him. Just then, another couple cleared the top of the waterfall and ran past them laughing. Several feet away, they stopped to embrace and indulge in a long and ardent kiss. A stab of longing hit Celeste deep in her core and she couldn't look away. She wanted what that couple had. That intimacy, that closeness. The clear passion between the two of them.

Heaven help her, Celeste had thought she'd given up on that longing three years ago. She realized she'd been fooling herself. She'd simply fallen for the wrong man.

She turned to see Reid watching the other couple also. His fist seemed to clench even tighter at his side.

"We should get cleaned up and dried off," he told her, gesturing to the building behind them that housed the shower and spa facilities.

But her feet wouldn't move. She didn't want this moment to end. The world around them seemed to fall away. Her vision zeroed in on one thing only—the man standing before her. The hunger in his eyes was as clear as the sunny sky above. Could he see that same hunger in her own?

"Lunch will be waiting for us soon," he reminded her. "We can use the time to go over your thoughts on ways to advertise this as part of the resort package."

It took a moment for her to register exactly what he was saying. How could she have forgotten even for a moment? She was only here because Reid was after her professional feedback.

While she stood here like a fool entertaining all sorts of romantic fantasies, Reid was simply utilizing her for her marketing expertise. His only concern was for his business.

The realization was like more cold water splashing over her skin. How could she have not learned her lesson? Technically, she was nothing more than Reid's employee.

Celeste certainly cleaned up well.

Reid watched as she found him at the wooden table where they'd be eating an authentic Jamaican lunch. She wore leather sandals, lace-covered shorts that showed off her long shapely legs and a thin-strapped tank top. She hadn't bothered to dry her hair and wore it in a loose pile atop her head.

She was a breathtakingly stunning woman.

It wasn't easy, but Reid was trying hard to ignore the sudden awkwardness that had developed between them. He could pinpoint exactly when it had happened. That darned couple with the passionate kiss atop the waterfall. Usually, the PDA of other people didn't bother him or so much as give him pause. He worked at a tropical resort that hosted numbers of couples, after all. But watching that kiss made him realize how badly he wanted to kiss Celeste.

That was unacceptable.

She was essentially working for him. After she left the resort, their paths may never cross again.

Oh, and there was also that whole other part where she'd been engaged to one of his closest friends. All that, on top of where he was in his life right now, Reid knew better than to acknowledge his growing attraction to a woman so clearly off-limits.

He cursed under his breath as she reached the table and sat down across from him. The smile she flashed him seemed forced and uncertain. She was aware of the awkwardness between them also.

Damn.

They still had a whole afternoon together. Not to mention all the activities scheduled for tomorrow. And the day after.

Maybe this whole thing hadn't been such a good idea. There was something developing between them that he hadn't expected or been prepared for.

Maybe he was deluding himself, but he was certain whatever was happening between them was mutual. That fact only made it all the worse.

He had a company to run, a devastated mother to look after, and he had to protect the family business from his reckless and disloyal father.

Nowhere in the scenario was there room to pursue any kind of relationship, let alone with a woman who'd once been engaged to one of his best friends.

"You look none worse for the wear," he said in a rather lame attempt at conversation.

Lord, he could use some of the rum punch this place was known for. Unfortunately, the next leg of this particular package happened to involve driving an ATV.

The waitress appeared with two loaded plates and a couple bottles of water before Celeste had a chance to respond.

"Hope you like hot and spicy."

She shrugged. "Depends on the heat level. Too much makes me uncomfortable."

He really couldn't read anything into that statement. Though he was sorely tempted to ask her if they were still speaking about the jerk chicken.

"I'll have a write-up ready for you before the morning. I made sure to dictate some notes into my phone before showering just now," she said.

She had turned all business.

Probably for the best anyway. But he found he'd lost some of his appetite. For her part, Celeste was barely picking at her own plate.

Reid took another bite and relished the punishing heat of the scotch bonnet pepper on his tongue. The silence between them grew. Finally, he threw his napkin down on his plate. Shameful waste of authentic jerk chicken but he didn't want any more.

"Something the matter?" Celeste asked.

This was ridiculous. They were both mature adults. Maybe it was time to address the proverbial elephant in the room. Yet another one.

"Yeah, I happen to have something on my mind," he admitted.

She raised an eyebrow in question.

"About what happened back there," he continued. "After we were done climbing."

Her eyes grew wide.

"Maybe we should talk about it," he added.

"Maybe we should. What would you like to say?" Her question sounded like a dare.

Well, he could play the game as well anyone. "I think we got caught up in an exciting moment. What about you?"

Her lips tightened into a thin line before she answered him. "I see. That's the conclusion you came to then?"

He nodded. "I'm interested in your opinion, however."

A glimmer sparked in her eyes before she leaned in closer to him over the table. "By that you mean you'd like me to confirm your convenient take on the matter so that you can rest easy."

"What?"

"Don't worry, Reid. We can forget the moment even happened. And ignore everything else too, for that matter. We'll play our roles as contract employee and boss man. That's the way you want things, isn't it?"

"Yes!" he said without taking the time to think. "I mean, no," he then corrected after a beat. "I mean, I don't know."

They were starting to attract the attention of the other diners.

The waitress approached, a look of concern as she eyed their still-full plates. "Is the food not to your liking, sir? Madam?"

"It's very good," he answered, not taking his eyes off the woman who had him so vexed at the moment.

"It's delicious, thank you," Celeste answered, somehow summoning a smile.

He'd been wrong. This was not the time or place to try to have this conversation. What did she want him to say anyway? It wasn't as if he could admit there was some kind of attraction there.

What good would that do either of them?

"Unfortunately, we're short on time," he explained to the waitress who didn't look any less concerned after their exchange. "If we could settle the bill. We'll be sure to come back another time," he lied. The chances of him coming back here with Celeste seemed slim to none right about now.

In fact, he'd be lucky if she didn't ditch the whole idea of his proposal and leave him to his own devices. That thought settled like a brick of disappointment in his chest. And though he was loath to admit it, the feeling had nothing to do with his professional goals.

At least the next activity would be on dry land.

Celeste followed Reid through the tree line down the dirt path where they were to meet their ATV driving guide. At least out of the water she wouldn't be tempted to look at Reid's chiseled chest and tanned, muscular arms. And she wouldn't notice how strikingly dark his sandy blond hair turned when it was wet. Nor the way his tanned skin glistened when wet.

He'd almost kissed her.

But he'd made himself stop, as if he'd immediately regretted the near lapse. She didn't want to acknowledge just how much that wounded her. Or why.

For then she'd have to admit what a glutton for punishment she was. She'd gone down this route before. Men like Reid and Jack knew exactly how to shut down their attraction or even affection for a woman when they realized she wasn't good enough for them.

She'd let her guard down and fooled herself into thinking that Reid might be different from Jack. Would she ever learn?

Finally, they reached a convoy of parked all-terrain vehicles, some of them were caked over almost completely with mud. Clearly, she'd overdressed for the occasion. By contrast, Reid had changed into dark green camouflage canvas shorts and a black T-shirt. His attire seemed much more appropriate. Looked like she should have gone over the details more carefully.

A guide came out of one of the banana-leaf roofed huts and the two men shook hands. After another safety lecture and being fitted with helmets, they climbed into one of the vehicles.

"You sure you don't want to drive one yourself?" Reid asked her, though they'd gone over this on the charter boat this morning.

"I'm sure. I have no desire to race down muddy embankments and treacherous curves in an open-top vehicle barely larger than a golf cart." She knew she sounded overly critical but she wasn't in the best of moods currently. This definitely wasn't an activity she would choose for herself when picking out an itinerary. In fact, she wasn't sure how to write about it in a way that might make it sound enticing.

"Let's go then."

With that, Reid revved the engine and peeled out into the wooded terrain. Celeste gritted her teeth. She'd been on smoother roller coasters. Reid was pushing the vehicle to the top edge of the speedometer. Trees and bushes zipped past her line of vision, her whole body jostled and bounced in the seat. He was driving perilously close to the edge of the cliff and she had to focus on her breathing as if in meditation to avoid a full-fledged panic attack. She thought for sure he'd slow down as they approached a hairpin turn, but if anything, he seemed to accelerate.

Celeste could have sworn they were riding on only the two side wheels for a brief moment.

Without warning, he suddenly veered into a more densely wooded area. Branches and brush whipped at the face mask of her helmet. Her panic grew by several notches.

The petrifying drive seemed to be having an opposite effect on Reid. Laughing and completely at ease, he was fully enjoying this. The next bump lifted her clear off the seat despite the tight seat belt. She landed back down with a thud that rattled her spine. Good thing she hadn't eaten much of the lunch earlier. No doubt it would have come up and lodged in her throat. Or worse.

An eternity seemed to go by before they turned back onto the beaten path. Reid started to slow the car and eventually came to a blessed stop. Reid let out another excited whoop and put the car in gear at the end of the line of the others.

Celeste uttered a small prayer of thanks to whichever deity was listening then wasted no time removing her helmet and jumping out of the car. Running to the nearest tree, she braced herself against the trunk and sucked in some much-needed air.

It wasn't long before she heard his footsteps behind her. "Uh…are you all right?"

Celeste summoned all the effort she could in order to try to keep her voice steady. She failed. "Did you have to go quite so fast? And you left the path. In fact, you ignored it altogether!" she blurted out, all too aware of the accusatory tone of her voice.

"Going fast is sort of the point," he countered. "And the guide said the path was a recommendation only. That more experienced drivers could use their best judgment."

"You consider yourself experienced, then, do you?"

She hated the high pitch of her voice. But, rational or not, she'd really been scared back there.

A muscle twitched in his jaw. "I do, as a matter of fact. I grew up riding such vehicles. As well as snowmobiles."

Of course he had. Was there nothing he wasn't good at? Or didn't have experience with? Whereas this was the first time she'd so much as sat on an ATV. The closest she'd come was the subway. Yet another example of how different they were, how their worlds had nothing in common. History repeating itself.

"Well, did you think about what might have happened if you'd lost control, even for a split second? I have a mother, a sister and a niece who need me alive to provide for them!" she almost shouted, then forced herself to calm down and take a breath. "I just need a minute to regain some balance here," she told him unevenly.

Reid took a step closer to her and frowned. "Take your time. You do look a little pale."

"I'll be fine." Once her pulse finally settled. Only that didn't seem like it was going to be anytime soon.

Just breathe.

"Why didn't you say anything?" he wanted to know.

Celeste didn't bother to answer. The fact was, she'd wanted to. But she hated that she'd gotten so panicky, that she'd felt so weak. She hated the idea of having to admit it to him. She'd just prayed that he'd eventually slow the cursed vehicle down. Only he hadn't.

As if reading her thoughts, Reid continued, "Look, I'm sorry if you were nervous or scared during the ride. And I'm even more sorry that I didn't notice. But I assure you that you were never in any danger. I knew exactly what I was doing."

That made one of them, Celeste thought.

CHAPTER SEVEN

THE FOLLOWING MORNING Celeste decided she was going to do absolutely nothing that day. Reid didn't have anything booked for them until tomorrow. Thank heavens for that small mercy. She punched her fluffy pillow and turned over in bed to stare at the ceiling.

So why did she miss seeing him so much already? Why had last night seemed so empty and boring? Barely twelve hours had passed since she'd seen him last and it wasn't as if they'd parted on the most positive note. Even after the awkward boat ride back to the resort where neither one had so much as spoken a word to the other, she wondered if that strained silence would have been preferable to the solitary dinner she'd had on her balcony before retiring early.

She'd somehow grown used to his company. That did not bode well at all.

Her phone screen lit up with a text on the bedside table next to her. She didn't need to look to know that it was Tara. She and her mother had been trying to get a hold of her all day yesterday. Celeste had no intention of returning the call just yet. Whatever it was could wait. She needed some downtime to process everything that had happened in the last twenty-four hours. The last thing that would allow her to do that would be to have any kind of toxic conversation with her family. If it was a true emergency, she knew they'd move all manner of heaven and earth to contact her.

No. Today she was going to linger in bed, then quietly meditate. Maybe afterward she'd take one of the yoga classes offered at the resort gym. Then she may or may not spend the afternoon in a lounge chair by the pool. Or back in her room with the gripping book she'd been neglecting.

Her idea of utopia. Usually, anyway.

Though she'd be alone the whole time. Normally, that would not have given her pause. In fact, it was the way she preferred to spend time on vacation.

She uttered a curse under her breath. The only reason she was questioning that now was because of one sandy blond masculine CEO with eyes the color of the deep ocean at sunrise and a dark beard. Celeste had never even liked facial hair before this. But on Reid, all she could think about was running her fingers through it. Or how it might feel against her skin.

She bolted upright before that thread of thought could go any further. Maybe her wayward thoughts about him were simply a result of her self-imposed celibacy these past few years. Maybe she'd do well to find a random single man on the beach and invite him back to her room for a no-strings-attached fun-filled afternoon.

Tara would be delighted for her.

Ha! As if she'd manage to let go of her inhibitions to ever allow that. As if she'd ever be so carefree. No. That was more her sister's style. That would take a level of lightheartedness Celeste had never achieved in her life. Plus, she didn't think it would do any good toward ridding her brain of Reid Evanson imaginings.

The ring of her room landline jarred her out of her

musings. Now she was concerned. Maybe there was some kind of emergency back home if her mother and Tara were trying to reach her through the hotel phone service. She grabbed the receiver.

"Hello?"

"Ms. Frajedi. Good morning. This is Prita at the front desk."

"Is everything all right?"

"Absolutely," Prita answered cheerfully with the slightest creole accent.

A wave of relief washed over her at the announcement.

"I'm just calling to let you know that you have a spa package waiting for you. You can come in anytime today."

"The spa? I didn't book anything at the spa."

"This is complimentary, Ms. Frajedi."

"I don't understand."

"It was booked at the direction of Mr. Evanson."

"I see."

"The package includes a full massage, facial, followed by a manicure and pedicure. It will take a few hours if you'd like to decide on a time."

"Thank you, Prita. I'd like to think about it and get back to you."

"Certainly, Ms. Frajedi. I'll give you the line to the spa and you can contact them directly."

Celeste made note of the number and disconnected the call. Reid had set her up with a day of luxurious pampering. She'd be a fool to turn it down.

Why had he done it?

Was this some manner of apology for the way things had turned out yesterday? Or was she to approach it as his employee and give him feedback on her spa experience? Perhaps he'd simply wanted to do something nice for her?

The latter was the least likely possibility.

So many lines were blurred between them now. They were former enemies but now she was technically working for him. She'd been engaged to one of his good friends.

She couldn't get the thought of kissing him out of her head. Or the way his touch had warmed her skin every time he'd caught her while climbing the falls. How it had felt to be embraced in his arms when he'd congratulated her afterward.

Enough already! What a pointless waste of brain cells to go over all of it repeatedly in her head. What was the use?

So much for staying in bed all day. Suddenly, she was too restless and wired up to just lay there. A day at the spa wasn't such a bad idea.

With a deep sigh, Celeste got up and made her way to the shower. She had some pampering to prepare herself for.

Thanks to Reid.

Reid's focus was completely shot. For what had to be the umpteenth time during their morning meeting, he tried to lure his concentration back to what Alex was saying. Instead, his mind kept wandering to thinking about what Celeste might be doing at this very moment. Had she taken him up yet on the spa offer? Was she there even now, lying on a massage table having some of the tension kneaded out of her muscles?

Would she accept his overture as the apology that it was intended to be?

Alex was making another point. "And I've spoken with the entertainment committee to put together a showing of *The Nutcracker* ballet with you dancing the major roles."

Reid nodded. "That's good, thank—"

Wait a minute.

Reid dropped his pen on the desk. "Ha-ha. That's really funny, partner."

"Just checking to see if you were paying attention. Where is your head at this morning, man?"

If he only knew. "I have a lot on my mind."

"Including the woman who's been helping you pull together a potential marketing campaign?"

Reid quirked his eyebrow. "Why do you ask that?"

"Let's just say you haven't quite been the same since she arrived on the island."

So it was that obvious.

Luckily, his partner wasn't the type to delve into his personal life. Not usually, anyway. "How's that whole project going anyway?" Alex asked, reverting back to business matters.

Reid wasn't quite sure how to answer. Where exactly did things stand now between Celeste and himself? "We just started yesterday."

Alex tilted his head. "And?"

"And we have a couple more excursions on the schedule tomorrow. She'll provide a written analysis and suggestions for each one we take."

Though, after the way yesterday had turned out, Reid wasn't even sure if Celeste was even still on board with it. He was half-afraid she'd already made the decision to end their agreement. Something told him she wouldn't do that. That she took her professional commitments far too seriously.

In fact, he was banking on it.

Still, she hadn't called to thank him or so much as acknowledge the spa day he'd arranged for her. An image of her lying on a massage table with only a narrow towel draped around her luscious curves flashed in his mind.

His partner was staring at him expectantly. Oh, yeah. He'd asked him a question, hadn't he?

Something about what he and Celeste were working on together. Reid decided to stick the truth. For the most part, anyway.

"Things are complicated between Celeste and me," he admitted, rubbing his forehead. "There's a bit of a history."

"I see," Alex responded. "And is that the only complication?"

"Absolutely," Reid lied. It wasn't an egregiously big lie however. Because he'd made something of a decision last night. As he'd lain there thinking about Celeste and the way she'd felt in his arms, he'd come to the conclusion that his dealings with her had to change.

From this point forward, he would maintain a safer distance. He would be at his utmost professional as they worked together. Though not technically his direct employee, Celeste was indeed doing work for him. He would treat her like the contractor that she was. No more touching, no more teasing. And definitely no more imagining her naked on a massage table or in the shower.

"Good," Alex interrupted that risky train of thought. "I'm interested to see what the two of you come up with. What's next?"

If Celeste didn't withdraw from the project altogether, they were due for a rather sublime activity tomorrow. "We're scheduled to visit the flower garden in St. Anne's Parish." An activity that would require no physical contact whatsoever, Reid thought with no small amount of gratefulness. The family owned and run botanical garden attracted tourists from all over the world to admire the striking flora that graced so much of the island. After a tour of the flower beds and exotic plants and trees, the excursion included some light shopping and a home-cooked meal.

Surely, he could get through something like that without laying his hands on Celeste's tempting body?

Piece of cake.

To make matters even better, they'd be fully clothed. No swimsuits involved for this outing. He wouldn't have to force his gaze away from the tiny dimple in Celeste's luscious thigh. Or the way her suit fit her like a glove and accentuated all those glorious curves.

"You just drifted off again, my friend."

Reid uttered a small curse. Thank heavens Alex had no idea exactly where his mind had drifted off to.

Who was he kidding? Celeste wasn't even here and he couldn't get her out of his head. He had his work cut out for him if he was going to maintain a professional distance tomorrow.

"Sorry. I was just mentally going over my to-do list." Another fib. He hadn't been this slippery with his friend and partner at any other time before this. He was behaving uncharacteristically in so many ways, he'd lost count.

Alex suddenly stood, apparently giving up on any kind of productive meeting given the state of Reid's mental sharpness at the moment.

"I should go get started on mine," he said, then turned to leave. He stopped at the door and turned back with a playful smile. "You sure you won't reconsider the *Nutcracker* gig now?"

"I'm sure, my man. No one needs to see me in tights."

Alex released a bark of laughter before exiting.

Reid turned to stare out at the glass wall behind his desk. In the distance, the ocean sparkled like a sea of precious gems. The sun shone bright in a clear, azure-blue sky. Another beautiful day in paradise.

The building that housed the spa could be seen at the edge of the property. Was she there now?

Reid stood and closed the lid of his laptop. Nothing wrong with taking a walk in that direction. He hadn't even been outside yet today. Some fresh Caribbean air would do him some good right now. He definitely wasn't trying to seek Celeste out. And if he did run into her merely by chance, what would be wrong with that?

No harm, no foul, he reassured himself. He'd simply be checking on a contract employee. Fifteen minutes later, after catching no sign of her, Reid resigned himself to acknowledging that their paths would not be crossing this morning. He also had to acknowledge the disappointment he felt.

CHAPTER EIGHT

Right on time.

Celeste's cell phone screen lit up with a text message as she was walking down the concrete pathway to the entrance of the resort property.

I'm here a couple minutes early. See you soon. R

She'd be arriving right at the time they'd agreed to meet at the bellhop desk to board the shuttle bus that would take them to the Flower Forest. Looked like Reid didn't want to take any chances that she'd be late. Or that she wouldn't show. If she was being fair, she would admit he couldn't be blamed for being uncertain. She hadn't so much as dropped him a thank-you text for the extravagant day of decadence he'd treated her to yesterday.

Even worse, she'd seen him approaching the spa building as she was leaving but had ducked for cover and turned the other way. Not that she'd meant to avoid him. But she had just needed one full day away from him to regain her equilibrium.

Truth be told, she was also a little embarrassed. Her reaction to the ATV ride weighed on her. Reid probably saw her as weak and fearful of new activities. It galled her to appear that way to anyone, let alone a man like

NINA SINGH   99

him. The temperature dropped several degrees as she entered the air-conditioned concierge lobby. She spotted Reid right away, but then he was particularly hard to miss. A head taller than most of the people in the room, he was dressed in khaki shorts and another formfitting T-shirt, blue this time. She had no doubt the rich color would serve to heighten the golden hue of his eyes.

Her conclusion was confirmed when she reached him. Yep, a girl could get lost in those beautiful golden depths if she didn't check herself.

Celeste would have to make sure to check herself.

"You made it."

She wasn't imagining the relief in his voice. He'd been afraid she wasn't going to show.

"All refreshed and ready to go," she answered with a smile. "Thank you for my day of pampering yesterday. I feel like a new woman."

His responding smile sent a bolt of awareness through her core.

"I'm glad you enjoyed it."

"Shall we?" Celeste prompted, before another one of those awkward silences could ensue that seemed to be so very frequent between them.

Reid nodded and led her outside to the waiting town car and held the back door open for her before climbing in the other side. Within moments they were pulling out of the long stone driveway and onto the main road. It always took Celeste a moment to adjust to the sensation of being driven on the opposite side of the street than what she was used to in the States.

Reid flipped open a console between their feet to reveal an assortment of drinks and snacks. "Can I get you anything?"

Celeste accepted some water and a rich chocolate bar

that seemed to melt in her mouth when she bit into it. Between hours at the spa yesterday and this luxurious ride, she could get used to this lifestyle. City life was overrated.

"So, tell me about this flower garden," she said between bites.

Reid uncapped a bottle of iced tea as he answered. "It's called the Flower Forest. It's one of the first excursions we contracted out after acquiring the resort. Owned and operated by the same family for generations. Now it's just the matriarch and her son and daughter. All three are delightful people. A bit on the traditional side. You'll enjoy meeting them."

"I look forward to it." She realized she was looking forward to the whole day, in fact. Unlike the adventurous feats of the previous excursions, this one sounded low-key and relaxing.

She'd have a chance to spend some time with Reid without a constant stream of adrenaline clouding her judgment. Maybe they'd even enjoy each other's company.

No. That was hardly the goal for today. She had to keep that fact in mind. They weren't a couple out enjoying an island getaway. They were barely friends, if one were to be completely accurate. Boundaries were important here.

Half an hour later, they pulled onto a gravel road and eventually came to a thick, green tree line.

Celeste had to suck in a breath when she exited the car at the sheer amount of color that greeted her. A flowing river could be heard behind the trees. The fragrant scent of exotic flowers filled the air. The entire scene could have been painted by a talented landscape artist.

Oh, yeah. This was much more up her alley than a jostling ride in an open-air vehicle as it straddled a cliff edge.

"Oh! It's so beautiful, Reid. Just lovely." This would be the easiest write-up she'd ever done.

A rotund woman who appeared to be in her early sixties appeared from behind a wooden gate and approached them. She was trailed by a young man and woman. Each had the same facial structure and eye shape. It was clear they were siblings.

"Mr. Reid. So nice to see you again," the woman said, giving Reid a hug and a small peck on the cheek.

"Uma, the pleasure's all mine," Reid answered over her head.

"You remember my son and daughter, Rinna and Theo," Uma added. The siblings nodded in acknowledgment.

"Of course." Reid motioned to where Celeste stood behind them.

"And I'd like you all to meet Celeste. She's a colleague of mine. She's going to help us bring some more attention and visitors to this lovely slice of paradise you have here."

Celeste reached out her hand but Uma ignored it and hugged her instead, as well. She mustered a smile as she returned the older woman's embrace but it was forced.

The word *colleague* had never sounded so disappointing.

"I have a confession to make," Reid said in a low voice as they trailed behind Rinna and Theo, their tour guides. Uma had left for the kitchen to start preparing the meal.

"What's that?" Celeste asked, her curiosity peaked. What in the world could he be referring to?

"I was a little concerned you'd back out of coming along today. After you know…the last time."

So he had been worried. Celeste felt a pang of regret. She had a stellar reputation as a competent and efficient businesswoman. To think that she'd given Reid the impression of unreliability would weigh heavily on her for some time to come.

Her professional reputation was a matter she took very seriously and an accomplishment she had worked very hard for over the years. Just made for another reason why she had to suppress whatever this attraction was between her and Reid. She had too much at stake. Theo stopped in front of a tree and turned to face them.

"This is Frangipani," Theo explained, pointing to the small tree adorned with white flowers. Celeste could smell the rich perfume of the petals where she stood.

They moved on. Theo and Rinna took turns pointing out and naming various flowers, bushes, and trees. Celeste was fascinated by the hibiscus flowers, which she'd seen on countless tea bag label ingredients but now had a picture of what the plant looked like.

All in all, it was a fascinating stroll. The weather was perfect, warm yet not muggy. A gentle breeze fanned her skin. By the time their tour ended, she felt both entertained and educated. A perfect tagline to advertise the attraction.

They'd reached the banks of the river when Uma came out to summon them to lunch. In moments, they were seated at a wooden picnic table by the water enjoying a mouthwatering meal of fried fish, rice and plantain.

"You were right," Celeste remarked between bites. "They are a delightful family. And Uma's a wonderful cook."

"Do you think you have a good idea of how to frame the description of this place?"

There it was again. Reid's sole focus was on the mission at hand. She wanted to kick herself for feeling any disappointment at his remark. It wasn't Reid's fault that she kept forgetting the true objective here. If anything, she should be thanking him for leading her back on track.

She nodded in response to his question. "I think so. The delicious food will play a major role."

Reid put his fork down and leaned toward her over the table. "Tell me something."

"Yes?" Celeste was fully expecting a question about her thoughts on the Flower Forest and what sort of features she would highlight in any summary she put together for him. So, his next words threw her completely off guard.

"Have you moved on? From your engagement to Jack and how it ended?"

Whoa. She had definitely not seen that coming.

Reid had an almost uncanny knack for throwing her off her feet. She swallowed the last bite she'd taken quickly, before she risked having it lodged in her throat.

She wasn't sure how to answer his question. If Reid was asking her if she'd met someone else in the past three years, the answer was no. But in every other sense, she'd moved on.

He suddenly looked away, out toward the water. "I'm sorry. I shouldn't have asked you that. It's none of my business."

"But you did ask. Why?"

"I'm not sure." He gave her a tight smile. "Like I said. I shouldn't have. I have no excuse for asking it."

Theo approached them before she could respond. He carried a sleek-looking professional camera. "Reid. Celeste. I hoped I might be able to take a few photos of the two of you."

Celeste couldn't decide if she was relieved or annoyed at the interruption. A little bit of both probably, she'd have to admit.

"I'm trying to do my own little bit of publicity for Mom. Just some photos to add to our website."

Reid looked at her in question. "That okay with you?"

Celeste shrugged. "Sure. Why not?"

They turned and smiled for Theo who snapped several shots in rapid succession.

"Let's do some by the water, yeah?" Theo suggested, and led them to the riverbank. "And I hate to ask…"

Reid gave him an indulgent smile. "Anything for you, Theo. What is it?"

"It's just that we're trying to appeal to a wider audience. Mainly couples. We seem to only get families with children. I was thinking it couldn't hurt to emphasize the romantic aspects of this place." He gestured around him.

Uh-oh. Celeste could guess where Theo was headed. He confirmed her suspicions. "You two mind posing like you're a real couple? You know, just so the photos look authentic?"

Neither one of them could seem to come up with an answer. Theo must have sensed their mutual discomfort. "Uh… Never mind. Forget I asked."

A pang of guilt settled in Celeste's stomach. What was the harm in a couple of photos? Theo, his mom and his sister had been the most perfect of hosts; gracious and accommodating. The least she and Reid could do was playact for a couple of stills.

"I'm okay with it if you are," she uttered, not quite able to look Reid in the eyes as she spoke.

Reid gave a slight shrug. "Sure. Go for it, Theo."

Theo flashed them a wide smile. "Thanks! So, just step together closer and, Reid, put your arm around Celeste's shoulders."

Reid did as instructed and Theo snapped away.

"That's great, you two. You both are naturals at this." He looked at the camera screen with a pleased smile. "It looks real. Like you guys are really together."

Celeste had to suppress an internal groan. Then things went from bad to worse.

"How about a pretend kiss?" Theo suggested.

CHAPTER NINE

REID HAD EVERY intention of simply dropping the slightest peck on Celeste's cheek. At the most, he might have softly brushed his lips along the corner of her mouth.

But somehow, after Theo made his suggestion, Reid's lips found hers and he seemed to have lost control of his intentions.

She tasted of berries and chocolate, her lips soft and luscious under his. Someone sighed heavily. He couldn't even tell which one of them it was. Her arms went up around his neck and it was all the invite he needed to pull her closer, deepen the kiss. Time seemed to stand still, their audience forgotten. Nothing of the outside mattered for him now. His one and only focus was the woman in his arms and how it felt to hold her, to kiss her.

He'd been imagining this, he had to admit. He'd had dreams at night where he held her, touched her, took her mouth with his exactly as he was doing now. The reality of it was so much more than he could have guessed. The clicking of Theo's camera suddenly registered in his brain. He couldn't be sure which one of them broke the contact first. Only that he felt the loss like a physical pang as Celeste pulled back and looked up at him. Her cheeks were flushed, her lips reddened from his mouth. It excited him to think that he'd been the one to put that color into her face, and her reaction to him only served to heighten his own desire.

"Reid?" she whispered softly, low enough so that he was sure Theo couldn't hear her question over the noise of his picture taking.

He wanted desperately to answer her. Not verbally but by kissing her again, he wanted to show her how much he desired her, how much of an effect she was having on him.

Theo's voice charged through his desire-fogged mind. "That's perfect, you two. These will work great. Let's move onto a different location, yeah?"

Reid couldn't seem to make his limbs work. He knew he should let her go. He knew they should turn around and follow Theo who had already stepped away and was walking toward the garden. But he couldn't so much as tear his gaze from Celeste's face.

Her breath had gone shallow. The one word question she'd uttered as simply his name still hung heavily in the air.

He couldn't help it, he touched his finger to her bottom lip and trailed it lower to her jaw.

Confusion grew in her eyes. "Uh. Theo's left. You don't have to keep pretending now."

The words felt like ice water thrown at him. They served just as effectively to pull him out of his desire-filled daze.

How foolish of him. Looked like only one of them had simply been pretending.

She'd never been good at pretending. The lines always became blurry for her. They certainly had just now. How much of Reid's kiss was real? How much was fake?

Dear heavens. She had to admit that everything she'd

felt as soon as his lips touched hers felt one hundred percent real. Well, she'd do well to snap out of it. Reid had already moved forward. He turned to see if she was following him.

"Coming?" he asked, completely nonchalant. Unlike her, he seemed far from affected in any way by the kiss they'd shared.

The fake kiss.

Celeste forced her feet to move and reached his side. Together they walked over to where Theo stood waiting for them by the Frangipani tree he'd told them about earlier when they'd first arrived. He motioned for them to go stand in front of it.

"How about you two hold hands?" Theo suggested after they'd complied with his request. Reid reached for her and she swore a bolt of electricity shot through her arm as she took his hand.

She had to clamp down on all this emotion. She couldn't let herself continue this way. She was only here in Jamaica for a few more short days. Soon, this whole adventure of a vacation would be over. She'd go back to her old life, her demanding job, and her draining family. She had neither the time nor the energy to spend her days pining over a man from her past. A man who was tied to her one majorly disastrous failed relationship. That life was her reality, those were the things waiting for her back home. A life full of responsibility and consequences. This was all a fantasy, a fake portrait that was meant to go into brochures and on websites.

It wouldn't do for her to forget that for even the slightest moment.

"You're not really smiling," Reid informed her through the side of his mouth. By contrast, he looked like a man thoroughly enjoying the day.

"Sorry. I'm not really good at this acting thing." Celeste forced her mouth to curve into a smile.

"Really? You could have fooled me."

What was that supposed to mean? She probably didn't even want to know.

"Let's just get this over with," Reid added. His grip against her palm lightened ever so slightly.

Well, that comment certainly cemented it. If she'd harbored any illusions that Reid was in any way as moved by their kiss earlier as she was, she could rest assured that he wasn't.

If only she could be like the tree behind her, Celeste thought, feigning another smile for Theo's camera. If only she could completely shed her unwanted feelings like they were discarded leaves. And then start anew. A whole new beginning, completely leaving the past behind.

The first metaphorical leaf she would drop would be her fraught and complicated feelings toward the man currently holding her hand.

Rinna approached them as they wrapped up the last few photos. It had taken some effort but somehow Celeste had willed her breath to return to a normal pace.

Well, as normal as she'd ever experienced while in Reid's presence.

"Momma asks that you two stay for dinner," the young woman announced when she reached them. "She says there's some type of holiday parade blocking the roads near the city. So you may as well wait it out."

As if on cue, Reid's phone lit up and he blew out a frustrated sigh when he glanced at it. "My driver has just confirmed exactly that." He turned to her. "Looks like we'll be here a bit longer than intended. Did you have any plans?"

Celeste shook her head. Of course, she didn't. She was here solo, after all. A warring flurry of uncertainty tightened her chest. Part of her didn't want this day to end. Another more sensible part warned her that any prolonging of time spent with Reid was a lethal threat to her inner peace.

"Excellent." Rinna clapped her hands in front of her chest. "I'll go let Momma know. She loves having company. We'll eat in about half an hour."

"This is good," Theo added after his sister left. "This will give you two a chance to see the holiday lights we set up this year. We decorated many of the trees. It's beautiful after dark."

"I'm looking forward to it," Celeste answered. She'd always been a sucker for Christmas trees and the sparkling lights during the season. One of the few aspects of the holidays she hadn't grown to resent.

Theo lifted his camera. "I'm going to go upload these images. You two take your time. See you at the house in a bit."

"Sorry about this," Reid said after the other man had left. "Things work differently on the islands. Holiday parades sometimes pop up without advance warning."

"It's all right, Reid," she answered. "Like I said, I didn't have any plans." She wondered if he thought that was pathetic.

"Well, good. If you'll excuse me, I should make a few phone calls given the change in my return time. I'm afraid I was due to meet someone who'll be arriving on the island tonight. Alex will have to take over."

Of course, unlike her, Reid would have a full schedule. No doubt this delay caused all sorts of disruption for him. A business owner like him had all sorts of demands on his time.

She wondered if one of the phone calls he was making was a personal one. Did it have anything to do with whoever he was expecting to fly in? He'd never mentioned being involved with a woman but why would he? It wasn't like it was any of her business. And though Celeste had never actually seen him with a lady so far on this trip, that meant nothing. She'd only been on the island a few days. While she'd spent a considerable amount of time during those days fantasizing and thinking about him, she'd steadfastly avoided wondering about his social life.

Now that she'd been confronted with the possibility he was attached, she felt even more foolish for pining for him for even a moment. Seemed she was a magnet for rejection. To imagine that someone like Reid would ever see her as anything like a romantic girlfriend was downright folly. She'd fallen for that fantasy once before, only to have reality come straight back and slap her into the truth. Men like Reid didn't end up with women like her.

No doubt the mysterious arrival was a beautiful, successful, and accomplished gem of a woman. Perhaps she was the model from the magazine cover she'd seen at the airport. Or maybe an actress. She vaguely recalled seeing a different photo several months back of Reid at some movie awards ceremony, attending as the guest of a Hollywood starlet.

She glanced at Reid's back now as he spoke into his cell phone, braced against one of the trees a few feet away. Slowly, she made her way toward the river. Watching the water stream by might be a soothing way to iron out her frazzled nerves. The whole day had been an emotional roller coaster. Correction, her whole trip had been a harrowing series of ups and downs. Definitely not what she'd expected to be in store for her. Just one more curve thrown at her. To think, she'd been so excited to leave the city behind her for several days.

Maybe this should have been the one year she stayed home for the holidays. The sadness the season always invoked in her might have actually been preferable to the assault to her peace that had been this trip so far.

She heard his footsteps behind her and instinctively took another step forward in a futile attempt at creating some distance between them. She really could use some time to think alone.

"Careful," Reid's voice warned from behind her. "You're awfully close to the edge there. The ground can be slippery. Unless you're looking for an impromptu swim."

An illogical surge of annoyance speared through her. She was a grown woman. One who certainly didn't need to be told what to do. In sheer defiance born of rebellion, she took another step.

Only to prove the worth of Reid's word of warning. Her foot slid out from underneath her as it landed on a slick patch of mud. She felt the shocking splash of water an instant later. Reid's shouted curse was immediately followed by another splash as he jumped in after her. Why in the world would he do that? She could swim, for heaven's sake. Now they'd both be a soaked, river-slimed mess. She opened her lips to tell him so only to have her mouth flooded with said slimy water. That couldn't be good.

"Hang on," Reid shouted over the splash of the water.

Even in the shock of her fall, only one thought crammed through her mind.

She hated that he'd been right. And that he was now attempting to rescue her.

* * *

Reid bit out another curse as he landed in the steadily flowing river. Grabbing Celeste by the waist, he began to hoist her onto the edge of the riverbank. Was she actually resisting? What the…?

He lifted her out of the water and followed her onto the land. "Are you all right? You didn't hurt yourself, did you?"

She ignored his question, posing one of her own. "Why did you do that?" she demanded to know crossly. "You did not need to jump in after me."

Well, if that didn't take the cake. "You have a funny way of saying thank you." Swiping the moisture off his face, he then ran his fingers through his hair.

Celeste was shooting fire at him. For helping her out of the water she'd fallen into, despite him having warned her.

He would never understand this woman, probably shouldn't even try. So he wanted to kick himself for the direction his next thoughts took him in. No woman should look that enticing dripping wet after a drenching in a green tinged, mossy body of water.

For that's exactly what she was. Enticing.

Her hair had turned a shade darker after the drenching, accenting the golden hue of her tanned skin. Her soaked white lace dress clung to her like a caress in all the right places. He had a clear view of her undergarments through the wet fabric of her clothes. Reid made himself avert his gaze. It wasn't easy.

He longed to slowly strip her of the dress, then rub his hands over every inch of her soaked skin to warm it up. His breath caught in his throat at the image. He couldn't deny it any longer. He wanted her. And he wanted her so badly it made him ache inside. How or when it had happened, he couldn't even try to place. Maybe it had all started that first day he'd seen her sprawled on a lounger on the beach. Perhaps it went back even further than that.

Not something he really wanted to examine at the moment. The better question was what he was going to do about it.

"Honestly, Reid," she huffed as she stepped around him. "Now we're both a mess."

He blinked. "Are you actually upset that I helped you out of the water?"

"I didn't need rescuing," she declared and tried to push past him.

Without thinking, he reached out to take her by the elbow and turned her around to face him.

"What is your deal?"

Her chin lifted in defiance. "I thought I already explained. I didn't need you to jump in after me. I'm perfectly capable of swimming out of a body of water."

He gave his head a shake. "Have you always been this difficult? I can't seem to remember."

It was the wrong thing to say. Celeste's eyes darkened with anger. "Is that what Jack told you?" she demanded to know. "That I'm difficult? That I'm hardly worth the effort? Did you two have fun talking about me and how sad and downright pathetic I looked waiting for him at the altar? Do you two get together at the bar on weekends and make fun of how ridiculous I looked on what should have been the happiest day of my life?"

Reid felt his jaw drop. Such an accusation was the last thing he'd been expecting. "What? Of course not."

"What exactly are you denying, Reid? That you think I'm difficult? Or that I'm a pathetic, dejected discard? Or that you and Jack get a kick out of recalling my humiliation?"

He couldn't seem to find the words to respond. The things she was saying were downright preposterous. Little did she know, he thought Jack's behavior was inexcusable that day. Friend or not, it had been a cowardly and treacherous way to treat a woman. Let alone someone like Celeste.

She pulled her arm free from his grasp. "Never mind. I'm going to ask for a towel."

With that she trudged away toward the house. He caught up to her in mere strides, though he didn't dare reach for her again. For he was far too tempted to shake some sense into her. Then he would tell her how ridiculous a notion it was to hint that she'd been at all responsible for the way Jack had treated her. That she was far too good for him and always had been. And then he would quiet any further protest by crushing his lips to hers and tasting her again the way he wanted to so badly.

"For the record," he bit out. "Jack and I never discussed you after that day. Not once. Even when the subject of his averted wedding came up. The conversation never turned to talk about you specifically." Mainly because Reid wouldn't allow it, he added silently. "And we certainly don't laugh at you over beers at the local pub!"

"Yeah, right," she answered, not breaking her stride. He had several inches on her and much longer legs, but somehow it was an effort to keep pace with her. Her anger seemed to be propelling her forward. Or her desire to get away from him.

"What reason would I have to lie about that?"

She shrugged, still moving ahead. "I don't know. Some misplaced sense of loyalty your friend perhaps? I know how charming and convincing Jack can be."

Reid rubbed a frustrated hand down his face. "Why

are we arguing about this? Now of all times?" But the answer occurred to him before he got the last word out.

She was thinking of Jack. She wanted to know if he asked about her, talked about her. And apparently, the answer mattered to her. Why else would she be so upset?

One thing was certain. The reverse was absolutely true. Even if Jack didn't think of her, Celeste still thought about her former fiancé. Jack was on her mind even at this very moment. Even after she'd spent the morning with Reid. After he'd kissed her under the native tree, held her hand and smiled with her at Theo and his camera.

A fireball of anger seemed to ignite in his gut. His vision turned gray and he had to bite back a curse. He stopped in his tracks and let her continue forward. He would have to meet her at the house later. Right now he needed to be alone. He needed to try to think straight.

A task he couldn't seem to do well whenever Celeste was near.

"Oh, my!" Rinna cried out when she saw the state Celeste was in. "I see you fell into the water."

"We both did," Celeste announced and climbed up the porch steps. "Well, to be more accurate, I fell in. Then Reid jumped in after me. For some inexplicable reason."

"I see," Rinna said simply. She glanced in the distance behind where Celeste stood. "Where is Reid?"

Celeste was vaguely aware that he'd stopped following her at some point. Thank heavens he had. Or she might have turned to him then and there and asked him exactly what he thought of her. How he *felt* about her. She might have run the risk of having him come and say straight out what she suspected—that he liked her enough as a person. But that there could never be anything between them. Hence, she'd be making a fool of herself over a man yet again.

"Um…could I borrow a towel?" Celeste asked just Uma stepped out onto the porch from behind the screen door.

The older woman clapped a hand to her face. "Of course, dear. Come in and let's get you dry."

Celeste went up the stairs gratefully and went to step inside, only to have her ankle give out.

Uma and Rinna both jointly caught her just before she could hit the ground. "Are you all right, dear? Did you hurt yourself in the river?"

Celeste gave her head a shake. "I didn't think so. But I must have sprained it somehow during the fall. And then the walk to the house must have aggravated it." She rubbed a hand down her foot, which was starting to swell and bruise right before her eyes.

"Let's get you to the couch," Rinna suggested. "Theo's gone back out for more pictures. Can you try to stand without putting any weight on that foot?"

She didn't get a chance to answer. A deep masculine voice sounded from behind the three of them.

"I've got her."

A set of strong, muscular arms suddenly wrapped around her waist and under her bottom. The next instant she felt herself lifted into Reid's masculine embrace. Heaven help her, she took a moment to simply inhale the scent of him. The same mixture of citrus and sandalwood combined with mint, somehow still present despite the river water soaking his skin. Without giving herself a chance to think, she rested her forehead against his broad chest, taking comfort in the warmth of his skin against her cheek. Reid nuzzled his jaw against the top of her head. She didn't dare try to read anything into his action. He probably just felt bad for her.

"Does it hurt badly?" he asked, his voice smooth above her head.

"No. Not really. Just a little achy."

"Sorry about all this," he spoke low into her ear as he carried her farther inside and toward the couch.

Great. Now he was trying to take responsibility for her fall. "I'm not sure why you're apologizing."

"You're only here in the first place because of me."

"That may be. But I fell into the water on my own. Due to my own carelessness."

He exhaled deeply as he set her down on the couch. "Anyone ever tell you that you can be stubborn?" he asked.

Was it her imagination or did his hands linger around her body just a bit longer than was necessary after he set her down on the cushions? She looked up to find the smallest hint of a smile on his face.

"As a matter of fact, I do hear that from time to time."

The smile grew. "I'll bet."

A strange sensation tugged at her heart. The warmth of his touch still lingered over her wet skin. The man did something to her insides she couldn't recall feeling with anyone else ever. Not even the man she'd been prepared to marry.

Rinna appeared from behind them with a couple of pillows. She placed one behind her back and the other under the offending foot. Reid leaned over her. "May I?" he asked, gesturing to her leg.

She reluctantly agreed and he ran a gentle finger along the arch of her foot and around her ankle. Then he went up higher, toward her knee. Totally innocuous as it was, tingles of awareness rippled up her skin at his touch.

Full-out kisses by other men had elicited less of a reaction from her than Reid simply examining her sore ankle. She had to suppress a shudder of reaction.

"It doesn't appear to be broken," he announced. "Just a sprain."

"You think so?"

"I'd place a wager on it if I had to." He nodded and gave her a teasing wink. "I've broken enough bones in my lifetime to be able to speak with some authority on the subject."

Celeste thanked the other woman for the pillows and allowed herself a groan of frustration. What a burden she was being to these people. And Reid, for that matter. All because she had been a careless klutz. She had no one else to blame but herself. Truth be told, she'd been distracted and dazed since that first day when she'd gone to find Santa only to discover Reid Evanson in his stead.

"Do you have any ice?" Reid asked Rinna.

"We do. But we can do even better than that. Momma has gone out to gather the plants she needs to mix up a medicinal balm." She laughed and shook her head. "I've had it applied to my various scrapes and bruises countless times over the years. She'll be back to prepare it soon. You'll start healing in no time," she reassured.

Celeste resisted the urge to ask if Uma might be able to come up with a balm to ease the ache in her heart.

CHAPTER TEN

THEY ALL ATE in the living room so that Celeste could remain lying on the sofa with her foot propped up. True to Rinna's word, Uma had wrapped a cloth around her ankle after applying the homemade poultice. Whatever the concoction was, it smelled heavenly. Miraculously, her foot started to feel better within minutes. Celeste didn't think it was the placebo effect. She could feel the swelling go down and the throbbing sensation had almost completely stopped. Between the filling meal and the relief from pain, she found herself drifting off into a comfortable sleep.

When she opened her eyes again, she was shocked that two hours had passed. She slowly roused herself to a seated position. Reid sat across from her at a wooden dining table, typing away at the keyboard of a laptop. He appeared to have showered and had changed into clean clothes. Oh, to be so lucky.

He glanced up when he realized she'd awakened. "You're up."

"It's dark out."

"That it is."

"Shouldn't our car have been here by now?"

"I asked for it to be delayed."

"Why?"

He shrugged. "You looked like you could use the rest. I didn't want to disturb you."

Great. Yet another misstep she could feel guilty about. "But I know you had to get back to the resort." And to finally meet whoever had been due to arrive earlier, she added silently.

Reid motioned to the computer in front of him. "It's okay. Theo was nice enough to lend me his laptop so I could get some stuff done remotely. How does your foot feel?"

Celeste wiggled her toes and moved her ankle from side to side. The pain had mostly subsided. Only a slight ache remained in the joint. "Much better. Rinna was right. Uma's potion has some sort of magical healing properties."

She huffed out a breath. "I feel so foolish for going and hurting myself like that. It must have been a terrible inconvenience for them to have to take care of me this whole time." And for him, too.

"Accidents happen. You're not at fault." He stood and walked over to stand in front of her. "If you're up for it, I can call for the car to come for us."

Uma entered the room at that precise moment. "It's much too late to try to make that drive," the older woman argued. "You two stay here for the night. We have an extra room."

Reid gave Celeste a questioning look. He was waiting for her to make the decision. "I don't want to inconvenience anyone," Celeste said to the room in general.

Uma waved her hand in dismissal. "It's not a bother. Everything is ready for you. The bed stays made as we have overnight guests quite often. And the sofa down here is large and comfortable enough for you to sleep on, Reid."

Reid turned from the older woman to address Celeste. "Uma's offer makes sense. I'd feel better if you stayed completely off that ankle at least for the night. Also, I'd hate to make the driver leave his house this late just to drive us across the island and then have to drive back home again."

Well, how could she argue with any of that? She'd already been enough of a burden to the people currently under this roof. She certainly didn't want to further inconvenience the poor nameless driver.

"Thank you, Uma. You're far too kind," she told her, vowing to come up with a way to thank the woman at some future date. She'd never experienced such hospitality from strangers she'd met only hours before.

"That settles it then," Reid announced before turning to Uma. "We'll take you up on your generous offer. Thank you."

Uma patted his cheek and left the room. Celeste made an effort to get up off the coach. Reid was by her side in an instant. "Whoa there. What do you think you're doing?"

Embarrassingly enough, she needed to use the washroom, for one. "Uh, I could use to freshen up a little."

He wordlessly leaned down and lifted her off the sofa. It was hard not to savor the feel of being in his arms again, despite the circumstances that had led her there. He carried her to the nearest bathroom.

"Just holler when you're done."

Celeste shut the door and took a moment to study herself in the bathroom mirror. She looked as if she'd gone toe to toe with some kind of swamp creature. Her hair was a tangled mess, dark circles framed her eyes and her clothes were in a wrinkled state of disarray. Oh, yeah, compared to the gorgeous models and actresses Reid was used to dating, she would definitely fall far short.

With a resigned sigh, she cleaned up as best she could, helping herself to some of the mouthwash sitting on the bureau behind her.

She may not look great, but by the time she opened the door, she at least felt better. Reid remained in the same spot, waiting for her.

"All set?"

She nodded, trying to maintain her balance on the one foot. With what seemed to be little effort, he picked her up and carried her once more. "This can't be good for your back," she commented.

"You wound me. Are you questioning my masculine strength?"

She had to smile. "I wouldn't dream of it."

To her surprise, rather than plant her back on the sofa, he walked toward the front porch.

"Where are we going?"

"You'll see." Kicking the door open with his foot, he took her out onto the porch.

Once they stepped outside, the sight before her took her breath away. The lights that Theo had referred to earlier were now lit up. The whole garden looked like a magical holiday light display. Several Christmas trees, a few bushes decorated like presents, glowing lights along the path leading to the river. She couldn't help her squeal of delight at the festive scene.

"It's beautiful, Reid! I'm so glad I got to see it." She knew it was silly, but part of her was almost grateful for the accidental fall that had led her to be able to be here for this sight.

Reid set her down gently on one of the outdoor patio chairs then took a seat of his own. The night was balmy with just enough wind to offer a refreshing breeze once in a while. A silver-gray moon floated above them in a velvet navy blue sky. Celeste couldn't guess how long the two of them wordlessly sat there simply admiring the view.

Her awareness of the man next to her was near tangible, so she felt it instinctively when his mood seemed to shift. A tenseness suddenly appeared in the set of his shoulders. His chin hardened. His shoulders slumped ever so slightly, yet enough for Celeste to notice. No doubt he was thinking of all the responsibilities waiting for him back at the resort.

"I'm sorry we got stuck here. Due to my carelessness."

He turned to her, surprise flickering in his gaze. "Don't apologize, Celeste. You had an accident." He gestured around him. "Besides, how can I possibly be upset about spending time here amidst all this beauty and calm? I dare say I needed the peace and quiet for an evening."

Did that include spending time with her? Silly question.

"But you seem quite distracted. I imagine you're thinking of all you need to get done."

He shook his head, turned back to stare at the navy blue horizon in the distance. "Just thinking about a phone call I have to make when I get back."

"Must be some phone call." The tension was practically vibrating off his skin as he talked about it. "Business or personal? If you don't mind my asking."

He crossed his arms in front of his chest. "Both. That's the problem."

"Want to tell me about it?"

He shrugged. "I have the very unpleasant task of dispelling the notion my father has that he can retake control of Evanson Properties."

Celeste didn't know much about Reid's company, nothing beyond what she'd read in the business papers. But his statement confused her, based on those reports. "I don't understand. I thought the company was on the brink of bankruptcy until you took over as CEO and turned it around." He'd done so in an astonishingly brief period of time, too.

"He's not exactly thinking straight. His motivation has more to do with an outside party. A woman."

Understanding dawned. She'd also read about the messy, bitter divorce of the elder Evansons. "I see."

He let out a grunt of a laugh. "My future stepmother has made it clear to him that she fell in love with a CEO, so she'd fully expected to marry a CEO."

"Sounds like a compromise might be difficult."

His eyebrows drew together. "Compromise?"

Celeste nodded. "There has to be a way for both you and your father to come to some kind of agreement."

He blinked at her. "Why would I bother? This is the man who let an uninformed, inexperienced outsider talk him into all sorts of bad investments. Everything from hiring social media influencers who simply took advantage of complimentary stays at our hotels, to investing in a failed music festival which resulted in countless lawsuits." He inhaled an agitated breath. "Lawsuits I'm still dealing with."

The underlying hurt in his tone was as clear as the flickering neon lights before them. His father's business failings were the least of the complicated scenario Reid was dealing with. No wonder he dreaded talking to the man.

"You feel betrayed," she supplied.

"How can I not? Evanson Properties was founded by my grandfather, it employs countless employees all over the globe. The Evanson name has been associated with luxury hotels for nearly a century. My father nearly destroyed all that with a few strokes of his pen. And for what? A midlife crisis?"

"But that's not all, is it?" she prompted.

"What else?"

Celeste bit the inside of her cheek. There was a chance she was overstepping here. But Reid was staring at her with expectation for an answer. "You also feel betrayed as his son."

Something seemed to have dislodged in his chest, some type of tight knot he hadn't even been aware of. He hadn't sat down and really discussed the disastrous events of the past couple of years or the hurtful actions of his father with anyone before this. He certainly wasn't about to burden his mother with any of it, she was a big part of the reason he'd worked so hard to rectify it all.

And his relationship with his closest male friend was far too strained and had been for the past three years. Unloading some of it simply by talking about it with Celeste felt like a bit of the burden being lifted off his shoulders.

You feel betrayed as his son.

He hadn't been able to come up with a response when she'd uttered those words. Her demeanor told him no response was needed.

Now they were both sitting in the balmy Caribbean air, enjoying a comfortable silence. He couldn't recall the last time he'd simply sat outside, chatting with someone. Someone who wasn't afraid to tell him what he needed to hear.

But it was getting late. And Celeste had had quite a day. Uma, Theo and Rinna had bidden them good-night several minutes ago and explained that the light display would turn off soon based on the timer system running it. Looked like the evening was coming to an end. And he'd already said more than he probably should have shared with her. He stood and stretched out his back.

"Guess we should head inside, huh?" Celeste asked.

"Guess so. Here, I'll help you upstairs to the spare bedroom."

Even in the relative darkness he could see her grimace. She didn't like being indebted to anyone. She might have read his thoughts based on her next statement. "I hate that you have to carry me, Reid. And I hate that you felt you needed to jump in after me when I fell." She inhaled deeply, her chest rising. "I'm not used to being dependent on anyone. It makes me uncomfortable. I'm afraid that's why I…lashed out…after my fall. I regret that. And I'd like to say I'm sorry for the way I behaved."

Huh. Reid couldn't recall the last time someone had directly come clean and apologized to him after making a mistake. Certainly not his father after the countless times he'd jeopardized the family business empire. And certainly not any of the women he'd dated in the recent past after a quarrel or spat. He'd always been the one to take responsibility and accept fault, regardless of whether it was deserved or not.

He checked his thoughts. It was way too late and the day had been way too long to become this pensive.

"Well, if it makes you feel better, you're probably one of the least dependent people I've ever come across," he told her with absolute sincerity. In fact, based on what she'd told him after the incident with the ATV, she'd made herself responsible not only for herself, but also for those she cared for. He hadn't known her that well three years ago, certainly hadn't been aware of the situation with her sister and mother. The knowledge now definitely shed some light on some of the mysteries he'd wondered about when it came to Celeste. In fact, if he'd been a betting man like his father, he would guess Celeste's family had been the real reason Jack had ultimately got cold feet over marrying her. He wasn't one to share. And he wasn't the type to appreciate a woman who came with that kind of baggage. Even a woman like Celeste.

Jack really could be incredibly selfish.

Reid couldn't help feeling somewhat sorry for him. The man had no idea what he'd had then foolishly lost. If Reid were in any kind of position to be with a woman like her, he'd hold on tight and refuse to let her go.

"Thank you for that," Celeste said. "It means a lot to hear you say so."

"You're welcome." Walking over to her chair, he cradled her in his arms and lifted her up. "Now I'm gonna get you to bed, beautiful."

He felt more than heard her sharp intake of breath, and couldn't decide whether she was reacting to the endearment or the loaded statement. He hadn't meant either, truth be told. He certainly hadn't meant to sound so provocative. "I'm sure you're ready to get some sleep," he quickly added.

Using his toe to nudge the door open, he carried her inside the house and up the stairs. He could get used to this, the feel of her in his arms. She was light and soft against his chest. Her shapely legs draped over his arms. The scent of her filling his senses. She belonged there, snuggled into him up against his chest.

Reid didn't bother with the light switch when they reached the room, the moonlight and glow of the still-lit display outside afforded just enough light to see. Reid stepped over to the bed to gently set her down. But two things happened at once. First, the bed was much lower than he was used to. Second, the lights outside suddenly went out right at that very moment. Rather than gently set her down, Reid lost his footing and they both stumbled onto the mattress.

"We have to stop meeting like this," he quipped as they both landed unceremoniously onto the soft surface. Her lips were inches from his, he could feel her hot, sweet breath against his jaw. His skin felt afire everywhere her body touched his; the softness of her chest, her long legs up against his.

Her response was to tilt her face up toward his. Reid didn't even know who moved first. But suddenly he was tasting her, devouring her the way he'd so often imagined doing. He thrust his hands into her hair, pulled her tighter against him and deepened the kiss. She tasted like fruit and honey and enticing spice. She tasted like home.

Her hands found his shoulders, then moved over his biceps, toward his back. She wrapped her arms around his neck and deepened the kiss. But it wasn't enough. He would never get enough of her touch, the taste of her.

The sound of a door shutting from somewhere down the hall served as a warning bell. Though it hurt like a physical blow, he made himself break the kiss and pull away. He had to suck in a breath to try to steady his pounding pulse.

Celeste's cry of protest nearly undid him. But as much as he wanted to continue kissing and exploring her, this wasn't the time or the place.

One thing was unarguable. He wanted her. And she wanted him. There was no doubt in his mind judging by the way she'd reacted just now and the shallowness of her breathing as she stared up at him in confusion. He'd had to fight hard the strong urge to throw all care aside and simply join her where she lay on the bed.

Instead, he leaned down and dropped a gentle, soft

kiss to her forehead. "Good night, Celeste." Then he forced himself to turn and walk away.

One and only one thought hammered his brain as he left the room to make his way down to the sofa on the first floor; he could make her forget she'd ever been committed to another man. Hell, he could make her forget that other man even existed.

There was no question of attraction. Not after what had just happened between them in that room and the way Celeste had melted in his arms. Under better circumstances, they could explore whatever this was between them and see where it might lead. If they were two completely different people, Reid would have no doubt in his mind about finding out once and for all.

No, the only question was whether he had any right to want her the way he did.

CHAPTER ELEVEN

THEIR TRIP TO the flower garden seemed like forever ago. Hard to believe only one day had passed. Celeste sank deeper into the Italian marble bath and took a deep breath. The hot water and luxurious fizziness of the scented bath bomb was doing wonders for her anxious nerves. But a dip in the bathtub could only do so much. She hadn't seen Reid all day yesterday once they'd arrived back at the resort, nor this morning or afternoon.

But she was due to spend the evening with him in a couple of short hours. The next item he had her writing up was a formal dinner cruise followed by live music and dancing aboard the boat.

What a fun, romantic evening it would have been if only it was all real. She had no idea what they would say to each other. The only words they'd spoken had been awkward and forced during their mostly silent drive back to the hotel yesterday morning after bidding Uma and her children goodbye. And then Reid had disappeared without a word to her except a brief text this morning confirming the time of the cruise. She'd been tempted to feign illness, to say that she wasn't up for it. But any fool would see right through that excuse.

Maybe he was avoiding her after what had happened in Uma's spare bedroom. Or perhaps he was busy with whoever had arrived that evening when the two of them couldn't return to the resort as expected. A pang of hurt she didn't want to identify as jealousy lodged in her chest.

The most probable explanation was that he was indeed avoiding her. He was no doubt embarrassed that things had gone so far between them that night. Heaven help her, she would have let things go even further if he hadn't suddenly stopped their kiss and walked out.

But he *had* walked out.

Reid had been the one to come to his senses. They had nothing in common, a shared brief past history which only complicated things further, and the chances that they would run into each other again once this trip was over were slim to none.

Unless, of course, she took him up on the free lifetime vacations he'd offered in return for her services. But she wouldn't. Her heart wouldn't be able to handle doing it. Seeing him every year, being tempted by a man she could never have.

A glance at the ornate clock on the wall above the sink counter told her she only had about half an hour left to get ready. With a sigh of regret, she stood and stepped out of the tub. There was no avoiding the inevitable. She could do this. She could dress the part, paste a fake smile on her face, and act like the all-business marketing professional that she was.

Toweling off, she walked over to the closet and removed the one formal dress that she'd packed. A silky black number that reached midthigh with red spaghetti straps and trim. Red leather high-heeled sandals and ruby earrings would complete the look. She'd included the outfit just in case when she'd packed, convinced she'd actually have no occasion to wear it.

If she'd only known.

About twenty minutes later, she was dressed and walk-

ing out the door of her suite to meet the man she'd somehow developed a devastatingly shocking attraction to.

This was a disaster in the making. The evening would
no doubt be a lesson in self-torture. How was she going
to playact the part of objective observer when the whole
night all she'd be thinking about was how much she
wanted him?

And heaven help her, she did want him. So much that
she'd been aching inside ever since the other night. If she
were honest with herself and looked deep within, she'd
have to acknowledge something much more worrisome
and disturbing: beyond the physical attraction, she'd developed feelings for him. Somehow, in the course of a
few short days, she'd started falling for a man who was
completely wrong for her. How many times in her life
could she make the same mistake?

There was no denying that mistake when she reached
the resort marina and found him waiting for her by the
water. Celeste had to remind herself to breathe. Dressed
in pressed dark pants and a midnight black fitted jacket
with a collared shirt, he took her breath away. Against the
backdrop of the luxury yacht and sparkling water, Reid
could have been posing for a men's cologne ad. In fact,
if she ever worked on a cologne campaign, this scene before her would serve as ample inspiration. She might find
a way to use this image in the very project she was working on for the resort.

*That's it, girl. Stay focused on the business aspect.
Steady now.*

Some protective instinct must have kicked into gear
in her head. The survival skills she'd built and developed
as an inner-city latchkey child were coming through for
her as they so often had throughout her life. She could
do this, she could get through this evening as an unemo-

tional, unaffected, driven businesswoman who was simply attending this event as part of a job commitment.

And for all intents and purposes, the man standing before her was simply her boss.

Never mind that she wanted nothing more at this moment than to run into his arms.

Reid had to clench his fists by his sides in order to keep himself from pulling Celeste tight against him and into his arms when she reached his side. He'd come close to canceling this evening. That option would have been the wisest course of action. But he couldn't bring himself to do it. He needed this marketing project completed and he needed it completed successfully. Distractions and delays wouldn't do.

Or so he told himself. If pushed, he would have to concede that he hadn't called it off because he hadn't wanted to. He'd wanted to see her. Avoiding her this past day and a half had been nothing short of painful. And what did that say about the sad state he currently found himself in? He'd been missing a woman he had no claim to. A woman who would walk out of his life in a few short days and most likely never return.

Given the way she looked right now, he knew he wasn't likely to stop wanting what he couldn't have anytime soon. The silky black-and-red dress she wore complemented her ever-deepening tan. Strappy red high heeled shoes accented her shapely legs, she'd worn her hair down cascading like an ebony dark curtain over her satin smooth shoulders.

He swallowed hard.

"Hey there," she greeted him when she reached his side.

Somehow, he got his mouth to work. "Hey yourself." He handed her the rose he'd thought to pick up on his way. Fake date or not, he knew when an occasion called for a flower.

She seemed surprised as she took it and inhaled deeply of the petals. He wanted to do the same. Only he would prefer to nuzzle his face against the gentle curve of her neck and inhale deeply of her now oh-so-familiar scent.

"Thanks. This was very thoughtful."

"You're welcome," he replied, then motioned toward the boat behind them. "Shall we?"

Celeste took the hand he'd extended and followed him on board. A group of uniformed crew members greeted them and they made their way below deck. A few other couples were already seated at elegant, candlelit tables. Yet others strolled in behind them.

A white tuxedoed crew member led them to their table and pulled out their chairs.

"How's your foot?" Reid asked.

"Completely healed, it seems." She took a sip of her water. "Uma's poultice is a wonder drug. She should bottle that stuff and sell it worldwide."

"I might have to suggest that idea next time I'm at the flower garden." It occurred to him that on his next stop there he'd mostly likely be by himself. Or with Alex. He'd never be able to visit the place again without remembering the time he'd spent there with Celeste. Just one of the many marks she'd be leaving on him when she left the resort for good shortly.

The waiter reappeared with a fruity, frosted cocktail complete with a swirly straw and placed it in front of Celeste. "The bartender's specialty drink, miss. Please enjoy."

He placed a shorter glass full of amber liquid in front of Reid. Top-shelf Jamaican dark rum. "Your usual, sir."

Reid made a mental note to sip the drink much more slowly than usual tonight. He couldn't risk a repeat of the other night when he'd completely lost control and practically ravished Celeste in Uma's spare bedroom. Though he'd been stone-cold sober then. Still, he didn't want to take the chance of lessening his inhibitions in any way.

Celeste took a sip of her drink and closed her eyes in pleasure. "Mmm, this tastes heavenly. Definitely something to note when writing about this outing."

Good for her for keeping her mind on the task at hand, Reid thought. At least one of them had their head in the right place. So why was a small part of him just a touch disappointed?

"I've also got some great things to say about the light show at Uma's place," she continued, then looked down at her drink.

Their thoughts must have drifted in the same direction; what had transpired between them after they'd admired said light display that evening.

Reid cleared his throat, trying to summon exactly what he wanted to say. They had to acknowledge what had happened. Or this awkwardness was simply going to continue to grow.

"Celeste, I'm not sure where to begin, but maybe we should be talking—"

But she held an elegantly manicured hand up to stop him. "Please, Reid. If it's just as well with you, I'd like to focus on the here and now. I need to if I'm going to be effective in what I'm trying to do here tonight."

All right. He would have to respect her wishes if that's the way she wanted to play things.

He sighed and took the slightest sip of his drink. "If that's what you'd prefer. But we're going to run out of small talk at some point. And you can only do so much observation and analysis."

She leaned over the table, resting her elbows on the surface. "Let's discuss some fun things then," she suggested.

"Fun?"

She nodded with enthusiasm. "What does the man I'm working for do to have fun?"

The man she was working for. He wanted to correct her description of him. He'd been so much more than that the other night, hadn't he? But again, he would respect her wishes. He would play her small-talk game.

"What do you do outside of work, Reid? Do you have any hobbies? What happens when you finally have some free time and want to enjoy yourself?" She paused to take a sip of her drink. "And who do you spend that free time with?"

So, that's what this was about. She was asking if there was a woman in his life. Celeste wasn't as unaffected by their mutual attraction as she pretended. A selfish part of him couldn't help but feel pleased. And if that didn't make him self-centered, he didn't know what would.

He took another swig of his rum and focused his gaze on her face. "Celeste, I believe you're asking me if I'm attached to anyone. Do I have that right?"

Celeste wanted to kick herself. She was usually much more subtle. In her defense, she hadn't realized that she planned to ask him that question. It had just come blurting out of her lips. Now it was too late to take it back.

"Just trying to learn more about you, that's all."

He flashed her a knowing smile. "All right, I'll bite," he stated. "I don't have much time for hobbies. But when I can get away, I enjoy a good getaway to the mountains for downhill skiing. In warmer climates, I'm an avid scuba enthusiast. Been certified since my teens. It's one of the reasons I started looking into the Caribbean as an investment opportunity."

So he was going to start with the less loaded questions. Then again, maybe he wouldn't answer her last question at all. Served her right. His personal life was none of her business, not really.

What did it matter that they'd lost control with each other on a couple different occasions? They'd simply both been carried away by the romantic setting and the adrenaline rush afforded by all the activities they'd done together. The strong possibility was that he probably had several girlfriends. He probably dated someone different in every city he traveled to. That was the impression she'd first gotten of him when they'd met three years ago at Jack's introduction. As a matter of fact, she distinctly remembered a conversation about which lucky lady Reid would bring to the wedding as his companion. Her bridesmaids had certainly fallen over each other trying to get his attention. She'd thought it rather amusing at the time. Not so much now. Now that he could also count her as one of the many females who had a thing for him.

They were interrupted by another server who appeared with a platter of cold shellfish. Everything from oysters, to clams, to chilled lobster garnished with lemons and capers sat on a bed of ice. Simultaneously, a sommelier appeared with a bottle of red wine and handed the cork to Reid. He simply nodded at the man after taking a small sniff. Another bottle of white wine was also placed alongside the table in a standing silver bucket sweaty with condensation.

Good thing she hadn't eaten all day. This was only the first course. Not that she had much of an appetite. Her frazzled nerves were wreaking havoc on her stomach.

Think of this as a straightforward business meeting.

Her own words mocked her. The way Reid looked in his suit and the romantic mood of the setting made that darn near impossible.

She vowed to try. "I've never been scuba diving," she

said, resuming their conversation after the servers had left. "I do ski occasionally. Nothing more than bunny trails. That's all I have the courage or the balance for, I'm afraid. I'm not much of an athlete." Unlike him.

His gaze dropped to her shoulders then traveled down and Celeste had to suppress a shiver of awareness. "If you don't mind my saying," he began. "You're clearly quite fit."

It was downright silly to feel as giddy as she did about that compliment.

"I do a lot of yoga. It helps center me. I started in college." Thank goodness she had. Between the stress of her job, the long hours, and the continuous mess that was her family life, she needed the release and quiet peacefulness of the practice.

"Makes sense." Reid offered her one of the lobster tails. "I've never tried it, but I hear some of the poses can be very physically demanding."

"Oh, yes. Definitely. Some of the more challenging ones can have me breathless with my muscles screaming and sweat pouring over my skin while I hold the pose."

"Sounds athletic to me."

She shrugged. "I guess."

He leaned back in his chair, studied her. "You do that a lot, don't you?"

"Do what?"

"Discount yourself. What you're capable of."

His statement surprised her. "I—I didn't realize I did."

"You were certain climbing the falls was going to be too much for you. Yet you handled it just fine."

"I had you there to guide and catch me."

He ignored that. "And the way you disparaged your karaoke performance."

Now he had to be teasing her. "Do you blame me? I sounded horrible. Pitchy and completely off key."

"Is that your takeaway from that night?"

"It's the truth! Please don't pretend I have any talent whatsoever as a singer."

"No. I won't."

She had to laugh at that quick response acknowledging her lack of singing ability. "Thank you."

"Does that mean you should never sing karaoke?" he asked with all seriousness. Celeste was beginning to wonder if this might be one of the most vexing conversations she'd ever had. To top it off, they were supposed to be talking about *him*.

"I dunno. I might say that's exactly what it means."

"You'd be wrong. You may be bad at singing. But you're great at karaoke."

Okay. Now he was making zero sense. "Uh... Come again?"

"You were magnificent up there when we sang together," he declared.

Magnificent? "Um... I was?"

He nodded with zero hesitation.

"How do you figure?"

"You were engaging and endearing, despite being scared out of your mind. Most important, you had the crowd entertained. Off key or not, they were with you through the whole song, some singing along. Others simply bouncing to the beat of the song."

Huh. Had that really been the way that whole scene had played out? She'd been so nervous, all she'd thought about was getting through the song and fleeing off the stage.

"I was?" she stammered, completely shocked at what he was telling her.

"Yes. You were. Everyone who witnessed it saw how amazing you were that night. Everyone but you."

CHAPTER TWELVE

HE'D IMPLIED THAT he found her amazing. Celeste couldn't seem to get that thought out of her head. They'd finished their dinner of salt fish and grilled vegetables moments ago and were now on the upper deck of the boat admiring the star-filled night sky and the tranquility of the Caribbean waters as they sailed over the surface.

For a conversation that had started out all about Reid, he'd certainly given her a lot to think of about herself. All her life she'd been told that she wasn't enough, that she had to try harder, be better, simply to be enough. Her mother certainly found her lacking. As did her younger sister. Her fiancé had left her emotionally bruised and publicly humiliated.

Yet here was this charming, enigmatic man trying to tell her the exact opposite—that she didn't give herself enough credit.

They'd carried their wine goblets up with them and Celeste took a sip of her drink as she admired the view. The band due to perform was setting up a few feet away toward the stern as she and Reid stood portside. They couldn't have asked for a more perfect evening for a dinner cruise. She couldn't deny that she was enjoying herself. Despite the somewhat awkward start to the evening, she and Reid had managed to lapse into an easy state of camaraderie and friendly conversation. But she couldn't get some of the things he'd just said about her out of her mind.

"You appear to have drifted off. Penny for your thoughts?" he asked, not looking away from the horizon.

Celeste gave a small shake of her head. "Just admiring the beautiful evening, I guess."

It occurred to her that he still hadn't answered her earlier question. This time, she'd take a different approach. "You were worried the other night about missing someone who was due to fly onto the island," she ventured. "Were they upset that you weren't there to greet them when they arrived?"

Perfectly innocent question. But maybe it would give her some kind of hint as to his relationship status. But Reid only shook his head. "No, they were perfectly understanding."

That told her absolutely nothing about who he was supposed to meet that night. Maybe a more direct approach was necessary after all. Though heaven knew she should just drop the entire matter altogether. But she couldn't seem to let it go.

Reid gave her a chance at an opening with his next question. "So, tell me. Is there no one at home upset that you aren't there with them to celebrate the holidays?"

"Not really. What about you? Is anyone unhappy that you're here, essentially working through the holidays?"

He smiled at her. "You first. I don't consider 'not really' much of an answer."

She blew out a long sigh. "Yes. My mother and sister are upset that I left the city for the holidays. But they're upset for all the wrong reasons." Celeste fought to find the exact right way to explain. She didn't particularly want to get into the whole matter of her family and all their dysfunction. It would only spoil the evening.

"I don't understand," Reid prompted.

"Christmas wasn't particularly a joyous occasion for me as a child. I grew up with a single mother who couldn't always make ends meet. Most years, she would have to work over the holiday, she usually waitressed. And I'd end up having to babysit my younger sister, who was usually upset and cranky that Mommy was gone and she was stuck at home with just her sister. Not much celebrating happened."

He'd turned to face her fully, listening intently to her every word.

"So, you see," she continued. "Christmastime wasn't exactly festive to begin with."

"And then your Christmas wedding happened," he supplied for her.

"Or didn't happen, to be more accurate. There's really nothing I find celebratory about it. Better to just take off for several days of fun and sun."

He reached for her hand over the railing, held it gently in his. "I'm sorry, Celeste. You didn't deserve that. Any of it."

Oh, no, they were not going to discuss Jack. Not here, not now. "Don't be!" she quickly countered before things headed in that direction. "I'd say I'm lucky. Nothing wrong with spending the holidays in paradise on a tropical island."

He looked less than convinced but didn't push. "Your turn," she prompted.

Reid let go of her hand and took a sip of his wine. Was it wrong that she wanted to reach for him again?

"No. My parents split wasn't terribly amicable. My mother's active with a lot of charities that ramp up their activity during the holiday season. And my father is in Aspen currently to spend the holidays skiing with his newly found love, a woman he left his wife of thirty years for."

"I see," was all Celeste could manage in response. For all the people the world over who looked forward to Christmas every year, there had to be just as many who dreaded it. "I'm sorry too, Reid."

He gave a small shrug. "No need. I have plenty that keeps me occupied during the holidays. The hospitality industry doesn't exactly slow down at Christmas. If anything, things are even busier. Then there's all the effort still required to clean up the mess made by Father's recent business decisions." He lifted his glass in mock salute before taking a long swig.

The resentment in Reid's voice was as clear as the starry sky above them.

"So, I guess you and I are a lot alike in many regards," he added, taking another sip of cabernet.

"How so?"

He turned to her once more. "Isn't it obvious? It appears neither one of us will be reveling in yuletide cheer anytime soon."

This conversation was becoming way too heavy. Reid shook off the melancholy that suddenly threatened the atmosphere between him and Celeste. He took the opportunity of a passing waiter to unburden them of their now empty wineglasses. Enough deep talk for now.

The band had finished setting up and began to play a reggae version of "Holly Jolly Christmas." The happy tune immediately lured several couples up and onto the dance floor.

"You think your foot might be up to a dance?" he asked Celeste.

At her somewhat hesitant nod, he gently took her by the elbow and they joined the other dancers. The tempo was just bouncy enough that they could sway easily to the beat. "I see you have yet another talent, Mr. Evanson. Consider me impressed with your footwork."

"Mother insisted on years of dance lessons. Said I needed to be cultured," he answered over the loud music. "You're not so bad yourself."

He couldn't recall going dancing with a woman and actually enjoying himself this much. Celeste seemed to be able to bring a level of energy and fun to whatever she was doing. It was infectious. The dance floor grew more and more crowded as the band started the next number. Celeste was a natural, her movements fluid and in tune with the music. He noticed several pairs of appreciative male eyes on her and reflexively stepped closer. Their bodies brushed against each other as they both moved. Hot, sharp need seared through him every time they made contact. When the band launched into a much slower song, Reid didn't give himself a chance to think. Her wrapped his arms around her and pulled her tight up against him. She didn't protest or make any effort to pull away. Thank the gods for he wasn't sure if he'd be able to let her go.

One of the band members began to speak through the mike over the music. "We're going to make sure everyone has a good time tonight," he announced to responding applause and cheers. He went on, "I hear there are a lot of couples here celebrating."

More cheers sounded. "Raise your hands if you're here to celebrate an anniversary."

Several sets of hands went up.

"How many of you are here on your honeymoon?" The bandmate asked.

Another round of hands responded along with raucous cheers, including from the young blonde woman and her companion who were dancing right next to them.

Celeste gave the couple a warm smile. "Congratulations," she said over all the noise around them.

"Thank you!" The woman responded with a grin. "We got married two days ago." She wagged a finger between him and Celeste. "How long have you two been together?"

"Oh, we're not—" Celeste began.

Reid decided to spare her the awkwardness. "We've known each other for about three years," he answered truthfully. The lady didn't need to know the details.

"That's lovely!" the other woman declared. "We only met last year. But it was love at first sight, you know? We've been inseparable ever since. When it's the right person, you just know. All the signs are there. I had no doubt he's the man I'm meant to spend my life with the moment I met him."

Her spouse nodded enthusiastically in agreement next to her as they continued to dance.

"That's really wonderful," Celeste said, her tone wistful enough that Reid instinctively pulled her closer against him.

"Thanks! I hope we're having as much fun in three years as you two are together."

Celeste seemed to deflate in his arms. He figured she could use a drink. "Why don't we head below deck for some refreshments?" he suggested.

She didn't hesitate, following him off the dance floor and to the bar down the starboard steps. He ordered them more wine once they were seated on the bar stools. But once their glasses arrived, Celeste didn't so much as take a sip. She merely rubbed her finger around the rim, deep in thought.

Reid cursed the loss of the easy companionship they'd been enjoying before running into the newlyweds. He could only guess what Celeste was thinking. She was wondering if she'd ever have what that couple had. If she'd experience the thrill of a honeymoon, or dancing with her new husband above deck aboard a dinner boat cruising over the Caribbean waters.

It was the strangest thing, but he was thinking along those same lines for himself. Definitely not something he'd ever considered before. He shook off the useless thoughts. He already had his hands more than full. Between the family holdings and his father's self-destructive behavior, Reid didn't have it in him to commit to any other kind of relationship.

His gaze fell on the woman sitting next to him.

No. He couldn't even go there, couldn't allow himself to think those thoughts. Celeste had been hurt enough in her lifetime. The last thing she needed was someone like him toying with her affections further.

But they had the rest of this trip. At the least, they had the rest of tonight. There was nothing wrong with enjoying each other's company.

Though Celeste looked far from joyful at the moment. He would have to do something about that. He couldn't have her this forlorn. The evening was much too beautiful to let it go to waste. They were the only people downstairs at the bar, with everyone else still at the dance party above.

He stood and took her by the hand. "Here, follow me." Acknowledging the sole bartender, he walked her behind the bar and led her to the kitchen area behind it.

Several cooks and servers waved as they entered. Reid walked over to the freezer in the center of the room and reached inside.

Celeste blinked at the carton he'd pulled out. "Ice cream?"

"Chocolate."

Her confusion grew into a wide smile. "Where do we find spoons?"

Five minutes later they stood at the hull of the boat with his jacket thrown over Celeste's shoulders and the wind blowing around them, spooning chocolate ice cream straight out of its container.

She didn't want the night to end. And it was just silly to think that way. It wasn't as if she and Reid were walking back to her room after any kind of real date. Foolish, really.

Reid's suit jacket still hung over her shoulders, the smell of him enveloping her, reminding her of the way it had felt to be in his arms on the dance floor. Not to mention, all those other times when they'd been alone.

A shiver ran over her skin. He must have noticed. "Are you still cold? I can call for a beach cart to drive you back to your room," he offered.

No. That wasn't what she wanted. She wanted to continue walking with him, to delay the inevitable. When they would part for the night. What then? Reid didn't mention any other activity he wanted her to attend, no other excursions were planned. For all she knew, this was it.

There would be no more opportunities to spend any time alone with him. Celeste felt an ache of pain in the center of her chest.

"I'm actually enjoying the night air. Thank you for walking me back."

"What kind of gentleman would I be if I left you to head back to your suite by yourself?"

"The kind that serves a girl chocolate ice cream on the hull of a boat during a dinner cruise?"

He laughed at that. The rest of their stroll continued on in pleasant silence, the night air balmy and comfortable. Celeste indulged in a slight fantasy and just let herself pretend. Just for these few short moments, she would make believe that she had what that couple on that boat had. That she'd found the man she was meant to be with and had known right away. And that, fanciful as it was, Reid happened to be that man.

Never mind that her reality was the complete opposite. By contrast, the one time she'd been engaged, it had been a mistake of epic proportions. And with Reid... She sighed. She honestly didn't know the true reality when it came to Reid. He was obviously attracted to her. But what did that mean when he was so quick to step back from her before things could go anywhere? The answer should be obvious, she figured. He knew they had no business being together, so he wasn't going to let things get too far. Wise of him. Unlike her, he was thinking straight.

Maybe she was done with having to do the wise thing, though. Maybe this one time she wanted more. Even if it was just temporary. It might shatter her inside afterward when it all ended and she had to leave, but in her heart she knew it would be worth it.

She just had to know. Without giving herself a chance to think, she blurted out one of the questions that had been on her mind. "I know it's getting late. Do you have to rush to get back? Is someone waiting for you?"

He turned and lifted an eyebrow in question. "What?"

"You were due to meet someone that day when we got stranded at the flower garden. You appeared upset to have to miss them. Are they waiting for you right now?"

The eyebrow lifted ever so higher. "My spirits supplier?"

She clasped a hand to her mouth. "Oh. You were due to meet your spirits supplier that night?"

He nodded once. "That's right. Who did you think it might have been?"

Celeste felt heat rush to her cheeks. Well, at least now she knew. And she couldn't help the sense of relief and giddiness that washed over her at the newfound knowledge. But it had all come at a price. Reid was on to her. He'd be stupid not to have figured out what she was getting at.

They'd reached her building and made their way to her door on the second floor. Celeste turned to face him, not even sure what she was going to say. The only thing she was certain of was that she wasn't ready to walk through that door just yet.

Her heart hammered in her chest as Reid stepped closer to her. She felt the wooden door up against her back as the warmth of his body seeped into the front of hers.

"Why did you want to know?" he asked on a strained whisper.

Her nerves completely on edge and with Reid standing so close, it was hard to think of an answer. The truth. She would go with the truth. She was done with the pretenses. "I think you know why."

"Spell it out for me, Celeste. I don't want to jump to any conclusions here."

Celeste sucked in a deep breath for courage. She was really doing this. "Go ahead and jump. You'd be correct."

Heat darkened his eyes and he visibly stiffened.

And then she couldn't take it anymore. Moving fully up against him, she slid her arms around his neck and brought her face up to his.

It was all the invitation he needed.

He hauled her tight into him and crushed his mouth to hers. He tasted of wine and chocolate and pure, unfiltered male. It was a taste she would never get enough of. The scent of him rushed her senses. His hands moved over her hips and up to her rib cage. All the while, his mouth continued pleasuring her lips, his kiss growing deeper.

"Reid, yes," she managed to whisper against his mouth.

She'd never been so wanton, so in need. But that was the only way to describe the state she was in. She *needed* this man. She needed his arms around her, and to have him hold her all night. And there was no reason not to give in to that primal desire.

Not for this one night, anyway.

Morning would come soon enough.

CHAPTER THIRTEEN

HE WAS GONE.

Celeste could feel his absence without even having to open her eyes. He must have left her bed in the middle of the night. Tears formed behind her lids and she opened them slowly to glance at the bedside clock. Just past midnight. There was no way she would be getting any sleep. Her body felt languid, the heat of Reid's touch still lingered on her skin. He'd brought her to a feeling of euphoria she'd never experienced before.

It was highly unlikely she would ever experience it again. Her eyes stung further before she shoved the sorrow aside. She was a big girl; she'd made her decision and would learn to live with it somehow.

A shadow moved outside on her balcony.

Celeste rubbed her eyes to make sure she wasn't seeing things. A surge of hope shot through her chest when she looked again. Reid hadn't left, he was standing on her balcony, arms draped over the railing, staring out at the ocean in the distance. He was still here. But everything about his stance told her that something was off.

Celeste stood and walked to the closet where the terry cloth robe hung on a hanger. Throwing it on, she took a deep breath. If she was smart, she'd go back to bed and feign that she was still asleep. But something about the rigid set to

Reid's back, the way his head hung forward, called to her. She just had to hope he wanted her to go to him right now.

Well, she was about to find out.

Sliding the glass door open slowly, she stepped out onto the concrete in her bare feet.

"Hey, there," she said softly.

He didn't turn to her. "Sorry if I woke you."

"I awoke on my own. Weren't you able to sleep, either?"

He shook his head. "Happens sometimes."

"I thought at first that you'd left."

"Would you like me to?"

Her answer was immediate. "No! Don't." *Please stay*, she added silently, hating herself for the despair flooding her insides at the threat of him walking out right now.

He simply shrugged. "Okay."

Okay? That was all he was going to say?

She sucked in a breath. "Would you like to be alone?"

He remained silent so long that Celeste was convinced he wasn't going to answer her. Which was answer enough in itself, she figured. But then he finally turned to her, reached for her hands.

"No. I've been alone long enough. Stay with me."

She wouldn't allow herself to look too deeply into his words. They'd just been intimate with each other, as close as two people could get. And heaven help her, she only wanted desperately to be back in his arms again, snuggled up against him in her bed. The next time she woke up, she wanted to be nestled in his embrace with his warmth surrounding her body.

Right now, she stepped into his open arms and let him hold her. After several moments, he exhaled deeply and turned her to face the ocean, her back up against his front.

She could feel his chest rise and fall with each breath he took. His strong, muscular arms held her tightly around her waist.

"It's beautiful out there, isn't it?" he asked, his breath hot up against her ear.

She nodded under his chin. "The whole resort is a sight to behold. You've really done well here, Reid."

He continued, "It's times like this when I wish I could simply take it all in and just enjoy this place. Rather than worry about how it's run. Or if we'll turn enough of a profit. It's all just so new."

He had a huge burden on his shoulders, she knew. She hadn't realized just how heavily it all must have weighed on him.

"I wish there was a way I could help."

"You are helping. You're helping me put the marketing plan together to help sell this place. I couldn't have asked for a better contractor."

Celeste tried not to bristle at the reminder that she was essentially his temporary employee. He had to see her as more than that after what they'd just shared.

Or was it simply wishful thinking on her part to think so?

"I'll do my best, Reid. But something tells me you would have figured out the marketing approach with or without me."

He turned her to face him then, dropped a soft kiss along the base of her neck. Red-hot desire had her shuddering all over. It was quite a marvel how the smallest peck of a kiss from him could make her insides burn with want.

"I'm glad it was with you," he said then took her lips in a hungry kiss. "So very glad."

Any thought of profits or marketing strategies completely fled her mind as soon as his lips touched hers. Her only focus was the man holding her, kissing her, making her *want*. Her arms instantly went around his neck as his hands found her skin underneath the robe.

The next instant she was lifted off her feet and carried inside.

Where he set her further aflame.

Reid woke up to find Celeste sprawled over his chest. She was still sound asleep. Her breath was hot against his chest, hair spread out fanlike over his skin. He took the opportunity to run his fingers over their silken strands, remembering the way he'd thrust his hands through them last night and the way she'd melted in his arms over and over again.

Morning had come all too soon. A glance at the tableside clock told him that it was much later than he usually started the day. Alex was probably wondering where he was.

Yep, reality had dawned just as clearly as the morning sun. He couldn't shove it aside any longer. Unwilling to let her go just yet, he pulled Celeste ever so slightly up against him. They would have some talking to do later. Though he had no real idea where he would start the conversation. He couldn't risk mucking it all up by trying before he'd even figured things out.

He had nothing to offer her. His world was hotels and resorts and meetings and investments. And somehow consoling his betrayed mother. Not to mention preparing for the fight he was certain was coming from his father. Dale Evanson wanted to regain control of the company he'd almost run into the ground. And he had enough cronies on the board who were ready to help him get what he was after.

A woman like Celeste had no room in her life for so many complications. Especially when she had enough of her own to contend with. Oh, and there was that whole former-fiancée-of-a-good-friend thing hanging above their heads, as well. He couldn't let himself forget that.

Yeah, reality could land a real kick to the gut sometimes.

Reid swore softly under his breath and made an effort to gently remove himself from bed without rousing her. She stirred but didn't open her eyes. It took a few more tries before he was able to disengage out of their embrace. He reached for his shirt and pants lying over the back of the leather chair. He had to go start his day. He would have to leave her a note or try calling her later.

But there would be no need to do either of those things. Celeste slowly opened her eyes and sat halfway up. She looked so alluring with her hair in complete disarray and her lips still swollen from his kisses. He could see the minor redness on her shoulders and around her chest where he'd rubbed his beard over her skin. He had to close his eyes to keep from crawling back into bed and joining her once more.

"You're up."

He nodded. "I have to get going. There's a lot happening today." *On and off the resort*, he added under his breath.

"Does that mean breakfast together is out of the question?" The look of longing in her eyes nearly undid him. He had to hold firm.

"I'm afraid so. I have one meeting after another." Starting with the business partner who was probably wondering where the devil he was at this very moment.

"I see."

He leaned over the bed, brushed a soft kiss across her temple. "You go back to sleep. No need for both of us to leave the warmth and comfort of the bed."

"It's not quite as warm anymore," she countered.

Reid ignored that, just turned to throw his pants on. Then he pulled his shirt over his shoulders. He had to turn away, if he continued looking at the enticing picture she made—with the sheet pulled up over the roundness of her breasts—he wasn't sure how much resolve he could muster. He wasn't made of stone, after all.

"I have to get you my written recommendations," Celeste said behind him as he sat in the chair to tie his shoes. "I've already got most of it written up on my tablet. I can use the business office to get it all printed once I finish."

"No need to do that," Reid threw over his shoulder. "Would you mind sending it via text? As an attachment. I'll look at it when I get a chance."

She sat studying him as he finished the last knot and stood. "Sure. I can do that," she answered.

"Thanks. I'm really looking forward to seeing what you have to say."

"Reid…"

"Yes?"

She opened her mouth but shut it again without speaking. Instead, she dropped back onto the pillow behind her and flung her arm over her face. "Never mind. It's not important."

Reid fought the urge to go to her side and indulge in another kiss, this time to her lips. But it would be dangerous to risk tasting her again. The sooner he walked out of this room, the better for both of them.

"Bye, sweetheart," he said and pulled the door open.

She didn't answer before he walked out.

She had no one but herself to blame.

Celeste turned the nozzle of the shower to the very end of the hot setting, allowing the punishing heat of the water to wash over her until she could stand it no longer. It did nothing to scorch away her internal anguish. What had she been expecting? To spend the day with Reid holding hands and walking along the beach? She'd understood last night exactly what she was getting into.

The fact that she was hurt and disappointed by the way he'd left this morning was no one's fault but her own.

She'd been naive, fooling no one except herself. She knew how ill-equipped she was for meaningless flings. She'd gone ahead and spent the night with Reid anyway. Worse yet, she'd fooled herself into thinking she could somehow conveniently forget that she'd fallen for him. It had only been a few days since she'd arrived on the island and run into him again. But it was like the newlywed on the dinner cruise had said last night—when you're with the right person, you just know.

Celeste just knew.

Though they hadn't been on the best of terms three years ago when she'd first met him, she'd noted Reid's determination and quiet strength. How hard he seemed to work as chairman of his family business. He'd always been a good friend to Jack, coming through for him with countless errands to help with the responsibilities of the would-be groom. Of all Jack's friends, it was only Reid whom she'd grown to admire.

And the time she'd spent with him these past few days had grown that admiration into so much more. Celeste bit back a sob.

She stayed under the spray until the water turned cold and her skin started to prune. Then she made herself take a deep breath and shake off the useless, defeatist thoughts. Celeste Frajedi had learned long ago that the best way to overcome any stumble or setback was to keep busy and work hard. Stepping out of the stall, she toweled off, threw on shorts and a tank top, then ordered coffee and breakfast from room service. Then she pulled up her tablet and got to work. She had a marketing report to complete.

CHAPTER FOURTEEN

HER SCRAMBLED EGGS sat cold and untouched an hour later when Celeste started putting the final touches to her write-up. Though the entire pot of coffee was gone. The next pot she ordered could be enjoyed relaxing on the balcony and watching the beach scene outside, now that she had the file mostly completed. And she'd done a good job with it too, if she did say so herself. There was a part of the report that could prove risky. A professional should never allow personal feelings to affect a business project, but she'd decided to take the chance. There wasn't much left to lose.

The ring of her cell phone pulled her focus.

Reid.

Her hand immediately reached for the device. Without stopping to glance at the screen, she immediately clicked the answer button, didn't even care how anxious she'd appear at having answered so quickly.

She was wrong. The voice that greeted her over the line was a husky feminine one. The first words spoken were slurred.

"Hope you're having fun lying on the beach while the rest of us are stuck here."

Her mother.

Celeste tried to clamp down on the alarm rising within

her core. This was twice in a matter of days. Wendy's problems appeared to be escalating. So far, this was turning into one sucker punch of a day.

"Hello, Mother. Is something the matter back at home?"

Her mother grunted in clear disgust. "Better believe there is."

An icicle of fear dropped into Celeste's stomach. "Is everything okay with the baby? What is it?"

"The baby's fine," her mother huffed. Celeste allowed herself a moment of relief before her mother continued. "Your sister needs to start looking for another job, ya know."

Celeste grasped for patience. What she did know for certain was that Tara wasn't in any rush to do any kind of job search. Especially now, mere days away from Christmas. "Mother, please tell me why you're calling. You said something was wrong."

"I'll have you know they're threatening to shut off my power. It's below freezing here. Not like that sunny, warm place you're at. And they're gonna try to cut my heat off."

Alarm tightened Celeste's muscles. "What? Why?"

"I don't know. They're saying the bill wasn't paid."

"Are they saying that because it's true? Did you neglect to pay the bill?"

"I don't remember."

"Just send the check out now. Pay it as soon as you can."

"I got nothing to pay it with, do I?"

Celeste rubbed a weary hand over her forehead. Her mother's account must be seriously overdue for the utility to be threatening to shut off supply. Which meant Wendy hadn't paid the bill for several months.

"Momma, I deposited more than enough money in

your account to cover all the expenses and utilities." And she'd done so consistently every month. "Why didn't you pay the bill?"

A muffled sound echoed from the tiny speaker. Was that a sob? Celeste's earlier alarm turned into an icy brick of fear in the pit of her stomach. "I kept trying to win the money, Celeste," Wendy said on a loud hiccup. "And I came so close, but then the table would turn the other way." There was no doubt now that Wendy was indeed crying.

"Have you been gambling?"

Another hiccup followed by a sniffle. "I was just tryin' a get some money to buy the baby some extra-special Christmas presents. Wanted to do it on my own, without help from nobody."

Celeste leaned back in her chair, her surprise almost too much to contain. Her mother had actually wanted to feel the pride of getting her first grandchild a holiday gift without asking for money from anyone else. Mainly her.

Celeste couldn't help but feel touched. But Wendy had gone about it in an oh-so-wrong way.

One thing was clear. Her mother needed to get help. It couldn't be put off any longer. Not only did her occasional alcohol benders seem to be growing more frequent, she now ran the very real risk of acquiring a gambling addiction, too.

"Mother, stop crying. I'll take care of the electricity bill, okay?"

"Th-thank you," Wendy was no longer trying to hold back the wails. "I didn't want to freeze."

"You won't. And we'll be sure to get Nat a wonderful present when I get back, okay? But you have to stop trying to win the money."

"Okay."

"Promise me, Mother."

"I promise," Wendy answered, and another loud sniffle followed.

Celeste squeezed her eyes shut and counted her breath for several beats after her mother hung up. It took some time, but finally her pulse started to slow and some of the tension left her midsection. She would need a full and long meditation session soon to try to take the edge off her frayed emotions. Given her day already, the session would have to be a marathon one.

She had so much to take care of once she returned to New York City.

But first things first. Saving the document she was working on, she switched browsers and called up her mother's electricity bill. The sum in arrears made her gasp. It was a wonder the electricity company hadn't shut her off already. With resignation and sadness, Celeste transferred the amount out of her own checking account to cover the debt.

This was her truth. Her reality.

Incidents like this were the reason she shouldn't have forgotten herself last night. Worse, they were the reason she should have never let herself fall for a man like Reid Evanson in the first place. Why hadn't she learned her lesson the first time?

For his reality was so very different from the one she lived in.

Alex made a show of glancing at his watch when Reid finally made it into the office later that morning. Reid braced himself for the inevitable ribbing that was sure to be headed his way.

"Yeah. I know I'm late, partner. How about giving

me some slack this one time, huh?" he asked, his arms spread out and his palms up.

Alex rubbed his jaw. The serious playacting he was attempting was severely undercut by the quiver of a smile at the corners of his mouth. "I don't know, man. I mean, you've been the one out enjoying yourself on all these various excursions with a beautiful woman by your side who you say is 'helping you.'" He added air quotes with his fingers as he spoke the last two words.

Reid had to groan out loud at the mention of Celeste. Alex noticed, of course. He immediately turned serious.

"What's happened?"

He really didn't want to get into any of this. Not ever. He didn't want to discuss Celeste at all. In fact, he didn't even want to think about her. Because doing that would undoubtedly tempt him to seek her out and drag her back to her room where they could run a replay of last night.

Just. Stop.

It was a risk he couldn't take.

"Nothing happened," he fibbed to his business partner. "I just overslept." That part was at least the truth.

Alex's eyes narrowed on him, clearly questioning whether to accept his answer as the whole truth. Reid knew he was too sharp and would see through it without effort. He was right. "I can't recall another time you've ever overslept."

"It was bound to happen sometime."

Alex gave a slight shrug of his shoulder. "Suit yourself. Don't tell me, then."

"What did I miss around here?" Reid asked, in a blatantly obvious move to change the subject.

Luckily, Alex was going to play along. "The usual," he answered. "A few minor guest complaints. The tennis pro asked that the courts be redone. And we're running low on chardonnay."

Reid gave him a nod. "Got it. I'll go make some phone calls." He pivoted toward his office.

"And then there's your father," Alex called out after him.

Reid stopped in his tracks and turned back to face his friend. "What about him?"

"He's been calling the office all morning. Says he got tired of leaving you messages on your cell just to have you ignore him."

Of course his father would say that. The truth was, Reid had given him every opportunity to change the course of the disastrous path they currently found themselves on.

"How's that whole thing going anyway?" Alex asked.

"About as well as can be expected. He wants full control of the company back." What made it so much worse was that Reid knew his father was ready to retire. The only reason he was doing this was to please his new bride-to-be.

"Any chance of that happening?" Alex wanted to know.

Reid shrugged. "He has some cronies on the board who are ready to vote as he wants." Reid would risk an all-out battle before he let that vote go his father's way—if it ever came to a vote.

Alex let out a low whistle. "Hostile takeover attempts can be brutal under any circumstances."

"Let alone amongst family," Reid finished his thought for him.

"I'm here if you want to talk," Alex said to his back as Reid walked into his office.

Once there, with the door shut, he finally let out the full brunt of the frustration he'd been feeling since leaving Celeste's bed this morning, by launching his priceless signed Red Sox vintage baseball across the room. It hit the wall with a loud thud and sent chips of paint flying.

Great. One more thing to have to fix. This time, he'd done it to himself.

If Alex heard the noise outside in the foyer, he was too astute to knock and ask him about it. Not that he ever actually knocked.

The angry calls from his father served as a reminder that he was right to leave Celeste this morning without lingering any further the way he'd wanted to. He'd so badly wanted to. The right thing to do was to leave her alone.

It wouldn't be easy, and it would take a great deal of effort, but eventually, he might even stop thinking about the way she'd felt in his arms last night.

An internal voice immediately mocked him. *Yeah, right.* He'd be thinking about her touch for the rest of his natural life. He could only hope to stop missing her at some point during it. Forty or fifty years apart might do it.

But she deserved to be able to move on. He didn't have the right to stand in her way.

He was going stir-crazy in this office. Reid cursed and threw his pen down on the desk blotter so hard it bounced off and landed on the carpet. He had to get out for a while. There were a dozen more calls to be made. Several documents to be signed and countless emails to answer. But he couldn't concentrate. Before the start of this week he might have boasted about his superior focus skills. It didn't help that he kept checking his phone to see if Celeste had sent him the text yet. As of three minutes ago, she had not. The short time frame didn't stop him from checking yet again. Nothing.

Not from her, anyway. By cruel contrast, his phone was buzzing with texts and voice mails left by his father.

He stood up and stormed out of his office. The desk attendant in the concierge area smiled at him when he approached. "Reid. I was just about to come knock. Someone left a file for you."

She handed him an envelope. He removed the papers within. Celeste's report. But she was supposed to have sent it electronically.

"How long ago was this dropped off?"

"Just a couple of minutes. The young lady used the business office to print it then dropped it off here. She said you were expecting it."

She couldn't have gotten far. Reid knew he shouldn't do it, but he found himself following the path she would take if she were to head back to her room from the concierge lobby. The least he could do was thank her.

The mocking voice reemerged. As if that's the reason you're trying to catch her.

He saw her moments later on the path by the kiddie pool. She stopped to retrieve and toss back an inflatable ball to a toddler when it rolled by her feet. The action stalled her long enough for him to catch up.

"Celeste." She froze.

"Reid?"

"Hey." He lifted the envelope in his hand. "Thanks for bringing this by."

"The text I attached it to kept bouncing back. The file must have been too big."

That explained the printout. He could release any notion that she might have come by the office hoping to run into him. He should have discounted that possibility in the first place. She had left it for him at the counter after all.

"Oh. Thanks for taking the time to print it out, then." How many times could he thank her in one conversation? He had no reason to be this tongue-tied around her. He had to get a grip already.

"You're welcome."

The toddler threw the ball back at her. Celeste flashed the child a bright smile and tossed the toy back once more.

"I'm looking forward to reading it," he told her when she'd turned back to him.

"I hope it helps."

"There's still the matter of your compensation. I can have papers drawn up—"

She held a hand up before he could continue. "That won't be necessary. I won't accept any type of payment from you."

A boulder settled in his chest. Part of him was convinced she'd take him up on the free annual vacations. That he would at least be able to see her again once every year. Though he'd feel gutted every time she left. "I don't understand. I don't feel right having you do all this work for nothing."

The ball landed between their feet again. They both turned to find the same toddler boy giggling.

Come on, pal, Reid thought, groaning inside. This was hard enough without a toothless lothario intent on a game of catch with his woman.

His woman?

He cleared his throat. "I'd like to talk about this."

She gave a slight lift of her shoulder. "If you wish. Sure, we can talk. But I won't change my mind."

Reid quickly took her by the elbow and led her to the poolside cabana bar before the beach ball reappeared. Celeste allowed him to guide her onto one of the stools. He motioned for the bartender and ordered two rum punches. He never drank during the day when he was working. But this was an extenuating circumstance if ever he'd encountered one.

He'd missed her. It had only been a few hours since he'd left her this morning. But he couldn't deny that he'd spent those hours wishing she was still by his side. He missed her smile, her wit. The way she smelled.

"Tell me why," he said once their icy drinks had arrived.

Celeste took a swig from her paper straw and his gaze immediately fell to her lips.

"I thought we had an agreement," he added.

"I've changed my mind. Consider it professional courtesy on my part. As your resort guest."

So that's all she was going to classify herself as. He had no business being disappointed. He wanted this distance, didn't he? It's why he had fled her room after the night they'd spent together.

For such a hot, pleasant day, they were the only two people seated at the bar. The bartender was busy at work several feet away with his back to them organizing bottles and tidying.

If they were a real couple, Reid might take the opportunity to kiss her.

His cell phone started to vibrate in his shirt pocket before he took that thought any further. He quickly removed the device and set it to do not disturb, ignoring the risk of missing an important business call. And if it was his father calling yet again…well, he'd had enough of his father's interruptions for a lifetime.

"I don't mind," Celeste said, pointing to his phone on the bar. "You can answer that, if you want."

"I don't want."

She lifted an eyebrow in question. "Oh?"

Reid blew out a deep breath. "I'm in the middle of something rather unpleasant. It involves my father. He wants to talk about it. Only there's nothing left to talk about."

"Ah." Celeste took another sip of her drink. "If it makes you feel better, I wish I hadn't received a call from my own parent this morning."

He laughed. "Yeah?"

"Oh, yeah. It was a doozy."

"Maybe we'll have to compare notes on our parents someday."

She ducked her head, suddenly serious. "I'd rather not."

"Tell me something," she asked, not meeting his eyes.

"Yes?"

"You said before that you and Jack didn't talk at all about me after we broke up."

Where was this all leading? Reid had no idea. He only knew that the reminder that she'd once been engaged to another man had his gut tightening. He really had no desire to talk about her ex-fiancé. "That's right."

"What about before the breakup? You two must have talked about the woman he was about to marry."

He shrugged, still confused about the direction this conversation had taken. He'd sat her down to try to convince her to accept payment for her hard work.

"What did he tell you about me, Reid? Did he say I was just after his money?"

He hadn't seen that question coming at all, wasn't sure how to answer. If he thought hard about it, Reid would have to admit that Jack had in fact insinuated that very thing. "Celeste, what's this all about?"

She took another sip from her straw, looked away toward the crystal-blue water of the pool. "See, he would have been right to say so if he did. It's the real reason he left me."

CHAPTER FIFTEEN

CELESTE COULDN'T REALLY say if her intention had been to shock Reid. But it sure looked like she'd done just that.

She hadn't had anything to eat all day, just that pot of coffee this morning. And the rum punch was so much stronger than any drink she was used to. Combined with the confusion that seeing Reid always seemed to bring forth within her, the alcohol had gone straight to her head and loosened her lips.

Reid suddenly stood. Dropping several bills onto the bar, he picked up his cell phone and the report. Then he gently nudged her up out of her stool.

"Let's go."

Celeste followed without question. The cat was out of the bag now. Might as well get everything out in the open.

He led her to a rental cabana that must not have been reserved for the day and pulled down the privacy flaps. A shiver of apprehension ran down Celeste's spine when he turned and fixed his gaze on her.

"Care to explain?" he demanded.

She dropped down onto the padded lounger and studied her toes. "I didn't grow up with any money, Reid. Unlike the way you and Jack grew up."

"Don't make assumptions, Celeste."

"What does that mean?"

But he wasn't going to allow the switch in topic. "Never mind. We're talking about you."

She let out a deep breath. "Why do you think Jack decided he couldn't go through with the wedding?"

"He got cold feet. It happens."

She laughed without any real mirth behind it. "He got cold feet because my mother and sister made no secret of the fact that they were very excited about how rich he was. They acted downright giddy."

Nausea roiled through her stomach at the memories. There'd been times when Momma had come right out and asked Jack about his net worth and how much he was willing to part with to help his future in-laws.

The humiliation had been unbearable.

She sucked in a deep breath. "Jack insisted we needed to get away from my mother and sister, starting with the wedding. Hence the desire to elope—so they wouldn't be there. He also suggested we consider living on the West Coast afterward. To stay far away from them."

"You said no."

"In no uncertain terms. I'm all the family Tara and my mother have. There is no one else. I couldn't just turn my back on them."

Reid remained silent, simply waited for her to continue.

"So Jack can't really be faulted for walking away, can he?" she asked. "I can't really blame him."

Reid crossed his arms in front of his chest as he analyzed her. "Is that what you really think?"

She could only nod silently, still staring at her toes.

"What about the fact that he waited until the last minute to do it? Or how cowardly it was to leave you waiting there with a church full of guests? Can you blame him for any of those things?"

"I'm not saying he's a saint. I'm not defending him. And I'm not defending my mother and sister. I'm just saying I understand why he did it."

"No, you're just finding ways to blame yourself. For the cowardly way he treated you. For the way your family members treated you. None of which had anything to do with *you*." He emphasized the last word with heavy inflection.

Suddenly, anger and frustration flooded her chest. She hadn't confided in him to be scrutinized or lectured to or somehow analyzed.

"Spare me the empty platitudes, Reid. I'm not telling you any of this to garner some sort of sympathy or for your pity."

"Then why did you tell me?"

"So that you know why I can't keep coming back here year after year. Seeing you again. That part of the deal is absolutely off the table."

She sucked in a labored breath. "And there's absolutely no way I'll take any money from you. I just wanted you to understand why."

She brushed past him and rushed through the canvas flap before he could see how close to breaking down she really was.

He didn't try to follow her.

Celeste hadn't stopped shaking by the time she reached her room and slammed the door shut. Her gaze immediately fell to the bed, bringing forth haunting and erotic images of all that she and Reid had shared the night before. How foolish she had been to fall in love with a man who was so terribly wrong for her. Her heart felt heavy and bruised in her chest. Like someone had struck a physical blow. She didn't know if the ache would ever heal.

Her breakup with Jack had been a hard hit to her ego. The loss she felt now felt like an open wound, one she might never recover from.

But now wasn't the time to dwell on any of that. She had a call to make. With shaky fingers, she reached for her phone and clicked on her mother's contact icon.

Wendy picked up after several rings. "Did you pay the bill?"

Not even a hello. Why was she even surprised?

"Momma. Listen to me. There's something very important I need to explain to you."

Celeste didn't give her mother a chance to protest. She just calmly and distinctly went over the decisions she'd recently made. Then she clearly explained the steps she planned to take in implementing them all.

Her determination must have rung through clearly in Celeste's voice because her mother didn't argue. In fact, Celeste thought she might even have heard a tinge of relief in Wendy's voice.

The perfect setting to fall in love...speaking from personal experience...

Reid reread the same passages from the file Celeste had turned in yet once more. He'd lost count how many times he'd already read them. As a marketing plan, she'd handed him pure gold. Her suggestions were sound, and many of her ideas could justifiably be described as brilliant. But those were the only lines he cared about.

She'd made it personal. And she was telling him she'd fallen in love with him. He was glad he'd made it back to his living quarters before taking the time to read her report. Something had told him he should be alone while looking at the file, someplace he wouldn't risk being interrupted. Finally putting the papers down, he walked over to the wet bar across the sitting area and poured himself a generous amount of aged dark rum.

She loved him. It said so in black and white. Written by her hand.

Lord knew he didn't deserve it. That he fell far short of the type of man someone like Celeste was worthy of. So now the only question was what was he going to do about it?

He downed the rum all at once, felt the satisfying burn of the spirit travel down his throat. It did nothing to ease his inner turmoil.

He'd called her ex a coward earlier today in the beach-side cabana when he'd pulled her in there after her so-called "admission." He had to examine whether he was the one being cowardly now. Was he going to let her walk off this island in a few short days and out of his life for good? Or was he going to be as brave as she was? The woman had fearlessly laid it all on the line by putting her feelings into words that the whole world was meant to see.

He wasn't worthy of such a selfless act done on his behalf. But he'd been bestowed with it nonetheless. He couldn't walk away. He would find her, and they would determine once and for all how to move forward. Together.

He had so much upheaval in his life right now, had no guarantee what the future held if this deal didn't work. His father was hell-bent on bleeding the company dry. He could only hope the board saw that fact and sided with him.

Because damned if he hadn't just realized that he'd fallen in love with her, too. He needed to tell her so. It was only right. He needed to follow her example and be as courageous as she was. He also needed to take her into his arms and make sure she understood that he was never going to let her go.

But first, a shower. It had been a long, grueling day that had left tension knotting in his shoulders and back.

Reid couldn't help the smile that tugged at his mouth as he walked to the bathroom and turned the water on. In a few short hours, if all went well and he could persuade Celeste to listen, he'd be holding her and kissing her again. That had to make him the luckiest man in the universe.

He realized all too soon that the universe had other plans.

Reid's phone lit up like a Christmas tree when he left the shower fifteen minutes later. With a chest full of trepidation, he returned the call to the number that had been trying to reach him for the entire time he'd been bathing.

One of his lawyers.

This was not a good sign.

The attorney answered on the first ring. "Bad news, Reid. We're going to need to do some damage control or you run the real risk of reverting all control back to Dale."

"I take it my father has managed to push through a vote?"

"You'd be right. You need to fly down to Boston first thing."

Reid disconnected the call and cursed the fates he'd been so sure were smiling on him just minutes before.

He tapped out Celeste's number on his screen but she didn't answer. His intended message wasn't the kind a man left on voice mail. He would have to try to get a hold of her later.

Right now, he had a flight to book and packing to do.

Celeste tried to focus on the same book she'd been try-ing to read ever since she'd arrived on the island. She'd barely gotten through the first couple of chapters. As gripping as the plot was, she couldn't seem to find herself immersed in the story.

She was much too distracted wondering whether Reid had read the file yet. There seemed to be no good conclusion. If he hadn't looked at it yet, what exactly was he waiting for? Why was he putting it off?

And if he had read it but wasn't reaching out to her... That scenario was the more heartbreaking possibility.

Well, she'd done all she could. She'd laid herself bare. Both with what she'd written and everything she'd told him in the cabana earlier. There was nothing more of her to expose to the man. Regardless of his ultimate reactions, she vowed to never regret her decision to do so.

She needed something to take her mind off him. The book wasn't cutting it. Celeste reached for her phone and dialed her sister's number. The gurgling, happy sounds of her baby niece would be like Uma's balm to her injured soul.

"Hey, Tara," she spoke into the phone when her sister answered. "How are you?"

"All right, putting up Nat's first Christmas tree. She's very confused about why there's a tree in the house. And why I'm hanging shiny things off its branches."

Celeste had to laugh at that. Maybe her little niece would be enough of a reason from now on to stay in New York for the holidays in the future. "I really miss the little tyke."

"She misses you, too."

"Can you put her on the phone? I just wanna hear her make noises for a bit. Maybe get her to say CeeCee again."

Her sister laughed. "I think you imagined that. She

is not trying to say your name already. She's only nine months old."

"I heard it loud and clear that day!" she exclaimed with a laugh.

"In any case, I'm afraid she's down for a nap right now."

"Oh. That's too bad." Celeste wasn't prepared for the depth of the disappointment she felt at the news. She really had missed the little girl, hadn't realized exactly how much until now.

Tara paused a beat before continuing. "You sound sad, sis. What is it?"

A sensation of warmth blossomed in her chest. She and Tara had their differences...what siblings didn't? But they somehow always knew how to read each other and tried to cheer each other up when it was called for.

"Nothing. And everything," she admitted.

"Does 'everything' include Ma?"

"So, you heard huh?"

"Yeah, she called here right after you told her. She knows it's the right thing to do. For what it's worth, I think you did the right thing, too."

Celeste sat upright on the bed. "You do?"

"Yeah. She's gotten bad. Doesn't pay attention to how much she's spending or what she's spending it on. She needs someone else to take charge of her finances. It might curb her drinking, too. Which also seems way out of hand lately."

"I set up an annuity for her," Celeste explained. "She'll get a certain amount every month as spending money. But I'll be the one in charge of her expenditures. And she has to agree to register for an addiction counseling service."

"I think that's wise." Tara hesitated before continuing. "Along those same lines, I've also been meaning to thank you. For setting up that trust for the baby. You know I appreciate it, right? And she will, too."

"I know, Tara."

This conversation was getting way too heavy. Celeste decided to change the subject. Though the next topic wasn't such a light one either. "How's the job search going?" she asked, knowing there couldn't be much of one.

Tara audibly sobbed into the phone. "Tara? Are you crying?" Not Tara, too! What was it with her family and all the waterworks today?

She heard a sniffle. "Maybe."

"What's wrong?"

"I just can't take it, sis. Those office buildings, sitting in those cubicles. It's not me. I feel stifled and caged. But office work is the only thing I'm qualified for."

Oh, dear. Celeste had no idea her sister felt that way. How had she never thought to ask? What kind of big sister did that make her?

None of which had anything to do with you.

Reid's words echoed in her head. He'd been right. This was about Tara, not about herself. She needed to find a way to separate herself from the needs of her family.

"What do you want to be qualified for?"

Another sniffle. "I don't know. But remember all those pictures I used to take before that camera Uncle Zed got us finally broke?"

The question invoked a vague memory in her mind. But apparently, the camera had meant a great deal to her sister. "Yes."

"I really enjoyed taking those pictures."

"You did?"

"Yeah, I did. And I was good at it, too. But you know how Ma is. She told me we didn't have the money to replace the camera. And that it was a stupid waste of time anyway."

That certainly sounded like their mother. Celeste had been so focused on her own treatment at her mother's hands, she'd completely missed the negativity that Tara had grown up with.

The answer came to her without question. "Then it's about time we replaced that camera, Tara." She told her sister. "And maybe we can find you a class that can show you how to take even better photos."

Her sister's gratitude came through loud and clear in her cheer of delight. "That's always been a dream of mine," Tara squealed into the phone. Again, Celeste had to wonder why she was first hearing this now.

"Careful," Celeste warned. "You'll wake up the baby."

Tara laughed. "I should probably go check on her. But just one more thing, sis."

"What's that?"

"I don't know why you sound so sad, you're on vacation in paradise, after all. But you deserve to have your dreams happen, too."

CHAPTER SIXTEEN

YOU DESERVE TO have your dreams happen, too.

Tara's voice still echoed in her mind the following morning. Celeste showered quickly then quickly got dressed and threw on her sandals. She fled out the door before she could change her mind. Step one in pursuing a dream was to have the courage to ask for what you wanted.

She wanted Reid.

Unlike the previous days since her arrival, this morning's sky was cloudy and gray. The air was thick with muggy moisture. She would guess a rainstorm was headed their way soon. Hopefully, the weather wasn't any kind of ominous sign regarding what she was about to do. When she reached the concierge level, she made a beeline straight to Reid's door. She had to do this before she lost her nerve.

Her knock went unanswered. She tried again with the same result. A pleasant male voice sounded behind her. "Can I help you with something, Celeste?"

She turned to face Reid's smiling, handsome business partner, Alex.

"I, um, was looking for Reid."

"Maybe I can help you."

She quickly shook her head. "I don't think so. I did some work for him, I just wanted to get his feedback on it." She had to tell the lie. She couldn't exactly divulge to Alex the real reason she was here. Kind eyes or not.

"Ah, right."

She shifted awkwardly. "Do you happen to know when he'll be in today?" she asked, knowing she sounded anxious and impatient but unable to help it.

"I'm afraid he won't be in at all today. I actually don't know when he'll be back. He flew out to Boston earlier this morning."

Celeste would have sunk into the floor if she didn't have an audience. Reid had left. Without so much as a goodbye. He hadn't even tried to find her first.

Alex continued to speak. She barely heard him over the pounding in her ears. "But I know he's read your file," he told her. "I'm sure he'll email you his comments in due time."

Celeste felt as if the wind had been knocked out of her lungs. Reid was going to email his comments. She'd laid her heart out on those pages. And he didn't think enough of that to so much as try to talk to her about it. He'd run off. Just like Jack had done on the day of their wedding.

Ridiculous as it sounded, Reid's betrayal felt like the bigger one by far. She'd recovered from Jack's desertion. She knew the same wasn't going to be possible this time.

She did her best to summon a smile for Reid's friend. "Thank you. I'll look for it in my inbox."

She could do so on her way to the airport. Looked like she would be cutting her trip short. She no longer had any desire to stay.

Or to ever come back again.

In his anxiousness and relief to be back in Jamaica, Reid exited the town car almost before the vehicle had come to a complete stop in the circular driveway of the Baja Majestic.

This had to be the quickest trip he'd ever taken to Boston and back. He usually booked at least one night at the Evanson Premier Boston Harbor hotel before taking a morning flight the next day. But he'd had no intention of sticking around the city this time. Once the confrontation with his father was over, he was more than ready to fly back to the Caribbean. Back to the resort he'd called home for weeks now. Back to Celeste. They had quite a bit to work out between them.

Though confrontation wasn't exactly the correct term for the meeting he'd had with Dale. Reid had arrived at Evanson Properties headquarters just in time to head off a vote of the board of directors. The clear relief on the expressions of the twelve executives told him the vote could have gone either way.

After that, he'd made sure to finally have the one-to-one with his father that he'd been avoiding for so long. It had taken Celeste to help him discover his avoidance had been more personal than business. He had yet to thank her for that.

In the end, Dale had seen reason and agreed to a limited role as a company president. Another weight lifted off Reid's shoulders, though he and his father had a long way to go before their personal relationship could begin to mend.

All in due time.

Nodding to the doorman, he passed through the sliding doors into the Baja Majestic lobby, gratified that several guests were milling about, ready to check in. So far, the holiday season could officially be called a success. Celeste's marketing plan would only help once it was implemented. Yet another thank-you she was due.

He stopped at the counter and removed his sunglasses. "Sanya, please deliver a cart with our finest champagne and a variety of desserts to Room B717."

The woman behind the counter smiled and started clicking at the computer keyboard in front of her. "Right away, sir." Her smile suddenly flattened with confusion. "Is that the correct room, Mr. Evanson?"

"Yes. Is there a problem?"

She returned her gaze to the monitor screen. "Our system says the room is empty, housekeeping is in there now. The guest has already checked out."

Reid felt all the excitement he'd experienced only moments before extinguish like a blown-out flame, replaced with a pounding sense of disappointment and hurt.

She was gone.

If she kept busy enough, and took on enough projects, she could almost push Reid Evanson out of her mind for several minutes at a time. The only problem was, the days between Christmas and New Year's didn't exactly bring in a lot of business activity. Still, Celeste made it a point to go into her Upper East Side office in every morning to find ways to keep herself busy. Never mind that she was one of only a few people there. Most of the other employees were out preparing to celebrate New Year's Eve.

So far, she'd gone over all her deliverables for the new year, and then she'd gone over them again. She'd studied past successful campaigns to analyze what had worked and why.

She'd even cleared out her inbox and organized her paper files via a new method. Today she figured she might tackle cleaning out the break room.

Despite the relatively empty floor, a flurry of noise

drew her attention from outside her door. What was that all about?

The commotion drew closer to her door. "Ho-ho-ho!"

She stood from her desk and opened her door. Someone dressed as Santa appeared to be approaching her office. Celeste rubbed at her temples. How had this guy gotten past Security? There were no children's daycares or anything of the sort on this floor. Not to mention Christmas was already over, thankfully.

"I think you're lost, Santa," she addressed St. Nick, her phone in her hand ready to call Security if need be.

His response was to reach for his jaw and pull down the pretend beard and mustache—to reveal the face she'd been dreaming of since she'd left Jamaica all those days ago.

"Reid?"

"Hi, sweetheart."

Celeste had to brace herself against the wall at her back. She couldn't be seeing or hearing any of this. She must be having some kind of *A Christmas Carol* hallucination or dream. Tiny Tim would pop out any minute now.

She blinked and rubbed her eyes. But Reid still stood there. As real as the hammering of her heart.

"What are you doing here?" she stammered out.

"I had an emergency business trip to make right before the holiday. As soon as I successfully wrapped it up, I realized I didn't get a chance to wish my lady a Merry Christmas."

His lady?

"You flew out here just to wish me a Merry Christmas?"

They'd drawn the attention of the few other people who'd come into work. Her colleagues were staring at them in astonishment. Two of the women looked like they were dabbing at their eyes.

"I did," Reid answered her, walking closer until he stood mere inches away. How did the man manage to look sexy in a bulky Santa suit, for heaven's sake? It took all her will not to throw her arms around him and nuzzle her face into his neck. She'd missed him so much, still couldn't believe this wasn't some fantasy or dream she'd be waking up from any minute now.

"Oh, I also wanted to give your Christmas present. Didn't get a chance to do that, either."

He reached inside the pocket of his red fleece pants. Then shocked her to her core by pulling out a velvet box and dropping to one knee.

Flipping the top over, he revealed a sparkling diamond ring surrounded by dazzling ruby red stones. He'd been thinking of the black-and-red dress she'd worn the night of the dinner cruise. There was no doubt in her mind.

Celeste had to remind herself to breathe.

"Celeste Frajedi. You're unlike anyone else I've ever known."

Her voice shook as she tried to answer. "I am?"

"Without a doubt. I would call you the most generous person I've ever met. And I'd like to call you my wife." He took her shaking hand in his. "Will you marry me?"

She couldn't stand any more. Literally. Celeste felt her knees give out and Reid caught her as she dropped to the floor in front of him.

"Yes!" She'd barely gotten the word out when applause and cheers erupted all around them.

"I can't believe this is happening," she said over all the noise. "I can't believe that you're really here."

"I am, sweetheart. And I want to promise you that I'll

do everything I can to make sure each Christmas we celebrate together is more festive than the last."

That settled it. Her tears would not be contained any
longer. The love she felt for this man overflowed through
every part of her being. "Oh, Reid."

"It's like a wise newlywed once said…" He laughed,
taking her in his arms and hugging her tight. "When
you know you're with the right person, you just know."

Celeste knew. Just as she knew that the holidays would
hold magic and happiness for her once again.

* * * * *

TEMPTATION AT CHRISTMAS

MAUREEN CHILD

To Patti Hambleton, because since we first met
at six years old, she has been the friend I could
always count on. The sister of my heart.
And the one person I never have to explain
the jokes to! I love you.

One

Sam Buchanan hated Christmas.

Always had, but this year, he had more reason than ever to wish he could wipe the "holiday season" off the calendar for good.

"So go on a Christmas cruise," he muttered darkly. "Good call."

He'd known it would be hard, but he wasn't one to step back from duty just because it was difficult. Sam had a business to take care of and he wouldn't let the personal get in the way of that.

Didn't mean he had to like it, though.

From the owner's suite at the top of the Fantasy Cruise Line ship, *Fantasy Nights,* Sam looked out on the curved bow with its sky-blue deck and the sea beyond…because he didn't want to look at the dock. San Pedro, California, harbor was crowded with passengers excited to get their cruise to Hawaii going and damned if he'd look down on a bunch of happy, celebrating people. Once the cruise got underway, he could hole up here, in his suite, only venturing out to check on his employees.

Sam took four cruises a year—on different ships in the Buchanan line—to maintain good communication with both crew and passengers. He'd always believed experiencing the cruises in person was the best way to keep his fingers on the pulse of what his guests and employees needed. Not to mention it was the only certain way to make sure those employees were doing their jobs to his expectations.

Gripping his coffee cup, he narrowed his gaze on the expanse of ocean waiting just beyond the harbor. Once they were on the open sea, he'd slip out of his suite, check in with the ship's captain and then do a walk through the restaurants.

He wasn't looking forward to it.

Normally, the Fantasy Cruise Line didn't allow children onboard. Adult-only cruises were their mainstay. But at Christmas, the rules were relaxed so that families could enjoy sailing together on their smaller, more intimate ships.

So for this cruise, not only would he be faced with miles of Christmas garland, brightly lit trees and piped-in Christmas carols, but there would be dozens of kids, hyped up on Santa and candy, to deal with as well. And still, he told himself, it was better to be on this cruise than in his own home where the *lack* of Christmas would taunt him even more completely.

"Yeah," he assured himself solemnly, "no way to win this year."

The phone on the wet bar rang and Sam walked to it. "Yes?"

"Captain says we sail in an hour, Mr. Buchanan."

"Fine. Thanks." He hung up and listened to the silence in the owner's suite. There would be plenty of it for the next couple of weeks and he was looking forward to it even as he dreaded it.

A year ago, things had been different. He'd met a woman on another cruise and two months later, they'd had a Christmas-themed wedding. And they had taken this Christmas cruise for their honeymoon. Yes, for Mia's sake, Sam had even given Christmas a shot. He hadn't thrown himself into it or anything, but he also hadn't been quite the Scrooge he usually was.

Now the marriage was gone. She was gone. And Christmas was back, just to rub it in.

He set his coffee cup down on the bar top, shoved both hands into the pockets of his black slacks and stared around the beautifully appointed room. The owner's suite was twelve hundred square feet of luxury. Teak floors gleamed in the sunlight, paintings of the sea and several of Sam's cruise ships lined the walls. On the ocean side of the suite, the wall was one-way glass, affording an incomparable view of the ocean and the wide balcony that stretched the length of the suite.

Leather club chairs and sofas were gathered atop a rich, burgundy throw rug in the middle of the living room and there were tables with lamps bolted onto them, in case of rough seas. There was a flat-screen television on the wall and a dining room off to one side.

There were two bedrooms and three bathrooms along with the private balcony/terrace that added an extra two hundred square feet to the suite. The master bedroom and en suite bath boasted a view of the sea from behind one-way glass. He could see out, but no one could see in.

And in spite of his surroundings, Sam felt…on edge. He stalked out to the terrace and let the cold wind slap at him. Glancing down at the nearly empty deck of the bow, Sam noticed a woman with long, wavy red hair and it felt as though someone had punched him in the chest.

"It's not her. Why the hell would she be on this cruise?"

Still, he couldn't look away. She wore white slacks and a long-sleeved green shirt and her hair lifted and twisted in the wind. Then she turned sideways and Sam saw that she was very pregnant. Disappointment tangled with relief inside him, until the redhead stopped, looked up and seemed to stab his stare with her own.

Mia?

His heart jolted and his hands fisted on the cold, white iron railing. She's *pregnant?* Why wouldn't she tell him? Why didn't she say *something?* What the hell was she doing here? And why didn't she take off her sunglasses so he could see the green eyes that had been haunting him for months?

But she didn't comply with that wish. Instead, she shook her head, clearly in disgust, and then stalked away, disappearing from view in less than a moment.

Mia. Pregnant.

Here.

Sam went inside, rushed across the room and hit the front door at a dead run. Somebody had better tell him something fast. He didn't waste time with a phone call. Instead he went down to the main deck where passengers were still filing onboard. The purser was there, along with two of the entertainment crew, to welcome people onto *Fantasy Nights.* Ordinarily, Sam would have been impressed with how easily his employees handled the streaming crowds—all smiles and conversations. But today, he needed answers.

"Mr. Wilson," Sam said and the purser turned. Instantly, the older man straightened up as if going to attention.

"Mr. Buchanan," he said with a nod. "Is there something I can help you with?"

"Yeah. Has a woman named Mia—" he almost said *Buchanan,* but Sam remembered at the last minute that his ex-wife had returned to her maiden name after the divorce "—Harper, checked in?"

The man quickly checked through the list of names on the clipboard he held. Then he glanced at his boss and said, "Yes sir. She did. A half hour ago. She—"

That was Mia. A very pregnant Mia.

"Which suite is she in?"

He knew she had a suite because all of the staterooms on the *Fantasy Nights* were suites. Some more luxuriously appointed than others but every suite on this ship was roomy and inviting.

"It's the Poseidon, sir. Two decks down on the port side and—"

"Thanks. That's all I need." Sam threaded his way through the crowd already spilling into the atrium, the main welcome spot on any ship.

On *Fantasy Nights,* the atrium was two stories of glass-and-wood spiraling staircases, now draped in pine garland. There was a giant Christmas tree in the middle of the room boasting what looked to Sam like a thousand twinkling, colored lights, along with ornaments—that the passengers could also purchase in the gift shop. There was a group of carolers in one corner, and miles of more pine garland draped like bunting all around the room.

Hanging from the ceiling were hundreds of strands of blinking white lights, to simulate snowfall and on one wall, there were tables set up, laden with Christmas cookies and hot chocolate.

Sam barely noticed. He didn't have time to wait for the elevator. Instead, he headed for the closest staircase and took them two at a time. He knew every ship in his fleet like the back of his hand, so he didn't need to check the maps on the walls to know where he was headed.

The Poseidon suite was one of their larger ones and he wondered why Mia had bothered to book a two-bedroom suite. If she was pregnant, why the hell hadn't she come directly to him months ago? He had no answers to too many questions racing through his mind, so Sam pushed all of them aside, assuring himself he'd solve this mystery soon enough.

The excited chatter of conversations and bursts of laughter from children and their parents chased him down the first hallway on the port side. On most cruise ships, hallways dividing the staterooms were narrow and usually dark in spite of carefully placed lighting. Fantasy Cruise Line hallways were wider than usual and boasted overhead lighting and brass wall sconces alongside every stateroom.

Here, the floorboards were also teak and on each door was attached a plaque describing the name of the suite itself. For example, he thought as he stopped outside Mia's suite, her doorway held the image of Poseidon, riding a whale, holding his trident high, as if ready to attack an enemy. He wondered if that was an omen for what was to come.

He didn't have long to think about it. He knocked and a moment later, the door was yanked open. Long red hair. Sharp green eyes. Green shirt. White pants. Pregnant belly.

But not Mia.

Her twin, Maya.

Was he feeling relief? Disappointment? Both? Sam just stared at her. Damned if he could think of anything to say.

Maya didn't have that problem. She glared at him then and snapped, "Happy anniversary, you bastard."

Almost instantly, Mia appeared behind her twin. Rolling her eyes at her sister's drama, she said, "Maya. Stop."

Her sister stared at her for a second or two. "Seriously? You're going to defend him?"

"Defend me from what?" Sam asked.

"*What?*" Maya repeated, shifting a hard look to him before turning back to her twin. "Really? Even now you want me to play nice?"

"Really." Mia tugged on her sister's arm. "I love you. Go away."

"Fine," Maya said, throwing both hands into the air. She threw one last hard look at Sam. "But I'm not going far…"

"What the hell?" Sam muttered, keeping a wary eye on the woman as she walked away.

This was not the way Mia had wanted to handle this. But then, nothing about this trip was how she'd wanted it. She hadn't planned on bringing her entire family with her, for instance. But there was nothing she could do about that now, except maybe keep Maya away from Sam.

"Yeah, she's not your biggest fan," Mia admitted, then

stepped into the hallway, forcing him to move back to make room. She pulled the door closed behind her, leaned against it and lifted her gaze to the man of her dreams.

Well, she amended mentally, the *former* man of her dreams.

He was tall. She'd always liked that. Actually, it had been one of the first things she'd noticed about him the night they met. She was five feet nine inches tall, so meeting a man who was six foot four had been great. That night she'd been wearing three-inch heels and she'd still had to look up to meet his eyes.

And they were great eyes. Pale, pale blue that could turn from icy to heat in a blink of time. His black hair was a little too long for the CEO of a huge company, but it was thick and shiny and she'd once loved threading her fingers through it. In fact, even after everything that had happened between them, Mia's fingers itched to do it again.

He was wearing a suit, of course. Sam didn't do "relaxed." He wore his elegantly tailored suits as if he'd been born to wear them. And maybe he had been, Mia mused. All she was sure of was that beneath that dark blue, pinstriped suit, was a body that looked as if it had been sculpted by angels on a very good day.

Her heartbeat jumped skittishly and she wasn't surprised. She had met him and married him within a two-month, whirlwind span and though the marriage had lasted only nine months—technically—she knew it might take her years to get over Sam Buchanan.

Then he started talking.

"What are you doing here?"

Mia scowled. "Well, that's a very gracious welcome, Sam. Thank you. Good to see you, too."

He didn't look abashed, only irritated. "What's going on, Mia? Why is my ex-wife on this cruise?"

Hmm. More 'wife' than 'ex', she thought, but they'd get to that.

"This was the only way I could find to get you alone long enough to talk."

He snorted and pushed one hand through that great hair. "Really. You couldn't just pick up the phone?"

"Please." She waved that away. "Like I didn't try? Your assistant kept putting me off, telling me you were in a meeting or on the company jet heading off to Katmandu or something…"

"Katmandu?"

"Or somewhere else exotic, far away and out of reach apparently, of my phone."

Sam tucked his hands into his slacks pockets. "So you take a fifteen-day cruise?"

Mia shrugged. "Seemed like a good idea at the time."

"With Maya."

"And her family."

He glanced down the hallway and then to the closed door, as if expecting to see Joe and the kids pop out of hiding. "You're kidding."

"Why would I kid?"

The door flew open and Maya was there, glaring at him. Mia sighed, but gave up trying to rein in her twin.

"Why wouldn't she bring her family along as backup when she has to face you?" Maya asked.

"Backup?" He pulled his hands free, folded his arms across his chest and glared at the mirror image of Mia. "Why the hell would she need backup?"

"As if you didn't know," Maya snapped. "And another news flash for you, Mom and Dad are here too, and they're not real happy about it."

He looked at Mia. "Your parents are here?"

She lifted both hands helplessly. Mia hadn't actually *invited* any of her family along on this trip. She'd simply made the mistake of telling her twin what she was planning and Maya had taken it from there. Her family was circling the wagons to keep her from being hurt again. Hard to be angry with the people who loved you because they wanted to protect you.

Also hard to not be frustrated by them.

"Are Merry and her family here too?" Sam asked. "Cousins? Best friends?"

"Merry didn't trust herself to see you," Maya snapped.

Thank God, their older sister Merry had decided to stay home with her family or things would have been even wilder. It was comforting to realize that at least one member of her family was sane.

"Maya," Mia said on a sigh, "you're not helping. Close the door."

"Fine but I'll be listening anyway," she warned and slammed the door so that the sound echoed along the hallway.

And she would be, too, Mia knew. "Merry stayed home to keep the bakery running," she said. "Christmas is our busiest time of the year."

"Yeah, I remember."

"So busy," she continued as if he hadn't spoken, "Mom and Dad are cruising to Hawaii, but they're going to fly home from there to help Merry."

"I don't get it."

"Which part?"

"All of it." He shook his head, took her arm and steered

her further from the door, no doubt because he knew that Maya was indeed listening to everything they said. "I still don't know why you're here. Why you felt like you needed an army just to face me."

"Not an army. Just people who love me." Mia pulled her arm free of his grasp because the heat building up from his touch was way too distracting. How was she supposed to keep her mind on why she was there when he was capable of dissolving her brain so easily?

And that, she told herself, was exactly why the family had come along.

"We have to talk."

"Yeah, I guessed that much," he said, shooting a glance at the still closed door.

Just being this close to Sam was awakening everything inside her and Mia knew that she was really going to need her family as a buffer. Because her natural impulse was to move in closer, hook her arms around his neck and pull his head to hers for one of the kisses she had spent the last few months hungering for—and trying to forget.

But that wouldn't solve anything. They would still be two people connected only by a piece of paper. They had never been married in the same way her parents were. The Harpers were a unit. A team, in the best sense of the word.

While Mia and Sam had shared a bed but not much else. He was always working and when he wasn't, he was locked in his study, going over paperwork for the business or making calls or jetting off to meetings with clients and boat builders and—anyone who wasn't *her*.

Passion still simmered between them, but she'd learned the hard way that desire wasn't enough to build a life on. She needed a husband who was there to talk to, to laugh with—and they hadn't done that nearly enough. She wanted a man who could bend and not be constricted by his own inner rules and Sam didn't know how to bend. How to compromise. Mia had tried. Had fought for their marriage but when she realized that only she was trying, she gave up.

If he'd been willing to work on things with her, they'd still be together.

"Fine then. We'll talk," Sam said, still keeping a wary eye on the door of her suite as if expecting Maya to leap out again.

Mia would not have been surprised. Her twin was very protective.

"But not here where Maya's listening to everything we say..." He frowned thoughtfully. "Once we're underway, I need to meet with some of the crew, check on a few things..."

She sighed. "Of course you do."

One eyebrow lifted. "You know I take these cruises to get the information I need on how our ships are operating."

"I remember." In fact, she recalled the cruises they'd taken together after they were married. Two of them. One to the Bahamas. One to Panama. And on each of them, the only time she really saw her new husband was at night, in their bed. Otherwise, Sam the Workaholic was so busy, it had been as if she were traveling alone.

"That's why we're here. On this ship," Mia said. "I knew you'd be taking this cruise."

He laughed. "Even knowing I hate the Christmas cruises?"

"Yes. Because it helps you avoid having to be at home with a non-Christmas," she said.

His frown went a little deeper. Apparently, he didn't like the fact that she could read him so easily. But it hadn't been difficult. Sam hated Christmas and no matter how Mia had tried to drag him, kicking and screaming into the spirit of the holiday, he would not be moved. Her family had planned their wedding and he'd been surrounded by holly leaves, poinsettias and pine garlands. After the wedding, he'd given in to her need to have a tree and lights and garland, but he'd admitted to her that if she weren't there, Christmas would have been just another day at his house.

She'd thought then and still believed that it was just sad. In her family, Christmas season started the day after Thanksgiving. Lights went up, carols were played, gifts were bought and wrapped and her sisters' kids wrote and then revised letters to Santa at least once a week.

She'd tried to get him to tell her why he hated that holiday so much, but not surprisingly, he wouldn't talk about it. How could she reach a man if every time she tried to breach his walls, he built them higher?

So yes, she'd known that Sam would take a Christmas cruise to avoid being at home in what was probably a naked house, devoid of any holiday cheer. It hadn't made much sense to her until she realized that Christmas decorations meant nothing to him, but a house devoid of those very decorations only made him remember that he was different than most people. That he'd chosen to live in a gray world when others were celebrating.

"These cruises are booked months out," he said. "How did you manage to get suites for the whole family?"

"Mike arranged it."

Sam's eyes flashed and she wasn't surprised. His younger brother had always been on Mia's side and thought their separation was the worst thing to happen to Sam. So Mia had counted on his brother's help to "surprise" Sam on this cruise.

"Mike? My own brother?"

She might have enjoyed the complete shock stamped on Sam's features, if she wasn't worried that this situation could start an open war between the brothers.

"Don't fault him for it either," Mia warned. "He was helping me out, not betraying you,"

"What did you think I'd do to him?" he demanded and she heard the insult in his voice.

"Who knows?" She threw both hands up. "Fly to Florida and toss him in the ocean? Keelhaul him? Throw him in a dungeon somewhere? Chain him to a wall?"

His eyes went wide and he choked out a laugh. "I live in a penthouse condo, remember? Sadly, it doesn't come equipped with a dungeon."

Oh, she remembered the condo. Spectacular with an amazing view of the ocean through a wall of glass. And she remembered spending too much time alone in that luxurious, spacious place, because her husband had chosen to bury himself at work.

Okay, that worked to stiffen her spine.

"Fine," she said. "Then we're agreed. You don't give Mike grief."

"Or a Christmas bonus," he muttered.

"He's your partner, not your employee." Shaking her head, Mia snapped, "You're going to give him a hard time anyway, aren't you?"

"I was kidding."

"Were you?" she asked.

"Mostly. You know what? Forget about Mike." Sam

looked her square in the eye and asked, "Why are you here, Mia? And why'd you bring your family with you?"

She had needed the support because frankly, she didn't trust herself around Sam. One look at him and her body overrode her mind. She had to be strong and wasn't sure she could do it on her own. Still, she wasn't going to tell him that.

"They wanted to take a cruise and I needed to be here to talk to you, so we all went together."

"Sure. Happy coincidence. And why did you need to see me?"

"That's going to be a longer conversation."

"Does it include why you picked our anniversary to ambush me on a cruise ship?"

She could have kicked her twin. Maya wishing him a *Happy Anniversary* had been exactly the wrong thing to say. Mia loved that her family was so protective of her— and so really furious with Sam. But this was her life and she'd handle it her way. And reminding Sam about their anniversary, as if she were upset about it, wasn't her way. Of course, she *was* shaken by the fact that she was here to talk divorce with her husband on their first anniversary, but that didn't matter really, did it? Their marriage had ended months ago. What was happening now was just a formality.

And if he'd forgotten their anniversary, then Maya had just reminded him and that was infuriating, too. How could he forget? Was their all-too-brief marriage really that un-memorable? Was she? God knew, she'd forgotten *nothing* about her time with Sam.

Heck, just remembering the nights spent in his arms made her heart beat faster and her blood heat up until she felt like she had a fever. It was so hard to be this close to him and not lean in to kiss him. Touch his cheek. Smooth his hair back from his forehead. She muffled a sigh.

And all of this would have been much easier to handle if he didn't look so good.

From the first moment they'd met, on one of his cruise ships, Mia had been drawn to him. It had felt then like an electrical attraction and it seemed that nothing had changed there. His pale blue eyes still looked at her as if she were the only woman in the world. His mouth still made her want to nibble at his bottom lip. And she knew firsthand what it was like to have those strong, muscular arms wrapped around her and oh boy, she'd love to feel that again—even knowing it would be a huge mistake.

She could be in serious trouble.

"Are you okay?"

His question snapped her brain out of a really lovely fantasy and for that she was grateful. Sort of.

"Yeah, I'm fine." She looked up and down the corridor before turning her gaze back to his. "I didn't choose to find you on our anniversary. It just worked out that way. And like I said, we need to talk and I don't think this hallway is the place to do it."

"You're right." He glanced at the closed door behind which Maya was no doubt lurking. "But I'm not doing it with your sister around, either."

Mia laughed shortly. "No. Not a good plan. I'll come to you once I make sure Mom and Dad are settled in. And I want to help Maya with the kids…"

"Fine. Once we get into open water, give me an hour, then come to my suite."

She watched him walk away and her mouth went dry. Mia hated that her instinct was to chase him down and leap at him. She'd been doing so well, too. She was only dreaming about him three or four times a week now. Seeing him again, though, spending the next two weeks together on the same ship, was going to start up the fantasies and the desire all over again.

And there was zero way to avoid it.

Two

Mia being onboard this ship had already destroyed Sam's concentration. For an hour, he talked with the Captain, studied weather patterns with the First Officer charged with navigation, then finally had a meeting with the Chief Security Officer to get a report on any possible situations.

Through it all, he heard his employees but didn't listen with the same intensity he usually brought to his visits. How could he, when his mind kept drifting to his ex-wife?

Why did she have to look so damn good? And smell even better? He'd forgotten—or convinced himself—that he'd forgotten that subtle scent of summer that somehow clung to her. Her lotion? Shampoo? He'd never really investigated it because it hadn't mattered to him *how* that scent appeared—he had simply enjoyed it.

And now it was with him again.

Haunting him again.

"And it's Michael's fault," he muttered. Standing on the private deck of his suite, Sam gripped his cell phone, ordered it to "Call Michael," then waited impatiently for his brother to pick up.

"Hey, Sam! How's it going?"

Scowling at the sailboats skimming the water in the distance, Sam blurted out, "You know exactly how it's going."

Michael laughed. "Ah...so you've seen Mia."

"Yes, I've seen her. And her twin. And apparently the rest of the family is aboard, too. What the hell were you thinking?" Sam curled one fist around the thick rail. The Plexiglas wall for safety only rose as high as the handrail. He wanted the feel of the wind against his face and right now, he was hoping it would cool him off. "I can't believe you did this. I'm your *brother*. Where's the loyalty?"

"Why wouldn't I do it?" Michael argued. "I like Mia. I like who you were when you were with her."

"What's that supposed to mean?"

His brother sighed. "It means that she was good for you. You laughed more back then."

"Yeah, everything was great until it wasn't."

That time with Mia hadn't lasted. As he'd known going into the marriage that it wouldn't. And even knowing that it would probably end badly, Sam had married her because he hadn't been able to imagine life without her. He'd risked failure and failed. Now, not only did he not have Mia, he had memories that continued to choke him during long, empty nights.

"We're divorced, Michael. It's over. You setting this up isn't helping any."

"It was helping Mia," his brother countered, then asked, "and if it's over, why is this bugging you so much?"

Good question.

"Look, I don't know why she had to see you, but when she asked, of course I did what I could."

Naturally, Michael would offer to help. That was just who he was. Some of the anger drained away as Sam realized how different he and his younger brother were. When their parents divorced, the kids were split up. Michael went to Florida with their mother while Sam stayed in California with their father.

They'd stayed close because they'd worked at it, even though they were only together whenever court-mandated visits to the non-custodial parent kicked in. Their father had been a hard man with strict rules for how Sam lived his life. Their mother was a kindhearted woman who hadn't been able to live with that hard man.

So Sam grew up with the knowledge that marriage was a trap and never lasted—his father after all, had been married four times. As a father, he was disinterested, barely aware of Sam's existence. While Michael saw the other side of things with a mother who eventually remarried a man who had loved Michael as his own.

Now Sam was divorced and Michael was engaged and Sam sincerely hoped his little brother would have better luck in the marriage department than he himself had.

Mike was speaking, so Sam tuned in. "Why don't you just enjoy the situation?"

Sam was stunned speechless—but that didn't last. "*Enjoy* having my ex and her family—who all hate me, by the way—traveling with me for the next two weeks? Yeah, not gonna happen."

Michael laughed, damn it.

"Are you *scared* of the Harpers?"

"No."

Yes.

He hadn't known back then how to deal with a family who defended each other. Who listened. Who actually gave a damn. And he still didn't have a clue.

His brother knew him too well, that was the problem. Once they were grown the two of them had made time for each other. Building a relationship that might have been denied them because of the way they were raised. When their father died, and the business had come to the two of them, they'd carved out a workable solution that suited both men.

Michael took care of the east coast cruises, Sam had the west coast. They made major decisions for the company together and trusted each other to do what was best for the growth they both wanted to see happen.

"Okay, I admit that having her family there might be a little problematic."

"Yeah, you could say that."

"So fine. Ignore the family, enjoy Mia."

Oh, Sam would love to enjoy Mia. Every instinct he had was clamoring at him to go and find her. To pull her into his bed and never let her out again. But going there wasn't good for either of them. In their brief marriage it had become crystal clear that Sam and Mia weren't going to work out. She wanted more from him than he could give. Bottom line? They didn't belong together and they'd both acknowledged that in less than a year. Why stir the embers just to get burned again?

"For God's sake, Sam," Michael continued, "you haven't seen her in months."

He was aware.

"Yeah well, she'll be here soon to tell me why she's on this cruise in the first place."

And he couldn't wait to hear it. Had she planned to be here on their anniversary? Or was that just happenstance as she'd said? Did it matter? Either way their anniversary wasn't a celebration, but more a reminder of mistakes made.

He never should have married Mia, Sam knew that. But he'd done it anyway and so he'd only set Mia up for pain. That he hadn't intended, but it had, apparently, been unavoidable. Hell, maybe that was why she was here. Just to let him know that she was over him and moving on with her life.

Why tell him at all?

And even if she wanted him to know, why book a cruise for that?

Scowling at an ocean that didn't care what he was feeling or thinking, Sam heard Michael's voice as if from a distance.

"That's great. Talk to her about whatever it is she needs to tell you. And when you're done, keep talking."

"What am I supposed to say?"

"Wow. This is embarrassing. You're my big brother. And you can't figure out how to talk to a woman you were married to?" Michael took a breath and sighed it out. "Maybe you could tell her you miss her."

He straightened up. "What would be the point? She left me, remember?"

Sam remembered it well and didn't really want to revisit the memory.

"Yeah, I remember. Did you ever ask yourself why?"

"The reason doesn't matter. She left. I moved on. Done."

"Sure you did," Michael said. "Talk to her anyway. Maybe you'll surprise each other."

Sam snorted. "I don't like surprises."

"How are we related again?"

In spite of everything, Sam grinned and stared out at the ocean. "Beats the hell outta me."

"Me, too," Mike said, laughing. "Good luck on the cruise. I hope Mia drives you insane."

"Thanks."

"No problem—oh and Sam, Merry Christmas!"

"Not funny."

"Yeah it is," Mike said, still laughing as he hung up.

Then Sam was alone with the wind, the sea…and the faint sounds of Christmas carols drifting up from the lower deck. Just perfect.

The Buchanan cruise ships were much smaller than the mega ships most companies sailed these days.

Instead of thousands of people crowding a ship that offered sometimes very small cabins, there were only two hundred passengers total on a Buchanan ship and each cabin was a suite that didn't make one feel as if the walls were closing in.

But, Mia thought, it also meant that she felt the movement of the ocean more than she might on the bigger ships. Some people didn't care for that, but she loved it. She'd discovered her sea legs on the first cruise she'd taken—when she'd met Sam and her whole life had changed.

A year ago, she'd fallen in love and felt that the cruise was almost magical. Now, the magic was gone, but she was once again sailing on a cruise with the man she had believed was her future. She'd been foolish, believing that love at first sight was real and substantial and that the two of them together could do anything.

It hadn't taken long before Mia had realized that it *wasn't* the two of them. It was just her. Alone in a beautiful home with a man who seemed reluctant to do anything to save their marriage.

"Mrs. Buchanan."

Mia looked up to smile at one of the crew she knew from other cruises. About thirty, the man had blond-streaked brown hair, green eyes and wore the short-sleeved red polo shirt and white slacks that were the Fantasy Cruise Line uniform.

"Nice to have you aboard," he said.

"Thank you, Brandon," she answered, and didn't bother correcting him about the whole *Mrs. Buchanan* thing. Because honestly, until Sam signed those papers, she *was* Mrs. Buchanan, watching him as he hurried past intent on whatever he was doing.

Brandon walked away at top speed and she watched him go. She had to wonder how many of this crew she knew from her time with Sam. And she knew that even if Brandon was the *only* familiar face, by the time the cruise was over, she would know most of them.

Smaller ships meant a higher than usual crew to passenger ratio. At the end of the fourteen-day trip to Hawaii, the *Fantasy Nights* would feel like a small, insular village, where everyone knew everyone else.

"There's an upside and a downside to that though," she murmured and continued along the deck to the nearby staircase. Gossip would fly through the ship. And no doubt people would be talking about her and Sam, just as they had talked about them a year before on that first cruise.

Shaking her head, she ordered herself to stop thinking about Sam and try to enjoy being on the ship, seeing the ocean stretch out forever. Feeling the wind on her face and through her hair and listening to the distant shrieks and laughter of the kids onboard.

Christmas was stamped all over the sleek boat and she knew that had to be irritating to Sam. He didn't like the holiday at all and had only grudgingly accepted not only their Christmas themed wedding, but the Christmas tree she'd brought into their condo last year.

Since he was a kid, Christmas had been an exercise in emptiness. Sam's world was so wildly different from anyone else's that he never even tried to explain what it was about that holiday that left him feeling hollowed out. Who would understand?

Thinking back on it now, Mia wondered if the fact that he didn't like Christmas was part of the reason they just hadn't worked out. Well, maybe not the reason. But certainly a sign of things to come. She loved Christmas and everything it promised—hope, joy, love. And Sam tended toward the dark side.

Even as that thought registered, she shook her head. It wasn't as if he was some evil mastermind or something— but he was more cynical than she was. More likely to see the downside than the up. Which was strange, since he was a masterful businessman and didn't you have to be optimistic to run a multimillion-dollar company?

She caught herself as she started going down the all too familiar path of trying to figure out Sam. It was an exercise in futility because the man simply didn't let anyone in long enough to actually *know* him.

"You've already spent months trying to figure Sam

out, Mia," she lectured herself. "It's too late now, so just give it up already."

Taking a deep breath, Mia let go of the convoluted thoughts roiling through her mind and instead focused on where she was at the moment. Even though the reason for taking this cruise was a hard one, there was no reason she couldn't appreciate her surroundings.

There were brass pots displaying poinsettias bolted to the deck. Pine garlands were strung along the railings and the cushions on the chairs and lounges were a bright red and white. She smiled to herself as she realized that the whole ship felt like a Christmas snow globe, with the decorations and the happy people trapped inside the glass, just waiting for a giant hand to give it a shake.

The only way it could have been more perfect was if she didn't have to face her ex-husband and tell him they weren't as "ex" as they'd both believed. But she was only on this ship to confront Sam and get this whole thing settled, so the best thing she could do was to just get on with it.

Mia had plans, starting in January and she had to get this taken care of before she could move forward. She was tired of standing still. She wanted a future and the only way she was going to get it was to build it herself.

And still, as she made her way along the deck, Mia looked out at the sea, and paused briefly to watch the waves froth. She heard the slap of the water against the keel and took a deep breath of the cold, salty air. She smiled, in spite of the turmoil grumbling inside her.

Her family was upstairs in the atrium, no doubt huddled around the cookies and hot chocolate. She knew Maya's kids, Charlie and Chris, were already planning to explore the Snow Room that had been set up for children's play. Artificial snow, made just for the holiday cruise, was going to be very popular, especially with California kids who didn't get many chances to throw a snowball.

She kept walking, taking the stairs up, because it was faster than going inside and waiting for an elevator. Besides, she thought, as she looked out at the ocean, you didn't get a view from an elevator.

But no matter what she tried to tell herself about the view, the truth was, she was stalling. The thought of talking to Sam again had her unsettled. Off-balance. He'd always made her feel that way, though. It looked to her like nothing had changed.

On the top deck, Mia walked toward the owner's suite. She knew exactly where it was, because that suite was positioned in exactly the same spot on every Buchanan ship. The closer she came to that wide, closed door though, the more her stomach jittered and the faster her heart raced.

"Damn it."

This should be easier. She'd cried Sam out of her system months ago. Their marriage was over. So why the hell could the very thought of him make her want to go all gooey?

"Because apparently, I have a masochistic streak," she muttered, then knocked before she could talk herself out of it.

When Sam opened the door, her gaze went straight to his. That cool, pale blue was fixed on her as if she were the only thing in the universe. Mia sighed. Sam was the one man who had ever looked at her like that. As if nothing else, in that moment, mattered. The only man who could make her knees weak with a glance. The only man who made her want to crawl into his bed and never leave it.

Which is exactly why you're in this mess, her mind whispered.

A year ago, she'd followed her heart—and her hormones—and had married the man of her dreams. Only to watch those dreams crumble into dust.

She kept that thought at the forefront of her mind as she said, "Hello, Sam."

Nodding sharply, Mia walked past him into the well-appointed suite. Her gaze swept the room in spite of the reason she was there. How could she not admire the space? The view of the sea, provided by the French doors and the wall of glass, was immense. It reminded her of the view from his condo at the beach, only here, she was much closer to that ocean, almost a part of it.

Breathtaking. And so was the rest of the room. Hardwood floors, jewel-toned rugs scattered across the honey-colored planks. A couple of sofas, that looked soft enough to sink into and easy chairs drawn together, facing the view that demanded attention.

"Well please," Sam muttered from behind her. "Come in."

She whirled around to face him, mindful of keeping a few feet of space between them. "Sam. We've got a problem."

"I don't think *we* have anything anymore."

He folded his arms over his broad, muscular chest and dipped his head down to stare at her. It was a technique he used. That professor-to-stupid-student glare. And as often as he might have used it on everyone else, that look had never worked on her before and it didn't now, either.

"You're wrong," she said shortly.

One eyebrow lifted.

She still didn't know how he did that.

"Okay," she said, "here it is. You know how *we* signed the divorce papers?"

"I recall," he said flatly.

"And *we* overnighted them in?"

"How about *we* get to the point?" His arms dropped to his sides. "What's this about, Mia?"

"Well, it seems we aren't as divorced as we thought we were."

Sam's brain short-circuited.

That was the only explanation for him being unable to think of a damn thing to say in response. Of course, it might have been being so close to Mia that was shutting his brain down, but that didn't make him feel any better about the situation.

The whole idea of what she was saying was preposterous. Ridiculous. He'd accepted his failure. Forced himself to acknowledge that he'd hurt the one woman in the world he valued. He'd lived through it, put it behind him.

Of course they were divorced.

But if they weren't…something that might have been hope rose up in him briefly, but Sam squashed it in an instant. No. Screw that, he wasn't going down that road. They were divorced. It was over.

"How is that possible?" He shook his head and held up one hand. "No. Never mind. It's not possible," he finally blurted.

"Apparently, it is." Mia tucked both hands into the pockets of her white slacks, then pulled them free again.

Sam wasn't surprised. She'd always used her hands when she talked. And she did now.

Waving her left hand, he noticed the absence of her wedding rings and felt a twinge—of what, he didn't know. He wondered what she'd done with the gold, diamond-crusted band and the matching engagement ring he'd given her. Wasn't his business, of course, and simple curiosity would have to wait for another time. But it surprised him to note that it bothered him to see her not wearing the damn things.

Besides, he had to hear what she was saying rather than concentrating on her hands or the way that emerald-green silk shirt made her eyes an even richer, deeper green than usual. Her golden-red hair was long and loose laying across her shoulders, sliding against her neck and it was all Sam could do to keep from reaching out and touching her.

"So it turns out the overnight driver who was supposed to deliver our divorce papers to the court…"

"What?"

"He didn't." She shrugged helplessly. "He had a heart attack at work and when they went in to clean out his apartment, they found *mountains* of undelivered mail. The poor guy was a hoarder, I guess, and kept most of the packages he was supposed to deliver."

Sam couldn't believe this.

"Apparently, they even found forty-year-old Cabbage Patch dolls!" She shook her head and sighed. "Poor little kids never got the dolls they wanted."

"Seriously?" he asked. "You're worried about kids who are now in their fifties or sixties?"

"Well, yes." She frowned at him and lifted both hands in a helpless shrug. "People are slowly being notified about this mess and I got word just last week."

"Last week?" She'd known they were still married for a week? "Why the hell didn't they notify me?"

"Probably because it was my name on the return address on the priority envelope."

Sam took a few long strides, taking him further away from the woman watching him so closely, then he turned around to face his *wife*. Not ex. Wife.

Scrubbing both hands across his face, he then let his hands fall to his sides. "So we're still married."

"I know what you're feeling. I couldn't believe it either. So now you see the problem."

He slowly walked toward her. "I see a problem, yeah. What I don't see is the big emergency that caused Michael to dump passengers off this cruise to make room for you and your family." Staring down into her eyes, he watched her closely as he asked, "Why the hell was it so important you get on this cruise to tell me something you could have handled back home with a damn phone call?"

She tipped her head back to look up at him. "This really isn't something I wanted to do over the phone and you were in Germany last week. This cruise was the first chance I had to talk to you in person."

"Okay. I get that." He hadn't exactly been easy to get a hold of lately. Since he and Mia had split up, Sam had kept even busier than he had been before and he wouldn't have thought that possible. Traveling, working, staying away from home as much as possible because the emptiness of his condo echoed with memories he'd rather not think about.

Mia kept her gaze on his as she dipped one hand into her black leather purse and drew out an envelope. Holding it out to him, she said, "My attorney drew up a new set of papers—same as the others. All you have to do is sign them and when we get home, I'll take them to the courthouse myself."

He looked at the envelope but didn't make a move to take it. They were still married. He didn't know how he felt about that. Michael had been right, Sam *had* missed Mia. More than he had expected. More than he wanted to admit. And now she was back. But nothing had changed. This delay in ending their marriage only meant the pain of failure would be drawn out.

"Why can't they just use the first set of papers?" he asked suddenly. "Why the need for new ones?"

"I don't know…" She waved her left hand again. "My lawyer thought it would be best this way and really? After I heard all about this, I didn't ask a lot of questions. I just want to get this done and over."

Looking into those forest-green eyes of hers, Sam felt a punch of heat and regret slam into him. Didn't matter that she'd left him. He thought that he would probably *always* want her. For the last few months, he'd tried to push her out of his mind. He'd traveled the world and still the memory of her had chased him. And now she was here, standing in front of him and it was all he could do to keep from reaching for her. Hell, they were still married. They had a fourteen day cruise stretching out in front of them. Why shouldn't they spend that time together? Call it one last hurrah? She wanted divorce papers signed. So, maybe they could make a deal, he thought suddenly. That all depended on just how important this divorce was to her.

"You seem pretty eager," he said.

Her gaze narrowed on his. "Sam, we were done months ago. This is just the final step—one we thought we'd already taken. Why wouldn't I want it all finished?"

"No reason," he muttered, wondering if a deal was a bad idea. Of course it was a bad idea—but that didn't mean he wouldn't suggest it. He had to silently admit that it stung to see how impatient she was to cut him loose. He could remember a time when all they wanted was to be together. Hell, he still wanted that. And he could see from the heat in her eyes that she felt the same.

They were still married.

He was here, with his *wife,* and suddenly, divorce seemed light-years away. Moving in closer, he saw her take a deep breath and hold it and knew she was feeling the same pull he was. Her eyes were flashing, her lips parted as her breath came in short puffs.

"What're you doing?" Her voice came out in a strained whisper.

"I'm saying hello to my wife," he countered and gave her a half smile.

She slapped one hand to his chest. "The fact that we're still married is a technicality."

"Always liked technicalities."

Especially this one. Hell, even knowing their marriage was over didn't get rid of the desire pulsing inside him. The ache he'd carried around in the center of his chest was easing now because she was here. Because her scent had wrapped itself around him. And one look into her eyes told him she felt the same, though knowing Mia, she'd never admit to that.

"Sam, we've already said goodbye to each other," she reminded him. "Why make this harder than it has to be?"

He laid his hands on her shoulders and the heat of her body rose up to slide into his. "Hello isn't hard, Mia. Unless you're doing it right."

"Sam…"

He bent his head to hers and stopped when his mouth was just a breath away from her lips. Waiting for acceptance. For her to let him know that she shared what he was thinking, feeling.

"This could be a big mistake," she said, with a slow shake of her head.

"Probably," he agreed, knowing it wouldn't change anything.

Seconds passed and still he waited. Damned if he'd take what he wanted if she wasn't willing. Finally though, she dropped her purse to the floor, reached up to cup his face between her palms and said, "What's one more mistake?"

"That's the spirit."

He kissed her, pulling her up against him, wrapping his arms around her and holding her tightly.

Three

Sam's mouth covered hers, his tongue parted her lips and she opened for him eagerly, willingly. Then he was lost in the heat of her. Her taste, her scent, filled him and he wondered vaguely how he'd managed to breathe without her these last months.

Their tongues met in a tangle of desire that pulsed between them like a shared heartbeat. Her breath brushed against his cheek, her sigh sounded in the stillness and Sam lost himself in her. For this one moment, he was going to simply revel in having her back in his arms.

However briefly.

When he dropped his hand to that sweet butt of hers though, she gasped and pulled back. Breathing deeply, she held up one hand and shook her head.

"Oh no you don't," she said. "A kiss hello is one thing, but we're not going to do what you think we're going to do."

"And what do I think?" he asked, grinning at her.

"The same thing I'm thinking," she said and when he took a step toward her again, she skipped backward. "Seriously, Sam, I'm not going to bed with you."

"Why not? We're married."

"For now," she said.

"I'm only talking about now." Sam moved in another step or two.

"That's the problem," she snapped. "Right there. You never thought about anything beyond the *now.*"

Okay, that stopped him. "What the hell is that supposed to mean? I married you, didn't I?"

"Please." Shaking her head firmly, she bent to snatch her purse off the floor. Her fingers curled into the leather until her knuckles went white. "You know exactly what I mean. Yes, you married me, but then…nothing. You never wanted to talk about a future. About making a family. Buying a house instead of that condo."

"What the hell was wrong with the condo?"

"Kids need a yard to play in."

"We don't have kids."

"Exactly!" And she'd wanted children. Her own family was so close. Her sisters both had families of their own and Mia's heart had ached to be a mother. But Sam wasn't interested in being a father. He never said so outright, but whenever she'd brought the subject up he'd closed down. She couldn't understand why, either. They'd have made beautiful children together and an amazing life—if only he'd cared enough to fight for their marriage.

"You're talking in circles, Mia." He couldn't look away from the fire in her eyes. Mia Harper was the only woman he'd ever known who could turn from desire to fury to ice and back again in thirty seconds. He'd always loved that about her. She was passionate and proud and so damn bullheaded that even their arguments had been sexy as hell. "Just say whatever it is that's clawing at you."

Shaking her head, she said, "You didn't want children, Sam. And you didn't bother to tell me that until *after* we were married."

True. Sam could admit that silently. Every time Mia had talked about raising a family, he had changed the subject. He'd wanted Mia more than his next breath, but he'd never wanted to be a father. How the hell could he? His own father had sucked at the job, so why would Sam think he would be any better at it? He had hoped that she would change her mind about children. Hoped that he and the life they could have together might be enough for her.

He was wrong.

"What's the point in talking about a future that might not happen?" He took a step closer to her again and he could have sworn he felt heat pumping off her body and this time it was anger, not desire, leading the charge.

"If you don't have a future all you ever have is a past and the present."

"The present can be enough if you're doing it right," he countered.

"Why settle for 'enough' when you can have more?" She stared at him and he saw disappointment in her eyes. He didn't like that but there was little he could do about it.

"How much is more, Mia?" His voice was low, tight. "When do you stop looking for the more and enjoy what you have? Why do you have to walk away from something great because it's missing something else?"

Her posture relaxed a bit and she took a long, deep breath before saying, "I'm tired of being the favorite aunt to Maya's and Merry's kids, Sam. I want children. That's the *more* I need."

He closed off at that because his brain drew up images of Mia, surrounded by nieces and nephews who adored her. Guilt poked at his insides. Sam knew he should have told her that he wasn't interested in having kids before they were married. But he'd wanted her too much to tell her the truth. He'd convinced himself that his lies wouldn't matter once it all ended.

Maybe he had been a bastard. And that was on him. He'd made a choice to have Mia for as long as he could, even knowing that they wouldn't be growing old together. Because he'd wanted her that much, despite knowing in his gut that he wasn't husband material. And how the hell could he be a good father when his father had been so damned bad at the job? Sam's only role model for fatherhood had convinced him to never try it.

"I should have told you," he admitted, though it cost his pride. He wasn't used to being wrong, so he hadn't had to become accustomed to apologies.

"I'm not mad at you about that anymore," she said softly. "We're divorced, Sam. It's over. We don't have to keep tearing at each other over the past."

He gave her a half smile. "But we're not divorced, are we?"

Instantly, she wagged a finger at him. "Oh, no. Don't do that. We may not be divorced, but we're not exactly married, either."

Sam smiled, one corner of his mouth lifting. "Until your new papers go through we are."

"And now you *like* the idea of the two of us married? Why do you care, Sam?" she demanded, pushing her hair back behind one ear to show off a long twist of gold dangling from her lobe. Her eyes shone with a light that was either passion or fury—or maybe a combination of both. "You didn't care when it actually would have mattered."

That slapped at him. Of course he'd cared. It was the only reason he'd tried marriage in the first place. He'd wanted her. Cared for her. Didn't want to lose her, so marriage had been his only option.

"I did care." He said it simply because if she honestly believed what she was saying, he wanted to convince her she was wrong.

"Really?" She tipped her head to one side and her hair slid off her shoulders to follow the movement. Then she shrugged. "Okay, maybe you did and I just didn't *see* you often enough to notice."

She might have a point, but damned if he'd admit it. He hadn't made a secret of the fact that he *liked* working. That his company was growing and needed close attention paid to it. "You knew when we got married that I run a big company and I work a lot."

Anger drained away and she sighed. "I suppose I did. I just thought that—"

"What?"

"Doesn't matter. Not anymore." Shaking her head, she set the papers down on the nearest tabletop and said, "I'll leave these here. Just call me when you sign them— or even better, have one of your minions bring them to my suite."

He might have smiled at the *minion* remark, but one look into her bruised eyes made that impossible. Whatever had erupted between them only moments before, was gone now. That kiss still burned inside him, but if Mia was feeling the same thing, she was better at hiding emotions than she used to be.

Hell, one of the first things he'd admired about her was her openness. The way her eyes lit up with pleasure over things most people wouldn't notice at all.

On the cruise when they'd met, she'd tried paddle boarding for the first time when they were in port and immediately fell off into the ocean. Sam had helped her up, thinking she'd be scared or want to stop and go back to the beach. Instead, she'd come up from the water laughing, eyes dancing. She'd climbed back on that board and no matter how many times she'd fallen off—dozens— she hadn't given up. Not until she'd found her balance and conquered that board.

Sam had never had patience for quitters. So watching this gorgeous woman's stubborn refusal to give up had appealed to him. Not to mention her eyes, her laugh, her body, her interest in *everything*.

He'd had an awakening on that cruise a year ago. Meeting Mia had opened his eyes to a lot of things he'd stopped noticing years ago. Sunsets. Sunrises. Pods of whales sailing past the ship. How good it had felt to sit beside her on the deck and watch the world drift by.

That's what had drawn him and what had eventually pulled him away. Sam had realized that he and Mia were too different. Too much opposites to last, and hanging around longer than he should was only making it harder on *her*. He wasn't built for cozy. For *intimate*. Sam Buchanan had been raised to be a hit-and-run lover. Don't stick around. Don't get close and for God's sake don't let anyone in.

And nothing had changed, he reminded himself. So he looked into her eyes and nodded. "Fine."

She almost looked disappointed at his response, but he thought he'd imagined that because a heartbeat later,

her features were cool and still. Polite and distant. Not
something he was accustomed to seeing from Mia. But
she was right. The more distance between them the
better.

When she left, he didn't watch her go.

"What did he do?" Maya was waiting for Mia on the
top deck at a table beneath a red-and-white umbrella.

Mia ignored the question and looked around for her
nephews. There were a dozen other passengers gathered
on the deck, talking and laughing, and from the deck
below came spurts of laughter from excited children.
No sign of Charlie and Chris, though. She looked back
at her twin. "Where are the kids?"

"You're stalling because you don't want to talk about
Sam."

Mia tapped one finger to the end of her nose. "Bingo.
So, where are the kids?"

Maya scowled at her. "Joe has them. I think they're
throwing snowballs already. And you know I won't quit
asking, so just answer already. What did your miserable,
no-good ex do?"

Mia groaned. "God, Maya, just stop, okay? You're not
making this easier."

"Sorry, sorry." She waved one hand in the air as if
she could erase her words. "Honestly, I'm not trying to
make things harder for you. It's just that Sam makes me
so furious."

"No. Really?"

Maya's lips twitched and Mia grinned. One thing she
never had to doubt was her twin's loyalty. When her marriage had fallen apart, leaving Mia in a soggy, weepy,
emotional heap, Maya had been there for her. She and

their older sister Merry had plied her with bottles of wine and sympathy until Mia had found her feet again.

Her parents had offered support, but had tried to maintain neutrality and though that might seem like a betrayal of sorts to someone else, Mia had appreciated it. Sam wasn't an evil person. Not the Darth Vader of Seal Beach. He just hadn't wanted to be married.

"Okay." Maya picked up her virgin mimosa and signaled to a nearby waiter to bring another for Mia. "Let's rephrase. How did your most wonderful ex take the news?"

Mia gave her a wry smile, then thanked the waiter who handed her a beautiful crystal flute. "Let's not go too far the other way." She paused, thought about it, then said, "He was…surprised."

"Well, yeah. Who wasn't?" Shaking her head, Maya sat back in her chair. "I still can't believe people weren't complaining about not getting their packages delivered. How does a delivery driver become a hoarder with other people's stuff?"

"I don't know. And it doesn't matter now anyway," Mia said. "All I need is for Sam to sign the papers so I can get the divorce filed before January 15th."

"So he didn't sign them." Maya nodded sagely.

"Not yet," Mia agreed. "But he will."

"And you know this how?"

"Because he didn't fight the divorce, remember?" That still stung whether Mia wanted to admit it or not. When she'd first broached the subject of divorce it had taken everything she'd had. She'd prepared herself for his arguments. For his request for a second chance. But she needn't have bothered. He didn't argue. Didn't really say much at all.

She could still see his face in her memory. Standing opposite her in the living room of the condo they shared, he'd simply stared at her, his features blank and hard—as if he'd been carved out of stone. When he finally spoke, all he'd said was, "If that's what you want, I won't stop you."

Well, she'd *wanted* him to stop her. Wanted him to admit that he hadn't given their marriage a real shot. That he'd been wrong to shut himself off from her.

Instead, she'd gotten an uncontested divorce.

"Damn it," Maya blurted, snapping Mia out of her depressing thoughts. "I hate this. I hate seeing shadows back in your eyes. You were finally okay. Moving on without him. Planning a life and a future and now you're right back where you started a few months ago."

"Stop being so dramatic," Mia said and took a sip of her drink. "I'm not going to throw myself off the ship. This is just a bump in my formerly tidy world."

Maya narrowed her eyes on Mia and studied her until Mia shifted uncomfortably beneath that knowing stare.

"Why are you looking at me like that?"

"Because you're right. You *are* fine. And I want to know why." Leaning forward, she kept their gazes locked. "You weren't there long enough to have sex with him."

"Maya!" Mia glanced around to make sure no one else had overheard her sister.

"Well, come on. Even distracted by kids, a house payment and his job, Joe can last longer than twenty minutes."

"Too much information, thanks. Now I'll have that in my head when I see Joe next."

"I know envy when I hear it," Maya said with a grin.

Mia snorted a laugh and took another sip.

"But there's something different about you. Something…" Suddenly Maya's eyes snapped. "You kissed him. Didn't you?"

No point in denying it. Maya had always had X-ray vision when it came to things like this. For a moment, Mia pitied her nephews when they became teenagers. They'd never put one over on their mother.

"He kissed me," Mia finally said. "There's a difference."

"And you fought him off, of course," Maya supplied wryly.

"Desperately," Mia assured her, then set her glass down with a click on the glass table. "Fine. I kissed him back."

Maya huffed a breath in disgust. "I knew this would happen."

The sun shone out of a sky so blue it hurt to look at it. A sharp, cold wind brushed past them, setting the fringe on the red-and-white umbrellas snapping and dancing.

"Wow, you're wasting time working at the family bakery. You should be on the Psychic Network or something."

Maya smirked at her. "Please. Like I have to be a fortune teller to know that you'd fall back into his arms."

"Okay," Mia said, defending herself, "I didn't do that. It was a kiss. And I ended it."

"Before or after he got your shirt off?"

"Maya!" Mia goggled at her sister. As twins, they were close. As best friends, they knew each other way too well, so she wasn't surprised at Maya, so much as disappointed in herself. She had pretty much given in to the urge to kiss Sam again. But why wouldn't she? Just because they were divorced didn't mean she'd stopped loving him.

Just because Mia knew she could gain ten pounds just by *looking* at chocolate cake didn't mean she'd stop eating it.

"I managed to keep my clothes on, thanks for your support."

"Oh, you have my support, honey. But trust me, I know what's going on between you two." She patted her baby bump. "Remember. I'm on number three child. Every time Joe walks into the room, I want to jump him. Heck, at this rate, I'm going to have ten kids. So believe me when I say I understand."

Mia sighed a little and quashed that twinge of envy she felt for her sister's life. Maya's husband was a firefighter and their two boys, Charlie and Chris, were funny, ferocious and all around adorable. Now Maya was pregnant with another boy and Mia knew that in a year or two, her twin would be trying for a girl again.

Maya had everything that Mia most wanted. She had love. Family. Children of her own. It's what Mia had hoped for when she'd married Sam. Building a life together. Raising some kids together.

But Sam hadn't really wanted children. Naturally, she hadn't believed him when he told her on their honeymoon. She'd wrongly assumed that he had simply never been around kids, so didn't know how much fun—okay yes, and trouble—they could be. And maybe he would have changed his mind at some point—if their marriage had lasted. But now she'd never know.

"But jumping Sam won't change anything," Maya said and thankfully her voice was low, soft.

"Yeah, I know that." Didn't stop her from *wanting* to jump him, but she was stronger than her hormones. She hoped.

"Honey, once he signs those damn papers, you can pick up your life again."

"I know that too, Maya," she said tightly.

Her twin must have caught the fine edge of tension in Mia's voice because she said, "Fine, fine. I'll stop."

"Hallelujah."

"Funny. Let's see if you're still laughing after you spend the day with my kids."

"Your kids are great," Mia argued.

"Yeah, they are," Maya said. "But don't tell them I said that." She scooted her chair back and held one hand out. "Now, help your prego twin out of this stupid chair, will you? I've got to figure out where I'm going to put that Christmas elf in our suite."

Mia laughed and pulled her twin out of the chair. "You brought Buddy the Elf with you?"

"Of course I did." Maya threw her hands up. "Both boys look for him the instant they wake up in the morning. And they know that Buddy reports to Santa so..." She shrugged. "It seemed like a good way to keep the boys in line while we're on this cruise."

"Uh-huh."

Maya gave her a hard look. "Just wait until it's your turn to hide that elf and you have to find a new spot every day!"

Mia could hardly wait.

For the next couple of hours, Sam buried himself in work. It was the best way. Always his answer to avoiding emotional issues, he'd been doing it since he was a kid.

Back then, his father had made it clear that a man's duty was to take care of his business and his employees. Emotions were something to be *avoided*. He would point out that marrying Sam and Mike's mother had been the biggest mistake of his life, since he'd had to settle an enormous sum on her when they divorced. He considered his sons to be his only compensation for his relationship with their mother.

His father had always demanded that Sam *think*. That he never allow his feelings, whatever they might be, to rule any decisions made. Well, Sam had broken that decree when he'd married Mia. He'd allowed emotion to swamp his judgment and now he was paying for it. He'd taken the risk—and lost.

"You're not getting any work done," he muttered and tossed his pen onto the desk in front of him.

Avoiding Mia wasn't going to do him any good if he couldn't get her out of his mind. He stared out at the ocean, letting his brain wander, hoping it would come up with a strategy for how to deal with this.

Deal.

At the thought of that word, Sam's brain leaped back to the idea that had occurred to him earlier. He'd dismissed it at first of course, because he might be a bastard, but was he low enough to actually blackmail Mia?

Slowly, his gaze slid to the envelope Mia had left behind when she walked out of the suite.

Divorce papers.

He hadn't signed them yet.

And he wasn't sure why.

He wasn't holding onto the past. He'd already come to grips with the end of their marriage. But she was here now, he reminded himself. She wanted those papers signed and he had to wonder what she'd be willing to do to see that happen.

A knock on the door had Sam's head snapping up.

Mia? Come back to…what? Was she looking to expand on that kiss that was still sending sparks sizzling through him? His body responded to that thought with a rush of heat that staggered him.

He walked to the door, yanked it open and the heat instantly drained away.

"Hi, Uncle Sam!" Charlie Rossi, Maya's five-year-old son, raced past him into the suite and on his heels was his three-year-old brother, Chris. Chris didn't say much, but he waved in passing.

"Hey you guys, don't run!" Joe Rossi, their father and Sam's brother-in-law shouted, then turned to Sam and held out one hand. "Good to see you."

"Yeah," he said, shaking the man's hand. "You too. And surprising."

He'd expected that Mia's family was onboard just to throw stones at him and protect Mia from him. He hadn't been prepared to see a friendly face in the bunch.

"I'll bet." Joe walked past him, looked for his sons and relaxed a little when he saw them jumping onto the couch. "Stop jumping, that's not your trampoline."

Chris stopped instantly. Charlie was a harder sell. "Uncle Sam, Dad says we can have a snowball war if we're good and don't bug you so do you have cookies?"

"What?" Sam looked at the boy, whose sun-streaked brown hair was dipping into green eyes much like his mother's. "Uh, no. I don't have cookies."

"Juice box?" Chris asked.

"No, sorry." He hadn't expected to be entertaining kids. And his features must have said so, because Joe came to his rescue.

"Relax you guys, you just ate lunch." Joe walked to the couch, picked up a TV remote and said, "Here. Watch that cartoon movie you like so much while I talk to Uncle Sam."

"Okay," Charlie agreed happily enough, dropping onto the couch hard enough to make his little brother bounce and fall over. "Then snowball war?"

"Yeah," Joe said. "If you're good."

"Be good, Chris," Charlie warned.

"Right," Joe muttered, with a laugh, "because he's the problem." Glancing at Sam, he added, "Should feel bad about that," he confessed. "Using the TV for a babysitter, I mean."

Sam watched Joe with his sons and thought how differently the Rossi kids were being raised than Sam had been. Hell, if he'd jumped up and down on a sofa, his father would have hit the roof.

Shaking his head, he pushed all of that aside and asked, "Want some coffee?" Sam asked. "And I've got water and probably sodas in the wet bar if the kids—"

"I'll take the caffeine," Joe said quickly, "and pass on it for the kids, but thanks. They're fine."

"Okay." Sam led the way to the coffee station along one wall and poured each of them a cup. "So, I saw Maya…"

Joe winced. "She's not real happy with you."

"Yeah, that was pretty clear." He could still see Mia's sister glaring at him like he was Jack the Ripper or something.

"The thing is," Joe said cautiously, "most of us aren't."

Sam didn't like hearing that and it surprised him. But Sam had always liked Joe, and Merry's husband Alan and Mia's parents, too. Of course, he'd known going into the marriage that it probably wasn't going to work out, so he hadn't gotten close to any of them. But still, they were good people.

"I can understand that," he admitted, and took a sip of coffee. "What I don't get is why you're all here on this cruise."

"Seriously?" Joe snorted a laugh, drank his coffee then shot a look at his sons, completely wrapped up in some movie apparently starring some weird-looking snowman. Turning his gaze back to Sam, he said, "You should know the Harper family well enough to know that when one of them's in trouble, they circle the wagons."

"Against me."

"Pretty much."

Nodding, Sam said, "Fine. But this is still between Mia and me."

"You'd think so, but no." Shaking his head, Joe continued, "Whatever happens between you two affects everything else. It's family, Sam."

On an intellectual level, Sam got it. But otherwise, no. He hadn't grown up with anything like the Harper family. He was taught to stand on his own—*don't let anyone close and if they do get past your walls, shut down so they can't affect you.*

He'd learned those lessons well. Sam had taken a risk, gone against everything he'd believed and married Mia even knowing it would all come crashing down. If he had regrets, they were his own. And he wasn't going to bare his soul for the Harper family, either.

"If you're here to push me into signing those papers, you didn't have to bother," Sam said.

"Yeah, that's not why I'm here." He broke off, glared at his son and said, "Charlie, I said no bouncing on the furniture." Looking at Sam again, he said, "My wife is pretty pissed at you."

"Yeah. I know."

"What you don't know is I don't agree with her." He held up one hand and added, "And if you tell her I said that, I'll claim you're a liar."

"Okay…" This was as unexpected as the surprise visit.

"You screwed up."

"Thanks." Sam lifted his coffee cup in a silent toast.

"No problem," Joe said amiably. "But the thing is, one screw-up doesn't have to end everything. You and Mia were good together. And hell, I like you."

Sam laughed shortly. "Thanks."

"So I'm thinking you shouldn't sign the papers. At least not right away." Joe shrugged, shot his bouncing son another warning look, then continued, "What the hell, Sam. You've got a two-week cruise. Use it. Talk to Mia. Figure out what the hell went wrong and maybe you can fix it."

Sam already knew what had gone wrong. And talking about it wouldn't change a damn thing. He just wasn't husband material. Probably never would be. How could he be? His own father had sucked at all four of his brief marriages and then had spent the next thirty years bouncing from one temporary woman to the next. Not exactly a sterling role model.

There were lots of things Sam wanted to do with Mia, but talking wasn't one of them.

"I appreciate the moral support, Joe. Seriously. But I don't think this is salvageable."

"Huh." Joe looked at him. "Never pegged you as a quitter."

Insulted, he said, "Yeah, I'm not."

"Could have fooled me."

Sam laughed again. "First a pep talk, then insults?"

Joe shrugged again. "Whatever works, man." He set his coffee cup down. "Look. Up to you, but you're both on this boat anyway. Might as well make the most of it, don't you think?"

Sam frowned thoughtfully, and realized that what Joe was saying almost lined up with his idea about making a deal with Mia. Probably not what the other man had had in mind, but it did slide right in there.

Joe wasn't waiting for an answer. He'd already turned to his kids. "All right you two! Snow time!"

"Yay!" Charlie jumped off the couch and his shadow, Chris, was right behind him. "Bye, Uncle Sam!" he shouted as he headed for the door.

"Bye!" Chris echoed, following his big brother.

"See you around, Sam…" Joe lifted one hand, then led his kids out the door. Before he closed it behind him though, he said, "Think about it. Talk to Mia. What've you got to lose?"

The TV was still on and some silly song was rolling through the suite. Sam didn't hear it. Instead, he was thinking about what Joe had said and wondering if he should give in to what he wanted—or just let Mia have the ending she was asking for.

Four

Make the most of it.

Sam snorted as he told himself that Joe probably hadn't meant his advice in the same way Sam was taking it. But for the next two weeks, Sam and Mia would be stranded on this ship. And the *Fantasy Nights* wasn't big enough for them to be able to ignore each other for long.

"And why should we?" Frowning, he stared down at the deck below, watching his employees working with the passengers, laughing, talking, making everyone at home.

But while he studied the small crowd, his mind was on Mia. Not married. Not divorced. So didn't that clear the way for them to be whatever the hell they wanted to be?

And that begged the question—what exactly *did* Sam want?

That was easy. He wanted Mia. Always had. Since the first time he'd seen her, all he'd been able to think of was getting her alone. Getting her into the nearest bed and keeping her there. That hadn't changed.

Their marriage had been a mistake, no doubt. But that failure hadn't killed his desire for her. He didn't think that was possible.

They could have two weeks together. Sam wouldn't promise her forever. Not again. But he could give her now.

Of course the moment that thought registered, he remembered that Mia had accused him of only considering the "now." But hell, that's all any of them were promised, right? There was no guarantee of tomorrow and yesterday was already gone. So why not focus on *now*?

All he had to do was bring her around to that same realization. He scowled as he acknowledged that wasn't going to be easy. But maybe, if she couldn't be convinced, he could try a little friendly blackmail.

She could move into his suite for the duration of the cruise—and he'd sign her divorce papers.

No. Though everything in him wanted to, damned if he wanted Mia back in his bed because she thought she had no choice. Scowling he was forced to admit that there were some lines he wasn't prepared to cross.

"Why did you bring the elf with you?" Mia shook her head as she watched her twin stalk around their suite.

"My choice was…what? Admit he's not real?" Maya gave her a hard look. "Want me to tell the boys Santa's not real, too?"

"Of course not." Mia loved those kids like her own and seeing their excitement for Christmas and Santa was wonderful. She couldn't wait to experience it all for herself with her own children.

"Well then, Buddy has to be here." Maya frowned to herself. "You know, he reports to Santa every night on the boys' behavior. Using that as extortion is the one chance I have to make sure they don't destroy this boat while we're on it."

Mia laughed. "They're not monsters, Maya."

Her twin smiled. "No. But they are little kids with too much Christmas excitement rattling around inside them and it's bound to erupt at some point. Buddy the Elf is my only hope to keep it contained."

"And you have to do this right now?" Mia leaned back into the navy blue couch, propped her feet on the coffee table in front of her and said, "We've only been onboard ship for a couple of hours. What's the rush?"

Maya sighed and laid her forearm on the crest of her sizable baby bump. "Because Joe's got the boys out exploring, so I want to take the opportunity to look for elf places while I can."

"Fine. I'll help."

"It needs to be easy enough for the kids to find him in the morning. And I'll need a few of them, to last over the whole trip." Maya frowned and shook her head. "I can reuse the spots of course, the kids are so little, they won't really pay attention. But I'm going to need at least three or four." She turned that frown on her twin. "When you said you'd help, did you mean today?"

Mia laughed. "Jeez, you're crabby when you're pregnant."

"You try having a tiny human jumping up and down on your bladder like it's a trampoline and see what kind of mood you're in." A moment later, Maya groaned. "I'm sorry honey."

"It's okay."

"No," Maya said, "it's really not. I'm not really mad. Just…tense. I guess I'm still worried about Joe. He was so tired when he got back from that Idaho wildfire."

"He looks good now," Mia said and knew her sister would worry anyway. Joe and several others had flown from their fire station in Seal Beach to Idaho to help fight a fast-spreading wildfire. And for the five days he was gone, Maya had hardly slept. So it wasn't just Joe who needed this trip to relax and catch up on some sleep.

"He does." Maya nodded firmly. "And I'm probably overreacting—hormonal and all."

"And you love Joe."

"I do."

"So…" Mia stood up and forced a smile. "Let's find some hiding spots for Buddy and then go sit on the deck so you can relax a little."

"That sounds great."

Mia looked around the suite. There were two bedrooms. Joe, Maya and the boys had one and Mia had the other. And the living area was a good size, so they could surely find someplace to hide an elf.

"Oh," Maya said, "you should know that Dad says he's going to talk to Sam."

"Great," Mia said on a sigh. "That'll go well."

"Oh come on. Dad won't hurt him," Maya said. "Much."

Mia sat down again. "Maybe it was a bad idea bringing all of you guys along on this cruise."

"Thanks a bunch," Maya said, opening a cabinet door and shutting it again. "I feel so special now."

"You know what I mean. Backup is one thing," Mia said, "but I didn't want you all to be an attack squad."

"God, drama queen." Maya laughed. "Nobody's attacking Sam. Yet," she added with a grin. "We just sort of want him to know what he lost."

"Well, if you have to *tell* him what he lost, what's the point?"

"To irritate him, of course." Maya walked across the room and dropped carefully onto the closest chair. Her smile faded and she looked at her twin with sympathy. "Sweetie, we're on your side. We won't do anything you don't want us to. We just want to be here so Sam can't crush you again."

Her head snapped back and she winced at the description. "I wasn't crushed."

"Please." Maya's eyes rolled.

"Fine." She had been destroyed when her marriage ended. But she'd mourned what might have been more than what *had* been. Because if she were honest with herself, the marriage itself hadn't been worth her tears. She'd been alone for the most part and even when Sam was home, she felt as if she were the only one in the room.

He'd managed to be close to her and as distant as the moon all at the same time. It was as if the moment they got married, Sam had turned inward, shutting her out. The worst part was, she didn't know *why*. And probably never would.

"You're right. It was bad at first. The difference is, now I won't be crushed."

"And how're you going to prevent it?" Maya watched her and Mia thought that sometimes she really hated how her sister knew her so well.

"Because I won't let myself. I learned my lesson. I'm not going to believe in Sam again."

Maya continued to study her silently for several long

seconds, then finally nodded. "Okay then. I'm going to hold you to that."

"Go ahead. In fact," Mia said suddenly, "I'll bet you twenty bucks that I'll leave this cruise Sam-free and my heart in one glorious piece."

That wasn't entirely true and Mia knew it. Just thinking about Sam brought up images of them together in her mind. She felt the heat of the flames licking at her blood and the ache inside her only grew. The next two weeks, being so close to Sam was going to be the hardest thing she'd ever done.

But any pain she felt…this time she would hide it from the family and instead bury it so deep within that she'd never really have to face it herself.

Quickly, her twin said, "I'll take that bet."

"Thanks for your support," Mia said wryly.

"Hey, twenty bucks is twenty bucks." Maya sighed a little. "And the truth is, Sam is your Kryptonite."

"He used to be," Mia corrected, ignoring the memory of the blast of heat that had seared her during that kiss she'd shared with him. She wouldn't allow him to be that important to her again.

Mia had plans for her life. And to make sure those plans came to reality, she had to get Sam to sign those divorce papers. Keeping that thought firmly in mind would see her survive this cruise without letting her heart drop into Sam's lap.

"Well," Maya said, "now that we have that settled, do you think it would send the wrong message if Buddy was hidden in the liquor cabinet?"

Laughing, Mia pushed thoughts of Sam out of her mind and concentrated on the magical elf instead. At least for the moment.

* * *

The next day, Sam met with Kira Anderson, the navigation officer, on the prow of the ship. Out there, with only the wind and the sound of the sea slapping against the hull, Sam fought to concentrate as she walked him through the latest weather reports.

"It looks as though we might catch a break," she was saying as she pointed to the graphic she'd printed out. "The storm isn't a big one, and it's moving at a pretty good clip. About a half hour ago, it shifted position here, heading further out of our path." She pointed to one of the red lines on the paper. "There's still a chance it will swing around and be waiting for us. But right now, it looks as though we'll miss it."

Sam studied the paper she handed him. Only their second day at sea and already a storm was brewing. Both on and off the ship, he thought wryly. Hell, with Mia here, everything had shifted and Sam was still trying to find his sea legs. He hadn't slept the night before, because every time he closed his eyes, he saw Mia. That kiss was still lingering on his lips and the burn she engendered in him had him feeling as though he was on fire.

Shaking his head, he pushed those thoughts aside and looked at Kira. "And what if we don't miss it? How big a storm are we talking about?"

She considered that for a moment and looked out at the ocean as if looking for confirmation before turning back to him. "Nothing that could endanger the ship or passengers, sir. But it could make the ship's doctor really busy doling out seasick pills."

His lips twitched. Didn't matter what time of year they were sailing, there was always going to be at least one night when the waves were high, and the winds strong enough to turn even the most practiced sailor into a whimpering shadow of himself, praying for death.

"All right," he finally said, handing back the papers. "Monitor closely and keep me in the loop about what you're expecting."

"Yes, sir." She practically saluted before turning to head back to the bridge.

"And Kira," he called out and waited for her to stop and turn to him before adding, "I want to know your best prediction by seven. Let's give our guests time to prepare. I don't want anyone unnecessarily scared over this."

"Understood." She nodded and hurried away.

Alone again, Sam thought about the possible storm and scowled to himself. He wasn't worried about what might happen. Sam had been sailing all of his life and faced the worst storm he'd seen before or since when he was fourteen.

He'd taken his skiff out alone, wanting to escape a house that had felt like a prison. Sam had been sailing for two hours when the clouds rolled in. Lightning punched the sky, rain fell as if it'd been poured from an upturned bucket. Fear was a living thing inside him.

Visibility was so bad he didn't know which way the shore was and he knew that one wrong decision and his boat would be pushed out into the open ocean with chances of a rescue slim. But he couldn't do nothing, either. The waves had battered his small boat until he was sure it would fall apart.

So he made a decision and headed toward what he hoped was the shore. He was out there, in the storm, alone, for what felt like years, though it was only an hour before he landed on the beach, exhausted, wet and cold.

By the time he'd walked home, it was late and his father was waiting. The old man didn't want to hear about the storm. He said Sam was irresponsible. He didn't deserve a damn boat and he wouldn't be getting another one. And if he didn't know enough to stay out of the ocean during a storm, he'd send Sam to a private school in the desert. Dear old dad had made it clear that night, just how low Sam was on his list of priorities.

But if one good thing had happened that night—besides surviving that storm—Sam had finally accepted that his father didn't give a damn about him. He was on his own and the sooner he stopped waiting for someone to care, the easier it would be. The memory faded away and Sam realized his hands were fisted around the iron railing. Deliberately, he relaxed his grip.

"Yeah," he muttered now. "Hell of a role model, Dad."

Shutting off the ancient images in his mind, he looked down at the pool deck. There were kids everywhere of course, with the ship lifeguards on red alert. Adults strolled the deck, huddled by the pool bar or tried to lounge in the water in spite of the splashing and shrieking coming from the kids.

The sky was blue and dense with heavy white clouds. Waves crested and fell across the surface of the water and made Sam wonder if they were closing in on that storm faster than Kira had thought.

Then Sam spotted Mia's parents. He took a breath and let it out again as he studied the couple. They were at a rail, staring out over the ocean. At five foot ten, Henry Harper was a good six inches taller than his wife, Emma. He had his right arm draped across his wife's shoulders and she was leaning into his embrace. A unit. That's how Sam had seen them from the beginning. They could have been alone in the world instead of on a cruise ship filled with Christmas-hyped kids.

And a part of Sam envied them their unity. The Harpers had welcomed him into their family when he married Mia. But he seriously doubted whether that welcome was still alive and well. Actually, he knew it wasn't. Knew that when he left Mia, the Harper family had left *him*.

Yet they were here, on his boat and trying to avoid them for the next couple of weeks would be ridiculous.

"Besides," he muttered as he headed for the closest staircase that would take him to the pool deck, "they should be thanking me." Staying married to Mia would have been a disaster. By leaving, he'd spared her a hell of a lot of pain further down the road.

"Sure. They're going to believe that," he said to himself. Hell, even he had a hard time with it.

Sam walked a wide berth around the pool area, then headed for the Harpers. As if sensing his approach, Henry turned his head and pinned Sam with a cold stare.

Sam kept walking, though it felt as though he was making his way through a minefield. When he was close enough, he said, "Hello Henry, Emma."

Henry nodded. Emma didn't so much as twitch. It was as if Sam was invisible to her.

The sun was bright, the wind was cold and the air was filled with the kind of noise only twenty or thirty kids could make.

"Sam," Henry said, giving him a brief nod. The man's reddish-brown hair whipped in the wind and the green eyes he'd passed on to his daughters focused on Sam. "Didn't expect to see you."

"Really? I thought that was why you'd come on this trip with Mia. To see me."

"No." Henry shook his head. "We're here to make sure you don't hurt our girl again. That's all."

Sam gritted his teeth against that verbal slap because he respected Henry. He wouldn't argue with the older man, and how could he? He *had* hurt Mia. But he'd hurt her far less than he might have if they'd been married longer.

He glanced at Emma, who hadn't once shifted her gaze from the ocean to him. Sighing, he turned his gaze back to Henry. "Okay then. I won't keep you. I only wanted to let you know, we may be heading into a storm later."

Henry took a brief look at the sunny sky and the water, choppy, but hardly threatening, before saying, "Is your boat up to it?"

Sam laughed shortly and tucked both hands into his pockets. "Every one of the Buchanan boats are built for stability as well as comfort."

"Stability," Emma repeated.

Sam's gaze switched to her, but she wasn't looking at him. Frowning a bit, he said to Henry, "We'll be safe, but it could be a rough night."

Henry looked around at the people enjoying the day, then said, "You're not telling the other passengers?"

"We will, later. If it looks as though we can't avoid the storm." Sam winced when a wet beach ball smacked the middle of his back. Looking over his shoulder, he saw a young boy hurry after the ball before heading back to the pool. Focusing on Henry again, he said, "I didn't see the point in worrying everyone until we knew for sure."

"But you didn't mind worrying us?"

"That's not what I meant." Of course, that's how Henry would see it. But the truth was, Henry was a coolheaded person and wasn't inclined toward panic. "I knew you weren't the kind of man to overreact."

"Uh-huh." Henry watched him. "Think you know me, do you?"

Confused and a little wary, Sam said, "Yes. I do."

"Well," Henry told him, "I once thought I knew you. But I was wrong. So you might be as well."

"Henry—" Sam didn't know what he could say. Hell, what he wanted to say. But it felt as though he should be trying, somehow.

"No," the older man said, dropping his arm from Emma's shoulders. "I didn't get my say when all this blew up. You just walked out on my daughter and acted like the rest of us didn't exist."

"I figured you wouldn't want to see me."

"You weren't wrong."

Sam really didn't want this confrontation, but there was no way to avoid it now. Thankfully, with the crowd around the pool, the noise level was high enough that it would keep anyone else from listening in. Pulling his hands free of his pockets, Sam folded his arms across his chest and met Henry's gaze straight on. "Mia asked me for a divorce. I gave her one."

"And why'd she need that divorce, Sam?" Henry tipped his head to one side and stared at him. "Could it be because you didn't mind having a wedding, but you really didn't want to be married?"

That skimmed a little too close to home. "I'm not getting into any of it, Henry. That's between me and Mia."

"You making my girl cry over you?" Henry countered. "That makes it my business, too."

She'd cried. Of course she had. Sam hadn't let himself think about that because he just couldn't take the image of a teary Mia. Especially knowing it was his fault. If he'd never married her, none of this would be happening.

But he'd been so blinded by desire—by feelings he'd never known before, he hadn't been able to stop himself even when he knew he was risking disaster for both of them. Sam had known that Mia wasn't a 'temporary' kind of woman and so he'd tried. He'd taken that risk because he'd wanted her so badly. Hell, he still wanted Mia more than his next breath. She was the only woman who had ever tempted him to try marriage. And look where it had gotten them both.

Still, it was over and done now. Everybody should be moving the hell on. Sounded great, he thought. But he wasn't thinking about moving on. He was focused on finding Mia and kissing her senseless. Letting himself feel the burn of her touch and the rushing slide into a heat he'd only found with her. Shaking his head, he let go of those thoughts and looked at his in-laws.

"Look, Henry," he said, done trying to apologize for doing the right thing. As a husband, he was a failure. Should he have stuck around long enough that Mia was begging him to leave? "I can't change your opinion of me and frankly, I'm not going to try. I only wanted to give you and your family a heads-up about the possible storm. Now that I have, I'll leave you to enjoy yourselves."

It looked as though Henry had more to say, but instead, he smashed his lips together as if locking the words inside. But before he could go, Sam heard Emma speaking.

"You know something Henry," she said, still watching the water as if she were mesmerized, "if Sam were here, I'd tell him what a disappointment he is to me."

Sam felt that sting down to his bones. Emma had always been good to him. He'd seen her relationship with her daughters and it had been a revelation to him. He'd never known a *real* family dynamic and he'd liked it. Enjoyed it. He was accepted as a son—much like Joe and Merry's husband, Alan. He hadn't even known how much that had meant to him until it was gone.

Now, Emma wouldn't look at him.

"Emma—" he started.

"And," she continued, "I'd tell him if he hurts my baby again, the storm won't be his only problem."

There was nothing he could say to turn things around, so Sam just kept quiet.

Emma looked up at Henry and said, "Let's take a walk, shall we?"

Henry gave him a brief look, then nodded at his wife. "Sure. Let's go check on the kids in the snow room."

"That'll be fun," Emma said and walked past Sam as if he were a ghost.

And to her, he told himself, that's exactly what he was. The ghost of a man who'd made promises he didn't keep.

Sam watched them go, then stabbed one hand through his hair. When his marriage to Mia had ended, so had everything else. He'd tried to be nice to Henry and Emma. They weren't interested. So why should he keep trying to be Mr. Nice Guy? This was his ship. His world. They were only passing through.

Being here with Mia was a gift from the universe. The fires between them were still burning. He still ached to have her with him and now he had his chance. Once, he'd married her because the desperate need inside him had demanded it—and he'd let her go because she'd needed him to. Now he needed and damned if he'd waste this opportunity. And once this cruise was over, they'd go back to reality and never have to see each other again.

So maybe it was time to rethink that "deal" he'd considered earlier. A nice guy wouldn't do it. But apparently, that wasn't who he was.

And that opened up a world of possibilities.

Mia spent most of the day in the ship's kitchen. She knew several of the chefs from her time with Sam and it was good to see them all. But she acknowledged, at least to herself, that the real reason she was in the kitchen, was that it was literally the last place on earth she had to worry about running into Sam.

The Buchanan ships were small enough that it wasn't easy to hide—it would have been much easier to disappear into a crowd of thousands on the bigger cruise ships.

Chefs were moving about the kitchen as if they were in a well-rehearsed dance. Miles of stainless steel countertops were stacked with dishes being readied for the dining room and a dozen conversations were happening at once.

"This is great, Mia." Holly Chambers, pastry chef on the *Fantasy Nights*, was barely five feet tall and wore her black hair cut close to her head. Her blue eyes were always bright and smiling and a pair of gold studs were in her ears. When Mia and Holly had met a year ago, they'd bonded over baking.

The Harper family bakery, Your Daily Bread, specialized in…naturally, bread. But as Mia and her sisters took over more of the bakery, they were growing the menu, too. Now they offered Italian cookies, English scones, cannoli, sticky toffee pudding and a tiramisu that could bring tears of joy to your eyes.

But today, Mia was showing Holly how to make her mother's amazing rosemary bread. As she kneaded the fragrant dough on the stainless steel counter, Mia said, "This is one of the best sellers at the bakery."

"I'm loving it already and it hasn't been baked yet," Holly said, checking her notes to make sure she'd written the recipe down perfectly.

Mia smiled to herself. This was therapeutic to her. Kneading dough, creating something amazing out of flour and herbs.

"Oh, and it smells like heaven when it's baking," Mia said. If there was one thing the Harper kids knew, it was baking. All three of her parents' daughters had started working at the bakery when they were kids. They'd grown up around the ovens, the proving room where yeast breads rose, and the front of the shop where customers lined up every morning to buy the day's special.

Mia's mom's family was Italian and English, which explained why their dessert menu was so eclectic. The Harper sisters had grown up making those treats and experimenting with new dishes.

Now, the sisters had serious plans for growth. Not only to open another bakery, but they wanted to start a traditional British tea shop as well.

But that was still down the road, Mia thought. She had her life to straighten out first and she couldn't move forward with any of those plans until she'd put her marriage—and Sam—behind her.

And *that* thought brought up an instant wave of heat. Ridiculous, that a simple turn of phrase "put Sam behind her" could remind her of all those times she'd *had* Sam behind her. Her breathing quickened and she told herself to stop it. Already, she was working on very little sleep because her dreams had been filled with Sam.

Memories crowded into her mind, forcing her to remember not just the pain, but the joy, the passion, the—

Okay, cut it out.

She punched the dough down a little more vigorously than required, and automatically began patting it into a domed circle.

Lost in her thoughts, Mia jumped when beside her, Holly called out, "Oh, hi, Mr. Buchanan."

"Oh, God," Mia murmured.

Five

He was watching her, his gaze fixed, his expression unreadable.

Mia took a breath, but it didn't stop her heart from jumping in her chest, or her blood from turning into steam in her veins. He wore a suit, of course. Navy blue, tailored to perfection, with a white dress shirt and a red tie. Cruise to Hawaii or not, Sam Buchanan was the picture of business elegance, with a touch of pirate, since his hair was a little too long.

Had she conjured Sam simply by thinking about him? No, that couldn't be true, or he would have been appearing in her apartment constantly over the last few months. He'd been the center of her thoughts since the day they'd met and even going through a divorce hadn't ended that.

Mia looked up and saw him, standing just inside the kitchen, watching her. Second day of the cruise and already she was seeing him way too often for her own good. How was she going to make it through two whole weeks?

"Hello Holly," he said, then added, "Mia."

The rest of the kitchen staff simply went about their business. They were busy prepping for dinner, so no one had time to talk—well, except for Holly. Her pastries wouldn't be part of the amazing onboard menu until morning and the breakfast buffet.

Mia said, "Hello, Sam," then turned back to the rose-mary dough. "You can bake it in a simple round, like this," she told Holly, "or, you can actually divide it into three, braid it and then draw the ends into a circle. Not only is it delicious, but it makes for a gorgeous presentation."

"I'm convinced," Holly said with a grin.

"Once it's risen," Mia said, "bake it for about a half hour at 375 until it's nice and golden."

"Got it." Holly tossed a glance at Sam again and Mia could see she was a little tense with her boss standing there watching.

Mia knew just how she felt.

"Let me know how it turns out," Mia said and patted Holly's arm. Then she walked toward Sam and his gaze narrowed on her as she got closer. It was as if the hundreds of kitchen workers didn't exist. She and Sam saw only each other. She wished she was wearing something more impressive than a simple pair of white shorts and a bright yellow, scoop-necked T-shirt. Her hair was pulled into a ponytail and she wore a pair of black sneakers that were now dusted with flour. Damn it. He looked like an ad in *GQ* and she looked…well, like *her*.

She could have sworn she actually felt her skin sizzle

under that stare of his. But she wouldn't let him know it. She stopped right in front of him and keeping her voice low, said, "You're making Holly and probably everyone else in here a little nervous."

One eyebrow winged up and he shot a quick look around the room as if to see for himself that she was right. Shrugging, he said, "I didn't come here for them. I came to talk to you."

"How'd you know I was here?" And she'd thought her hiding place would see her through this cruise.

"It's my ship, Mia," he said, his gaze boring into hers. "I know everything that happens on it."

"Right." Someone had tipped him off. How nice to be a god in your own little world. She sighed. "Okay, you found me. Let's take this somewhere else, all right?"

Mia headed out the door and into the main dining hall. Scores of tables were set up, each of them covered in pristine white cloths. Waiters were already hustling around the room, setting up carafes of ice water while others placed water and wineglasses at every setting.

She didn't have to look behind her to know he was hot on her heels. Mia *sensed* his presence. The man was a force of nature. At least that's how it had always seemed to Mia. Her very own, personal Category 5 hurricane.

He had swept into her life and turned everything upside down. And even when he had left her, there was rubble in his wake.

Through another door and they were outside on Deck Two and the wind slapped at her. Mia turned her face into the cold, salty sting of it, hoping it would clear her mind. She walked to the railing, looked out at the choppy sea, then turned to Sam as he moved up beside her.

"Why were you looking for me?"

"Just wanted to talk to you."

"The papers?" she asked. "Did you sign them?"

"No."

She sighed again. Why was he making this so much harder than it had to be? "Fine. What is it, then?"

"Wanted to tell you that I spoke to your parents."

She laughed shortly, imagining just how that conversation had gone. Her parents were still furious with Sam and nothing Mia had said so far had done a thing to cool them down. She knew why, too. Her folks had welcomed Sam into their family. He'd been one of them. Then he'd walked away. From her. From the whole family. And the hurt was as real as the anger.

Maybe she hadn't been able to cool them down because *she* hadn't cooled off, either.

"Well," she said wryly, "I bet that was fun."

He rolled his shoulders, as if he were shrugging off a heavy weight. "Yeah, it was a party." He scowled, then said, "Look, I talked to them because I wanted to give them a heads-up about the storm we might run into tonight."

She blinked at him. Mia had been through storms at sea before and it was never fun. And having a storm so early on the cruise was harder still, because the passengers weren't even accustomed to being on the ship yet— let alone having to deal with high waves and seasickness. "Really? Second night at sea and a storm?"

"Yeah, I know." The wind ruffled his hair and he pushed it off his forehead impatiently, only to have it tossed there again. "We might miss it, but the way this day's going, I think we'll hit it dead-on."

He stared into the distance as if searching for its arrival on the horizon.

"Are you worried?" Mia knew that was a pointless question. Even if he were worried, he'd never admit it. Sam was a man who always projected an aura of calm command.

"No," he said, quickly. "And if it looks like a sure thing, we'll give the other passengers fair warning. But I wanted to tell you and your folks first."

"I appreciate that." She looked up into his eyes and told herself that the coolness reflected there didn't bother her a bit. That was a lie, of course. But then, she was lying to herself about Sam a lot these days. "Now, I'm going to go talk to Maya and Joe, tell them about the storm, so they're prepared just in case."

"That's fine. Just don't tell anyone else," Sam said. "Not yet."

"I won't," she said. "After I talk to my sister, I'm taking Charlie and Chris to the pool. I told them I'd swim with them this afternoon, so their mom and dad can have some time alone."

"Right." He nodded. "They probably need the break from the kids."

Mia cocked her head to one side. "You know, they actually like their children. Most people do."

"Not all," he muttered darkly. His eyes instantly shuttered and Mia recognized the look. Sam was shutting her out of his past, out of whatever it was that had made him so determined to go through his life alone.

She had tried for nearly a year to get past the walls he'd built around himself and hadn't succeeded. Maybe if she had, none of this would be happening. Regret and hurt rose up inside her and Mia had to choke it down.

He stepped aside so she could move past him, then he caught her upper arm and held her in place. "Mia…"

One touch and she was on fire. Mia really resented that he had that power over her. She looked from his hand to his eyes and when he immediately released her, she was sorry for that too. The silky burn of his fingers on her skin remained though, as if to taunt her.

"Was there something else, Sam?"

He looked as though he wanted to say more, but a moment later, he clamped his lips together and shook his head. "No. It's nothing."

Mia's breath caught in her throat and her heartbeat hammered. Standing this close to him was unnerving. She wondered idly if it would always be that way. Would she, in thirty years, run into Sam somewhere, shake his hand and instantly dissolve into a needy puddle?

That thought brought a sting of tears she didn't want to shed. Thirty years without Sam? When she'd been without him for only a few months and already his loss was tearing her apart? How would she ever go the rest of her life without seeing him? Being with him?

By building the kind of life you want, she reminded herself.

And that started in January. All she had to do was get him to sign the papers, survive the rest of this cruise and then she'd be free and clear to begin the journey she'd mapped out for herself.

"Well then. Like I said," Mia whispered, "thanks for the warning about the storm." She left quickly, because if she didn't, she might not leave his side at all.

And where would that get her?

Of course they hit the storm.

Alone, Sam told himself he should have proposed his 'deal' to Mia when he'd talked to her last. He'd thought about it, but the timing had felt…off. And now, that deal had to be put on the backburner.

"Have to give Kira a raise," Sam muttered. "She called it right down to the hour."

At seven, the first of the heavy waves began to push at the ship, as if trying to turn it around. But the Captain was experienced and one of the best in the world—Sam knew this because he and his brother Michael only hired the best. The ship pushed on and the sea fought them for every mile.

The sky shattered with crashes of thunder and splinters of lightning, illuminating the waves and the empty decks of the ship. The crew were hustling, checking on the passengers, and helping to keep everyone calm, by singing Christmas carols in the dining hall. The youth counselors were keeping the kids busy with games and crafts. For those passengers who'd elected to stay in their suites, their bedroom stewards were doing all they could to help.

Sam spent most of the early evening up on the bridge, where he could watch his employees defy the storm as the ship punched right through the middle of it. By midnight, the waves were a little higher, the decks a little emptier and Sam was tired of being shut up on the computerized bridge that looked futuristic enough to be a spaceship.

Braving the howling wind and the cold sea spray jetting up when wave met hull, Sam stalked the decks, doing his own wellness check. Walking wasn't easy and more than once, he had to make a grab for the railing. But he'd grown up around ships, so he was more than prepared to deal. He didn't run into another soul until he came around the corner on Deck Two, where ordinarily, lines of chaise lounges were set out, tempting passengers to stretch out and enjoy being waited on while they took in a spectacular view.

Now though, the lounges had been folded up and stowed away for safety. It was like a ghost ship—there was only the storm and Sam.

Then he saw her.

His heart leaped. His body burned and he knew that the backburner thing was done. Just one look at her and Sam was in a tangle of need and emotions that both confused and aroused him.

Mia was at the rail. Her hair was a twisted tangle in the wind and she wore jeans, sneakers and a windbreaker that probably wasn't doing much good.

Irritated that she was out by herself in a storm, all he could think was, she might be swept overboard and no one would know it until it was far too late to save her. That thought and the resulting images that appeared in his mind made his blood run cold. With the thought of losing her at the forefront of his mind, Sam stalked to her side and grabbed her arm.

Mia jumped, startled. "Damn it, Sam! You scared the crap out of me!"

"Good," he retorted. "Then we're even. Hell, when I saw you standing out here it damn near stopped my heart. What are you doing out here in this storm?"

"I like it," she said, then pulled her arm from his grasp and turned her back on him as if expecting him to turn around and leave her there alone.

Not going to happen.

He grabbed her again. Hell, the wind was strong enough to pick her up and toss her over the railing. "If you went overboard in this storm, no one would even notice until it was too late to save you."

"I'm not a complete idiot, Sam," she said, not bothering to turn her head to look at him. "I'm not going to fall overboard."

"Yeah, nobody *plans* to fall."

"Honestly," she snapped, finally looking up at him and tugging her arm free again. "I'm not your responsibility. Don't you have something more important to do?"

"Not at the moment," he said, glancing around the empty deck. Close to midnight, the night was quiet but for the thunderous slap of waves against the hull and the now distant growl of thunder. Deck lights threw puddles of lamplight into the darkness, illuminating the deck enough that any late-night wanderer would be safe. When they weren't in a storm.

"I couldn't stay in our suite any longer." She raised her voice to be heard over the cacophony going on around them. "You know I love a storm. At least you should know it."

"I do," he said. And memories crowded his mind. Any time a storm blew in off the ocean, Mia would head out to the balcony off the condo living room to watch it. Most women he'd known worried about their hair, their makeup, but Mia walked into the rain and the wind and never cared what she looked like. Which only made her more beautiful.

And he remembered a night like this one when they were on a cruise to Bermuda. They'd stayed on their private deck and let the storm howl around them like a living thing. They'd laughed like fools as the sea spray and rain soaked them and then the laughter had ended when they made love right there on the rain-slicked private deck.

His body twisted tight and hard and he nearly groaned

at the ache that settled on him. That night, Mia had said that the storm was magic—but Sam had always believed that *she* was the magic. Letting her go had been the hardest thing he'd ever done. But if he'd known, even then, that staying with her would have dimmed that magic and he couldn't take the thought of that. He didn't know how to be what she wanted him to be. So for her sake, he'd let her go.

"It's still dangerous, Mia."

"I'll risk it, Sam."

Hardheaded woman. Why did he like that so much? "You should head back to your suite."

"Are you?"

"No, but it's my ship. I want to check a few things."

"Isn't that your crew's job?"

There was an old argument. She'd always believed that he should delegate more. "They're busy. Why are you out here, anyway?"

"I told you, I like storms." When he only stared at her, she blew out a breath, curled her fingers around the top rail and said, "Well, the boys got seasick—though I think it had more to do with the gallons of hot chocolate they had after dinner than the rocking of the ship. That was an ugly hour or so." She grimaced. "Anyway, Maya was cleaning up and then she got sick. Between the ship rocking and the boys—well, another ugly hour. Joe put the boys in my bedroom so Maya could rest and I moved out to the couch to sleep."

"You're going to sleep on the couch?" The sofas were nice, top grade, but sleeping on one wasn't the best idea.

She shrugged. "It's not that bad. So far. Ask me at the end of the cruise. Anyway, I couldn't sleep with all the moaning going on, so I came out here to be *alone*."

He ignored that not-too-subtle hint, because Sam wasn't about to leave her alone on deck in a storm. "I can have maintenance go to their suite and clean things up."

She tipped her head to one side and looked at him. "Thanks. But not necessary. Our Bed Steward, Robert, helped Joe and I clean things up and most of the misery was over before I left…"

Sam made a mental note to give Robert a bonus. It sounded like he'd earned it. "You don't have to sleep on the couch, Mia."

"Well, it's better than the floor," she said on a half laugh. "And it's not the first time I've slept on a couch."

"No." He took her arm and turned her to face him. The wind buffeted them and sea spray soaked the air from the incessant crashing of the waves against the hull. Her long red hair was tangled and wet. Droplets of water clung to her cheeks and her green eyes were like a forest at twilight in the shadows.

Sam didn't want to feel this need for Mia clawing at his insides. But he didn't know how to make it stop—and even if he could, Sam knew deep in his soul, that he would miss it if it ever ended. What he felt for Mia was unlike anything he'd ever known before and maybe, he thought, that's part of why he'd had to walk away.

It seemed though, that desire for Mia was simply inevitable. She'd had this effect on him from the first moment he'd met her. Nothing had changed. Leaving her hadn't done it. A divorce wouldn't do it. Mia was his wife. Mia was the woman he wanted.

The one he couldn't have once this cruise was over.

His 'plan' rolled through his mind and he smiled to himself. The situation Mia found herself in right now, could feed directly into that plan of his. Now, his idea didn't only benefit him—but her, too.

"You don't have to sleep on a couch, Mia—"

"Well," she said, "I'm not staying in my parents' suite. What if they get frisky? I can't hear that."

"Yeah, I don't want to think about that either," he said. "And I have a solution. You can stay in my suite."

The ship rose up on a wave, then slapped down, making her stagger forward. She slapped both palms on his chest to steady herself. Sam's heartbeat jumped into overdrive.

As if she knew what he was feeling, she shook her head and said, "Oh, no. That is so not a good idea."

"What's the matter?" he asked, a smile curving his mouth. "Don't trust yourself around me?"

"Hah!" She grinned and shook her head. "You would think that, but no."

He didn't believe her. Even over the roar of the storm, he could hear her short, sharp breaths. "Then what's the problem?"

"We're divorced, Sam."

"Not yet."

"Not officially," she amended, shaking her head. "But still."

"It's a two-bedroom suite," Sam reminded her, his voice compelling. "You'd have your own room." *However briefly.*

As if she'd heard his thoughts, she snorted. "And how long would that last?"

"As long as we need it to."

"So," she said, "ten seconds?"

He grinned. "I think it's a great idea."

"Of course you do," she countered, shoving her wet hair off her face.

"Think about it." Sam kept his gaze fixed on hers and he could see, even in the dim light, that in spite of her arguments, she was tempted.

Damn, he'd missed this. Just talking to her. Standing so close to her that he could see her pulse pounding. Looking into green eyes that danced with magic or flashed with fire. He hated that he still missed her. Hated knowing that he probably always would.

He leaned one hip against the railing. Below him, the ocean churned, crashing against the boat. "If you were staying in my suite, Maya and Joe would have a room to themselves…"

"Yes, but—"

"Maya could probably use the break…"

She laughed. "Now you want to do Maya a favor?"

He shrugged. "I'm a great human being."

"Sure." Shaking her head, she looked out to the sea again, so Sam couldn't read her eyes. But he heard the indecision in her voice when she said, "Us sharing a suite would just create more problems, Sam."

"How? Like you said, we're already divorced. What else could go wrong?"

She looked at him. "You know exactly what."

"So again. Don't trust yourself?"

"It's not me I don't trust."

He slapped one hand to his chest and feigned innocence. "Hey, I'm a boy scout."

"Not how I remember it," she muttered.

Sam grinned. He knew how to manage a negotiation and the first step was always, don't show how much you want something. So he'd back off. For now. Let her think

about his offer for a couple of days. Always allow the
target to think they were in charge. Even when in reality it was Sam's game.

"Think about it, Mia. A room to yourself. Gotta be
better than the couch in Maya's suite…"

Shaking her head, she stepped back and looked up at
him. "You're doing this on purpose."

"Damn straight."

"Well, that's honest at least."

"It's a new thing I'm trying." He ran his fingertips
down the length of her arm.

She shivered and said, "You're staring at me."

"Yeah," he said, moving in closer.

"You're going to kiss me." Her tongue swept her bottom lip and sent a shot of fire racing through him.

"Yeah," Sam said. "You have a problem with that?"

"No." She shook her head slowly for confirmation and
added, "I should, but I really don't."

"Good to know." He took her face between his palms,
let his gaze slide over her features, painting new memories in his mind. The curve of her cheek, the sigh of her
breath, the dip in her top lip that made him want to bite it.

Slowly, so slowly it ached inside him, Sam lowered
his head and slanted his mouth over hers. That first taste
of her filled his head, his body. She swayed against him
and Sam held onto her as if it meant his life. And maybe
it did. Because kissing her, feeling her kiss him back,
made his heart jolt in his chest as if he were being elec-
trocuted. Every cell in his body sparked into life and
hunger for her grew.

Mia wrapped her arms around his waist and he
threaded his fingers through her hair, holding her head
still. His tongue danced with hers, their breaths min-

gled, becoming one, then sliding apart again, separate but joined, apart but together.

Seconds ticked into minutes that flew past and at the same time seemed to last forever. And when he finally lifted his head to look down at her, the wind died, the thunder stopped and it felt as if the world was holding its breath while a different storm raged between them.

"This is crazy, Sam," she whispered.

"I don't care," he admitted.

Six

Mia didn't care, either.

Crazy or not, she wanted Sam so badly, it was all she could think about. All she could see. Her hand in his, she held on as he practically ran to the stairs leading up to his suite.

The ship rose and fell with the still roiling waves and Mia hardly noticed.

At the top of the stairs, Sam stopped and took the card key from his shirt pocket. Mia shifted from foot to foot—edgy, needy and well beyond trying to hide what she was feeling.

"Hurry, hurry…"

He shot her a fast look, grinned and quickly slid the key card in and out. The door clicked open and he stepped inside, pulling her in behind him. The room was dark, with only the palest of light streaming through the wall of windows, displaying the stormy ocean beyond the safety of the ship.

She didn't care. She didn't need light. She needed *him*.

"Now, Sam," she whispered, "*now.*"

"You got that right," he muttered and yanked her into his arms. Burying his face in the curve of her neck, he kissed her throat, tasted the pounding pulse point there and Mia let her head fall back on a sigh of pleasure.

It had been so long. Too long since she'd felt his hands and mouth on her.

He lifted his head long enough to claim her mouth with his and when their tongues tangled together, Mia was lost. She met him, stroke for stroke, as he walked her backward until her back slammed against the closed door. He broke their kiss as his hands moved up and down her body, cupping her breasts, sliding down to cover her core until Mia writhed against him, arching into his touch.

It wasn't enough.

"Damn it," she whispered, "we weren't supposed to do this."

"Baby," he countered with a half smile, "we were *born* to do this."

Hard to argue.

She unbuttoned his shirt and slid her palms across the broad chest she remembered so well. He hissed in a breath and she smiled to herself, loving that he was as affected as she was. He was beautiful. Muscled, tanned, and so strong, he took her breath away.

"That's it," he muttered, lifting his head to look into her eyes. "Clothes off."

"Oh yeah." She pushed at his shirt, dragging it off his shoulders and he did the same for her, tearing off her windbreaker and then the shirt she wore beneath it.

Then his clever hands unhooked the front closure of her bra and a heartbeat later, his palms were covering her breasts. She hissed in a breath and let it slide from her lungs. "Sam…"

His thumbs and forefingers tweaked and pulled at her nipples until Mia whimpered and bit down on her bottom lip to keep from moaning. "That feels so good," she said brokenly.

"Tastes even better," he assured her and bent his head to pull one erect nipple into his mouth. His lips and tongue and teeth pulled at that sensitive bud and Mia was helpless against the onslaught of sensation.

She held his head to her with one hand when he suckled her and she felt that pull deep into her center. Mia licked her lips, watched him sucking her nipple and whispered, "You're killing me."

"No," he murmured against her skin, then lifted his head again to look at her. "I want you alive and screaming my name."

"Good chance of that," she admitted and swallowed hard as one of his hands dropped to the unbuttoned waistband of her jeans and shoved them and her black panties down. Instantly, she stepped out of them, kicked her jeans and panties aside and gave him free rein over her body. His palm covered her heat, his thumb rubbing, rubbing over that tiny bud of coiled need until she groaned aloud and swiveled her hips against his hand.

While he stroked her into mindlessness, she quickly undid Sam's pants, then freed him, curling her fingers around the hard, thick length of him. Sam growled and she smiled to herself, loving the power she had over this strong man. She stroked him, rubbed the tip of him and listened to the harsh, fast breaths that shot from his lungs.

Mia trembled from the need coursing through her. Hearing his response to her, seeing it reflected in his eyes, fed the desire consuming her. And every time he touched her, that pounding drive inside hammered harder, faster.

He dropped both hands to her butt and lifted her off her feet. A rush of fresh excitement slammed through her as she wrapped her legs around his hips and felt his erection brush against her core.

"We're not going to make it to the bedroom this time," Sam murmured.

"Not even close," she agreed and gasped when he pushed himself inside her.

This was what she'd needed. What she'd missed so desperately for the last few months. The way Sam filled her. The way their bodies fit together—as if they were each the missing part of the other.

Mia took a breath and held it, savoring the feel of Sam buried so deeply within her. It was, as it always had been, *magic.* Then he moved and she moaned, letting him hear what he was doing to her. The amazing friction of bodies sliding together. His fingers curled into her butt hard enough to leave imprints on her skin. His breath filling her lungs as he kissed her again, driving his tongue into her mouth, claiming everything she was, silently demanding she hold nothing back. And she didn't. Mouths fused, they tormented each other with the tangle of tongues, the rasping breaths that slid from one to the other of them.

Her hands moved over his back, her nails dragging across his skin and he shuddered as a groan rolled from his throat. His hips rocked hard against her, pushing his erection deep inside. She wiggled against him, wanting more of him. "Harder, Sam. Harder."

"Hold on, honey," he said and quickly set a rhythm that she fought to match.

Desperation fueled his moves and her reaction. There was so much here, so much she'd missed. This was the danger with Sam. That she'd never felt like this with any other man. He was the only one who could make her experience the physical and emotional at the same time.

Again and again, he rocked in and out of her body, pushing her higher than she'd ever been before. Her heels were locked at the small of his back and she pulled him closer, silently demanding more of him.

The low tingle of expectation erupted at her core and Mia chased it, knowing what was waiting for her. She wanted it. Wanted him. He kept her racing toward completion, not giving her a chance to think, hardly allowing her time to breathe. And she didn't care. Who needed to breathe when there was so much more?

His fingers dug into her butt and she squirmed against him. "Sam… Sam…"

"Come on baby, go over," he whispered, staring into her eyes as he claimed her over and over. "Let me watch you. Let me see your eyes."

She wanted him to see what he did to her. Wanted him to know what she was feeling. Mia met his gaze, and held nothing from him. For this moment, all that mattered was Sam and what he was doing to her. She read her own need in his eyes and that was all she needed to finally rush toward the cliff's edge and eagerly jump over.

Mia screamed his name and held onto him tightly as her body exploded from the inside out. Wave after wave of pleasure rocked her, taking her beyond what she thought she could stand, forcing her to feel more and more.

She clung to him, the only stable point in a suddenly upside-down universe. Mia had missed him so much. Missed these moments. The touch of his hand, the warmth of his mouth and the incredible explosions of sheer pleasure that they shared.

Moments, hours, *years* later, Sam finally let go, gave himself up to the same release she'd just experienced, and Mia tightened her grip on him. Holding him to her, loving the way his body bucked and how his eyes went dark, nothing there but the glint of passion.

He called out her name as she held him and locked together, they slid down the other side of need.

When his head cleared, Sam looked into Mia's eyes and gave her a smile. Their bodies were still joined together, and the hum of release was still swimming through his veins. Being with Mia again smoothed out every jagged edge inside him. Sam felt as if after months of being stranded in the icy cold, he'd somehow found his way to a fire that warmed every inch of his body and soul.

And need erupted inside him again. He knew he'd never have enough of her. Be close enough to her.

His hands cupped her behind and his dick jumped to life inside her. "That was…"

Mia took a deep breath. "Yeah, it really was."

"But I'm not done," he admitted, leaning toward her to kiss her once, twice. He wanted more of that fire. The welcoming heat.

When he pulled his head back, she licked her lips, as if savoring the taste of him. And again, his dick reacted.

"I should go," Mia said softly and he felt a sharp stab of disappointment. That lasted only a moment though, before she said, "But I'm not going to. Because I'm not done, either."

"Thank God," Sam murmured and tightened his grip on her, easing her away from the wall.

She laughed and the shuddering of her body sent jolts of new pleasure through his. "I can walk, Sam."

"Yeah, but I like you just where you are."

"Hard to argue," she said as he headed across the darkened room to the master suite. Wiggling against him, she moaned softly at the resulting buzz of sensation.

"You keep that up, we're not going to make it to the bedroom this time, either," he warned.

"Right." She nodded solemnly, then grinned. "So hurry up."

"Yes, ma'am."

Sam had always liked that about Mia. She had no problem letting him know how much she enjoyed sex. How willing she was to try anything.

Instantly, his memories filled with images of her in his bed, against a wall, on the floor, on his kitchen's granite countertops, laid out like a goddess waiting to be adored. And he'd done his best. That night stood out in his mind and had haunted him ever since they'd split up.

It hadn't lasted. He'd lost her. Lost everything because as amazing as the sex was between them, it hadn't been enough to keep them together. But this time with her was something different. Impermanent. Perfect. And he wasn't about to question it.

Now he had her to himself again and he didn't want to

waste a second of it. Sam pushed through the open door to his bedroom, stalked across the floor and then laid her down on the king-sized mattress. They were still joined and he didn't want to break that bond, but he did anyway. It almost killed him to pull free of her body and hearing her groan of disappointment didn't help any.

"Don't," she whispered, lifting her hips, letting him see her need. "Be inside me, Sam. I need you inside me."

"I need that too, Mia," he assured her, then went up on his knees and leaned over her.

He dropped his head to her breasts and took first one then the other of her hard, dark pink nipples into his mouth. He loved the taste of her. Always had. And her scent filled his head, fogging his brain as he inhaled her deeper, making that scent a part of him.

Mia held his head to her breast and arched her back, moving into him and when he suckled her, she gasped. His dick aching, his blood pumping, he forced himself to slow down. To appreciate everything about her that he'd missed.

Her skin was so soft, her body so curvy and lean at the same time. And so willing. So eager.

He trailed his mouth down her rib cage, across that flat abdomen of hers and down to her center.

"Sam?"

"I'm hungry for you, Mia," he said, catching her gaze with his. He paused briefly to watch her eyes flash and then he knelt between her legs, held her open for him and covered her with his mouth.

"Sam!" Her shout echoed in the room and reverberated in his mind, his soul.

He ran his tongue over her center, licking, nibbling. Her legs trembled in his hands, but she lifted her hips blindly, helplessly, trying to feel more. He sucked at the nub of sensation crowning her core and he felt her body shake. Her breath quickened with every stroke of his tongue.

Sam listened to her whimpers, moans, pleas for release and those soft sounds fed the fires inside him. He pushed two fingers into her depths while his mouth worked that tiny nub of passion until she was a breath away from completion.

Then he stopped.

"What? What?" Her eyes sprang open and she stared at him. "You can't stop now. What are you doing to me, Sam?"

"Enjoying you, Mia," he said, then took hold of her hips and with one quick move, flipped her over onto her stomach.

"Oh." She threw her hair back out of her eyes and looked at him over her left shoulder. A tiny smile tugged at one corner of her mouth and then she licked her lips again. Slowly, slowly, she went up on her knees and Sam smoothed his palms over her behind.

"That's my girl," he murmured and edged off the mattress, pulling her along with him. When he was standing behind her, he held onto her hips and drove himself inside her.

Mia tipped her head back, pushed hard against him and moved in time with the rhythm he set. Back in her heat, Sam gave himself over to the moment. Rocking into her body again and again, he took them both as high as they'd ever been and then went further.

"Sam! Sam!" Mia's body shattered quickly, because she had been so close when he'd changed things up. She trembled and cried out again and now, when he was so close to joining her, he changed again.

He pulled free of her, flipped her onto her back and lay down on top of her. Sliding into her once more, he stared into her eyes, shadowed, passion-glazed, and let himself take that long, last leap into the kind of passion pool he'd only found with Mia.

Exhausted, energized, Mia lay on Sam's big bed and looked over at the wall of windows. She knew the glass had been treated, so that no one could see *into* the suite. Which made it easy to feel decadent, naked with her lover—her husband—and displayed to a world who couldn't know what was going on behind the glass.

She hadn't meant for this to happen, but maybe it was always going to end here. In bed. She and Sam had always had an extremely physical relationship. When everything else in their marriage had begun to dissolve, the sex had never lost its magic.

Turning her head on the pillow to look at the man sprawled beside her, Mia had to smile. Even in sleep, he was contained, pulled into himself. There was no leg tossed over hers. No arm reaching out for her. And that broke her heart a little, as it always had. She wished she knew why Sam spent most of his time trying to keep her at a distance. But his brother Michael had refused to talk, insisting it was Sam's story to tell.

She agreed. The only problem was, Sam wouldn't tell it. And until she knew what she was fighting against, how could she win? She couldn't. Which was why Mia had finally admitted defeat and accepted that their marriage was over. Outside, the storm had passed and moonlight was fading into the first hint of the coming sunrise. That thought propelled her off the mattress, which instantly brought Sam awake.

"Where you going?"

She stood up and scooped her hair back from her face. "I have to get back to the couch in Maya's suite."

He went up on one elbow. "Why? Just stay here."

Mia laughed and shook her head. "I don't think so. Maya doesn't need to know what happened here."

That was all she needed. Wasn't this exactly what her twin had been warning against? She really didn't want to hear Maya on the subject because Mia was already giving herself a stern, internal talking-to.

"Ashamed?" he asked.

"No."

The one-word answer encompassed everything she was feeling. She wasn't embarrassed or ashamed or whatever else he might accuse her of being. Heck, she couldn't even regret this because she hadn't felt this good in months. Her body was loose and limber and her mind was filled with new memories that would have to last her a lifetime. Because this time with him hadn't changed anything.

"Great," he said. "Then stay."

The man was almost impossible to argue with because generally, he could *not* be budged from his point of view. That's the way it had been throughout their marriage. Sam did what he wanted when he wanted. He'd never learned to bend. To give a little.

And she needed more than that.

"I can't." She turned then and walked naked out of the bedroom.

Outside the sky was lightening and she knew that soon, the boys would be awake and Maya only moments later. Mia really had to hurry.

Of course, Sam followed her into the living room, as naked as she and so tempting, she couldn't trust herself to look at him for long.

She passed the dining table and noticed the envelope containing their divorce papers. "Did you sign the papers?"

"Not yet," he said from right behind her.

Mia grabbed her jeans and panties from the floor. Stuffing her torn underwear into one of the pockets, she pulled the still damp denim on and shivered with the cold. "What's the problem?"

"What's the rush?" he countered.

Sighing, Mia bent over to pick up her bra and shirt. Thankfully, Sam hadn't ripped her bra as casually as he had her panties. She pulled on the black lace bra and hooked it. "I have plans," she said. "Starting in January. I need you to sign those papers."

"What plans?" he asked, crossing his arms over his chest. His feet were braced apart and he stood there staring at her like an ancient god.

Her mouth went dry, but still, she managed to say, "None of your business."

"It is if you want me to sign."

Mia paused to slip on her cold, damp blouse. "Blackmail? Really?"

"Oh, I haven't given you the blackmail offer yet."

Staring at him, she said, "You're serious."

"Damn serious." He walked toward her and Mia backed up. A naked Sam was far too dangerous. "You want those papers signed. I want more time with you in my bed. And I want to know your big secret plans."

"Sam."

Shaking his head, he said, "Think about it. You move

into my suite for the duration of the cruise. When we're back in Long Beach, I sign the papers and we're done."

Her heart was pounding and her mind whirling. She should have expected this. Hadn't he been trying to get her into his suite all along? Of course the businessman in him would use whatever leverage he had to get the outcome he wanted.

"So you're blackmailing me into having sex with you to get what I want."

"To get what we *both* want," he corrected.

She could fight him on this, but what would be the point? She'd proven only moments ago how much she wanted him, too. They had a little less than two weeks on this cruise together. Was she going to pretend that sex wouldn't happen between them again? Would she pretend she wasn't going to spend her nights slipping out of Maya's suite to come up here and be with Sam, then sneak back to that couch in the morning?

Sam walked closer and Mia knew she should move back, but she didn't. It was a little late to be circumspect. Barn door open. Horse gone.

He stepped up to her and slid his hands beneath the open edges of her shirt, skimming his fingertips across her skin until she sighed with resignation. There was simply no denying this. She wanted Sam. Always would.

So if the next two weeks was all she'd have of him, then she could be called the world's first willing blackmail victim.

"What do you say, Mia?" Sam bent his head to the column of her throat and kissed his way up to her mouth. By the time he got there, she was weak-kneed and helpless to say anything but what he wanted to hear.

"I say it's a deal." When he lifted his head, she met

his gaze and tried to read everything written in those depths she had once thought she knew so well. But he was a master at negotiations and all he allowed her to see was his satisfaction.

"So you'll move in here tonight."

It wasn't a question. "Yes," she said, and batted his hands away so she could button up her shirt. Looking around, she spotted her shoes where she'd kicked them off a lifetime ago.

She walked over, stepped into the slip-on sneakers then looked at Sam. He was exactly what Maya had always called him. *Mia's Kryptonite.* Even now, all she wanted to do was step into his arms and let him carry her back to the bedroom.

"And you'll sign the divorce papers." Also not a question.

His eyes flashed, but he nodded. "I will."

"Okay then. I'll see you later." While she still could, she opened the door, slipped outside and hurried back to Maya's suite. And on the way, she tried to come up with the words she would use to tell her family about what she was doing.

By the following afternoon, it was as if the storm had never happened.

Passengers were out enjoying the pool area, the spas and the shopping pavilions on the Sun Deck. At one end of the Sun Deck, the pool, hot tubs and the swim-up bar were busy. But at the opposite end, passengers were crowded around the five food stations, offering everything from sushi to sandwiches to stuffed Belgian waffles. And the shops were just as crowded. It looked to Sam as though everyone on board ship was determined to celebrate the end of the storm and the return of smooth sailing.

He walked the perimeters of the crowd, because he'd learned long ago that the best way to learn what people thought of your business was to interact with them. Watch them with the employees, and make mental notes of where to improve.

It was a party atmosphere, and even Sam couldn't help smiling at the small group of children playing by one of the Christmas trees set up on the promenade. When he realized what he was doing, his smile slipped away. Kids? Really? What the hell was that?

Were Mia and her family getting to him?

He shook his head and kept walking, skirting the edges of the crowd, making more mental notes on the waiters, the stewards, the chefs working the food stalls. Nothing escaped Sam's attention. Not the smallest detail. Though the traffic flow through this section seemed to be working well enough, Sam realized that putting more distance between the food stalls themselves would allow the passengers to get a better idea of what was being offered.

Waiters worked the crowd, delivering meals and drinks and the shops on this level were packed with customers. He appreciated how well the Christmas-themed cruise seemed to be working. The passenger list was mostly families and he told himself that it might be time to consider adding a few family cruises to their yearly lineup.

By banning kids from most of their voyages, they were cheating themselves out of hundreds of thousands of potential passengers. His brother Michael had made that same argument many times, but Sam had never been interested. Their father had started the adults-only cruises and Sam had never seen the point in changing something that was clearly working.

But now, he had to admit that family cruises could be very successful for the Buchanans. He'd have to talk to Mike about it. And even as he told himself that, Sam realized that he never would have considered making the change before this trip and a part of him wondered why he was doing it now.

He remembered the looks on the faces of his nephews—the excitement. The...well, the *joy* and multiplied it by the number of kids onboard. Maybe it was because this was a Christmas cruise and the kids would be excited by the holiday no matter where they were, but Sam had the feeling that being onboard a ship sparked the same kind of excitement in most of them.

"Sam!" He stopped, looked around until he spotted Joe Rossi, sitting at a table with their father-in-law.

Joe waved one hand and said, "Come sit down for a minute."

Sam hesitated, trying, he could admit to himself, to find a way out. But there wasn't one. And damned if he'd go into hiding on his own damn ship. He could handle a quick conversation for God's sake. He threaded his way past the crowded tables and stopped beside Joe and Henry's. Each man had a beer in front of him and in the center of the table was a huge bowl of nachos, corn chips smothered in cheese, onions, peppers and shredded beef.

"You make it through the storm all right?" he asked, looking from one man to the other.

"It was rough for a while," Joe admitted with a laugh. "But things are looking up now." He pulled out a chair. "Sit down, Sam."

He glanced at Henry and the older man nodded. With

no way out of spending a little time with his in-laws, Sam took a seat and signaled a passing waiter for a beer. He had the feeling he was going to need one.

"Mia told me the kids and then Maya were sick last night."

Joe's eyebrows arched. "She did, huh? Well, she wasn't lying. But everyone's better today. My A plus mother-in-law has the kids in the craft room making Christmas presents and Maya's relaxing with Mia at the spa."

That explained why he hadn't spotted Mia anywhere on the ship during his walkabout.

"When did you see Mia last night?" Joe asked.

Sam shifted a look to Henry. The older man was pretty cagey and always seemed to know more than he let on. So that led to the question—*what did he know about what had happened last night?*

"During the storm, late last night. I found her at the railing by the pool." Of course, that wasn't where he'd left her, but they didn't need to know that.

Joe winced. "That's probably our fault. Between the kids and then Maya getting sick…"

Henry nodded, never taking his gaze from Sam's. "No, Mia's always loved a good storm. And living in California meant she didn't get to see many."

"She does love the wind and rain," Sam said. He remembered again how Mia would stand out on the balcony of their condo to watch anytime there was a storm. Be a part of it.

Henry leaned forward, picked up his beer and sat back again. "I wanted to talk to you, Sam. Without the women around."

The waiter delivered Sam's beer, then disappeared into the crowd again. Sam lifted it, took a sip, then held onto the icy bottle as he waited for whatever it was his father-in-law was going to say next. He didn't have to wait long.

"I'm listening," Sam said tightly, waiting for the man to come down on him for breaking up with Mia. Or for hooking up with her last night. Or for not signing the damn divorce papers. Whatever it was though, Sam would take it. Out of respect for Mia's father.

He just hoped that Henry didn't somehow know what had happened between him and Mia last night during the storm. And what was going to happen the minute he got her alone again.

"You made a big mistake, Sam."

Well, that caught his attention. Sam didn't make mistakes often, but when he did, he surely didn't need someone else to tell him about them. "I don't think so, Henry."

The older man laughed shortly and shook his head. "That's because you can't see far enough ahead of you yet."

"Henry..." Sam paused, took a sip of beer and used that moment to think of something to say. But Henry beat him to it when he continued.

"Yeah, this is my talk, Sam," he said. "So you just sit there and listen, all right? I want you to know, Emma's still pretty pissed at you."

"Yeah, I caught onto that yesterday," Sam said wryly, remembering how his mother-in-law had talked *about* him as if he didn't really exist.

Henry smirked and shrugged. "She protects our girls with everything she's got. And when one of them gets hurt, then God help whoever caused that pain."

"Yeah," Joe put in. "We've been married eight years and Emma still hasn't forgiven me for standing Maya up one time when we first started dating."

"You're kidding." Sam just stared at him.

"I wish."

"The point is," Henry said, getting both of their attention again, "I want you to know that I get it."

All right, that he hadn't expected to hear. "You do?"

"You're not the first man to have the crap scared out of him by marriage."

Well, that was insulting. If he'd been scared of marriage he wouldn't have married Mia in the first place. He was scared of dropping his own issues onto Mia and corrupting her with them. He'd wanted her—loved her—enough to try, though in spite of the niggling doubts inside him. Hell, a part of him had hoped that she would be his cure. But he hadn't been able to let her get close enough to try. "I don't get scared, Henry. And I sure as hell wasn't scared of Mia."

"Didn't say you were. Said you were scared of marriage."

"And you're wrong again. I just wasn't any good at it." It cost him to admit that.

"Hardly gave yourself long enough to find that out, did you?"

"It was long enough, Henry." Sam set his beer down and looked at the older man. He had never liked explaining himself and didn't want to do it now. But maybe he owed Henry something. "I thought it was better that I leave when I did than wait until we were farther down the road."

"Uh-huh."

There was a smirk on Henry's face that irritated Sam so that he spoke up again quickly. "Better I left when I did. Yeah, she was hurt. But if I'd stayed, it would only have gotten worse."

Joe gave a long, low whistle and Sam frowned at him. What the hell did that mean?

"So you're the hero, is that it?"

His head snapped around to Henry again. "I didn't say that, either."

"Son, I'll tell you right now, you've cheated yourself and Mia out of what you might have made together. I don't believe you've got the first clue about what you're doing here."

Sam had had the same thought many times, but he knew himself. Knew that if he'd stayed with Mia, it would have become a misery and he wanted to save her—and himself—from that kind of pain.

"Maybe not, but it's my decision. Mine and Mia's."

"No, just yours. If it was her call to make, you wouldn't have split up."

"Mia's the one who asked for the divorce, Henry."

"That's true, but I'm guessing she didn't expect you to agree."

"You should ask her how she feels about it now," Sam muttered and took another drink of his beer.

Sex didn't count.

The sex between him and Mia had always been amazing. He'd never been with a woman he could laugh with during sex. Never had a woman touch him the way she did. But that wasn't enough to build a marriage on. It wasn't enough to make up for the fact that Sam had no damn idea how to be in a relationship for the long haul.

"All I'm saying is you should use this cruise to take a hard look at what you gave up," Henry said. "And ask yourself—was it worth it?"

Sam had been asking himself that question for months. And he still didn't have an answer.

"One more thing," Henry said, his voice low and tight. "If, when the cruise is over, you can't see what a treasure my daughter is—then you sign those papers and you let her go."

Seven

While Joe and Maya's dad were having a beer, the kids participated in a Christmas-themed scavenger hunt. Under the supervision of what appeared to be a battalion of crew members, children raced around the boat trying to find all of the objects on their lists.

When that was over, Emma Harper took her grandsons to the Christmas craft room to make presents for their family. Which gave Maya and Mia time to enjoy a spa day. After facials and a mani/pedi, the twins lay stretched out on plush, luxurious chaises waiting for their nails to dry.

"You don't have to stay on the couch," Maya said for what had to be the tenth time that morning. "The boys are feeling better so you can have your room back."

Mia had made it back to the couch before everyone got up and she was grateful for that. But the truth was, Maya and Joe both looked rested after getting a good night's sleep and the boys had a ball in their adjoining room. Sam had been right about that. Joe hadn't complained about anything, but she knew that part of the reason for this trip had been to give him a chance to rest up, too.

Joe and several other firemen from his company had just returned from fighting a fire in Idaho and he could use all the rest he could get.

"Yeah, about that," Mia said. "It's better with you and Joe having your own room. The boys get to laugh and talk to each other half the night."

"Sure," Maya said, pausing for a sip of her pomegranate fizz, "but you deserve more than a couch."

"I agree." She took a breath and added, "So, I've found a room and I'm moving into it when we're finished here." Of course, she knew her twin and was absolutely sure that Maya wouldn't accept that statement at face value. Mia had been dreading this conversation all morning. But the time had come, whether she liked it or not. Besides, this wasn't about Maya or what she thought. Mia was moving in with Sam because she wanted this time with him. It wasn't forever. Heck it wouldn't last longer than this cruise. But God, she needed him so badly, she was willing to put up with the inevitable pain to come just to have him now.

Maya pushed herself up on her elbows and looked at her. "How'd you find a room? The ship is sold out. Did you toss someone overboard?"

"No."

"What's going on with you? You keep getting really quiet, like you used to in school when you were figuring out how to do something without me."

Mia forced a laugh. "You're paranoid."

"No, just hugely pregnant and out of patience. So why don't we cut through everything else and you just tell me what's going on?"

"Okay, fine." Mia swung her legs over the side of the chaise and faced her sister. "I met Sam last night…"

"When?"

"Right after the hot chocolate plague."

Her features screwed up. "Ew. Don't blame you for leaving, even if it was in a storm. And you saw Sam where?"

"Out on the Sun Deck and…"

"And?" Maya's eyes narrowed on her and Mia wondered why she was feeling guilty. For heaven's sake, until they were divorced, she and Sam were married. Why was it bad that she'd had sex with her husband? And why was she leery about telling Maya?

"And we went back to his suite."

"God. You had sex, didn't you?" Maya struggled to sit up and lost. The mound of her belly kept getting in the way. She held out one hand to her sister and Mia stood up, grabbed that hand and hauled her twin into a sitting position. "My God, I forget what it's like to just sit up whenever the hell you want to," Maya grumbled.

Then louder, she said, "I knew you had a *just had sex* glow and I told myself I had to be wrong because my twin wouldn't be so stupid as to waltz right back into Sam's bed."

"Not stupid."

"Just horny?"

"Maya." Exasperated, Mia sighed heavily. "He's still my husband."

Maya waved that off. "A technicality."

"A fairly important one." Mia sipped at her drink and paced the small, private room. The spa treatment rooms were, of course, luxurious and soothing, with their cream-colored walls dotted with pastoral paintings and thick, pale blue carpet. The furnishings were designed to calm, relax. But, she told herself, it was going to take more than that to cool Maya down.

"Mia, you're supposed to be over him, remember?" Maya stared at her. "We're here so he'll sign the divorce papers and let you start the life you want to have. And you're sleeping with him?"

"Not sleeping," she mused and couldn't quite keep a half smile from curving her mouth.

"No need to brag," her twin snapped. "Has he signed the papers yet?"

"Not yet, but he will."

"And you know this how?"

"He told me he would." She took a sip of her fizz to ease a dry throat. "When we get back to Long Beach, he'll sign."

Maya studied her through narrowed eyes. "Why are you so sure all of a sudden?"

"I just am, Maya. Leave it at that." She really didn't want to confess that she'd been blackmailed into this deal, because even though it had given her the excuse she'd needed to do what she wanted all along, the truth was just too humiliating to admit that she was a willing victim.

"I don't think so."

"How about looking at it like this—if I'm right there with him, I can make sure he signs those papers."

"Sure. You sharing a suite with Sam and you're going to be thinking about business."

"He'll be a captive audience, won't he?"

She wanted her sister on her side because it would make things much easier. But the bottom line was, she'd already made her decision. She didn't like sleeping on the couch. Sharing a suite with her sister and the family was harder than she might have thought. Just the bathroom situation alone was enough to make her go for it.

And she almost laughed at her own ridiculous explanations for what she was doing. The simple truth was, she wanted to be with Sam. They had this cruise together and then they were finished.

She wanted this time with him.

Still…when they were married, Sam was rarely around. He didn't spend time with her—except at night in their bedroom. So wouldn't he find ways to stay busy somewhere on the ship? Probably. But the ship was a lot smaller than the city of Long Beach. He'd have a much harder time avoiding her, especially if she was sharing his room.

"Oh man…" Maya shook her head. "This is what I'm worried about."

"What?"

"You *want* him captive. You still *want* him."

"I didn't say that."

"You didn't have to."

"You're wrong," Mia lied and silently congratulated herself on sounding so convincing. "What I want is the future I'm planning. To get that, I have to deal with Sam."

And that's all she would do. She'd already made arrangements to move her life forward. That began in January and Mia wouldn't let anything stop it.

"Look, this will work out for all of us. You guys get your own room. I don't have to stay on a couch…" She threw up one hand. "Why shouldn't I stay with him? He's got the room. We're still married."

"And Sam's doing this just to be nice?"

"You have a suspicious mind."

"I know. I like it." Maya sighed. "What I don't like is that you're getting drawn back in when you were fighting your way out. I don't want to see you crying for him again, Mia."

She didn't want that either, but she had a feeling there was no way to avoid it. So if she had to pay later for what she wanted today, then she'd pay. She'd missed him too much to deny herself this chance to be with him again, however briefly. He was worth the coming pain. He was worth everything to Mia.

"I love you for that sweetie, I really do. But this is my decision."

Maya nodded grimly. "And your plans for January? Is that still a go?"

"Yes," she said quickly. "This doesn't change that. I still want children. I'm still going to keep my appointment at the sperm bank. But I need Sam's signature on those papers so there's no legal confusion when I do get pregnant."

She didn't want to risk still being married when she was pregnant through a donor. It might bring up custody issues and who knew how many other problems. No, she would stay with Sam until he signed the papers and then she would be free to build the family she'd always wanted. If she had to do that alone, she was ready. She had her extended family to stand with her and though her baby wouldn't have a father, Mia would make sure her child would never doubt how much it was loved.

"Okay, I won't say anything else about it…"

"Thank you."

"But—"

"I knew it," Mia muttered.

"If Sam makes you cry again, I make no promises."

She'd just make sure Maya never saw her cry. "That's so reasonable, I'm not sure who you are now."

Maya laughed, drained her pomegranate fizz, then set the glass down. "Okay, I'm done. Let's go pack your stuff so you can get started on your hormonal journey."

"Maya…"

After that "talk" with Mia's father, Sam had had enough of people. He went back to his suite and busied himself with the blueprints for their new ship. Sipping at coffee he really didn't taste and staring at the intricate details of what would be the Buchanan line's first Clipper ship, he tried to concentrate, but how the hell could he?

Ridiculous. When he and Mia were together, he hadn't had any trouble focusing on his company. All he'd had to do was remind himself that their marriage was doomed and that was enough to keep himself laser focused on business. He'd known that Mia wouldn't be satisfied with a husband who couldn't give her what she needed—real intimacy. And he couldn't bring himself to tear down the walls he'd built around himself. Not even for her. They were too strong. Too implacable. But he hadn't been scared.

"Scared?" He snorted, picked up his coffee cup and took a swallow, only to gag when he discovered it had gone icy cold.

He set the cup down, pushed away from the dining table and the detailed plans he'd been trying to study.

Instead he walked to the French doors and stepped out onto his private balcony.

The ocean wind rushed at him as if welcoming a long-lost friend. The scent of the sea and the distant sounds of people having a good time reached him and Sam wondered why the hell he felt so alien on his own damn boat.

He didn't fit in with the passengers. Or with Mia's family. Or hell, even with Mia. And yet she was all he could think about. He didn't much like that and hated admitting it, even to himself. But the truth was there and couldn't be avoided.

Mia's eyes, her smile, her laugh, plagued his memory. The way she moved, the way she sipped at a glass of wine then licked her bottom lip in a slow swipe. The sounds she made when they had sex. The way her hair fell around her shoulders as if it were caressing her.

The last few months without her hadn't been easy, but at least not seeing her had allowed him to tell himself that his memories were cloudy. That he was remembering everything surrounded by some stupid rosy glow.

But being with her again forced him to acknowledge that there was no rosy glow. It was all true. Every memory. Every haunted dream. And now she was moving in here with him just so he could what? Torture himself further?

"What's the damn point?"

Sex, his brain shouted at him.

And yeah, true. But also true was that being around her now wouldn't change anything. He'd still be a bad bet for marriage and that's what Mia wanted. What she deserved. A family. Husband. Kids. And as bad as he was as a husband, Sam felt sure he'd fail even more spectacularly as a father. Since he didn't allow himself to fail, he wouldn't put himself in a position to do just that…again. Marrying Mia the first time, when he'd known going in that it wouldn't last, had been the exception. He shouldn't have done it. He knew now he couldn't give her what she wanted so why was he going to take this time with her only to cut ties and leave again?

Because he wanted her.

More than his next breath, Sam wanted Mia.

Whatever it cost him.

Whatever it cost them both.

The knock on the door brought him up from his thoughts. He stalked across the living room, threw the door open and stared at Mia. She wore a pale yellow, short-sleeved shirt with a deep neckline and a string of tiny buttons down the front. The shirt was tucked into a pair of cream-colored slacks and her heeled brown sandals displayed toes painted a dark purple.

Her long, reddish-gold hair was a tumble of waves around her face and draped across her shoulders. Her green eyes watched him and, in the sunlight, he noticed the spray of golden freckles across her nose and cheeks.

In her three-inch heels, they were nearly eye to eye and all Sam could think was that he'd always liked that she was tall. Made it so much easier to kiss her.

"Are you just going to look at me?" she asked, tipping her head to one side. "Or are you going to help me carry my stuff inside?"

"I can do both," he assured her and still bent down to grab her suitcase. He stepped back and waved her inside, then followed and closed the door behind them.

Glancing at him, she said, "I thought I'd put my things in the second bedroom."

He'd wondered if she would try to back away from their deal. "You did? Why?"

"Because we're not here to play house, are we?" she asked. "It's sex we're both after, not *real* intimacy, right?"

He set her bag down. "I think we were pretty intimate yesterday." And he couldn't wait to be *intimate* with her again.

"Our bodies, sure," she said, dropping her brown leather bag onto the nearest table. "But that's all."

"Not enough for you?" he asked, even knowing the answer. Of course it wasn't enough. The sex they'd shared when they were together had been amazing, and it hadn't been enough. She'd still wanted out. Just as he'd known she would.

"It shouldn't be enough for anyone," she countered.

"Fine. Stay where you want," he said tightly. Damned if he'd *ask* her to stay in his bedroom. "But no matter where you sleep, our deal stands."

"I won't back out. And you won't back out of signing those papers, either."

"I won't."

"Good, then it's settled."

If it was, it sure as hell didn't feel like it.

She walked to the second bedroom and stepped inside. Sam followed after her, carrying the hot-pink suitcase. He set it down on the queen-sized bed, then folded his arms across his chest and watched her as she moved about the room.

It was smaller than his suite and the bathroom wasn't nearly as impressive, but he guessed she didn't care about any of that. "It suit you?"

She turned toward him, swinging her hair back from her face. "It's fine."

Nodding, he asked, "What did you tell Maya about where you were going?"

"The truth."

Perfect. "Bet she was happy to hear that."

Mia smiled briefly. "Believe it or not, she used to like you. A lot."

Wryly he said, "She hid it well." Why were they so stiff and polite all of a sudden? What had happened to the woman who'd been completely free and open with him yesterday? Was she rethinking their deal? And if she was, why was she here at all?

"Why are you here?" he asked aloud.

"You know why," she answered. "I need you to sign the divorce papers."

"And…"

She took a deep breath and let it out again slowly. "And, because I want you. I never stopped wanting you."

"I feel the same," he admitted. Then felt as though he should say more. Should make sure she knew that whatever they shared for the next ten days or so, nothing would change the reality between them. "You need to know, Mia, and to remember, that when we get back to Long Beach, everything between us ends. Again."

Mia laughed shortly and shook her head. "Do you think I'm daydreaming about white picket fences, Sam? No. I learned my lesson. You're a very good teacher."

The expression on her face tore at him. Hurt. Anger. Disappointment, before she buried it all beneath a small smile and cool green eyes. He pushed one hand through his hair, then scrubbed the back of his neck as he searched for the words he wanted.

"I didn't set out to hurt you, Mia."

"Imagine if you'd put some effort into it," she quipped and the sting of the words stabbed at him.

"Right. Hell, I knew before we got married that it wouldn't work out. I knew it was pointless."

Pointing her finger at him, Mia said, "And that's the attitude that killed it."

"What's that supposed to mean?" He hadn't killed anything. He'd married her, hadn't he? Even when he knew it would fall apart.

"Oh Sam." She sighed. "That's so pitiful. You knew it wouldn't work out. Don't you get it? That was a self-fulfilling prophecy."

"Seriously?"

"Yes. If you were so sure our marriage would fail, then you didn't have to try to make it work. So when it ended, you could pat yourself on the back and say *See? I was right.*"

While she opened her suitcase and unpacked, Sam stood in the doorway, considering. He'd never thought of it like that before and he didn't much care for the idea now, either. Besides, did it matter why their marriage had come apart? The point was that it had and the only thing Sam was interested in was *now*.

Then he scowled again when he realized that not long ago, she'd accused him of thinking only of the now. Her being right about that was more irritating than he wanted to admit. How the hell had they gotten onto this anyway? He didn't need therapy and if he did, he wouldn't go looking for it from his almost ex-wife.

"So why did you ask me to marry you in the first place?" she asked.

"Now you want the answer to that?"

"Better late than never," she quipped. "You said you knew it would fail, but you did it anyway. Why?"

"Because I wanted you."

"Not good enough."

He pushed one hand through his hair. "I wanted…"

"What, Sam? What did you want?"

"To belong, I guess." Sam's mouth snapped shut but it was too late, a bit of the truth had slipped out.

"Oh Sam, you did belong. With me." She shook her head. "And you let me go."

Yeah he had and she had no idea how much that had cost him. Losing Mia had been like ripping his own heart out. And still he'd done it because he'd believed it was better for both of them.

"So the plan is to give me a hard time?"

Her mouth worked and her eyebrows arched. "I don't think I'm in charge of the hard time."

"Funny. But the question stands."

"Oh relax, Sam. I'm not going to torture you or anything. It looks like you're doing a good enough job of that on your own." She carried a toiletry kit into the bathroom and glanced around. "Hmm. Tiny."

"You can use mine," he said.

"Thanks. I might." She came back into the room and looked up at him. "Anyway, you barely listened to me when we were married, so why would you listen now?"

"I listened."

She rolled her eyes and he gritted his teeth. Maybe having her stay with him hadn't been such a great idea after all.

"I thought we'd have dinner on our balcony tonight," he said, changing the subject. "I'll have the chef send up his specialties."

"Oh." She bit her bottom lip.

"Problem?"

Shrugging, she said, "I already ordered an early dinner to be sent up. It should be here any minute, actually."

"Really?" He smiled, feeling better about this whole thing. An intimate dinner, just the two of them, then to bed. Worked for him. "That's great. I'm glad you're comfortable here."

"Oh, absolutely." A knock on the door sounded and Mia patted his arm. "That's dinner."

It was only five, but if she wanted dinner now, Sam would find a way to be hungry. Besides, the earlier they ate, the earlier he could get her into bed, where he most wanted her. He followed her out and saw her open the door to two crew members carrying trays. Whatever she'd ordered, there was plenty of it.

"Oh, thanks, Brian," she said. "Can you guys just put it on the dining room table?"

"Sure thing, Mrs. Buchanan."

Sam moved fast, getting to the table first and sweeping up the ship blueprints he'd been studying earlier. Two covered trays were set down on the polished teak table and then the first steward asked, "Is there anything else we can get you?"

"No," she said, "that's great. Thanks again. Oh, is Steven on his way?"

"Yes, ma'am. And Devon's bringing the rest of the stuff you asked for."

She beamed at him and Sam couldn't blame the kid for flushing bright red. "Terrific."

"What stuff?" Sam asked and Brian slipped out the door to avoid having to answer the boss.

"You'll see," Mia told him.

"Fine." Sam looked at the trays a little warily. "So what's for dinner?"

"That's a surprise, too," Mia said with a grin, then turned to the door at the sound of a kid shouting.

Sam frowned but couldn't look away. As the stewards left, a young woman in a crew uniform approached, holding two kids by the hand. Maya's kids. Sam just barely muffled a groan.

"Aunt Mia, hi!" Charlie pulled free and raced to her.

Mia bent down to hug him, then grabbed Chris close too, as soon as the young woman got him up the stairs. "Hi you guys! Are you ready for your party?"

"Christmas tree?" Chris asked, looking past her into the barren, if luxurious suite.

"Soon, sweetie," she assured him. "Now why don't we go have dinner? It's your favorite. Hot dogs!"

"Yay!" Charlie raced to the table, shouting "Hi Uncle Sam," as he passed.

Both kids raced across the elegant carpet, leaving a trail of sweaters and what looked like bits of snow in their wake.

"Hot dogs?" Sam looked at her as she led Chris to the table, too.

"I thought it would be nice for us to give Maya and Joe and my folks an evening off. We can spend some time with the kids and the adults can go have dinner together." She shrugged and gave him a wide-eyed, innocent smile.

"Uh-huh." He glanced to where Charlie was standing on a hand carved chair, trying to lift one of the tray covers. Sam moved fast. He lifted the heavy cover, then told Charlie to sit down.

"I like ketchup," Chris said, scrambling for a seat himself.

"Mine's mustard, right Aunt Mia?"

"Right, sweetie." Mia moved up to the table and set out plates for both boys and fixed hot dogs for each of them. "Here's some mac and cheese, too. Don't use your fingers, Charlie. Chris, do you want some? And we've got juice boxes here somewhere too." She lifted the other lid, found juice and glasses and ice, along with a plate of chocolate chip cookies for dessert.

Chris reached for a juice and tipped the glass over. A river of what looked like cherry juice ran across the table and over the edge to land on the hand woven rug.

Sam muffled a groan and dropped a stack of napkins on the puddle. He was not set up for small children.

"I need more juice," Chris whined.

"Sure sweetie," Mia cooed and took care of that.

Sam was watching it all as if from a distance. His personal space had been invaded by a horde of barbarians and all he could do was watch.

"Yay! Can we watch a movie about Christmas because we get to decorate a Christmas tree and where is your tree, Uncle Sam?"

Sam's ears were ringing, but he stared at Mia as if he'd never seen her before. He should have suspected something when she'd arrived. She had been too smiley. Too accepting of the whole situation. Of course she'd had something planned.

"Christmas tree?" he asked.

She shrugged and smiled again. "If I'm going to stay here with you, we need to get into the spirit."

"Mia…" He didn't do Christmas and she damn well knew it. What was she up to? Trying to drag him, kicking and screaming, into the holiday? And using the kids to guilt him into agreeing?

"Steve, the cruise host is bringing in one of the trees that wasn't set up." She paused and said, "You had way more trees than you needed, so at least someone who works for you likes Christmas. Anyway, Steve said the extra trees were stored in the hold."

"Movie!" Chris shouted and took a bite of his hot dog.

"Small bites, Chris, and chew it really well," Mia warned. Sam looked at the kid like he was a live bomb. He really did not need one of the boys choking on a hot dog.

Mia picked up a remote, and turned the wide screened TV on. She hit the right channel and played *Home Alone* for the boys who started laughing the minute they saw their favorite classic.

Then she got back to her subject as she tossed a few silk pillows to the boys so they could lay on them. "So anyway, Steve's bringing the tree and Devon, the Assistant Cruise Director, said he'd find the decorations that were set aside in case they were needed and I thought we could have a decorating party with the boys."

"I'm *good* at decorating," Charlie told him. "Can we get snow from the snow room to put on it?"

"No," Sam said and ignored the kid's crestfallen expression. Looking at Mia, he said, "You got my employees in on this?"

"Yep, and they were really great. Everyone was so anxious to help out the boss's wife."

Yeah, he bet they were. "You set me up."

"I really did." Mia grinned, patted his arm, then leaned over to pick up a hot dog. Layering it with mustard, she added, "Now all you have to do is enjoy it."

Enjoy Christmas trees and decorations and kid movies and two kids laughing and talking at pitches only dogs should be able to hear? Yeah. He'd get right on that.

"I don't—"

"Like Christmas. I know. But it's just a tree, Sam." She pushed her hair back from her face and held her hot dog out to him. "Want a bite?"

He shook his head and she grinned at him. "So the question is, are you going to disappoint the boys—and me—or are you going to pretend to be a Christmas elf?"

"Our elf went swimming in the toilet today," Charlie said around a bite of hot dog. "Chris said Buddy wanted to swim so Chris put him in the toilet cuz it's like a little pool for elfs."

"Elves," Mia corrected.

"Mommy used her hair dryer on him, but he was still wet, so he's going to get a tan out in the sun tomorrow."

"A tan," Sam repeated.

Chris piped up and added, "Mommy says elfs can't swim good so I shouldn't put him in the pool again."

"Good plan," Sam said, then took a breath and blew it out.

Elves in toilets. Christmas trees. Hot dogs. He looked at Mia and he was lost. Her green eyes were sparkling with suppressed laughter. She was really enjoying all of this. The shouts, the kids kicking their heels against the chairs, the movie turned up to a deafening level and his consternation at what had happened to his nice, orderly world and his seduction plans.

What the hell was a man supposed to do with a woman like that?

A knock on the door sounded again before he could figure it out, and both boys shouted "Christmas tree!"

Mia just looked at him. Waiting.

He could leave. Do some work. Make some calls. But he wasn't going to. He may have blackmailed Mia into moving in, but it seemed, she was getting him to do things he wouldn't normally do, too. And, he thought, they both knew it. Shaking his head, Sam said, "I'll let them in. And I want mustard on my hot dog."

Eight

Three hours later, the boys were exhausted, the Christmas tree was beautifully decorated from the middle down and the scent of hot dogs was clinging to the air.

Mia smiled to herself. The evening had gone better than she'd hoped. Even though he'd been coerced into taking part in their festivities, Sam had come around. He'd put the lights on the tree, watched the kids hanging ornaments as high as they could reach and joined them for some chocolate chip cookies during the *Rudolph the Red-Nosed Reindeer* movie.

But the best part, she told herself, was seeing little Chris climb up on the couch to cuddle with his uncle and Sam automatically wrapping his arm around the boy. He probably hadn't even noticed when it had happened, but she had and Mia was still smiling to herself over it.

When Maya and Joe showed up to collect their kids,

Joe scooped Chris into his arms and Maya took Charlie's hand in hers. Looking around at the detritus left behind by her children in what was usually a tidy, elegant space, Maya grinned.

"Seems like everyone had a good time," she said, looking directly at Sam.

"It was fun," Mia told her and bent to kiss Charlie goodbye.

"Thanks for watching them," Joe said. "It was nice having dinner and only cutting up my own meat."

Sam laughed and Mia beamed at him. Really, he'd been great with the kids and her heart was feeling so full, she might burst. This was what she'd hoped for in her marriage. What she wanted most in her life. And this, she told herself had been what she and everyone else had worried about. Being around Sam, spending time with him, had her falling in love with him all over again.

Yes, he was a little stern and so dedicated to his business he barely noticed life around him most of the time. But oh my when she did have his attention, when he was relaxed, he made her feel so much. Made her think about possibilities.

Made her remember how much she loved him.

Her heart did a tumble and roll in her chest and she knew she was in trouble. She was supposed to be here to get the man she loved to sign divorce papers when all she really wanted was for him to stop her. For him to say he didn't want to split up. That he loved her and wanted to be with her always.

That he wanted this life they could have together.

And what were the chances of that happening?

Slim, she told herself firmly. So what she had to do, was remember *why* she'd wanted the divorce. It hadn't been because she didn't love him. But because she was tired of being married all alone.

Maya's expression was wary, as if she couldn't really believe that any of this was happening and Mia couldn't blame her twin. She'd hoped of course, that Sam would go along with her plan to watch the kids and have a Christmas evening, but a part of her had been sure he'd find a way to disappear. After all, when they were together, disappearing had been his superpower.

He'd surprised her tonight and clearly her sister was a little stunned, too.

"Thanks again," Maya said, holding onto her oldest son while cradling her baby bump with her free hand. "We're taking these two off to bathe and go to bed."

"Good idea," Sam said, tucking both hands into his pockets. "We've all got mustard, ketchup and mac and cheese on us."

Maya laughed and winked at her sister. "So, a typical dinner. Good to know."

Joe headed for the door and Maya was right behind him. But when she got to the door, she paused as Charlie broke free of her grip and ran to Sam to hug him around the legs.

"Thanks Uncle Sam. That was great!"

Clearly a bit embarrassed, Sam gave the boy an awkward pat and said, "You're welcome."

Charlie grinned up at him, then darted back to his mother. "Is Buddy the Elf dry yet, Mom?"

"Let's go check," she said and gave Sam a nod and a slow smile before they left.

Mia closed the door behind them and leaned against the heavy panel. Amazing how two little kids could completely exhaust you in a matter of hours. As much as she loved her nephews, she was grateful for the sudden silence that dropped on the suite. Looking at Sam, she asked, "Should we call the kitchen, have someone come and take away the trays?"

"What?" He shook his head, then reached up to push both hands tiredly through his hair. "No. Let's not. They can come for them tomorrow. I've had enough of people for tonight."

"Me too," she said and moved away from the door to walk to him. He had mustard on his shirt, dried ketchup on his chin and a stray macaroni noodle stuck to his collar. Smiling, she reached up and plucked it off, then showed it to him. "A different look from those tailored suits of yours. I like it."

"How the hell—"

"No one knows," she said. "Get too close to children and you'll come away covered with all kinds of interesting things."

"How do they have so much energy?"

"Another mystery." Mia moved into him, wrapping her arms around his waist, laying her head on his chest.

His arms came around her and he rested his chin on top of her head. "Did you enjoy all of that?"

She leaned back to look up at him. "I really did. How about you? Were you completely miserable the whole time?"

Sam frowned at her. "You know I wasn't."

"Yeah, I know. I just wanted to hear you admit it."

"Fine. Here it is then." Taking a breath, he looked into her eyes and said, "I admit it. It was fun. Watching the kids put the ornaments on the tree—" he glanced across the room to where the brightly lit, artificial tree almost seemed to be leaning to one side because the kids had clumped everything together. Looking back into her eyes, he continued. "Hot dogs for dinner. The mac and cheese was good…"

She held up the one dried-up noodle. "So I noticed."

Sam snorted. "I even liked that movie—*Home Alone*?"

Stunned, she asked, "You've never seen that before?"

"Why would I?" He shrugged. "I don't do Christmas, remember?"

"Sometimes you amaze me."

"Thanks." One corner of his mouth quirked up. "Anyway, it wasn't as terrible as I thought it would be."

"High praise indeed," she said, then went up on her bare toes to plant a quick kiss on his lips. "And now… I think I need a shower as badly as the boys need their baths."

"Right there with you."

"That's what I was hoping," she murmured, staring into his eyes.

"What?"

"I said," Mia trailed her fingers down his shirtfront. "I was hoping you'd be right there with me, in the shower— unless you're too wiped out."

Slowly, a wide grin curved his mouth. "Yeah, I think I'm getting my second wind."

"Good to know," she countered and headed for his bedroom and the massive adjoining bath. "We'll use your bathroom. I think we're going to need the space."

In minutes, they had stripped and were walking into the enormous, connected bathroom. The wall of glass lining one side allowed for a really astonishing view of the moonlight-kissed ocean and the cloud-tossed, starry sky above it.

The tiled floor was heated and felt delicious as she

walked unerringly toward the impressive, if a little scary, shower. It was completely made of glass and cantilevered to jut out from the side of the ship, so that she could literally look down at the ocean below while she showered. Naturally, the glass was treated so that the view was definitely only one-way. No one could see in. No one would know anyone was in that shower.

She turned to face Sam as he approached and her stomach jittered with expectation. There were no nerves between them. Only exploration. Mutual desire. Need.

Sam joined her in the middle of the shower, and said aloud, "Shower on."

Instantly, water, heated to the perfect temperature, erupted from six different showerheads placed at all different angles and heights. Surprised, Mia laughed and swiped wet hair from her face. "A voice-activated shower?"

He grinned at her. "Hands-free, so I can keep busy in other ways."

There were two dispensers attached to one wall and Sam reached for one of them, squirting body wash into his palm. The hot water pummeled them both as he lathered the soap then ran his hands all over Mia's body.

Slick. Slick and strong, each stroke of his hands drove her along the path she was so ready for. She rubbed her own palms over her soapy breasts then transferred that soap to Sam's chest, and smiled to herself when he sucked in a breath. Mia instantly reached for the dispenser herself and when her hands were soapy, she did to him exactly what he was doing to her.

She defined every muscle, every line of his amazing body and felt her eager response to him climb. Her right hand curled around his hard length and began to slide rhythmically. She watched his eyes, heard his tightly controlled groan and smiled to herself again.

The hot water continued to cascade across their skin and as they moved together, bodies skimming against each other, the heat in the shower intensified.

Yet it wasn't enough.

Sam called out, "Shower off," and the spray of water instantly stopped.

He picked her up and Mia sighed into his neck before running her lips and tongue along his throat. Her heartbeat thundered and her blood was racing. Sam's long legs carried them into the bedroom quickly and when he laid her down on the mattress, she reached her arms up for him.

"Just a minute," he murmured and reached for the bedside drawer. He grabbed a condom and in a second or two had sheathed himself before coming back to her. "We forgot last time," he whispered, "no sense pushing our luck."

"Right." A small curl of disappointment unwound in the pit of her stomach, but when Sam took one of her nipples into his mouth, that feeling was pushed to the back of her mind.

He joined her on the big bed and knelt down before sitting back on his haunches. Mia looked up at him and smiled as he reached for her. Lifting her easily, he settled her on his lap and Mia braced herself on her knees. She ran her hands through his still wet, silky black hair and leaned in to kiss him long and hard, letting her own need guide her.

Why was it that she never seemed to get enough of him? She wanted to keep touching him, to hold him, to have his mouth on hers and his body locked deep within.

And on that thought, she rose up on her knees and then slowly lowered herself onto his erection. Inch by tantalizing inch, Mia tortured them both by moving as slowly as she could.

Until finally, Sam muttered thickly, "Enough!" His hands at her hips, he pulled her down hard, pushing himself high inside her.

Mia groaned, let her head fall back and then deliberately swiveled her hips, creating a delicious friction that reverberated all through her. And when she lifted her head to meet his gaze again, she saw fire in Sam's eyes.

"You recovered from being tired really well."

"Just what I was thinking about you," he said and leaned close enough to taste the pulse point at her throat.

Mia shivered and moved on him again. He hissed in a breath and dug his fingers harder into her hips. Guiding her movements, he set the rhythm they danced to and she raced to keep up. Her arms around his neck, she locked her gaze with his and when the first ripples of completion gathered in her like a storm, she welcomed them.

"Let go, Mia," he crooned. "Just let go."

"No," she insisted, her voice broken, halting. "Together. This time we go together."

"Stubborn woman," he muttered and made a fast move, flipping her onto the bed and covering her body with his.

He lifted her legs and hooked them on his hips, then leaning over her, he drove into her heat with such a quickness Mia's breath was lost. Her head tipped back onto the mattress and she stared blindly at the ceiling as he rocked his hips against hers in a frantic rhythm.

Mia felt his body tighten, his muscles flex and she knew that he was as close to shattering as she was. She fixed her gaze on his again and he stared back, just as determinedly.

"Together," he whispered, through gritted teeth.

"Now," she countered. "Please, *now.*"

"Now," he agreed and stiffened against her as her body splintered around his. They clung to each other like survivors of a shipwreck and when the tremors finally stopped, they collapsed together to ride out the storm.

Sam threw one arm across his eyes and waited for his heart rate to slow down to less than a gallop. Every time with Mia was like the first time. Every time with her only fed his hunger for *more* with her.

He dropped his arm away and turned his head to look at her. The satisfied smile on her face made him smile in return, though she couldn't see him. The woman was a mystery to him in so many ways. Whenever he felt as though he had her completely figured out, she threw another curveball that knocked him off kilter.

Most women he'd known would use those moments after sex to ply him with questions, or prod him to make promises he wasn't interested in keeping. But not Mia. From the first time they'd been together, she'd simply enjoyed that afterglow and had accepted what they had for what it was.

He was the one who'd proposed, though he knew she wasn't expecting it. *He* was the one who had taken that step though he'd known it wouldn't work out in the end. And now, here she was, forgetting about how he'd blackmailed her to get her into his bed and instead, enjoying this time together for however long it lasted.

"You're staring," she murmured.

"Guess I am," Sam admitted and she finally turned her

head to look at him. Her mouth curved and her eyes shone as her red hair spilled across the white pillowcase. His heart fisted as he watched her. "You're beautiful, Mia."

She blinked and he could see she was surprised at the comment. Had he not told her before? Had he kept that to himself even when she took his breath away? Was it so hard for him to give a compliment?

"Okay, now you're scowling. What's going on, Sam?"

"Good question." He wasn't sure and he didn't like the feeling at all. Indecision was a foreign concept to him. And it made him uncomfortable enough that he shifted the conversation to her rather than him. Staring into her eyes, he blurted out, "I'm curious. Why'd you want the divorce in the first place?"

"What?"

"You heard me." He went up on one elbow. "I didn't get it then—oh, I wasn't surprised by it, but I didn't understand your reasoning for it and I still don't. We almost never argued. The sex was great. So what was the problem?"

Shaking her head, she turned on her side and propped herself up. "Let me answer that with a question. Do you remember my grandparents' sixtieth anniversary party?"

Thinking about that, he had to frown. "No, I don't."

"Yeah, that's because you didn't go." She pushed her hair back from her face. "You promised me that you'd be there, but at the last minute, you 'had' to fly to Florida for a meeting with Michael."

Sam's frown deepened. He remembered that now. The truth was, even after they'd gotten married, he'd focused on the company because he'd known even then that the business was all he could really count on. His marriage would end, eventually. But Buchanan Cruises would be there forever—as long as he was a good custodian. "Sometimes business has to come first."

"Uh-huh," she said. "But the party's only one example of you disappearing without thinking about how it affected me." She shrugged, but Sam could see she wasn't taking this conversation as lightly as she was pretending to.

Then she was talking again. "You could have taken a later flight, but that didn't occur to you."

"Mia, I have a company to take care of."

"You had a marriage to take care of, too," she reminded him. "You were always so busy, Sam. If we had dinner plans, it was because you had decided that we could be together. When I decided I wanted to buy myself a car—suddenly one was in the driveway."

He remembered that. Sam had bought her a fire-engine red SUV because it was the safest car on the market. "That was a good car."

"It was the car *you* thought I should have. Even though you knew that I'd already decided to get myself a VW."

"The SUV was safer."

"And not what I wanted," she countered, shaking her head. "You never listened. You simply pushed your way down my throat, expecting me to roll along."

Sam decided he really didn't care for this conversation.

"My fault too," she added quickly, "because I *did* roll along. For a while. But being in love with you didn't mean I stopped having a mind of my own. Honestly, I think the real problem was that you never learned to bend. To give a little. Basically, Sam, I got tired of being all alone in our marriage. It's hard to be the one always giving and getting nothing in return."

He could see that and he didn't like having to admit that she was right.

"And I wanted kids, Sam," she said softly, her gaze locked on his. "I wanted a family with you—and you didn't."

It wasn't so much what she said as her expression when she said it. Sam could see the shadows of old pain in her eyes and knew that it hadn't been any easier for her to say all of this than it had been for him to hear it. He wanted to defend himself, damn it. He wanted to say that he'd known that he would be a lousy husband. That marriage to him was a losing bet right from the start. But that he'd married her anyway because he'd loved her.

He didn't say any of it though, because it felt to Sam as if he were trying to make excuses and he didn't do that. Ever. He took responsibility for his actions. Which was why he'd agreed to the divorce when she'd first broached the subject.

He'd failed. Not something he did often. Not something he really ever admitted to. Not something he was proud of. But his mistake—his duty to fix it.

"I'm not saying any of this to make you feel bad, Sam," she said and reached out to lay her hand on his forearm.

He felt that soft, warm touch right down to his bones.

"I accepted that our marriage was over months ago and started making plans for my future." She smiled. "I'm not broken anymore."

Broken.

He hated the sound of that. She was so strong, so confident, he'd never even considered that he might have the power to break Mia Harper. Knowing he had was like a knife to the heart.

The darkness of the bedroom was only relieved by the moonlight beyond the glass wall. And in that pale wash of light, her eyes were shadowed and almost impossible to read. Maybe, he told himself, that was a good thing.

When they returned to Long Beach, he'd be signing those papers, as promised. The two of them would no longer be linked, in any way. She had plans, as she'd said many times, for her future, plans that didn't include *him*.

Suddenly, he wanted to know what they were.

"You keep talking about your plans," he said, initiating an abrupt change of subject. "What are they?"

"Why do you want to know?" she asked, honestly curious.

"So, when I *do* take an interest and ask a question, you're not happy?"

"Fair point," she said and he saw the quick flash of a smile. "Okay. If you really want to know. I need you to sign those divorce papers soon because I have an appointment to keep on January twenty-fifth."

Now he was more curious than ever. "What kind of appointment?"

"At a sperm bank. I'm going to be a mother just as soon as I can arrange it."

Whatever he'd been expecting, that wasn't it. He was stunned. Okay, yes, he knew she wanted kids, but to do it on her own? Be impregnated by a stranger?

"*Why*?" he asked and sat up, drawing up one knee and resting his forearm on it. "Why would you do that?"

"Why wouldn't I?" she countered and sat up to face him. Both of them naked and not caring, they glared at each other for a long minute before Mia started talking again. "I wanted kids with you, but you shot that down."

All right, there was still some guilt left there. He lifted one hand and nodded. "I know. I should have told you where I stood before we married. It's not that I don't like kids. Your sister's boys are great. It's just that I'd be no better at being a father than I was at being a husband."

"That's crazy. You were great with the kids tonight."

"For three hours," he pointed out. "They weren't my kids."

"No, they weren't," she said. "And as much as I love them, they're not mine, either. And I want my own children, Sam. Why should I wait to try to find someone else to love?"

He didn't like the sound of that, either. "What's the big rush?"

"I'm thirty years old and I don't want to wait until I'm forty to get started. That's okay for some women, but not for me." Shaking her head, she lifted her chin, took a deep breath and said, "That's why I'm taking my future into my own hands."

"To get pregnant by a nameless guy who left a sample in a cup." He couldn't believe this. "Doing this alone, Mia? Not exactly easy."

"Nothing worthwhile is easy," she said and shrugged. "And I won't be completely alone. I'll have my family. They're all behind me on this."

He knew she was right there. The Harper family would circle the wagons to protect and help one of their own and just briefly, he wondered what that must feel like. To be able to count on people.

"Yeah. You said *children*. You're going to do this more than once?"

"Hopefully. I've always wanted three kids."

Stunned, he asked, "Have you always wanted to do it alone?"

"Of course not. I wanted to do it with my husband."

He gritted his teeth to keep from saying the wrong thing.

"But the fact that I am alone isn't going to stop me."

His brain was buzzing with too many thoughts at once. He didn't even know what to say to all of this. Imagining Mia pregnant with another man's child hit him hard, leaving behind an ache in his heart and a knot in his gut. But surely insemination was easier to consider than picturing Mia naked in some other man's bed.

He shouldn't care, either way. He knew that. They weren't a couple anymore and really—they never had been. They were married, but they weren't a unit. They lived together but led separate lives. So why the hell was this bugging him so much?

Sam climbed off the bed and stalked across the room to the balcony doors. Tossing them open, he let the cold wind rush into the room. Instantly, Mia yelped and he glanced over his shoulder to see her grab the quilt off the bed and wrap it around her. She clutched it to her chest as she walked toward him. The wind lifted her hair and drifted her scent to him and that did nothing to ease his mind.

"Why is this bothering you so much?"

He pushed one hand through his hair, then scrubbed that hand across his face. "I don't know."

"Geez. Good answer."

"What do you want from me, Mia?"

"Just what I've always wanted from you, Sam. Honesty."

"You want honest? Okay, how's this?" This idea had

just occurred to him a moment ago and now he found himself blurting it out.

"When we had sex the night of the storm, we didn't use a condom. Were you hoping you'd get pregnant then?" He kept his gaze fixed on hers and waited for the answer.

"Of course not." Her eyes went wide and in the moonlight, the insult stamped on her features was easy to read. "I wasn't thinking about protection any more than you were."

She had him there. That first night with her after months apart, a condom was the last thing on his mind. He'd been desperate to have her and he hadn't been capable of rational thought at all.

Still… "Okay, I grant you that. But you wouldn't have minded if you did get pregnant."

"You say that like it's some great shock to you. I've already taken steps to start my own family and that's why you signing those papers is so important. I don't want any custody questions later. But if I had gotten pregnant that night—no. I wouldn't have minded. Why would I mind getting pregnant by my *husband*?"

"And yet you keep saying we're not married."

"Oh for heaven's sake, Sam. I want kids. You know that. If I got pregnant the other night, of course I wouldn't care. But I also wouldn't have expected anything from *you*."

"Meaning…"

"Meaning," she said, "I would sign whatever you wanted, releasing you from child support or any other connection to my baby."

Hearing that he'd have been tossed aside once his usefulness was done wasn't easy to hear. "Just like that."

"You don't want children," she said. "I do."

He wouldn't be used. He wouldn't be discarded. He would, though, let her know where he stood on this.

Sam tipped her chin up with his fingertips. When her gaze locked with his, he said, "If you are pregnant because of that night…you might find that I'm not so easy to dismiss."

Nine

"Tell me something, Sam," Mia said, ignoring that last statement as she stared up into his eyes. "Why don't you want children? Why do you hate Christmas? You never would tell me before, but tell me now."

"Why would I do that?"

"Consider it part of our bargain," she said. "Once this ship docks we'll never see each other again. Don't you think I'm owed an explanation finally?"

"Maybe." He stared out at the darkness and she studied the tightness in his jaw as she waited. Finally, after what seemed forever, he started talking, his voice low and dark.

"Christmas doesn't mean anything to me because it never did," he muttered thickly. "Decorations...just empty gestures. Like putting a mask over the ordinary to pretend it's special even though it's not."

"I don't understand," Mia said softly, though her heart was already breaking a little.

He glanced at her. "My father was busy with his wives, then his girlfriends." He snorted as if choking out a laugh at his own pitiful memories. "There was no Christmas at my house. No Santa. For sure, no elves. The housekeeper put up a tree and some garland and crap, but it was still an empty house."

It was so hard for Mia to hear this. To imagine the boy he'd once been, alone and forgotten, watching the world celebrate without him.

"It sounds like the housekeeper tried," she offered, though she knew it was a lame attempt.

"Maybe," he said with a shrug. "But all it accomplished was defining the emptiness." He turned to look at her and her breath caught at the glint of old pain in his eyes. "Garlands and trees and all the other holiday crap doesn't mean anything to me because it was never special. Never a true celebration, so I don't have them. But not having decorations up, only reminds me of their lack. So yeah, no winning at Christmas time for me."

"It doesn't have to be that way." Mia reached for him, but let her hand fall without touching him. "We could have made new memories together, Sam."

"Empty is all I know," he muttered and looked back out at the ocean. Moonlight peeked out from behind the clouds and painted the foam on the waves a pale silver. "And trust me. You don't want a man who was raised by my father, being a parent to your kids."

"You're wrong. About all of it, Sam."

He didn't look at her and maybe that was best for both of them. At the moment, her heart ached for him but she was sure he wouldn't appreciate any semblance of pity or sorrow. And at the same time she wanted to shriek because he'd given up on them because of things that had happened to him before they'd ever known each other.

"I'm sorry Sam," she said.

"Don't want your sympathy."

"That's too bad." Mia reached up and touched his cheek gently. "Because I do feel sorry for that little boy. But now, I'm furious with the grown man."

"What? Why?"

"Because you let that lonely child decide your whole life. You wrapped yourself in the past so tightly that you can't even see a future, let alone build one."

Shaking her head, Mia said, "You should have trusted me, Sam. Together we might have found a way."

"This is crazy, Mia."

The following day, Mia's mind was still whirling with everything she and Sam had talked about the night before. And dealing with the family at the moment was dancing on her last nerve.

"No, it's not," she argued, meeting her twin's worried gaze. "And it's really not worth an *intervention*." She glanced from her mother to her father to Maya, then sat back and folded her arms over her chest.

Mia loved her family, but sometimes they didn't make it easy. Maya had invited her to come over for coffee and doughnuts—something everyone knew Mia wouldn't refuse. But when she walked into the suite, Maya and her parents were at the table, Joe had taken the kids to the snow room and Merry was on the computer via FaceTime.

They all had something to say about her relationship with Sam. But gathering everyone together to form a united wall was a little much, even for them. And all because she'd moved into Sam's suite.

"Don't think of it like that, honey," her mother said and reached over to pat her hand.

"That's exactly what it is, Mom." Mia looked at her father. In a houseful of women, Henry Harper had always been the voice of reason. "Dad, you can't really be okay with this."

He glanced at his wife, then said, "I don't want to see you get hurt again, Mia. But it's your life and you should run it your way. Your mother and sisters just want to talk to you. They're worried, is all."

"I'm not." Merry's voice came from the laptop open on the table.

Mia looked at her. "Thank you for your sanity."

"You're not helping, Merry," Maya said, then looked at her twin. "She's in love. Again. And not thinking about what that means."

Mia glanced at her twin. "I'm not an idiot, Maya. I love him, but I'm not expecting anything from him anymore." Especially after last night.

Once Sam had told her his secrets, he'd kept his distance from her—just like old times. The walls were down and now he was more defensive than ever.

"That's where you're making your mistake," Merry said and everyone looked at the computer screen.

"What do you mean?"

Sighing a little, Merry said, "Honey, you love Sam. But instead of fighting for what you wanted, you walked away."

"Um, he's the one who walked away, Mer."

"No, honey. You're the one who asked for the divorce. He just agreed."

Huh. That was true.

She hadn't considered it like that before, but Merry was right.

"If you want Sam, tell him," Merry said.

"And have him say no thanks? Yeah, that doesn't really sound like a good time."

"Mia, you don't know that's what he'll say unless you try it. If you love him, say so. See what happens. If he's not interested, you'll be no worse off than you are right now."

Maybe she had a point, but it was a step that Mia hadn't considered taking. Being Sam's lover again was supposed to be a short-time thing. She'd gone into it knowing that no matter how good it was, there wouldn't be a future for them. But what if there could be?

Maya leaned in closer to the screen. "What kind of feminist are you anyway?"

"Oh, stop it," Merry said, waving that off. "This is love, Maya, and all bets are off."

"Really? Why would you want a man who didn't want *you*?"

Merry laughed. "Since you guys called home to tell me that Sam and Mia are shacking up—I think we can reasonably assume that he *does* want her."

Maya grimaced, but said, "Okay, fine. But I don't trust him."

"Not up to you."

"It's not up to either of you," their mother said and caught everyone's attention.

Emma smiled at her husband then looked from one to the other of her daughters. "Your father made me see that as much as I want to protect Mia from being hurt again, it's not my decision to make. And it's not yours, either, girls. This is all up to Mia." She looked at her. "You know your own mind, Mia. You'll do what's best for you. And *we*," she glanced at everyone else in turn, "will support you no matter what you decide."

Quite a concession from her mother, Mia thought, then wished she actually knew what to do. That got Merry speaking again.

"Sweetie, stop thinking so hard and start feeling. Yes, you were unhappy in your marriage and I'm sorry about that. But maybe now, you're ready to fight for what you want."

"Why should I have to fight?" Mia asked. "He either loves me or he doesn't."

Her mother spoke up then. "Honey, sooner or later, you realize that everything worth having is worth fighting for."

Mia grabbed a doughnut, took a bite and only half listened as her family continued to argue and talk about her life, without *her*.

It didn't matter though, because her older sister's words were echoing inside her mind. Mia hadn't really fought for her marriage. Stood up for herself. Demanded that he pay attention. She'd simply given up on ever reaching Sam and had asked for a divorce. Sam hadn't fought either, but now, she knew enough about how he was raised to know that he wasn't used to being loved. And maybe she'd done exactly what he'd been expecting her to do all along.

Well, that was irritating. There was just nothing worse than being predictable.

"We're docking in Hawaii today, Merry," their mother said. "So we'll have a few days here and then fly home."

The trip was moving on. Soon her parents would be

gone and not long after that, the ship would be back in Long Beach and this whole interlude would be over.

Mia could either go back to her life not knowing what might have happened if she'd only spoken up. Or, she could take a chance, tell Sam she loved him and maybe get everything she ever wanted.

When his cell phone rang, Sam looked at the screen, rolled his eyes and answered. "Michael. Everything all right?"

"That's what I was calling to ask you," his brother said. "How're things going with Mia?"

There was a loaded question, he thought. Sam had been up and out of the suite before Mia woke up because last night's conversation was still running through his mind and he wasn't in the mood to continue it.

His sleep had been haunted with the kind of images that would probably keep him from sleeping for the rest of his life. Mia. Pregnant with a baby that wasn't his. Raising kids on her own—unless of course, she married some other guy and then she'd be having *his* babies and Sam would go on as he had been.

Alone. Wasn't that better, though, he asked himself. He'd already proven that he couldn't be the kind of husband Mia wanted and deserved.

"That doesn't sound good," Michael said and snapped his brother's attention back to the conversation.

"Let it go, Michael."

"Damn it, Sam," the other man said, clearly exasperated. "This was the perfect opportunity for you to get past what our dear father did to your brain and have a real life."

Sam scowled at the phone. What he did not need was a pitying lecture from his younger brother. "I have a life, thanks. And it runs just the way I want it to."

"Alone. Forever."

"I'm only alone when I want to be," Sam argued.

"Great," Michael said. "So you're going to be a man just like our father. A long string of temporary women coming and going out of your life and not one of them meaning a damn."

He didn't like the sound of it, but the truth was, that was what he'd been raised to be.

"Is there a reason you called besides a chance to hammer at me?" Sam demanded.

"Yeah. I wanted to let you know the new Clipper ship is taking shape. They've got most of it built out and it looks like they'll beat their own deadline."

"Finally," Sam muttered. "Good news."

"Even better news? They're thinking she'll be ready to take her first passengers in another six months."

"Good timing. Ready for the summer sailing crowd."

"That's what I thought. If this one works as well as we think it will, we should put the next Clipper ship on the routes leaving Long Beach."

"I think so too. Lots of people would want to take that kind of ship to Hawaii or Panama…"

"And since we agree on that, I'm going to push my luck," Michael said. "Don't blow this second shot with Mia, Sam. You don't want to be Dad, the sequel."

When his brother hung up, Sam stared out at the sea and told himself that his brother just didn't get it. But as he stood there at the bow of the ship, watching the waves slash at the boat, an idea began to form in his mind.

It was a damn good idea, too. He hoped to hell it would work out better this time—and he thought that maybe it could.

All he had to do was convince Mia.

Once they were in port and docked in Honolulu, the passengers fled the luxurious ship to explore the island. Mia's family was no exception. She watched her sister's family, along with their parents, take off for a day on land. She hadn't gone with them, because she needed to see Sam. To decide if she should try Merry's advice or not.

The notion of risking her heart again wasn't easy. Living through losing Sam once had nearly killed her. If she allowed herself to hope and lost again…the pain would be so much worse.

Still, it wasn't in Mia's nature to give up, so it had cost her to admit that her marriage was not what she had hoped it would be. But she'd finally come to terms with it and now, she was supposed to take a chance again? She didn't know if she was willing to or not.

"You look deep in thought."

That voice reverberated throughout her body. Mia's heartbeat jumped as she slowly turned around to look at Sam. Surprising to see him in khakis, a dark green, short-sleeved shirt and casual brown shoes. She was so accustomed to seeing him in a suit, she hardly knew what to make of casual Sam.

"No business meetings today?"

"No," he said and moved to stand beside her at the railing. In port, they could watch surfers and day sailors on their little skiffs with jewel-toned sails. The view, complete with huge white clouds and a heartbreakingly blue sky, was like a living painting.

"Where's the family?" he asked, and glanced around, as if expecting Maya to come growling around a corner.

Mia laughed a little. "They all went ashore. Mom and Dad for shopping, Maya, Joe and the kids to hit the beach."

"But you didn't go with them." His gaze was fixed on hers now and Mia thought that his eyes were an even nicer view than the one she had just admired.

"No, I wanted to stay here. Maybe…" she paused. "Talk to you again."

Nodding, he leaned his forearms on the railing and glanced at her. "Don't you think we said enough last night?"

"I don't know," she admitted. And that was part of the problem. Last night, he'd let down some of the walls surrounding him and maybe she was hoping he'd open up some more. Really let her in. If he didn't, would she push? Sex with Sam was wonderful, but it didn't clear up the situation either, it only confused things further.

"Well." He straightened up and laid both hands on her shoulders.

Heat swept through her and Mia felt powerless against it.

"Why don't we go ashore, too?" Sam asked. "Do the tourist thing. We can talk while we go."

Like they had before on the cruise when they'd met.

"That sounds good," she said.

"Great." He smiled at her and took her hand. "Let's go."

Sam took her to every spot they'd visited the year before. From the beaches on the north shore to the shops and restaurants in the city. In the rental car, they were out for hours, and it seemed that once away from the ship, the tension between them slipped away. They laughed and talked as they had when first getting to know each other and when they stopped for lunch Mia smiled at him and said, "Thanks for this."

"You're welcome. But it was for me, too," Sam admitted. "Seeing you again made me remember a lot of things I forced myself to forget."

She picked up her iced tea and took a sip. "That's the difference between us. I didn't want to forget."

"Didn't say I wanted to," Sam countered. "I said I forced myself to."

"Why?"

He laughed at that. "Seriously. Why? Because we weren't together anymore, Mia. Remembering was pointless. Painful."

"Was it?" she asked. "Painful, I mean."

He gritted his teeth and chose his words carefully. "Did you really believe that breaking up meant nothing to me?"

"It didn't seem to bother you," she said quietly, so that others in the tiny restaurant wouldn't overhear.

The restaurant was very small and obviously designed to attract tourists as there were grass skirts tacked to the walls and tiki torches along the patio outside. But the servers were friendly, the views were beautiful and the food smelled delicious.

"What would have been the point of indulging pain? It was over," he said, remembering the look on her face when she'd asked him for a divorce. He'd taken the hit because he'd been prepared for it from the moment they'd taken their vows. Sam was expecting the marriage to end, so pain wasn't unexpected.

"If you're so okay with this, why didn't you just sign those divorce papers the first day I gave them to you?"

Yeah, he didn't have a ready answer for that question. He wasn't even sure *he* knew the reason he'd delayed. A little self-torture?

"Never mind," she said, waving one hand in the air as if to erase her question. "Let's just have lunch and enjoy the rest of the day."

A tiny smile tugged at one corner of his mouth. "You mean, we should enjoy 'the now'?"

Her gaze snapped up to his and she grinned briefly. "Okay, yes. Let's enjoy the now."

"Welcome to my world," he said and lifted his glass of beer in a toast.

She did the same. Then there was silence for a couple of long seconds while Sam watched her, indulging himself by looking into her green eyes and admiring the fall of that red hair. Finally, he heard himself say, "Come to dinner with me tonight."

She blinked at him and he could see the surprise in her eyes. "Dinner?"

He shrugged, to downplay what he was feeling. "Why not keep enjoying the now?"

Mia looked at him for what seemed forever and he knew she was trying to figure out what he was thinking. He wished her luck with that, because even he couldn't make sense of his jumbled thoughts at the moment. But finally, she nodded.

"Okay. Dinner."

And after that, he promised himself, they'd celebrate by doing what they did best.

* * *

"Have I told you yet, that you look beautiful?"

Mia smiled at Sam. "You mentioned it, but thank you. It's nice to hear."

She was wearing a sleeveless, sunshine-yellow dress with a short, full skirt and a pair of taupe, three-inch heels. She'd left her hair down and the humidity had zapped some dormant curls into life.

Sam of course, looked gorgeous in a black suit with a white dress shirt and a deep, magenta tie.

And the setting was both lovely and curious. The Sunset Cliffs restaurant was just what the name implied. It sat high on a cliff side with a breathtaking view of the ocean and the beach far below them. The stone patio was dotted with a dozen cloth-covered tables—empty now—that each boasted a hurricane lamp where candle flames danced in a soft, warm breeze.

And at sunset, she remembered, the view was staggering as the sun turned the ocean orange and gold, scarlet and purple. She remembered everything about the night she was last here, a year ago when Sam had brought her here to propose.

She could see it all in her memory as clearly as if it had happened the night before. But she didn't look at it. Instead, she watched Sam and wondered why he'd brought her to this particular restaurant. She wouldn't have called him a sentimental man, so why?

Sipping at her glass of crisp, white wine, Mia tilted her head to one side and studied him until he shifted under that steady stare.

"What?"

She shook her head. "It's just—I'm glad you brought me here for dinner."

"Best restaurant on the island."

"And is that why we're here?"

"No," he admitted, then shifted to look out at the horizon where the sun was beginning to dazzle. "We took that trip down memory lane today, I thought we should finish it up right."

That made her sad and happy, which was just ridiculous and a total sign of how messed up she was over this situation. Was the restaurant just a memory to him?

Or was it that he wanted to experience that night all over again? Was there more to his motivation in bringing her here than he was admitting? She'd like to think so, but how could she be sure?

"Well, if you wanted to really relive that night we were here," she said, with a knowing smile, "there should be other diners at the tables."

He glanced around, then looked back at her and shrugged. "Buying out the patio just for the two of us seemed like a good idea. This way we can talk and not have people listening in."

Huh. What was it he wanted to talk about? Was he going to suggest they stay together and have those babies she wanted so badly? Had he realized that life without her wasn't nearly as good as life *with* her? Oh, Mia really wanted to think so. And in spite of her efforts to keep it in check, her heartbeat sped up, racing with possibilities.

Maybe Merry was right. Maybe this was the time to tell him that she loved him. That she didn't really want the divorce. She wanted him. And a family.

"What did you want to talk about?" she asked instead.

He reached across the table for her hand and folded it into his. "I wanted to tell you that these last few days with you have been…"

"…I think so, too."

"Good," he said, nodding, keeping his gaze fixed on hers. "Because since last night, when we talked, I've been thinking about a lot of things."

"Okay…" There went her heartbeat again as hope rose within in spite of everything.

The waiter brought their meals and Sam released her hand and waited until the man had left again before he started speaking. "When you said you were going to a sperm bank," he admitted, "I didn't like it."

She hadn't expected *that*, so she said, "I'm sorry, but that's my choice."

"I understand that." Sam lifted one hand for peace. "I do. And I get why you've decided to do it. But hearing your plan started me thinking and kept me up most of the night. Today, something occurred to me and that's been racing through my brain until I can't think of anything else."

"What are you talking about, Sam?" She held her breath because hope was a dangerous thing. Not enough hope and life wasn't worth living. Too much and you were setting yourself up for constant disappointment.

Their dinners were ignored as they stared at each other, while the sky went lavender and the dancing candle flame reflected in their eyes.

"I'm talking about what happened the night of the storm."

Confused, she asked, "You mean when we had sex?"

"Unprotected sex," he corrected.

Now her stomach jittered in time with her galloping heartbeat. She didn't know where he was going with this, but she really hoped she would like where they ended up.

"You could be pregnant right now," he said tightly.

She hadn't allowed herself to think about the chances

of that happening. Because the truth was, she would love being pregnant with Sam's baby. True that hadn't been the plan. But if she were pregnant with Sam's child, she wouldn't be disappointed. Even if it meant she still wouldn't have Sam.

"I suppose so." Instinctively, Mia's right hand dropped to her belly as if to protect the child that might be there.

"When I realized that, I decided something else." He paused, reached for her hand again and held on. "You want kids," he said. "Have mine."

She gasped. Had she heard him right? Of course she had. She wasn't deaf. She was just…stunned. Had he brought her back to this special place to propose again? To renew what they'd promised each other a year ago?

"Are you serious?"

"Why not?" He held her hand tighter, as if half-afraid she'd pull away before he was finished. He didn't have to worry, Mia thought. Now that he'd started, she had to hear the rest of his plan.

"We're still married, Mia."

"Yes, but—"

"We're good together."

"Okay…" Still confused, still hopeful, Mia told herself to wait. To keep hoping.

"So have my children," Sam said. "Stay married to me."

"You want us to be together again? To have a family?"

"That's what I'm saying."

"And how will it be different this time?" she asked.

"You'll have the kids you want."

Slowly, the air in her balloon of hope began leaking out.

"I will," she mused. "Not *we*."

"Mia, I've told you already," he explained. "I don't

know how to be a father. All I do know, I learned from watching my father and believe me, that's not a role model you want to emulate.

"I told you some of it last night. Understand that my father was a bastard and his kind of parenting is all I know."

"You're not him, Sam."

"That's the thing," he admitted. "I don't know if I am or not and it doesn't seem fair to some innocent kid to take the chance. I'm just not good with kids."

She hated hearing him say that because it wasn't true. Mia had seen him with Maya's children. And the boys loved him. Kids were always good judges of people. If they loved Sam, then he was better with kids than he believed he was.

"Yes you are. Charlie and Chris love you. So do Merry's kids."

Sam released her hand and sat back. His gaze stayed on hers. "That's different. Being an uncle doesn't require the same amount of patience and—never mind, I'm not going to get into this again."

"Afraid I might convince you?"

He shook his head. "Don't make what I'm offering something it's not."

"Then what is it, Sam? Be specific."

"It's simple. We stay married. You get the kids you want. And we go on as we were before."

And with that, she thought, the balloon was flat and dead.

"No, Sam," she said and felt him loosen his grip on her hand. "I can't do that. What we had was an empty marriage and it almost cut my heart out."

Frowning, he argued, "Come on Mia, it wasn't that bad. We got along great. We had a good time."

"When you were there," she said softly. "But you

stayed away as much as you could. Now you want to go back to the same thing that hurt me so badly? And worse yet, you want to add children into the mix—kids who would have their hearts damaged because their father wasn't fully there for them."

A chill dropped across the surface of his eyes. "I would make sure they had everything they needed."

"Except love." Mia sighed and looked out at the sunset, sorry to see the glorious colors had already faded and the ocean was going dark. "We missed it."

"What? Missed what?"

"The sunset," she said, though her heart was breaking. "We were arguing and we missed the beautiful show."

"It was a sunset," he said. "There's another one tomorrow."

She looked at him and really hoped she didn't start crying. She did not want to do that until she was alone and could really give in to it.

"Don't you see, Sam? Missing that sunset is a metaphor for what our lives would be like if I agreed to your plan."

"What the hell are you talking about?"

"If we got back together, doing the same thing that didn't work before, we'd miss the beauty."

"What beauty?"

"Of family," she said. "Of love. Of really being together."

"Mia…"

"No, Sam, let me finish." She looked at him, staring into those blue eyes of his until she felt steady enough to say, "I love you, Sam. I always have. Probably always will."

"That's a good thing, Mia."

"It should be," she agreed. "But I can't set myself up

for more pain when I know that nothing has changed. You still believe that marriage is a nightmare and I still want a family."

He leaned in toward her. "I can give you that family, Mia."

Yes, he could, but he didn't see the whole picture. He would hold himself back from her, and from any kids they had. And that sounded like an empty life.

"It's tempting, Sam. So very tempting because I love you so much. But I can't do it. I deserve more," she said softly. "*We* deserve more. Don't you see, Sam? If you had children and never shared yourself with them, then you would be doing exactly what your dad did to you. You say you don't want to risk being him, but this …offer, is exactly that."

He stiffened and she knew she'd struck a chord. "You don't want that, do you Sam?"

"Of course not."

"I'm sorry. But I can't go back to having to fight for any scrap of attention from you. And I will not put my children through that."

"And that's it." It wasn't a question.

"That's it," she said sadly, then she picked up her purse. "If you don't mind, I'm not really hungry anymore. You stay. I'll take a cab back to the ship."

"Don't be ridiculous." He stood up, called the waiter over, handed the man a couple hundred dollars and told him to keep the change.

They walked out together—but separate—and Mia knew that's how they would always be.

It broke her heart all over again.

Ten

Sam drove in silence. What the hell could he say? He slanted a sideways glance at Mia and told himself that he'd tried. He'd offered her a life, the children she wanted, but it hadn't been enough.

The silence stretched on until it became a huge presence. A third passenger in the car, impossible to ignore and just as impossible to address.

From the corner of his eye, he saw Mia clutching her brown leather purse on her lap as if it were a lifeline. She sat poker straight and kept her gaze fixed on the road in front of them.

Man, this day had gone to hell fast.

At a stop light, his fingers drummed on the steering wheel, but he stopped when she said, "I'll move back to Maya's suite tonight."

He cursed under his breath and wished—hell, he didn't

even know what he wished anymore. All he did know was that he wasn't going to send her back to sleeping on Maya's couch. They might not share a bed anymore, but there were two bedrooms in his suite. No matter how hard it would be, being around her and not touching her, damned if she would move out.

"No you won't." He turned to look at her and found her gaze locked on him.

"Sam—"

"Let me finish." The light changed and he stepped on the gas. Steering through the traffic, headed for the port, he said, "You can stay in the second bedroom. There's no reason for you to go back to Maya's couch."

"I'll be fine," she said, her voice determined.

"Yeah, but why should you have to just be fine?" He shook his head, but kept watching the road. "You can even lock the bedroom door if you feel like you need to."

"That's not it," she argued and he believed her. "I just don't want to make this harder on either of us than it has to be."

"Right. But do you really want to talk to Maya about why you're moving back?"

"No," she admitted and her body slumped, her head dropping to the head rest. "I really don't. Not tonight."

"So stay." He felt her gaze on him and sighed. "Damn it, Mia, we're adults. I can be in the same room with you without making a move. And I think you're capable of saying no, even if I did."

"I know that. I told you, it's not about that. It's just—" She shifted in her seat so she was facing him. "I don't want it to be awkward between us now, Sam. And staying in your suite, seeing each other all the time, but not being together anymore—not even temporarily—will just make things that much harder to deal with."

"Relax, Mia. If you can handle it, so can I." He scowled at the thought, but said, "We go back to being what we were to each other when the cruise started. And when we get to the ship, I'll sign the damn papers for you. Sharing a suite doesn't have to be intimate. We'll avoid each other when we can and that should be good enough."

Though he was sure as hell going to miss being with her. Having the right to touch her. To hold her.

He already felt the loss of her as he would a limb and the real torture hadn't even begun yet.

"You'll sign the papers before we get back to Long Beach?"

He threw a quick glance at her. "Is there any point in waiting?"

"No," she said softly, "I suppose not."

"Okay then. This isn't anything new to us, Mia." Though it was. Because he had offered her family. Kids. Everything he'd thought—hoped—she'd wanted. And she'd turned him down. That truth sank like a stone in the pit of his stomach. "We'll get through it."

And the silence crept back, settling down between them and this time, each of them hid behind the silence and were grateful for it.

For two days, Sam was like a ghost, slipping in and out of the suite at all hours and somehow managing to avoid seeing Mia completely. Clearly, he was doing everything he could to make it easier on both of them.

She didn't know whether to be angry about that or to leave him a thank-you note.

It was hard not seeing him, but it would have been so

much harder to spend time with him and know that now, it was truly over. But God, she missed him so much.

"He asked you to stay married."

She looked at Maya. "Yes."

"And have kids."

"Yes."

"And you said no."

Mia took a deep breath, turned her head on the pool-side chaise and said, "Yes. We've been over this a dozen times in the last two days already. For God's sake, Maya, why can't you let this go? Can't you see I really don't want to talk about it anymore?"

"Well, I'm still stunned. He stepped up, Mia. He agreed to kids."

"Yes, but he didn't agree to being part of that family he offered to build with me." And that still stung.

Ever since Mia had told her family that it was really over between her and Sam, Maya had been doing inter-rogations that the CIA would have been proud of.

"But you're still staying in his suite."

Mia groaned dramatically. "Maya, I beg you…"

"With no fun stuff."

"None." Mia sighed. Her twin was not getting past this anytime soon. But then, neither was Mia. And oh, how she missed the fun stuff with Sam. Every time she took a shower now, she remembered being with him, his hands sliding over her skin, caressing her breasts until she was mindless with need.

But strangely, even more than the sex, she missed having coffee with him in the morning. Missed laughing with him. Missed curling up next to him on the bed—until he stretched out his arms and legs in his sleep and nearly pushed her off the mattress. She missed laying out on their private deck holding hands and watching the stars. Missed…oh hell.

She just missed *him*.

"Did you know he took the boys up to the bridge yesterday?" Maya smiled and shook her head as if she still couldn't believe it herself.

Mia was stunned. Sam had spent time with the boys without her nudging him? "He did?"

Maya nodded and added, "He even got the Captain to let them take turns steering the ship. I've got to say, I'm glad I didn't know that the boys were in charge, even if it was only for a minute or two."

Mia's heart squeezed. "He didn't tell me."

"Well," Maya pointed out, "you did say you two aren't even talking now."

"No, we're not. In fact, I've hardly seen him in two days."

"Well, the boys were so excited after all of that, he and Joe took them for ice cream."

"What?" Mia shook her head as if she hadn't heard her sister right. That was so unlike Sam, she didn't know what to make of it. And in the end, it only made her feel worse, knowing that he was so good with kids—seeing that he was good with them—and he didn't realize it.

"I know," Maya agreed. "Shock time. That's one of the reasons I keep asking you about what happened. I mean, this sounds like a man who loves you."

The surprises just kept coming. "I can't believe you're defending Sam."

"Yeah, it's stunning to me, too." Maya tugged her hat brim a little lower onto her forehead. "You know how furious I was when you guys broke up?"

"Yeah," Mia said wryly. "I remember the fury and some mention of putting a curse on him."

Maya ignored that. "What I didn't tell you was the reason I was so mad? I *liked* Sam. And when he hurt you, I was furious at myself because I hadn't seen it coming."

Mia smiled at her twin, reached out and grabbed her hand for a quick squeeze. As irritating as family could be, Mia couldn't imagine her life without a twin who was so fiercely defensive of her.

But Maya wasn't finished. "And then we come on this ship and I watch him watching you and I'm pretty sure he loves you and then it all blows up again and he still loves you. And he's good to my kids. So I'm furious all over again."

They had all been on a roller coaster for far too long. The adrenaline rushes alone were exhausting. And Mia had cried herself out so that she woke every morning feeling dehydrated.

"You really need to dial it down, Maya. I know you're upset and I love you for it, but that baby you're carrying needs peace and quiet."

"Then he's coming to the wrong house," Maya said with a half laugh.

They sat beneath a red-and-white striped umbrella and watched everyone in the pool from the safety of shade. The breeze was lovely and the cruise would be short as the ship made its way to Kauai for two days. For the first time since boarding the ship, Mia was wishing the cruise was over. But there was still a week to go before they were home again. Would she make it through another week in that suite with Sam?

Mia was thankful that their parents had flown home

the night before, ready to get back to work at the bakery. At least, she only had Maya's sympathy and outrage to deal with.

"I know you don't want to move back to our suite," Maya was saying, "and I get it, since just sitting on that couch hurts my back. But if you really don't want to stay with Sam, maybe you could take over Mom and Dad's suite."

Mia shook her head. "No good. I already checked. The suite was booked a week ago. Someone taking the trip to L.A. and then back again on a different ship."

"Well then, maybe you should take that as a sign."

"A sign of what?"

Maya shrugged. "Maybe the universe *wants* you and Sam to work this out and that's why it's keeping you together."

"The universe can butt out. Besides, I'm sorry," Mia said, turning to face her twin. "Aren't you the one who was telling me to run fast, run far from Sam just a few days ago?"

"I was," Maya admitted with a gracious nod. "And I changed my mind."

"As historic as that is," Mia commented, "I don't think talking is going to change anything."

Maya sighed. "Fine. I'll stop now."

"Thank you."

"After I say—"

"Maya…"

"After I say that I'm on your side in this, Mia."

She sighed and smiled. No matter what, she could count on her sister. Her whole family, for that matter. So she would keep doing her crying in private so she wouldn't worry them. And then on the twenty-fifth, Mia would begin her journey toward a family of her own and Sam would be only a memory.

A wonderful, haunting, memory.

"Mrs. Buchanan?"

She turned to face the waiter standing beside her chaise. "Yes?"

"Mr. Buchanan asked that this be delivered to you at noon." He held out an envelope and when Mia took it, he turned and went back to work.

"Wow," Maya said. "He *really* doesn't want to talk."

Mia ignored her, opened the envelope and pulled out the single sheet of paper. Sam's bold, handwriting sprawled across the page.

Mia—I took an early flight out this morning. I'm headed to Bermuda on business. The suite is yours, so enjoy it.

It was good to be with you again. However briefly.

Be happy.

Sam.

"He's gone," Mia whispered.

Maya snatched the paper from her suddenly nerveless fingers. "He left? Without a word?"

"He sent word, Maya. You're holding it."

"Yeah, but come *on.* He couldn't look you in the eye to tell you he's leaving?"

"It's over," Mia whispered, finally accepting that Sam didn't want what she did. Sam didn't feel what she did.

"Well, look out," her sister grumbled. "I'm changing my mind about him again."

"Don't," Mia said, looking at her twin. "Just accept it for what it is. Sam and I just weren't meant to be, I guess."

And saying that out loud ripped at Mia's heart. She'd let herself hope and even though that particular balloon was now flat and empty, it was hard to let go of it completely. But then, she had years ahead of her to face the emptiness that was waiting for her.

So she'd build her own family, love her own children and dream about what might have been if Sam had only trusted himself as much as she'd trusted him.

Sam stayed in Bermuda for two weeks. He spent most of his time at the shipyard, consulting with the builders, going over every detail of the new build.

He buried himself in work so that he didn't have time to think about Mia and how silent his life felt without her in it.

He stood at the window of the house the Buchanans kept on the island. Sam's grandfather had built the house, saying that he spent so much time there with ship builders, he needed his own place rather than a hotel. And then Sam's father had used it—as a place to bring the long string of women he'd been involved with.

But for one week every year, Sam and Michael had been together at this house. Every summer, the boys had a week to explore, to play, to be the brothers their parents had kept them from being. So there were good memories here for Sam. And he tried to focus on them, to keep the thoughts of Mia at a distance.

It didn't really work.

He hadn't expected to miss her so much. But he did. Waking up next to her, talking over coffee, listening to her laugh. Hell, he even missed how she shoved him over in the middle of the night and fought him for blankets.

And he remembered that night with the boys, decorating a Christmas tree, and how Mia had shone brighter than the twinkling white lights. For the first time in his life, Christmas decorations had been…beautiful.

Though he kept her out of his mind during the day, at night in his sleep, she was there. Always. Her sighs. Her smiles. The way she touched him and the way she came apart when he touched her. He woke up every morning, dragging, his mind cloudy, his chest tight as if he'd been holding his breath all night. And maybe he had been.

All he knew for sure was that getting over Mia was going to take years.

"You look lost in thought."

Sam turned and saw his younger brother standing in the doorway. He'd never been so glad to see anyone.

"I am—or was. Now that you're here, maybe that'll stop."

Michael moved into the main room, walked to the wet bar on the far wall and grabbed two beers from the under-the-counter fridge. He carried one to Sam, then opened his own.

"So what thoughts are you trying to get rid of?" He looked at the ceiling, tipped his head and said, "Hmmm. Let's think. Could it be, Mia?"

"Knock it off," Sam said, opened his beer and took a sip. "Didn't I just say I was glad I could stop thinking?"

"Okay, I'll think for you," Michael said and dropped into a chair. "I think you miss Mia. I think you had a great time on the ship and I think you didn't want to leave."

"I think you should mind your own business."

"You're my brother. You are my business."

"Fine. Mind a different business." Sam took a sip of beer and looked away from Michael so the other man wouldn't notice that he'd really struck a chord with Sam. "Don't you have a fiancée you could be bugging?"

"Alice is nuts about me," Michael said with a grin that slowly faded. "So tell me about you."

"Nothing to tell," Sam lied easily. He wasn't going to dump everything on Michael. There was no reason for it. He'd made his decision and like his father, once his mind was made up, there was no shaking him from it.

"Right." Michael looked around the room. "Hey. When did you paint in here?"

"When I first got here," Sam said. He'd hired a crew to come in and redo his father's office. Hell, he'd been meaning to do it for years but he'd never made the time. But during this trip, the dark maroon walls with their white crown molding had felt as if they were closing in on him.

His father had insisted on dark colors because he claimed they made him calm. Well, Sam didn't remember a time when his father was calm. Or relaxed. And maybe this place had fed into that.

But whether it had or not, Sam hated the darkness of the place, so he'd paid a premium to get a crew in and completely redo not only this damn office, but the whole blasted house. Now the walls were cream colored with pale blue molding and Sam had felt years of depression slide off his shoulders with every room completed.

"It looks better," Michael said. "Wish you looked better, too. But damn Sam…"

"Thanks." Sam sat down and kicked his legs out straight ahead of him. "Maybe I just need a fresh coat of paint."

"We both know what you need, Sam."

He sighed, stared down at the open neck of his beer bottle. "I got a call from my lawyer this morning. He says the divorce papers have *definitely* been filed this time. It'll be official in a couple of months."

"Good news, is it?"

Sam shot him a hard look. "Of course it is. Mia wants a family. Kids. I can't do that."

"Can't or won't?"

"There's no difference."

"Sure there is." Michael took a sip of his beer. "You choose to say no to something—someone—you want. That's won't. Not can't."

"I offered to give her the family she wants. She still said no." Hard to admit. Pain shook him, but he pushed it aside.

"Because she wants you, Sam. She wants you to be there. A part of it all."

"Damn it Michael, I was raised by our father. And you know damn well what a crap role model he was."

"And yet, you're letting *him* decide your life."

"Oh, that's bull." Sam snorted.

"Is it? You're walking away from a woman you love because you think you'll be like Dad."

"Won't I be?" Sam jumped up from the chair because he suddenly couldn't sit still. He walked out onto the stone patio at the rear of the house and looked out over the exquisitely trimmed lawn, the gardens and the ocean beyond.

It was paradise here and yet, for all he noticed, he might as well have been living in someone's garage with a view of a brick wall.

"I can give you one example right now of how you're not like Dad." Michael walked up beside him, sipped at his beer and stared out over the yard.

When his brother didn't continue, curiosity got the better of Sam. "What?"

"You married Mia. Did Dad ever once marry for love?"

"Well, there's our mother…" Though he'd never seen evidence of love in that relationship.

Michael snorted and as if reading Sam's mind, asked, "Did their marriage look like love to you?" He shook his head. "When I got engaged to Alice, Mom told me how happy she was. She said when they got divorced, Dad told her the only reason he'd married her was *his* father had ordered him to marry her and have at least two children. He wanted to assure the whole Buchanan legacy thing."

That hit Sam harder than it should have. He felt an instant stab of sympathy for his mother that made him even more glad that she'd finally found real love in Sam and Michael's stepfather.

"Yeah, Dad was a prince," Michael muttered. "But my point was, you married Mia because you loved her."

"It still ended."

"Because you let it."

Sam glared at him. "There was nothing I could do. She wanted the divorce, Michael."

"Because you weren't there for her." Michael took a step and stood in front of his brother, forcing Sam to meet his gaze. "I think you were so worried about screwing it up, you stayed away as much as you could. Which was stupid."

"Thanks." He had another sip, but even the beer tasted flat, flavorless. Like the rest of his life.

"No problem. But the solution here is to see what you did wrong and change it."

"She wants kids."

"You do, too," Michael said on a laugh. "You're just scared of screwing that up—and news flash, so's everyone else. So you work at it. You love your kid and you do your best. And I know you, Sam. When you do your best, you never fail."

Was he right? About all of it? Though Michael had been raised by their mother, he'd spent enough time with their dad to know what he was talking about.

Most of his life, Sam had been trying to avoid turning into his father. Yet he'd never noticed that he was nothing like the old man. Just this house was proof of that. The darkness that Sam's father had surrounded himself with had been banished for good. So couldn't he banish darkness from his life, too?

Thinking about Mia again, Sam saw her face in his mind, felt that hard jolt of his heartbeat and knew that whatever else he did in his life would never come close to being as important as his next move would be.

"She filed the papers, Mike," he muttered.

"You've got at least two months before it's final."

Was he right? Should Sam take a good hard look at who he really was? Was it too late?

He looked at his brother. "You gave me a lot to think about, Michael. Thanks."

Michael slapped him on the shoulder. "Any time. Oh. Did I mention that Mia's coming to my wedding?"

Sam looked at him as a slow smile curved his mouth. Suddenly, his breath came a little easier and the day looked a little brighter. "Is that right?"

Mia had to go to Michael's wedding.

She'd always liked Sam's brother and his fiancée was just as nice as he was. Besides, just because she and Sam were finished didn't mean she would give up her relationship with Sam's brother.

But seeing Sam. Being in the same small church

with him. Was so much harder than she'd prepared herself for.

The papers had been filed. The divorce would be final in a couple of short months and yet, love still flavored every breath she drew. She'd lived through Christmas with her family and managed to keep her pain from shadowing everyone else's good time.

But she'd gone home from the cruise once again inflating that hope balloon. This time hoping that she might be pregnant. But when that dream died, she had to accept that it was time she let go. Get ready for her appointment at the end of the month. Prepare to welcome her own child and start building the family she wanted so badly.

Sam wouldn't be a part of it and that would always hurt. But she would smile anyway and live the life she wanted.

During the ceremony, she tried to focus on the bride and groom, but her gaze kept straying as if on its own accord, to Sam. So tall, so handsome in his tailored tuxedo. He stood beside his brother and she wondered if he thought about *their* wedding, a little over a year ago. Mia did and the memories brought a pain so bright and sharp it was hard to breathe.

Of course, the two weddings couldn't have been more different. She and Sam had been married on a cliff in Laguna Beach during a bright December morning. Michael and Alice were having a black-tie, evening ceremony in a tiny church that was draped in flowers of white and yellow.

She slipped out of the church from the back row before the bride and groom had a chance to rush smiling down the aisle. She had to try at least to avoid Sam. Otherwise, she'd be a masochist.

Mia hurried out to one of the cars provided by the couple to transport everyone to the reception. The party was being held on one of the Buchanan ships and when she arrived, she saw balloons, streamers, flowers and yellow-and-white garland wrapped along the gangway.

Once aboard, waiters with silver trays holding flutes of champagne greeted the guests. Mia took one and immediately had a long sip. She was going to need it if she was to face Sam.

Flowers lined the route to the main reception, where a band was playing and every table was decorated with more flowers and candles in hurricane globes that sparkled and shone in the twilight.

She sipped her champagne and avoided the growing crowd in the room by stepping out onto the deck. Here in Florida, the weather was warm, even on a January evening, but the ocean breeze sighed past her in a cool embrace.

"This is good," she whispered to herself. "I'll have to see Sam, but maybe that will help me get over him." It didn't make sense even to her, but Mia hoped it was true.

"Don't get over me."

She took a deep, quick breath and steadied herself by laying one hand on the railing in front of her. Sam. Right there. Behind her.

"Mia—"

"God, Sam," she said, not turning to look at him. "Don't do this to me. Please. Just let me enjoy Michael and Alice's wedding and go home again."

"I can't do that," Sam said softly, then laid his hands on her shoulders and slowly turned her until she was facing him.

He was so handsome he took her breath away. And he

wasn't hers. Even the heat slipping into her body from his hands at her shoulders was only temporary. Not hers to keep.

"I'm sorry," he said and simply stunned Mia speechless.

She took a sip of champagne and let the icy bubbles wipe away her suddenly dry throat.

"You're sorry? For what?"

He released her, swept both hands through his hair and then shrugged. "For everything, Mia. I'm sorry I didn't show up for our marriage. Sorry I made you feel as if you weren't important to me when the truth is, you're the *most* important person in my life."

Cautiously, Mia watched him, tried to read his eyes, but too many emotions were dazzling them for her to identify them all. So she waited. To see where he was going with this.

He laughed shortly. "Before I say everything I need you to know, I have to tell you that you're so beautiful, it makes my chest tight."

She laughed too. Mia wasn't a fool. She knew she looked good. She'd made a point of it, since she'd known she'd be seeing Sam. She had wanted him to see her and to be filled with regret for letting her go.

She'd bought a dark red, off-the-shoulder dress with a sweetheart neckline, a cinched waist and a short skirt that stopped mid-thigh. Her black, three-inch heels brought her nearly eye to eye with him, so she could see that he meant what he was saying.

"Thanks. I bought this dress on purpose. To make you suffer."

He laughed again and some of the shadows left his eyes. "Well, mission accomplished."

"What is it you want, Sam?" she asked, bringing them back to the reason he was standing there in front of her.

"You, Mia. I want *you*."

Her heart clutched. "Sam…we've been over this."

"No, no we haven't. Not like we're about to."

She bit her lip and took a breath. "What's that mean?"

"It means," he said, with a rueful shake of his head, "that I finally understand that I'm not just my father's son, but my mother's as well. Mom got past her time with my father. She found love with her second husband and I saw it. They were happy. Hell, Michael grew up in Disneyland comparatively speaking."

"I know your dad was hard, Sam, and I'm sorry about it."

"This isn't about him anymore, Mia." He cupped her face with his hands and stroked his thumbs over her cheekbones. "I've let him go. At last. I finally get that it's my choices that will define my life. Not who my father was."

She stared up into his eyes and read only love shining back at her. Her heart started racing again and that silly balloon of hope was back.

"I want to believe, Sam. I really do."

But how could she? He'd chosen his work over her so many times, she didn't know if he even *could* change.

"Do it, Mia. Believe me. Take one more chance on me. I won't let you down this time. I'm tired of emptiness, Mia. I want the magic and the magic lives inside you. I want real Christmases. I want laughter. Joy. Passion. And that's all with you." His cell phone rang and grumbling, he took it out of his pocket and never checked the screen before he wound up and pitched it over the rail and into the ocean.

"What?" Shocked, she turned to look at the sea then back to him. "What did you just do? That could have been work calling."

"I hope it was," he said firmly and held her again, looking into her eyes, willing her to believe him. "I hate that you're surprised by me choosing you over a business call. You shouldn't have to be. You should have been able to expect that your husband—because we *are* still married—would choose you over business or anything else.

"I'm so sorry for that, Mia. Sorry for not realizing what I had while I had it."

"Oh Sam." Her heart was full and her hands were shaking so badly, champagne sloshed out of her glass onto her hand.

Sam took it and tossed it, too.

"Stop doing that!" Shaking her head, she said, "I never expected you to ignore your work. I love my job at the bakery. I only ever wanted to know that I was important to you, too."

Sam threaded his fingers into her hair and let his gaze move over her face. "You are more important than anything else in my life."

It was so hard to breathe with her heart pounding and the hope balloon swelling until it filled her chest.

"What does that mean for us, Sam?"

"It means I want to stay married. We can have the lawyers pull the divorce papers before they go through."

"Sam…"

"Stay with me, Mia." He kissed her fast. "Make babies with me."

"Really?" She blinked up at him and her eyes filled with tears. She had to blink faster just to clear them.

"I want a family with you. Maybe I always did but I

was too scared to even consider it." He bent down and kissed her again, harder, faster. "But I'm more scared of losing you than I am of trying to be a good father."

"You will be a good one," she said. "A great one."

He gave her a half-smile. "I can promise to do my absolute best. I love you, Mia. I will love our kids and we'll have as many as you want. A family with you—a future with you—is all I really want. Mia, you're all I can see of the future. Without you, I don't have one."

"Sam, you're making me cry."

"That's a good sign," he said with a grin. "I like it."

"Of course you do," she said on a laugh.

The first stars appeared overhead and the sounds of the party drifted to them as they stood alone on the deck.

"We'll buy a house anywhere you want," he said quickly as if trying to convince her before her tears dried. "Hell, we can live next door to Maya and Joe."

Now she laughed harder. "Next door might be a little *too* close."

"Okay. That's fine, too. Anything, Mia. Anything to make you happy. I swear I'm a different man."

"Not too different I hope. I always liked—loved—who you were, Sam. I just wanted more of you."

"You'll have it," he swore. "And if I ever do screw up again, you have to call me on it and I'll fix it. I never want to lose you again."

Smiling through her tears, Mia said, "I can't lose you again either, Sam."

"You won't. I swear it." He let her go long enough to dip into his pocket and come out with a ring. He took her right hand in his and slipped the emerald-and-diamond band onto her finger.

When he looked into her eyes this time, he said,

"We're already married, so I expect you to put your rings back on when we get home."

She laughed and nodded, looking from the ring to his eyes.

"But this one," he said softly, "I want you to have to mark my promise to you.

"I will love you forever, Mia Harper Buchanan. And I will love the children we make together and I will give you all everything I have."

Mia looked down at the glittering ring on her finger, then up into the most beautiful blue eyes she'd ever seen. "I love you, Sam. Always have. Always will. And I'm so glad you came home."

"You're my home, Mia. My home. My heart. My everything."

And when he kissed her, Mia felt her whole world come right again and she knew that the future stretching out in front of them was filled with all the love she'd ever dreamed of.

* * * * *

A CHRISTMAS
PROPOSITION

JESSICA LEMMON

To Dad, for always making Christmastime feel special (PS: you can stop reading now).

One

December 20
Source: thedallasduchess.com
EXCLUSIVE:
STEFANIE FERGUSON AND BLAKE EASTWOOD
REUNION

Good morning, Dallas!

As maven of this fine city, the Dallas Duchess makes it her job to know the happenings of local royalty. In this town, no royalty is finer than the Fergusons.

"Princess" Stefanie Ferguson, socialite, heiress and party girl, has been spotted once again on the arm of cunning and charming Blake Eastwood, who just so happens to be the mayor's *biggest* opponent. (Naughty, naughty!) And, my savvy duchess dolls, you're all aware that the mayor=Stefanie's gorgeous and recently betrothed brother. Yes, ladies, another of Dallas's eligible bachelors is about to bite the dust.

(As an aside, you longtimers may recall my breaking story about the mayor shacking up in Montana during a snowstorm with his old flame. Hotcha! You always hear it here first.)

But back to Princess Stef and her dashing bad boy... By now you've no doubt seen the photo circulating on social media of Blake and Stefanie dancing cheek to cheek at a Toys for Tots fund-raiser. And if you're an astute observer like moi, you felt the sparks flying from that photo. As of right this very minute, I can confirm what my pitter-pattering heart was hoping for the most:

Stefanie and Blake are together!

Recently, I spoke with Blake and while I couldn't get him to commit to a timeline, I did learn a verrrry juicy bit of intel.

Dallas Duchess: I have to ask for the sake of my readers. Are you and Stefanie Ferguson seeing each other again?

Blake Eastwood: [emits a sexy chuckle] Um. Yes. We are.

DD: [squeals of delight] Can you tell me more?

BE: I can tell you that it's new, but serious.

DD: Put-a-ring-on-it serious?

BE: Come on, Duchess, I can't let every cat out of the bag.

DD: But it's almost Christmas! Surely you can give us one teeny-tiny hint?

BE: Christmastime is Stef's favorite time of the year. She whispered in my ear just yesterday that it's the perfect time to shop at Tiffany & Co. I'm a man who knows how to take a hint.

Ladies, gentlemen. If that's not a confirmation that Blake is popping the question Stefanie is begging him to ask, I don't know what is!

Go forth and share across social media with the links below. Looks like a Christmas engagement could be forthcoming!

Stefanie Ferguson paced the shining white floor of her sister-in-law's home office in a pair of knee-high, spike-heel Christian Louboutin boots. Unlike the last public relations hiccup she'd gotten into with Blake, this one couldn't be handled over a cup of coffee at Hip Stir.

Late last night, she'd been sipping on hot cocoa with Sambuca when she received a text from Blake.

Dallas Duchess has some news to share tomorrow. Me and you, gorgeous.

She'd pecked in an angry "Go to hell" followed by "Leave me alone" and then erased both lines in favor of ignoring him.

Lord only knew what he would've done with the screen-shots if she'd texted him. It had taken everything in her not to respond to his baiting. Blake was Bad News with a capital *B* and *N*.

Last year, he'd gone to the Dallas Duchess via one of her brother's staff members to break the story about Miriam Andrix returning to Chase's life. The write-up was in defense of Chase and almost lecturing Miriam for ruining the city's chaste mayor. Ridiculous. It was clear to anyone who saw them together that Miriam and Chase were gaga over each other—even Stefanie could see that, and she was Chase's sister.

Blake's original motivation for his nefarious smear campaign was building a new civic center, which he wanted to erect *very close* to Ferguson Oil property. Chase had been saying no for years. Blake had promised to "ruin him" if it was the last thing he did, as if he were some sort of mustache-twisting bandit.

Stef reminded herself, again, that she hadn't known the dirty details when Blake charmed her into his hotel bed one lonely night a few years back. She certainly had never expected him to release pictures of them leaving the hotel together.

Penelope Ferguson had summoned a PR magic spell to bail Stef out of her Blake-related problem then, and she'd had a hand in smoothing over Chase and Miriam's relationship last year. With Chase's imminent reelection looming—Stef refused to consider the possibility of him losing—she had zero worries that Pen would be able to work her magic again and smooth this one over, as well.

"You should've called me the second Blake the Snake sent you that text," Penelope scolded from where she sat in front of her computer screen. Her full mouth was a firm line of displeasure, her eyes narrowed in frustration.

Stef stopped pacing and wrapped herself protectively in her own arms. "It was late. I didn't want to bother you."

And she hadn't wanted her sister-in-law to hear the raw vulnerability in her voice. Stef might have refused to respond with the intent of letting Blake know how little he'd affected her, but in truth he had. Like the first time those hotel photos saw the light of day, she felt cheap and used.

He'd been charming and—she'd thought—vulnerable the night he'd told her he wanted her. She'd been fresh off a breakup and vulnerable herself. A night with an attractive man who appreciated her—even one who disagreed with her brother the mayor—was supposed to have boosted her confidence and relieved a long drought of physical affection.

They'd both been attending a boring fund-raiser at the time. Champagne had flowed and he'd been accommodating and, she knew now, lying. He'd been seeking revenge on Chase and would take any of the Fergusons as his pound of flesh. She'd allowed herself to be talked into going to bed with him and she still felt the sting of embarrassment and anger at her naïveté.

The next day, the photos had surfaced and she'd been accused of slutting around with the mayor's nemesis.

And now this.

"When was the fund-raiser where this was taken?" Pen turned her laptop screen to show the most recent leaked photo of Blake and Stef cheek to cheek on the dance floor.

"Last weekend."

"You're looking cozy."

"He asked me to dance by taking my hand and dragging me to the floor. I didn't want to cause a scene by telling him where to shove his invitation."

She'd caused enough problems for her brother and his campaign. Chase didn't hold her accountable, but she couldn't unshoulder her fair share of responsibility.

"What you don't see in this photo is that I'm telling him off. I used some very unladylike language, hence my leaning in close. I told him if he didn't leave me and my family alone, I'd castrate him with a pair of dull shears."

Stef smiled, proud. At least she'd stood up for herself then. Pen wasn't smiling with her.

"What you did was step into a snare of his making, Stefanie. *Again.*" Pen shook her head. "He timed the release of this photo on purpose, to coincide with the reelection. Why is he hinting that you two are going to be married?"

Stef felt her cheeks warm as she recalled the rest of her conversation that night. "That…is partially my fault."

Pen raised her eyebrows and waited.

Stef, you'll be single forever with a mouth like that. You have to be a good little girl if you ever hope to land a husband. Blake had swept her in another circle on the dance floor while her ire had risen to dangerous levels.

Ha! You're one to talk. Is there a female on this planet who would willingly perch in your family tree or do you have to trick them all into going to bed with you?

You came willingly. A few times if memory serves.

"He was holding me tight, and twisting away didn't loosen his hold on my waist." Stef licked her lips, regretting her words now that she'd felt the sting of retaliation. "I may have mentioned something about a 'tiny prick' and 'faking it' and that if he didn't let me go, I'd tell everyone within earshot how unsatisfying it was to be bedded by Blake the Snake."

Pen's eyebrows climbed higher on her forehead, and just when Stef was sure she'd be read the riot act, her sister-in-law's smile burst forth like the sun after a hard rain.

"You know how to find trouble, don't you?" Pen asked through a laugh. She must've caught Stef's crestfallen features when she looked up because she was out of her chair in a shot. "I'm sorry I said that. Ignore me."

Pen grabbed Stef's shoulders and Stef felt the wobble in her chin paired with heat behind her eyes.

"I don't try to."

"I didn't mean it that way. Seriously." Pen pulled Stef into a hug.

Stef felt like a fragile piece of china lately, not wanting to be in the way of Chase's campaign or too involved while Pen and Zach raised their daughter. Heck, even Mom and Dad were going through a second honeymoon phase, so Stef was trying to stay out from underfoot in that capacity, as well.

"You can fix this." Stef swallowed her budding tears. "You have unraveled some of the biggest knots in Dallas since you moved here. Tell me the easiest, fastest, most succinct way to crush this fake news."

"As a woman who had her own false engagement to contend with—" Pen smirked "—I *have* had experience with this sort of thing. Only the 'groom' was your brother and part of the plan."

"And Blake's a renegade douchebag."

Of all the bad decisions Stef had made during her thirty

brief years on this planet, why this one? Why had she fallen victim to that man's false charms?

"If you were anyone other than my sister-in-law, I'd advise you to get married."

"To Blake?" Stef practically shrieked.

"No! My God. *No.* I'm saying the best way to trump Blake's claim that he's engaged to you is to marry someone else. Know any eligible bachelors?"

Stef was staring in shock. This certainly wasn't the advice she'd expected to get from Penelope.

"I'm *joking.*" Pen gave Stef's shoulders a little shake before moving back to her desk. Laptop open, she started typing. "I'll craft a plan to detangle this mess that will work for you and your brother the mayor."

"Thank you."

Pen smiled up at her. "And I promise it *won't* involve nuptials."

Two

Emmett Keaton had been Chase Ferguson's close friend, arguably his best friend, since college.

He could say with authority that Chase rarely allowed his feathers to ruffle. But today his feathers weren't only ruffled, they were scattered to the four corners of the earth.

Since it was Emmett's job to keep the mayor's office safe, he'd have to assume the role of "the calm one" today. As the scandal currently wreaking havoc had to do with Stefanie, he found it challenging to bank his own anger.

The youngest Ferguson had a talent for finding trouble.

"When I get my hands on that sniveling weasel," Chase grated out through teeth that were welded together, "I swear on everything holy—"

"Chase." Penelope—wife to Chase's brother, Zach—stood in front of Chase's desk, arms crossed. She was dressed in a white pantsuit, her long blond hair pulled into a neat twist at the back of her head. Her stance broadcast one undeniable truth: she wasn't intimidated by power. She'd handled many a powerful man as a public relations specialist over the years, and had become a trusted friend when Chase hired her to care for Stef the first time she stepped in it with Blake fucking Eastwood.

Because Chase trusted her, Emmett did, also.

"I've got this," Pen said. "You have nothing to worry about."

A muscle in Chase's jaw ticked but he gave his sister-in-law a curt nod. She returned it with one of her own and spun on one very high-heeled shoe to leave.

Once she was out the door, Chase glanced at Emmett with irises so dark they bordered on black.

Chase punched a button on his phone. "Cynthia. Get my sister on the line."

"Yes, sir."

"Sure you want to do that, boss?" Emmett asked.

Chase didn't answer.

A moment later, the desk phone rang.

"Where the hell are you?" Chase barked into the receiver. A brief pause and then, "You have thirty seconds." He slammed the phone down on its base and glared at the only target in the room. Emmett took the blow without flinching. "She was already on her way."

"Good."

Chase needed to redirect his anger? *Fine.*

It was better than him unleashing it on Stefanie.

The door burst open almost exactly thirty seconds later. Stefanie strode into the office in a short red designer dress, tall boots with dangerous-looking heels and a painted pout in siren red.

"I saw Pen on my way in." Stef tucked her cell phone into an oversize handbag. "She warned me that you weren't in the best mood. I'm assuming you're mad at me."

Nostrils flared, Chase pulled in a deep breath through his nose. When he spoke, his words were carefully measured. "I'm not angry with you, Stefanie. I'm—"

"Don't say *disappointed*." She dropped the handbag onto the leather chair in the corner of the room and sent Emmett a derisive glare.

Typical.

She hated him for reasons he'd yet to discern. He'd only ever offered assistance when she'd needed him—whether she'd asked or not. If memory served, she'd never asked.

"I'm *concerned*," Chase said, and her head swiveled back to her brother. "Your Christmas retreat is soon, yes?"

"Yes." A smile of pure delight crested her red mouth.

That smile lit her face like a string of holiday lights. Emmett had never seen someone so in love with the idea of Christmas. Loving the holiday was as foreign to him as understanding anything else about the lush lifestyle his best friend's family led. In spite of his own amassed fortune, Emmett had no desire for frills of any kind. And he certainly had no desire to celebrate an occasion that brought forth bad memories and worse consequences.

"Where is it this year?" Chase asked.

"San Antonio."

"Cancel it."

Her face morphed into tortured shock. "What? Never. Absolutely not."

"That wasn't a request. There was no question mark at the end of my sentence." Chase pointed at her, his quaking arm revealing his anger. "Because you don't have the sense to stay away from Blake Eastwood, my campaign is suffering from the fallout."

Emmett's hands balled into fists at his sides.

He was rarely in disagreement with his friend, but in this case, Chase's comments were out of line. Stef had been briefly involved with Blake—whom Emmett would love to go a round or two with, bare-knuckle—but the accusation that she was to blame was harsh.

"Whatever you have to do in San Antonio with your girlfriends can be done from Dallas just as easily. You're not leaving the city, and if you do go out, you're going to be chaperoned. Do you understand me?"

Her stricken expression faded into a laugh of disbelief. "You can't ground me, Chase. You're not my father. And even if you were Dad, he can't ground me, either. I'm thirty years old!"

"Then why are you acting like a spoiled teenager?" Chase roared.

"Hey!" Emmett's outburst was so unexpected that both Fergusons faced him wearing shell-shocked expressions.

He took a step closer to Chase, instinct more than decision driving him. "Let's keep the blame where it should be. *On Blake.* Stefanie's been through enough. She doesn't need you piling on."

Chase's lips pressed into a thin, frustrated frown. Then he pinched the bridge of his nose, took a deep breath and leaned both hands flat on his desk.

Emmett flickered a glance over at Stefanie, who, for the first time in her life, regarded him with something akin to gratitude. He wasn't sure what to do with that.

"I'm asking, Stefanie—" Chase addressed his blotter before sitting in his chair and meeting his sister's eyes "—for your cooperation."

"Penelope is amazing at her job. There's no reason she can't—"

"I'm *asking*," Chase repeated, his voice firmer.

"I look forward to this retreat every year. I can't cancel an event that happens in four days."

"Why not?" Chase's forehead dented. "Can't you and your girlfriends drink champagne and talk about fashion another time? Mail them their gifts. Hell, invite them here. You can host at my mansion."

"I…can't do that." She regarded her impractical boots, appearing tormented by the idea of canceling.

Disappointment, Emmett could understand. Torment didn't make a hell of a lot of sense.

Stef loved her family above all else. Over the years, Emmett had witnessed the special bond she and Chase had—she respected her brother. And she would never lie to him. So why was Emmett getting the distinct impression that she was trying hard not to do just that? Why couldn't she party here in town? Why did she have to travel to San Antonio?

She wasn't lying—not yet—but she was definitely keep-ing from saying too much.

"Plans can be changed. I'll foot the bill for it, if you like," Chase told her. "I'll grease some palms and find you a last-minute venue in Dallas. You can't leave town with this mark on your back. I forbid it."

"What mark? Do you think I'm going to be kidnapped by Blake's henchmen or something?" Stef let out an exas-perated laugh. Emmett didn't find it funny. His back went ramrod straight, his senses on high alert at the idea that any harm would befall her.

He forbade it.

"You do things without thinking," the mayor said. "Who knows what could happen?"

"Chase, that's enough." Emmett took a step closer—to Stefanie this time.

His friend was right to watch out for his youngest sib-ling, but he was handling this wrong. Not that Emmett had much experience with sensitivity—he had been raised by Van Keaton, after all. But Emmett knew Stef and he also knew the situation. He couldn't keep from stepping at least one toe in her corner.

"You can stand down," Stef snapped. "I don't need your protection from my stupid brother."

"You need protection from yourself," Chase interjected.

This conversation was getting nowhere.

"I'm going to San Antonio tomorrow," she said. "I'll be back in a few days. I'm sure your *precious* campaign will be intact when I return." She grabbed her handbag and slung it over her shoulder as Chase rose from his chair, his face a beet-worthy shade of red.

"I'll drive you," Emmett blurted.

Again he was faced by both Fergusons. But only one of them looked upset by his offer. The cute blonde one.

"Yes. Great idea." Chase nodded. "Emmett will be your escort."

"I don't want an escort!"

"I don't care!"

"Knock it off." Emmett bodily moved himself to stand between Stefanie and Chase. "I'll drive you to San Antonio. Book me a room wherever you're staying."

"It's a bed-and-breakfast and it's *full*." She raised her chin, her aquamarine eyes flashing in warning.

"I'll sleep in my SUV." Emmett tipped his head in challenge. "It's either this or you don't go. Your brother's right about it being dangerous. Your image is plastered all over social media. I've seen you in the spotlight before. Paparazzi chase you, Stef."

She was beautiful and young and easily the most famous female billionaire in Dallas, if not the state of Texas. The combination of her it-girl reputation and a rumor that she was going to marry the mayor's sworn enemy made for tempting media fodder.

She opened her mouth, probably to argue.

Emmett lifted his eyebrows, silently communicating. *Give me a break, okay?*

Miraculously, rather than arguing, she gritted out, "Fine."

"Great. Get out," Chase said. "Both of you."

So, his best friend was prickly. So what? Emmett wasn't one for being handled with kid gloves. His rhino-tough hide had been hewed at a young age.

"Come on," he told Stef, opening the mayor's door for her to exit. "I'll give you a ride home."

Emmett held open the passenger door of his black SUV, a gas-guzzling, tinted-windowed, way-too-big-for-a-road-trip vehicle.

"You can't be serious about taking this beast to San

Antonio. We'll have to pull over every fifteen miles to re-fill the tank."

"Get. In."

She glared up at his chiseled jaw and perfectly shaped head beneath very short, dark brown hair. He wore it cropped close and rarely was it more than a few inches long on top. He was bedecked in what she'd come to think of as his "standard uniform." A crisp white shirt open at the collar and dark slacks. His brawn and bulk and attitude were better suited for a T-shirt and sweats, but his job title required a dab of formality.

She tossed her purse inside and grasped the SUV's door handle and the front seat to climb in. Emmett's warm, broad palm cupped her elbow to steady her, and she nearly jerked away in shock. If she wasn't mistaken, that was the first time he'd ever touched her.

It was...alarming.

And not in the get-your-damn-hands-off-me kind of way. His touch had felt...*intimate.*

Once she was inside he dropped his voice and leaned close. She ignored the clean leather smell of him. Or tried to, anyway.

"Heads up. There's a suspicious cyclist over there." He shut her door and walked around to the driver's side.

She scanned the immediate area outside her brother's office twice before she spotted a casual-looking guy on a bike with a cell phone conspicuously propped on the handlebars and pointing at the SUV.

Damn.

As much as she hated to admit it, Chase might have had a point about media attention.

Emmett settled into the driver's seat and turned over the engine, sending her an assessing, stony gray stare. Typically, his eyes held a note of blue, but today they mirrored the cloudy skies above.

"What?" she barked. "Do you want me to congratulate you because you're right?"

He smirked. "Buckle your belt."

"Let's get one thing straight, Neanderthal," she said as she jerked the belt over her torso. "You may believe a woman's place is in the passenger seat. Or that I can't handle anything on my own without one of you *big strong* men to help me out, but FYI, I am not yours to command."

Though some foreign tingly part of her suggested that Emmett might be the perfect specimen to take commands *from*.

She swallowed the rest of her speech about being an adult and handling her own problems, mainly because they both felt like stretches of the truth. In all of her attempts not to involve her family in her life, she'd somehow managed to tow them in. Her parents, Chase, Penelope, Zach and now Emmett.

Angry with herself more than her driver, she stared out the window in silence as the SUV pulled away from the curb.

Three

Stef had gone to bed late last night, staring at the ceiling for a long while, her mind lost on her current predicament.

She hadn't stayed up late to pack—she'd done that already and her matching luggage was lined up dutifully next to her apartment door. Knowing that Emmett would pick her up promptly at 7:00 a.m., she also hadn't indulged in more than one glass of sparkling rosé before bed. No, her insomnia couldn't be blamed on a lack of planning or too much alcohol. She'd lain awake, earning this morning's puffy eyes and groggy brain for one reason.

She was tired of being everyone else's problem.

It wasn't enough to tell her parents and her brothers that she was an adult. She had to *show* them. In order to show them, she needed to take care of the Blake situation herself.

Penelope was equipped to handle any PR disaster, but the more Stef thought about it, the more Pen's plan to "wait and see" sounded like a slow track to a solution. Chase's election was less than six months away. Stefanie refused to let Blake continue to drag her family's good name through the muck.

Chase had made it clear last fall that he didn't hold Stefanie accountable for her act of indiscretion with Blake. In spite of his absolving her, her guilt remained.

That Blake held this much power over her infuriated her. She refused to let him cause her to lose even one more minute of sleep.

Last night while staring at the ceiling of her apartment, she'd decided not to let Blake have that power over her family, either.

Penelope's words rang in her ears.

If you were anyone other than my sister-in-law, I'd advise you to get married.

Well, why hadn't that been Pen's suggestion? It shouldn't matter that Stefanie was her sister-in-law. A solution was a solution! There was only one *eensy-weensy* problem. Stefanie would have to find someone to marry, and fast.

She wasn't sure who to approach, let alone how to ask. She'd climbed out of bed during the wee hours, unhooked her phone from the charger in her kitchen and poured one more small glass of wine. Then she started scrolling through her contacts in her phone's address book.

Every prospect she thumbed through seemed worse than the last. She passed over ex-boyfriends, hookups and acquaintances alike. None of them were marriage material— not even temporarily. Plus, how would she ask for a favor like that from someone she hadn't talked to in months, or years in some cases?

Hi, I know you haven't heard from me for a while, but would you mind marrying me for a few months?

Not to mention she would need her groom to keep their marriage arrangement a secret. The entire purpose of the ruse would be to convince the press and that horrible blogger woman that Stefanie wasn't involved with Blake. Then Blake would be forced to recant his bullshit statement.

After she'd thought it through, she decided an engagement announcement would look like a desperate cover-up. It gave Blake too much wiggle room, and she couldn't risk him slithering into her family's life again.

Wineglass empty and fatigue finally overcoming her, Stef had dragged herself to the couch, pulled a blanket over her body and caught about three hours of tossing-turning sleep.

The knock on her front door came way too early, even

though she was ready for it. She'd pulled her hair into a sloppy bun on top of her head, dashed on a layer of makeup and donned big, dark sunglasses so that *if* a photo was snapped of her in the wild, she wouldn't look like she'd had a sleepless night fretting over Blake.

Stef had called Pen yesterday afternoon and suggested releasing a statement that she was no more marrying Blake than she was marrying Kermit the Frog, but Pen had recommended against it.

We can't turn this into he said, she said, especially while you're out of town. Let's let the dust settle and we'll handle things in the new year. Enjoy your Christmas party!

Despite what she'd led everyone to believe, Stef wasn't going to a Christmas party with her girlfriends. She was hosting a massive charity dinner that she'd arranged for some of the poorest families in Harlington, a city outside San Antonio.

Over the last three Christmas Eves, she'd hosted similar dinners and, so far, had kept her little Christmas secret. She didn't want publicity or attention for it—not yet. She wanted to do it her way, and *without* input from family members on how to arrange the place settings or what kind of food to serve.

Providing for the less fortunate and giving back filled her with a sense of satisfaction like nothing else. To Stef, this dinner party was about more than writing a check. She'd personally witnessed gratitude and happiness on the faces of men, women and children who otherwise wouldn't have had a merry Christmas.

Hiding what she was doing from her family wasn't too difficult, but keeping her identity a secret from her guests was a bit trickier. So far so good—no one had recognized her yet. She might be widely recognized by the snooty Dallas upper crust, but to the hardworking people of Texas proper, she was simply a young woman helping out.

Her goal was to grow the charity event larger starting next year, which would mean she'd need to reveal her true identity in order to expand and give it the attention it deserved. But she couldn't do that while living in the Ferguson shadow or tiptoeing around her brother and his career as mayor.

Yes, going public would mean she'd have to do a bit of pruning to her own reputation before next Christmas.

"Coming!" she called when the knock at the door came again.

She rushed to the door and held it open, but rather than ushering Emmett forward, she ended up walking outside into the cold with him.

"Is that snow? Oh my gosh, that's snow!"

Snow in Texas was a rare occasion. Typically this time of year temperatures hovered in the forties.

"Yeah—hey, where are you going?"

She ignored him to step out onto her upstairs front stoop. The snow wasn't sticking, sadly, but the flakes were enough to fill her heart with joy. Each delicate, sparkly and, yes, *sloppy* flake was a reminder that her favorite holiday was nearly upon them.

"It's beautiful."

"It's wet. Inconvenient. And not why I live in Texas."

She frowned at Emmett. In a black leather coat, his white collared shirt visible just beneath the open zipper, and his standard black pants and leather boots, he should look like a tall, attractive, sturdy man she could count on. Instead, he was a grousing, grumpy individual set on ruining her good mood.

"It's *magical*. And I refuse to let you make me feel bad about that."

She slapped a palm against his broad chest, shoving him aside. Okay, so she didn't so much shove him as push against a chest made of solid muscle that had no give whatsoever. No matter! Emmett Keaton was not going to ruin her day. She'd already given that power away, and all too recently. It was a mistake she vowed not to repeat.

"I'll just take these *magical* bags out to my *mystical* SUV and wait for you to float on down, then," he said as he picked up her luggage.

Humming a Christmas tune to drown out Scrooge Keaton, she snagged her coffee thermos out from under the single-cup coffee maker and snapped on the lid. She might have to spend several days with him, but thank God the car ride was only four hours long.

How much damage could he do in four hours?

Hour One

"No Christmas music."

"That's inhumane."

She stabbed the button on the radio to turn it on and Emmett pushed a button on the steering wheel to shut it off.

"Can you explain to me how I am on my way to a Christmas celebration—that you have volunteered to drive me to, by the way—and yet I'm not allowed to listen to Christmas music on the drive over?"

"My car. My rules."

"That was rhetorical. Don't be a grump." She turned on the music again, and again Emmett turned it off. "What if the volume is really, really low?"

He didn't pull his eyes from the road, not even to glare at her.

"Fine. I'll talk instead." She cleared her throat. "So, I found this dress for my mother's art show next month. It's blue and sparkly and goes perfectly with my new shoes that I bought from—"

A long-suffering sigh sounded from his chest, and Emmett powered on the radio in surrender. He thumbed down the volume button on the steering wheel, but she considered it a win.

Hour Two

"I don't see why we couldn't stop at a decent restaurant and order takeout." She held the fast-food bag between a finger and thumb and eyed the grease spots that had seeped through the paper dubiously. "There are approximately a million calories in this bag. If I'm going to consume a million calories, it'd better be a gourmet meal."

Emmett stuck his hand into the bag and came out with one of the cheeseburgers. She watched as he unwrapped the sandwich, took a huge bite and, because that move took both hands, drove with his knee.

Because he was big enough to drive with his knee.

One booted foot firmly on the floor, his left knee kept the SUV perfectly positioned in the center of the lane.

What an irritatingly sexy move that was. Why did he have to be so damn capable at everything?

She rummaged through the bag until she found her sandwich. A fish sandwich had been the least calorie-laden item on the menu. It was roughly the size of a silver dollar, smashed flat, and half the cheese was glued to the cardboard container rather than on the bun.

"Great."

Emmett's hand plunged into the bag again and he came out with a container of fries. The burger held in one hand, he wedged the fry container between his big thighs and shoved three or four fries into his mouth. Even with one cheek stuffed like a chipmunk's, he didn't appear any less capable.

She'd been around strong men all her life. Her father and her brothers were all strong, commanding, decisive men.

Emmett had those traits as well, but it came in a less refined package. Sure, he dressed well, but there was a rough-
hewn edge beneath that Armani shirt.

It bothered her. It bothered her because it didn't make
any sense.

It bothers you because you find it attractive.

Just like she'd found Blake attractive? Just like she'd
found plenty of other men who were all wrong for her attractive?

She nibbled on the edge of her fish sandwich, sending
a longing look to the fries nestled between Emmett's legs.

"See something you like?" He crumpled the empty
burger wrapper and tossed it into the fast-food bag at her
feet.

She jerked her gaze to his face and was alarmed to find
him smiling over at her.

"No. I don't," she argued a little too fervently.

His smile remained. Eyes on the road, he proffered the
container of fries.

Rather than resist, she plucked out three perfectly golden,
salty potatoes and reminded herself that the bossy, attractive man in the driver's seat was as bad for her as this meal.

Four

Hour Three

Emmett slid a look over at Stefanie, who was intently scrolling through her phone and had been for the last several miles. What the hell was she doing?

"You're going to make yourself carsick," he grumbled.

He could feel her eyes on him. Wide, innocent eyes.

He didn't understand that observation about her, but it was nonetheless true. The only Ferguson daughter wasn't naive or immature. She was headstrong and mulish, and he knew from experience, since he had both those attributes in spades. When they belonged to a woman, however, people saw her as a trite, vapid troublemaker.

Frankly, it pissed him off. He'd known Stef for as long as he'd known Chase, and she wasn't any of those things. But she must've been immune to what the public said about her. She never complained about her image or tried to make herself smaller because the media talked about her.

"You do your thing, I'll do mine." Her snide remark made him smile in spite of himself.

His "thing" at the moment was chauffeuring her safely from Dallas to San Antonio so that she could hobnob with her friends and ignore him. Which was what being around her was always like. He'd been joking about sleeping in the SUV, but he assumed he could find a last-minute room. San Antonio was a big city.

He checked the rearview mirror and noticed the same black sedan he'd clocked earlier. It trailed three or four cars behind him. He wasn't so paranoid that he believed they were being followed—it was a highway and they were all heading the same direction—but neither would he take Stef's safety for granted.

He'd been in the habit of looking out for her over the past couple of years, so he supposed that was the reason he'd offered himself up as the human sacrifice rather than asking her to change her plans.

First off, he knew she wouldn't. And if she'd gone anyway, he'd have been the one tailing her right now.

Another glance showed the black sedan sliding into the same lane and vanishing behind a semi.

It was early yet. He'd keep an eye on it.

Both eyes.

Hour Four

Stef paused her scrolling through her address book, which she'd been desperately searching for a man to marry her for show.

She was young, rich and attractive, yet this was proving to be an insurmountable task. Every name she passed on the list was either seeing someone or the wrong choice. Like Oliver James, for example.

She and Oliver had casually dated for three months last summer. He was a successful commercial real estate buyer and a few years older than her. They'd stopped seeing each other mutually when things had simmered down.

She'd been contemplating texting him to find out if he was still single when Emmett spoke up to ask her if she was cold and snapped her out of her imaginings. Just as well. Oliver was a nice enough guy, but she didn't know if she could trust him when it came to being discreet. He was showy with a big personality. Always telling a joke or commanding the attention of the room.

Definitely not a good choice for an undercover marriage.

Now, though, her eyes rested on a name that she hadn't considered before. She blinked, considered what she knew of the man and wondered if she could slot him into the role of groom even on a pretend-temporary basis.

Emmett Keaton.

She wrinkled her nose, but the distaste she tried to feel wasn't there.

Stefanie Keaton.

It might work.

At first blush, the idea seemed insane, but when she allowed herself to walk through the steps of arranging a wedding to the man driving, it wasn't so insane.

Emmett didn't like her and she didn't like him that much, either. Ending a marriage when it was time would be as natural as breathing for them.

She looked up "marriage licenses in Harlington" on her phone and Google provided the website for the city. She hadn't exactly lied about going to San Antonio. The smaller district was located about thirty minutes outside San Antonio. If she had told Chase that she was heading to the one-horse town to visit her high-class friends, he would've known something was up.

She hadn't told Emmett yet, but they weren't close to where he needed to pull off the highway. She opened a map. In about twenty miles, he'd need to reroute.

Back to the issue at hand: marrying Emmett.

The marriage license had a seventy-two-hour waiting period. If they applied today… She counted the days on her fingers. They'd be good to go by Christmas Eve. The question was, could she find someone to marry them at the last minute on a holiday?

She opened her email app and pecked out a correspondence to the woman who ran the B and B where Stef had made her reservations.

Hi, Margaret,
Do you know anyone who could marry a couple on Christmas Eve?

She watched out the windshield, considering the timing of the charity dinner. It was a six o'clock dinner, and even with cleanup she'd be out of there by ten o'clock. Once they returned to the B and B, changed into whatever wedding attire she was able to scrounge up in the three-day gap between license and "I do," that'd mean…

Preferably midnight, she typed. As Christmas Eve turns to Christmas day.

She smiled to herself as she finished the email. Married at midnight on Christmas day. Could it be more perfect?

She slanted a glance at Emmett and frowned. Maybe *perfect* was overshooting it. She hoped he could summon up an expression other than "The Grinch Who Stole Christmas" for a few of the photos.

She should probably make sure Emmett didn't have a secret wife or girlfriend first. He kept his personal life in Stef's blind spot. She knew him in relation only to what he did at the mayor's office, and even then it looked to her like a bunch of walking around while wearing a starched white button-down shirt and a stern expression.

"Do you date?"

Emmett snapped his head around, a look of incredulity on his face. "What?"

"Date. Do you date?"

If she wasn't mistaken, he squirmed in his seat.

"Women. Men. Anyone?"

"Women." His frown intensified.

"Are you dating anyone right now?"

He said nothing, both hands on the wheel in an elbows-locked position.

"Why?" he finally muttered.

It seemed too early to blurt out that she wanted to marry him. She'd have to ease into that request.

"Just making conversation. I never see you with anyone whenever you're at a family function."

"That's work."

"You can't work all the time."

"I can. I do."

Yeah, this was getting her nowhere.

"Your head is the perfect shape. Not everyone can wear their hair that short."

"The deep car chatter continues."

"I'm just saying, I'm sure you can find a date even though your personality is basically the worst."

His shoulders jumped in what might have been a laugh, but no smile yet.

She smiled, enjoying a challenge. "So? Do you date?"

"Not as much as you do."

She ignored the jab. "Are you seeing anyone right now?"

"Yes. You. *Exclusively.*"

He didn't take his eyes off the road to look at her so he didn't see her bite her lip in consideration. As segues went, this was pretty much her only chance.

"I talked to Penelope about how to handle the Blake situation. Know what she said?"

"Stay out of it and let her do her job?"

Almost verbatim, but that wasn't what Stef was getting at.

"She said that if I were anyone else, she'd suggest I get married."

"She would suggest you pretend you're married?" he asked, his tone flat.

"No. She would suggest I literally get married. Marriage licenses are public record. Any reporter worth her salt could verify if it was real or not."

Emmett said nothing.

"I've been scrolling through my phone in search of Mr. Stefanie Ferguson, but no luck. I'm almost halfway through the alphabet."

He changed lanes, the mar in his brow deepening.

"You're going to have a lot of wrinkles when you're old because of the frowning. Did you know that—"

"It takes more muscles to frown than smile? Yes. I knew that."

"Anyway, when I find my husband-to-be, it'll only have to last until the election. Once Chase is reelected as mayor, I can annul it, no harm no foul."

A minute of silence passed, the only sound in the car a Mariah Carey holiday tune playing quietly on the radio. Emmett stabbed a button on the steering wheel to shut it off.

"You have to take this exit for where we're going."

"I don't think so."

"I know so." She held her phone up and showed him the map.

"Where is that?" he asked, even as he dutifully changed lanes.

"I lied about San Antonio. We're going to a town called Harlington. It's just outside—"

"I know Harlington." His visage darkened.

"You do?" She'd assumed he was from a similarly wealthy Dallas background as her family. At least upper middle class. "Here. This exit." She rested her cell phone on the dash, and though he mumbled a swear word under his breath, he pulled off the exit.

"From here take route—"

"I can read the map, Stefanie."

Yeah, proposing should work out great, she thought with an eye roll.

She waited a few more silent minutes before turning on the radio again. The Sting song didn't cause her driver to visibly wince.

Her email notification lit up her phone and she opened her inbox to read Margaret's reply, whose answer was an exuberant "Yes!"

Evidently Margaret's son was a minister and available on Christmas Eve for a midnight wedding. In the next paragraph of her reply, Margaret went on and on about the beautiful decorations in the sitting room of her old Victorian house.

Stefanie responded with a quick message. I'm working out the marriage license now.

Little did Emmett know, the address she'd keyed into her map was for city hall downtown.

Five

"Which building?" Emmett drove through the thick traffic of downtown Harlington.

Yeah, he knew this town. He'd grown up not far from here. Before he'd escaped to go to college. Before happenstance had put him at the same wild frat party as Chase Ferguson. They'd stopped in the center of the room en route to flirt with the same girl. Neither of them had won the girl, but they'd forged a strong friendship.

From there, Emmett's world had forked. He'd left behind his former life as a rough kid from a lonely home. He'd dropped out of college and never finished, but his old man hadn't noticed. Van Keaton had been lost in his own prison of grief since the Christmas that'd robbed both him and Emmett of all that was good.

Since then, Emmett had been determined to create good. In addition to working with Chase as his head of security, Emmett had also learned how to invest well. Hell, he'd mimicked his friend's financial habits, had read every book Chase recommended and had listened to countless podcasts on the topic. It never would've occurred to Emmett that he could live the way he lived now if it wasn't for the Fergusons. They took the idea of "living well" to an advanced level.

Emmett's work at the mayor's office might as well be his source of oxygen. He had the Fergusons, who had been a placeholder for the family Emmett rarely saw. His father was a lonely man determined to bask in his own misery, so Emmett let him do it. And he'd never gone home on a holiday. Van didn't do holidays. Not anymore.

And neither did Emmett.

Stef squealed from the passenger seat, going on about how "beautiful" the red bows and pine boughs tied to paint-chipped lampposts were, but he could only offer a grunt.

Those tattered pine boughs had seen better days and the red ribbons drooped. The shop windows downtown covered in spray snow would require tedious scraping with a razor blade to come clean, and the strings of white lights wrapped around every lamppost served as a reminder of what once was but could never be again.

"Where the hell is this place?" he asked at a stoplight. He didn't see any building resembling a B and B.

"Oh. Um. I have to stop at city hall first."

She directed him to the tall brick building between a shoe shop and a store called the Fan Man, which, as far as Emmett could tell, sold ceiling fans and lighting fixtures.

"What for?" He navigated to an open parking spot, but when she took off her seat belt, he caught the strip of nylon in one fist. She sagged back into her seat.

"I know you think the idea of me marrying someone sounds—"

"Insane," he finished for her, letting her go.

"Think about it, Em. Blake won't have a leg to stand on. I refuse to let him use a mistake I made in the past against my family."

Every time he pictured her with that guy, rage spilled into his bloodstream.

"It was the worst mistake of my life."

"Huge," he grumbled in agreement.

Guilt outlined her pretty features.

It was the wrong thing for him to say. Blake was predatory and single-minded. And when Chase had found out his sister slept with that pig, his reaction had mirrored Emmett's. Emmett would've happily castrated the bastard to ensure he'd never hurt anyone again.

"There are worse things in life," he told Stef. "Trust me."

Christmas shoppers flooded the streets, bustling around to finish their shopping before it was too late, many with small children in tow. One little boy with dark hair and pink cheeks rode in a stroller and pointed with one mitten as snow began to fall, and Emmett's heart crushed.

That kid was the same age as his brother, Michael, when he'd passed.

"I was awake for hours last night trying to think of a suitable groom, but after a quick scan of my contacts I came up empty-handed. I decided to check again today in case I'd overlooked someone and then I found myself lingering over a name…"

"Completely insane." He shook his head.

"Do you know why?"

He did look at her now, having neither any idea why nor any clue as to how she thought this was the best way to proceed.

"Because I came across the only name in my address book that belonged to someone who cares enough about my brother to agree to my plan."

Something tender invaded her expression. He'd never until this moment been regarded by Stefanie Ferguson with "tenderness."

Hell if he knew what to do with that.

"You." She said the word with finality.

"Me what?" he asked, the question loud in the cab of the SUV.

"You are the only man who would be discreet, go along with my plan and, provided you don't already have a girlfriend, fiancée or wife—"

"You think I have a wife?" There was a crazy idea. Even crazier was the idea that Stefanie would *be* that wife. He reached for his cup of gas station coffee, wincing when the mouthful was cold instead of hot.

"There's a seventy-two-hour waiting period, so we have to apply for the license today. Then we can be married on Christmas Eve after my…um… After I visit my friends."

"Forget it." He put the SUV in Reverse to wiggle from the parking space when her hand—and cold, delicate fingers—brushed his.

Her touch was foreign, as most touches were to him, yet familiar in a way he couldn't understand. Maybe because he'd known her for so long. Other than her mother, Eleanor Ferguson, Stefanie had been the only constant woman in his life since he was a very small boy.

"I've worked out everything. All you have to do is agree and smile for the camera so I can leak a few photos to social media. That's it. Two little things."

"Little?" His incredulous laugh cracked the air. "You're suggesting we get *married*, Stef. There's nothing little about that ask."

"The end game is to screw over Blake and save Chase's campaign. It's noble. You'd be doing your civic duty."

"There's got to be another way."

It was nuts. He couldn't consider this.

So why was he?

"Well. I guess I could pay someone to marry me."

"Absolutely not."

Anger filled him to the brim at the idea she'd sell herself to the highest bidder. And what goon from her dating past would be the lucky lotto winner? The idea of Stefanie being taken advantage of again made his blood pressure climb to dangerous levels.

"Listen. It's a surefire plan. This is the ultimate undo button for me. Haven't you ever wanted to go back in time and stop a tragedy from happening?"

Her pulled-up blond hair revealed a sweet face silhouetted by the cheesy town holiday decorations and winking lights in every window of city hall. Hell yes, he'd wanted to go back in time. He'd fantasized about going back for a huge "undo" for most of his childhood life.

"Yes," he answered honestly. She beamed, but that grin was erased when he spoke again. "Then I grew up and learned that what's done is done. There is no going back. There is no undo button on tragedy."

She squeezed his fingers as if apologizing for the tragic evening that changed his and his father's lives forever. She had no idea what had happened to him and his family— no one did. Save Chase, but Emmett had sworn his best friend to secrecy.

"Help me, Emmett. I'm begging." Against his will, the plea in her eyes took root in his chest. "You know it's serious if I have to beg. If there were anyone else, I'd ask them. But there's only you."

The sentiment was strange to hear in any context, especially in one where he was being proposed to, but it didn't stop him from reconsidering.

"I'm not going in there," he said. Stefanie's shoulders slumped in defeat before he added, "Until you explain every last detail of how this will work."

Thirty minutes later Stefanie walked out of city hall with her fiancé.

Her big, brawny, silent, scowling fiancé.

"There." She pointed across the street at a jeweler and marched over as soon as there was a break in traffic. She was a woman on a mission.

A cheery bell jingled as she pushed open the door of the jewelry store. Emmett did a neat jog to catch up and join her, but his expression remained as unreadable as it had when they'd applied for their marriage license.

It was so simple it was sort of unbelievable. It was like they'd let anyone get married these days.

"Hello." A saleslady scanned her new customers, ring-laden fingers clasped at her front. "What can I help you find today?"

"Wedding bands. And an engagement ring."

"Congratulations."

"Thanks." Stef peeked over her shoulder at Emmett, who was standing by the door looking unhappy.

She jerked her head, widening her eyes to communicate her meaning: *get your ass in here.*

He strode in, a reluctant lurch to his walk, as the saleslady led them to a glass case filled with sparkling diamond bands. She pulled out a tray of platinum settings at Stefanie's request. Stef leaned over them, fingering each one.

"They're beautiful."

She reached for a princess cut but before she had it lifted from its velvet bed, Emmett pushed the ring back down and plucked a band featuring a trio of marquise-cut diamonds instead. Rows of smaller diamonds winked from their homes on each side of the band.

"Great choice," the saleslady praised. "That's an old set. It was traded in yesterday by a woman whose husband passed away ten years ago. They were married forty-eight years and she had no children to leave it to. She said their marriage was a happy one, but she was remarrying and felt wrong keeping it. She thought bringing it here would allow another couple to give it new life for another four decades or more." She eyed Emmett and then Stefanie. "You two look young enough to make it to your forty-eighth wedding anniversary."

It was both a sad and sweet sentiment since Stef knew that her marriage to Emmett wouldn't last until summer.

"Go ahead and slip it onto her finger," the saleslady told Emmett with a wink. "Practice for the big day."

He lifted Stef's left hand, the ring gripped between his blunt fingers.

"Maybe this ring is the wrong choice for us." She started to tug her hand away, but her betrothed didn't heed her warning, instead slipping the ring past her third finger's knuckles, where it sat as snugly as if it'd been sized for her hand.

"It's perfect." His gruff voice held a note of surprise.

"It's beautiful." The saleslady took Stefanie's hand and turned the diamond this way and that. "I tightened those prongs myself."

It was beautiful. And Emmett was right. It was also perfect. The woman handed over the matching band, and he pulled it onto his finger—again, a perfect fit.

"It was meant to be." The saleslady let out a gasp of delight. "We have financing and we also accept credit cards."

"Cash." Emmett wiggled the ring from his finger and placed it onto the counter as Stef was reaching into her purse for her wallet.

"Splendid. Let me grab a few boxes." The saleslady dashed off to the back, rings in hand and a spring in her step thanks to the hefty price tag.

"I'll pay for it," Stef said.

"No. You won't."

"Em—"

"Let me." He grasped her hand where the engagement ring sat, his palm big and warm. An answering warmth curled around her heart and sent a flush up her neck.

Speechless, she let Emmett take care of the purchase.

Six

Emmett drew the line at shopping for clothes.

Applying for a marriage license and purchasing the rings they'd exchange during their vows had been surreal enough. If she added a wedding dress to the mix, he'd have to call a shrink.

Agreeing to her harebrained plan would work twofold. It would defuse the threat to Chase's campaign and keep Stefanie out of one of her boneheaded exes' beds.

Emmett couldn't stomach the idea of her stooping to offer herself to another man who likely had his sights set on the Ferguson fortune. Not when Emmett himself was perfectly able to fill the role of temporary husband—and would sooner die than be compensated for the task.

He'd slid that band onto Stefanie's finger in the jewelry store, the tale of the ring's past eating into his soul. What he hadn't been able to deny was his desire to protect her at all costs. The rest of the Fergusons weren't going to approve, but Emmett didn't care. Stefanie needed him, and in the same way he'd been protecting the Ferguson family since Chase hired Emmett onto the security team, he'd protect Stef now. She didn't need him to leap in front of a bullet. She needed him to commit to a vow that was temporary for both of them.

He could hardly believe he'd let her talk him into it.

"There it is." She pointed out the window at a tall Victorian home. The painted wood siding was slate with brick red shutters. The matching sign was dusted with a thin layer of snow and the wood-carved lettering read Lawson Bed and Breakfast. "It's as pretty as the online photos."

It was a regal house in an older neighborhood of Harlington, probably from before the oil wells dried up, back
when the residents believed it to be a forever home. It was
impressive that it'd been kept up. He pulled down the driveway and into a parking area with four spots. Three of which
were taken.

"Margaret Lawson runs the B and B," Stef said as they
walked to the front door. She rang the buzzer. "Her son will
be officiating our wedding. We'll have to share a room, I'm
afraid. Otherwise, it'd look weird."

"Gee, I'd hate to look weird." He caught sight of the
engagement ring when she tugged off one glove, then the
next. It was odd seeing it there—the ring he'd *put* there.
It filled him with a propriety he had no right to feel. As if
she were *his* to care for and watch over.

A cheery redhead answered the door. "You must be Stefanie. And this is your…"

"Emmett Keaton." He thrust a hand forward in introduction.

"Nice to meet you. Your room is ready whenever you are."

"Is there a couch or extra bed in our room?" he blurted.
When Margaret's smile vanished, he covered with "I toss
and turn. Wouldn't want my future missus to lose any
beauty sleep."

The older woman glanced from Emmett to Stefanie,
who was regarding him like she wanted to strangle him.

"There's a love seat," Margaret answered. "A rather
small one."

"We'll make do. Thank you, Margaret," Stef said.
"Honey, won't you grab the luggage?"

He could take a hint. He excused himself to unload the
SUV as Stefanie followed their hostess into the house.

Granted, this was her idea, but could Emmett at least
appear to like her? First, he argued that she was insane for

suggesting a marriage of convenience, then he asked the owner of the B and B for separate sleeping accommodations. At least he'd been game for the ring buying or else she would have developed a complex.

He stomped into the room in heavy boots and unloaded their luggage—several bags for her and one duffel bag for him.

"Do you have a suit and tie in there?" she asked.

"I have what you see me wearing in there." He unshouldered his coat to reveal his white-shirt-black-pants combo. His broad frame filled the room—which was small by anyone's definition of the word. Having him in it shrank it to cracker-box size.

She tapped a key on her laptop, having extracted the computer from her bag first. "I'll look into tux rental."

"What's it matter?"

From her cross-legged seat on the center of the bed, she slapped the laptop closed. In a voice low but firm, she told him exactly why it mattered.

"This isn't going to work unless you pretend to at least like me. I've been doing a good job of cordiality but you are failing with a capital *F*. Margaret patted me on the arm after leading me up here and assured me men always behaved strangely before a wedding and not to take what you said to heart!"

"I don't see how that is any of her business."

"I don't see how you're missing the point I'm so clearly conveying," she snapped. Closing her eyes, she pulled in a deep breath. *Serenity now!* "We need everyone to buy into the farce or else it'll leak that this is fake, which will give Blake even more ammunition and ruin my reputation."

"What do you suggest I do, Stef? Follow you around like a puppy? Hold your hand? Nuzzle your neck?" he bit out.

The idea of Emmett holding her close and nuzzling her

anything had her growing warm—and not in a good way. She'd obligated him enough. She couldn't ask that he force a reaction he wasn't comfortable with. That would be sexual harassment.

"Of course not." She craned her chin as he stepped closer to the bed.

He folded his arms over his chest and looked down at her, his weighty presence stifling and strangely sensual. Flummoxed by her reaction to him, she changed the subject.

"I have errands to run over the next couple of days. Wedding dress and shoe shopping."

She also needed to go to the site of the charity dinner and make sure everything was coming along as planned. Caterers would be delivering tables and chairs, and decorating no fewer than three Christmas trees. Not to mention that the volunteers from the community church would be wrapping presents for the invited families.

"I'll need you to drive me." She half expected resistance but Emmett nodded easily. "I won't make you wear a tux."

"Fine."

"Great."

"Great."

He eyed the bed where she was sitting, legs folded pretzel-style in front of her. Then he sent a glance at the diminutive love seat on the other side of the room.

"You can have the bed," she told him. "I'll sleep on the couch."

"Nice try." He grinned, an almost jovial light in his eyes. It faded as fast as it appeared, but damn, what she wouldn't give to see it again. That smile had transformed his entire face. "I'll take the floor."

"It's cold down there."

"I'll live." He walked to the door and when she asked where he was going, he turned to answer her, his body taking up most of the doorway. "I have a sleeping bag in the SUV, Stef. Stop worrying about me, yeah?"

Then he patted the doorway and was off.

She wasn't worrying about him, but she was trying to accommodate him. Clearly, he was uncomfortable, and now that they were to be wedded she was feeling equally awkward about their suddenly intimate situation. How was she going to manage an "I do" kiss and sharing a room with him if she could barely talk to him when they were alone?

And it wouldn't end in Harlington.

No, this decision would follow her home. Follow her around until she and Emmett were *un*married. And what would they do until then?

She didn't want to think about it. She opened her laptop and started typing a list of to-dos for her wedding. After a few minutes of crafting a list, she realized that even the basics were going to take plenty of time and energy and effort.

In order to pull off a wedding as well as a successful charity dinner, she would have to either make a clone of herself or do some delegating. And there was only one other person to delegate *to*.

That person strode back into the room with a rolled sleeping bag tucked under his arm. He hadn't bothered with his coat for the quick jaunt outside, so his face and nose were red even from the brief exposure. Before he dropped the bag, she made her request.

"I need your help with a few things while I'm here." Realizing that sounded demanding, she added, "If you can take the time away from your job."

"You are my job while I'm here." He crossed the room and dumped the sleeping bag onto the love seat.

It was easier for her to admit this next part while looking at his back...

"One more thing…" He turned before she could finish and she gulped, a dry sound that caused her throat to click. "I need to tell you the truth about why we're here."

Seven

"You mean there's more to it than cornering me into matrimony and eating a fancy dinner with your fancy friends?"

But that last bit didn't make much sense, did it? Not now that they were in Harlington, where the "fanciest" restaurant in town was a Chili's.

"You're joking with me. That's new. Usually you're frowning at me." Her smile was tentative. She leaned back on the bed, the pair of leggings making her slim legs look a mile long and the oversize pink sweater hiding her petite curves. She looked comfortable and relaxed, which was as crazy as the fact that he felt the same way.

Stefanie didn't like him—he'd have lost a bet that she'd smile at him let alone *propose* to him even if it were up to them to repopulate the planet. There were a million strings attached to the proposal, and it was an arrangement for the greater good, but…shouldn't they both be more on edge?

She picked at a thread on the quilt rather than look up at him. "Does this mean we're becoming friendly instead of mortal enemies? That someday I could be more than a job to you?"

Ah, hell. Surely she didn't think that. He didn't consider her an enemy—he liked her.

He cared about her safety.

And about her as a person.

"I only ask because we need to make this marriage look real if we go forward. How good of an actor are you?"

His face scrunched at the question.

"Can you hold my hand in public? Open a door for me?

Be a gentleman? I don't think the public would believe I'd fall for someone who didn't do those things."

"Who cares what the public thinks?" he barked, stung at her accusing him of not knowing how to treat a woman. He was accustomed to protecting—to watching other people's backs. That was why he brought up the rear whenever they walked anywhere together.

"Do it for Chase if you can't do it for me." Hurt flooded her eyes.

Did she really believe he found her so unsavory? Emmett wouldn't stoop to defend himself aloud, but his thoughts went there. He *was* doing this for her. So that she could come out here to…do whatever she was doing.

"You owe me the truth," he reminded her. But when she took a breath, presumably to tell him, he held up a hand. "Not here, though. I'm hungry."

Stefanie had never set foot inside a Chili's restaurant until today. It wasn't that she was too good for a burger and fries; it was that there wasn't much of an opportunity to go to a chain when there were hundreds of other unique restaurants to choose from. Any man she'd dated had endeavored to impress her with meals that had cost hundreds of dollars.

Emmett didn't apologize for choosing a restaurant that had nary a word of French on the menu. She appreciated being treated as an equal and not catered to like some spoiled rich girl. She wasn't sure if it was because he was stubborn or because he knew her better than anyone else, but the latter seemed impossible. They barely knew each other at all.

Once they were settled in with their drinks—wine for her and beer for him—and a bowl of warm tortilla chips and a dish of salsa, Emmett gestured with a chip for her to speak. "Go."

"I'm not in Harlington for a girls' getaway."

"I gathered." He piled salsa onto another chip.

"For the last three years I've been hosting charity dinners for families who can't afford a Christmas on their own." She reached for her wine, her throat dry. "I'm planning on taking it public next year, maybe recruit some 'elves' to help me throw more than one charity dinner at a time. I guess I'm saying…this will be my last year for anonymity."

He said nothing, regarding her with a narrowed gaze. Stefanie could understand why. It probably didn't make sense to him why she would keep a noble cause quiet.

"I wanted to do it on my own," she supplied. "In case you haven't noticed, my parents and two older brothers, not to mention my oldest brother's best friend—" she paused to give him a meaningful eyebrow raise "—don't let me do much on my own. I don't want anyone's input. Succeed or fail, I wanted the outcome on me.

"It's been a success. I've hired assistants over the years to help me pull it off, but I do most of the work. I'm a party planner and an organizer by nature. It's a challenge I enjoy."

Emmett crunched another chip as if she hadn't revealed a huge secret or exposed her tender underbelly to him. Either he was too hungry to comment or…

Well, she didn't know *or what*.

Guessing what was inside his head was a challenge she was not equipped for.

"Say something."

After a long guzzle of beer, he did. "You provide Christmas dinner for poor people."

"And gifts. That's simplifying it, but yes. The idea that a little boy or girl wouldn't wake up to gifts or a Christmas tree made me want to change all of that. I've always had magical Christmases. I couldn't imagine not having them."

He nodded, but the reaction was noncommittal at best. Not that she wanted praise for her charitable work, but she had expected a more favorable reaction. She'd always assumed Emmett considered her the shallow end of the Ferguson gene pool. Much as she'd convinced herself she didn't care what he thought of her, she did. It was her plight.

In a dark corner of her heart, she cared what a great many people thought of her.

"You'll be glad to know that your standard attire for work is acceptable for the dinner."

"I'm not going."

She blinked at his reaction.

"You're my fiancé. Of course you're going. What else are you going to do?" She tried a tactic she was sure would sway him in her favor—making him believe she could be in danger at the event. "I never know what kind of people could show up, so it would be nice if you were watching out for me and the volunteers. I won't make you talk to anybody. You can be your lovely, quiet, unsociable self."

He sat back in the booth and crossed his thick arms over his thicker chest.

"I bet you would enjoy it. It's rewarding to give back to those who have little when you have so much."

Since she was looking right at him she didn't miss one of his eyes twitching or the frown between his eyebrows deepening.

She didn't understand. What kind of person wouldn't support a charity that provided Christmas for underprivileged kids? Had she pegged Emmett wrong? Was he truly the scrooge she'd labeled him as?

"Anyway…" she said when it was clear he wasn't going to say another word. "Now you know the real reason I'm here. And it's not to gallivant with my friends. I'll just gallivant with you instead."

It was like delivering a speech to a stone wall…one that ate chips and salsa.

"You'd be pretty if you smiled more." She batted her

eyelashes coyly, but Emmett didn't smile. "Yeah, that line never works when a man says it to me, either." She reached for a chip and shrugged, giving up.

After dinner, they returned to the B and B, where they passed Margaret in the kitchen. Their hostess was pouring steaming mulled cider into red and green mugs.

"Emmett and Stefanie!" she greeted. "Your timing is perfect. I was about to take a tray of drinks into the living room. There's a fire in the fireplace, pine garlands draped over every surface and Christmas music playing."

"That sounds absolutely dreamy." Stefanie inhaled the scent of warmed cinnamon and clove and citrusy orange rind. "Let me take my purse upstairs and we'll be right down."

Around the corner at the stairs, she stopped on the second step, alarmed to feel Emmett's palm at her lower back. She turned and regarded him curiously.

"Isn't this a gentlemanly thing to do?"

"Unless you are trying to steady me because I had a second glass of wine, then yes." She had to smile as she ascended the steps, his hand on her lower back before it slipped casually to her hip.

He'd been listening to her, after all.

He'd also opened the door for her when they exited Chili's, and then he made a point not to unlock the SUV so he could open that door for her, as well.

The conversation at dinner had been mostly one-sided as she'd chattered about the charity. She was trying to be friendly, but it was hard to be friendly with someone who… was introverted? Didn't know how to be friendly? She had no idea what Emmett's issue was, and she was tired of guessing.

Tonight, she'd enjoy warm cider and Christmas music in front of a crackling fire.

In their shared room, she hung her coat on a hook on the

wall and deposited her purse on the bed. When she turned and found Emmett untying his boots, she asked, "Why are you taking off your shoes? We're going to the living room."

"Pass."

"Emmett. We're engaged. People expect to see us together."

"People get tired. You can tell them that's what happened to me." He took off his other boot and dropped it with a *thunk*.

"This is a perfect opportunity for you to practice being with me around people."

He let out a grunt before standing in front of her. Almost *over* her. He took a step closer, his hand going to the shiny metal buckle of his belt. She watched as he pulled the thick leather through the buckle and she licked her lips, her mouth practically watering. It took everything in her not to drop her attention to his waist or lower.

"What are you doing?" she croaked when he reached for the button on his slacks.

"I'm going to take a shower. And then I'm going to bed."

"How about one mug of cider?" She tried again, blinking out of the pheromone haze saturating the air between them.

"Knock yourself out. I'm not going down there." His eyes on hers, he slowly pulled the belt through the loops of his pants and began rolling it.

Was it hot in here or was it just him?

When he reached for his zipper, she shut her eyes.

"Can you at least wait until I leave the room?"

"Aren't we supposed to be practicing?"

Her eyes flew open, her cheeks heating with…something. Lust? Frustration? Frustrated lust?

But before she could take him to task, she saw one corner of his mouth lift in amusement.

"Thought you liked it when I joked."

"All joking aside—" she cleared her throat "—there's no need to practice the physical part."

"You sure? A lengthy kiss usually follows the 'I dos.'"

"I'm pretty sure I can wing a chaste marital kiss. Even with you."

"You're the boss."

His gaze drifted to her mouth, that move as sensual as if he'd leaned forward to press his lips to hers.

"Right. I'll be back up in an hour."

"Take your time."

She fished her room key out of her purse as she heard the rustle of clothing that—she guessed—was Emmett taking off his pants. Hand sweating on the knob, she exited and walked into the hallway, shutting their bedroom door behind her. No way was she turning around to see if he was a boxers or briefs guy.

No freaking way.

Eight

Emmett was lying on the hard floor, the thin carpeting doing his back no favors. And the sleeping bag wasn't helping after a long day of driving, getting engaged and the bonus of being pummeled by memories.

Stef had gone downstairs well over an hour ago, and now his little social butterfly was taking her sweet time delighting the guests of Lawson B and B. He could imagine her broad, infectious smile. The way she stood when she told a joke and almost always flubbed the ending.

He closed his eyes and shook his head, wishing she'd come back if for no other reason than to distract him. He could go downstairs, he supposed, but after he'd found out the real reason for her being in Harlington, something inside him had cracked open and out seeped decades of toxic waste.

He'd been in one of those families she was planning on serving. After his mother and baby brother had passed away, his father quit working. They'd had financial help from the state, and his old man had qualified for disability thanks to an unsuccessful attempt at suicide.

That'd been a shitty Christmas.

Emmett had worked hard to escape his past, to make up for the assistance his father sponged off the system. He'd done well for himself, and always worked harder than expected to make sure he earned every cent of his paycheck. As his check was signed by a Ferguson, it was no surprise that Stef's sharing that she was in town to help the less fortunate had struck a raw chord.

As if he needed a reminder that she was better than him in every way.

Uglier thoughts like that one had traipsed around his mind in a demented square dance since he'd climbed out of the shower. Thoughts like, if Chase knew who he really was, would they even be friends? Emmett had shared everything with his best bud save what income bracket he'd hailed from. He'd also wondered if Stefanie ever would have approached him about marrying her if she knew he'd once qualified to be one of the guests at her dinner.

The entire scenario sickened him. He couldn't escape the loss that came back like the Ghost of Christmas Past. He couldn't shake the feeling that he was a sheep in wolf's clothing—and underneath the tough exterior was a tender boy with a broken heart.

"Fucking Christmas." He pushed himself to sitting, ran a hand over his short hair and sighed. Sleep was so far away he'd need a passport to get there.

Dressed in only boxer briefs and a sleeveless tank, he braced himself against the chill in the room when he climbed to his feet. The Victorian was an old house and drafty as hell.

He knelt to check the fridge beneath the television, praying for a few of those miniature overpriced bottles of booze to take the edge off. He never made a habit of drinking away a mood, but in this case, it would serve a dual purpose. He'd warm up, too.

He inspected the fridge's contents—OJ, milk and water. Not a bottle of liquor to be found.

The sound of a key card sliding through the pad drew his attention to the door. Stefanie stepped into the room, her smile slightly wonky but no less charming. She carried two steaming mugs.

"I was hoping you'd be awake." She smiled brightly, and even in the meager light leaking in from the streetlamp through the lace curtains he could see the pink tinge of her cheeks. "I had Margaret heat up a few more of these—and add some bourbon." She bared her teeth in a bright grin. "I've already had one with bourbon."

In spite of all that had haunted him this evening, he felt better already. She'd walked into the room and her presence had slain the demons.

"I'll take it." He flicked on a nearby lamp. "Nothing but nonalcoholic beverages in the room."

"Well then. You're welcome." She handed over the cider topped with whipped cream. He wasn't sure this concoction would make a difference in his mood, but it was worth a shot.

She sipped and then licked the whipped cream off her upper lip. At the same time, they moved to sit on the end of the bed.

"Sorry," she said.

"Go ahead." He gestured, remaining standing.

She sat, patting the bedding next to her. He regarded the quilt for a beat before easing down next to her.

Curling her legs beneath her, she held the mug with both hands and hummed. "I love being warm."

"In this drafty house that might be a challenge. I didn't see a thermostat in this room."

Her eyes went past him to his bed on the floor. "Is it cold down there?"

He shrugged.

"You could always—"

"It's fine." Whatever she was about to suggest, he couldn't let her. She wasn't sleeping down there—or wedging herself onto the tiny sofa.

He drank his cider carefully to make sure it wasn't too hot. It was perfect, and the sweet tang of bourbon welcome.

"Margaret has the hearth decorated with thick greenery and gold ribbon. Glass-and-glitter ornaments and nutcrackers that her children buy her every year." Stef's eyes were bright and happy. "Don't you love Christmas?"

He nearly choked on his next sip.

"No." He wasn't sure what possessed him to tell the truth, but there it was.

"At all?" She regarded him like he'd announced he kicked puppies in his spare time.

"Not at all."

"Why?"

He turned to face her and was struck dumb by the blue of her eyes. Stefanie Ferguson was a beautiful woman. He'd noticed before—it was impossible not to notice—but until now he'd never given himself the luxury to truly look at her.

She was royalty and he was more like a stable boy. In his mind, there'd never been a misconception about who she was and who he was—where she hailed from versus the rock he'd crawled out from under. She was whole, and he'd lost a chunk of himself a long time ago. Whatever passing admiration he'd felt for her in the past, he'd shut it down immediately.

"Did something bad happen?" she pushed.

"Yes." He cleared his throat and stood, setting aside his warm drink, the whipped cream melted.

"Will you tell me about it?"

He faced her, hyperaware that she was dressed from head to toe and he was in his underwear. She noticed, too. He watched her take him in, her eyes sliding down his chest and lower.

Interesting.

Had she ever looked at him with anything other than disdain?

"It's not a happy story, Stef. I'd rather let you keep your delusions that Christmas is magical and wondrous."

A line formed between her eyebrows. "I'm not a child because I choose to see the good. Why not admit you're too much of a coward to share what's bugging you rather than lash out at me?"

Ah, familiar ground. With a sigh, he returned to the bed, arms resting in his lap. Maybe she was right. Maybe he was lashing out. His blurred reflection watched him from the dark television's screen. His broad shoulders were slumped as he sat there like a stubborn giant. Stefanie sat delicate as a fairy, blond hair out of its ponytail and spilling over her shoulders, her chin down as she watched him through her lashes.

They were contrasting in every way.

The filthy-rich girl. The wrong-side-of-the-tracks guy. She'd been blessed by the gods and his luck always felt like it was on the verge of running out. He didn't talk about his family tragedy for a lot of reasons, the dominating one being habit.

"Fine. Don't tell me." She stood and set her mug aside, but before she could huff off to the attached bathroom, he wrapped his fingers around her arm. Her eyes widened.

"Sorry." He held up both hands. "I didn't mean to—"

Rather than finish the thought, he scrubbed a palm over his short hair. "If you really want to know, I'll tell you."

Arms crossed, she hoisted an eyebrow in a proprietary manner and waited.

The floor was his.

Standing over Emmett was an odd juxtaposition.

She'd never seen him like this. In his underpants, sure, but she'd also never seen him look so…tired.

She had the irrational urge to touch him. She curled her fingers into fists to keep from reaching for him.

How could he not like Christmas?

"It was a long time ago," he started.

Her stomach tightened at his foreboding tone. She'd wondered at first if he'd suffered a bad breakup over the holidays, but the hollowness in his voice suggested this tale was much, much worse than a broken heart.

"I was...six years old." He palmed the back of his neck, clearly uncomfortable sharing this story. "My dad and I went out. I can't remember why. The grocery store, maybe? Gas station? Whatever was open at 6:00 a.m. on Christmas morning."

His throat bobbed as he swallowed, his gaze unfocused on a spot across the room.

"We returned to our street and fire engines were lining both sides of it. Police cars wouldn't let us close, so my dad climbed out of the truck and busted through the cops to see what happened."

He sighed and paused as if gathering the strength to continue.

"The house was a total loss. My mom and my baby brother, Michael, didn't survive the fire. They said later it was caused by faulty wiring." The tilt of his lips was dark, humorless. "Half my family...gone, thanks to a shoddy electrician."

She let out a sound between a whimper and a gasp. What a horrible tragedy.

"I don't remember a lot from that day. More what happened in the years that followed. Sadness hovered in our apartment like a gas leak. There was no escaping. Until I did."

"Oh, Emmett." She gave in and sat, grabbing his hand, holding it with both of hers. He stiffened next to her, his arm going taut, his expression unreadable.

He shrugged one shoulder as if to assure her it was okay, but it wasn't okay, was it? Losing a parent and a brother in a house fire when you were six years old could never be okay.

She stroked her hand up his arm in an attempt to warm him, or maybe warm herself. Since he'd spoken it was as if a chill had come over the room. Like a ghost had passed by them both.

Or two ghosts.

She shivered.

"Like I said, it was a long time ago."

Still. It wasn't like losing half your family was easily forgotten. And he'd been a little boy.

"Anyway." He straightened his back, pushing the conversation aside. "Dad never was much of a Christmas guy, and I followed suit. And I'm not big on strings of cheap lights in my house decorating a highly flammable dead tree."

His hand was still in hers and she squeezed his palm.

"It was an awful tragedy, Emmett. I'm so sorry."

He faced her, his expression younger somehow, or maybe lighter. Like unburdening that story had taken years off him.

"I don't normally share that."

"I understand why." Who would want to relive that pain?

His eyes dipped briefly to her lips, igniting a sizzle in the air that had no place being there after he'd shared the sad story of his past. Even so, her answering reaction was to study his firm mouth in contemplation. The barely-there scruff lining his angled jaw. His dominating presence made her feel fragile yet safe at the same time.

The urge to comfort him—to comfort herself—lingered. This time she didn't deny it.

With her free hand, she reached up and cupped the thick column of his neck, tugging him down. He resisted, but only barely, stopping short a brief distance from her mouth to mutter one word.

"Hey…"

She didn't know if he'd meant to follow it with "This is a bad idea" or "We shouldn't get carried away," but she didn't wait to find out.

Her lips touched his gently and his mouth answered by

puckering to return the kiss. Her eyes sank closed and his hand flinched against her palm.

He tasted...*amazing*. Like spiced cider and a capable, strong, heartbroken man who kept his hurts hidden from the outside world.

Eyes closed, she gripped the back of his neck tighter, angling her head to get more of his mouth. And when he pulled his hand from hers to come to rest on her shoulder, she swore she might melt from that casual touch. His tongue came out to play, tangling with hers in a sensual, forbidden dance.

She fisted his undershirt, tugging it up and brushing against the plane of his firm abs, and Emmett's response was to lift the hem of her sweater, where his rough fingertips touched the exposed skin of her torso.

A tight, needy sound escaped her throat, and his lips abruptly stopped moving against hers.

He pulled back, blinking at her with lust-heavy lids. She touched her mouth and looked away, the heady spell broken.

She'd just kissed her brother's best friend—a man who until today she might have jokingly described as her mortal enemy.

Worse, Emmett had kissed her back.

It was okay for this to be pretend—for their wedding to be an arrangement, but there was nothing black-and-white between them any longer. There was real attraction—as volatile as a live wire and as dangerous as a downed electric pole.

Whatever line they'd drawn by agreeing to marry, she'd stepped way, *way* over it.

He sobered quickly, recovering faster than she did. When he spoke, he echoed the words in her mind.

"That was a mistake."

Nine

The following two days passed in a flurry of activity.

Stefanie didn't take the time to sit around and wonder what motivation lurked beneath her kissing Emmett, and she certainly didn't give any brain space as to why he'd kissed her back.

Until this morning.

She'd slipped into the bathroom and showered, replaying the kiss and Emmett's reaction to it. He wasn't wrong. It had been a mistake to kiss him. And yet she'd wanted to kiss him again ever since. She had the tendency to lean in whenever she felt the urge, and that night she'd *literally* leaned in.

After climbing out of the shower she blow-dried her hair, her mind a tangle of confusion. Mostly because kissing Emmett had felt undeniably right when it shouldn't have felt anything less than...wrong.

With no resolution in sight, she tabled the thoughts and set out from the B and B with a list and Emmett in tow. She had plans to finalize not only for the charity Christmas dinner but also for the wedding in which she was one of the main participants.

She could hardly believe she was going to be married tonight.

"May I help you?" a pretty dark-haired woman at the counter of the bridal boutique asked.

"Yes, I purchased a Vera Wang wedding dress yesterday and paid extra to have it taken in by today."

The small boutique in San Antonio had displayed the Vera Wang on a mannequin in a glass case under lock and key. It was one of a kind, and exactly the type of wedding dress she would've picked out for a real wedding. Not that this wasn't real, but she wasn't in love, so that made it *less* real.

"Tonight's my wedding night."

"Congratulations!"

But announcing it hadn't made it any less surreal.

"Sandy Phillips." An older woman emerged from the back and greeted Stefanie using her alias. The last thing Stef needed was word leaking to the media that she was buying a wedding gown. "Danielle, could you please pull the vintage Vera Wang for Ms. Phillips?"

"Of course." Danielle vanished behind a curtain and Nancy, who was also the owner of the store, patted Stef's hand.

"Are you excited? It's the big day!"

If by excited she meant nauseous and ready to get it over with, then yes. Yes, she was.

"Very."

"Is that your beau out front?"

Stefanie turned to the wide plate glass window. Emmett's SUV idled at the curb, the passenger-side window cracked, probably to release some of the warmth from the cab. He'd accused her of "cooking him" by turning up the heat on the passenger side, but she couldn't help it that San Antonio was suffering a cold spell.

"That's him."

"Yum." Nancy gave her a conspiratorial wink.

After Stef had slipped into her dress to ensure the alterations were perfect—they were—she carried her dress to the car and draped the opaque black bag over the back seat.

"Need help?" Emmett asked over his shoulder.

"No. I have it." She closed the back door, then opened her own, climbing inside and buckling up. At least the sun was out today. The snow had turned into rain and what white stuff was decorating the ground and windowsills had melted away. "That's the last item on my to-do list."

As he pulled onto the highway, she spotted a Starbucks sign on the horizon, and her mouth watered for a cinnamony, nutmeggy, sugary concoction.

"Coffee!" she exclaimed. "Coffee and then I'm done with my to-do list."

"Here?" He pointed at a fast-food place as they passed by. At her aghast reaction, he chuckled, the sound low and comforting. "Kidding."

The thirty-minute drive back to the B and B was quiet, mostly because she was cocooning a toasted-marshmallow white-chocolate mocha. Seriously. So good.

"Is this how you imagined your wedding day?" Emmett broke the silence, glanced in the rearview and changed lanes smoothly.

"Every detail. Right down to the mocha and a fiancé I had to beg to enter with me into holy matrimony." She smiled and he returned it, holding her gaze for a beat before he put his eyes on the road again.

An odd ripple of comfort spilled down her spine. How was it that he made this outrageous situation seem normal?

And how strange was it that she was proud to have chosen him as her groom, and relieved that he'd said yes to her proposal?

Emmett had experienced many catered charity dinners as a kid. Up close and way too personal. More than a few times his father had dragged him to a local church that hosted Christmas dinners for the "needy." Emmett had always hated that word. To him, it implied that he was taking what he hadn't earned, even though the parishioners never made them feel anything less than welcome.

He remembered wearing his coat to fend off a draft in a dusty gymnasium and squeezing in with strangers and no

elbow room at a battered plywood banquet table. Not that
he hadn't appreciated the efforts of the volunteers serving
those dinners—he had. But the food had always been accompanied by a hefty dose of shame. He'd kept his ball
cap pulled low and his head down, fearing he'd run into
someone he knew.

He'd vowed, while eating many meals of oversalted vegetables and tough meat, that the very second he was old
enough to find a job, he would. *And* he'd make enough
money to eat Christmas dinner at his own table in his own
house. He'd never liked being served, and it took him several years to warm to the idea of going out to restaurants.

But setting foot inside the venue Stefanie had prepared
for her charity dinner didn't bring back memories of those
days. Mainly because the venue was nothing like the dusty
gym packed with wobbly tables.

The former banquet hall and restaurant had been maintained by a private owner in Harlington for rental during special occasions. Unlike a YMCA or gymnasium, the
room was outfitted with wide round tables covered with
shimmery gold tablecloths. The entire setup—from the
elegant white plates to the stemware and the regal center-
pieces of pinecones and white flowers—reminded him of
a fancy Ferguson affair.

"What do you think?" Stefanie looked up at him, her
grin proud.

He nodded, and then figured that after her hard work she
deserved an actual compliment. "I'm impressed."

"Thanks!" She skipped off to the catering staff and another gaggle of people he assumed to be volunteers.

Hosting a party. Yeah, she was in her element all right.

The families had yet to arrive, but everyone else was
in place. Volunteers dressed in T-shirts emblazoned with
the words HARLINGTON CARES waited at the mouth of
what Emmett assumed was the kitchen—no buffet setup

here. Stefanie directed a few of the volunteers toward different points around the room. Three enormous trees dripped with ornaments and were surrounded by teetering stacks of wrapped gifts.

The air smelled of roasted meat and underlying scents of herbs and butter. Emmett's stomach rumbled. Lunch had happened too long ago, especially now that his nose had caught a hint of what awaited him.

"Hey, this is where we're sitting." Stef grabbed his hand and tugged him to a table in the rear of the room, near one of the trees. A metal sign in the center read VOLUNTEERS.

"I'm here as your security guy, not a guest," he said as his stomach clenched in protest.

"Hank and Albert over there are police officers, so you may stand down. Besides, what better way to protect me than sitting by my side?" She leaned in, her hand still warming his. "And it's your last chance to eat and gather your strength before our wedding."

At the reminder of what was to come tonight, his stomach clenched for an entirely different reason. Her beautiful blue eyes, flaxen hair and indelible smile hadn't changed, but since he'd allowed himself to taste those lips, the way he saw her *had* changed. No longer was she the untouchable sister of the mayor. Not since she'd touched him and he'd touched her back. The idea of having her as his had taken root and, without his permission, had outgrown Jack's bean stalk.

He'd felt the burn of lust for her since that unexpected kiss, and after they exchanged vows, he'd be damned if he'd back off.

There was only one way to go with this woman, and that was forward.

"You're the one who'd better gather your strength." He

leaned in, his breath warming her ear. "Tonight I'm not sleeping on the cold floor alone."

Her mouth dropped open but no words came out.

"What we do in bed is your call." This close to her he could watch as her pupils darkened. "But we're sharing the covers tonight."

"I thought—" she blinked a few times until she found the rest of that sentence "—the kiss was a mistake."

Yeah, well. He'd thought it was, too.

And then they spent the next two days together and all he could think about was taking her lips captive again. Running his fingers into her soft hair this time, tilting her head and stroking her tongue with his...

Easy.

Last thing he needed was to get hard at a charity dinner.

"There's no taking it back now." There wasn't any forgetting it, either. Last night he'd lain awake in the chilled room wondering if Stef was awake, too, eyes on the ceiling, her mind on him. "You'll have to kiss me one more time before we return to our room. Together. On our wedding night."

"Your wedding night!" A plump, smiling, dark-skinned woman approached and wrapped Stefanie in a hug. "Sandy, you didn't tell me you were engaged! Introduce me!"

"Emmett, this is Lakesha. Lakesha, Emmett." Evidently there was no need for him to have a fake name.

"I've worked with Sandy for two years in a row and I love her to bits and pieces. Probably as much as you do." Lakesha shoved his chest and then squeezed one of his pecs. "Oh, and he's solid as a rock. Nicely done."

She high-fived Stef and Emmett snapped a look from one to the other. Never before had he been *high-fived* over. A reluctant smile itched the corner of his mouth.

Not only had Stef proposed to him, she'd initiated a kiss and now *claimed* him. He straightened his shoulders, forcing his posture into a stance that he hoped made him look like he belonged with her. A bizarrely heady thought since he knew he didn't.

Stef lowered her voice to just above a whisper. "Do me a favor and keep it under wraps. My family doesn't know yet."

Lakesha visibly bristled and peeked around to make sure no one had overheard. Then pulled an invisible zipper over her lips and winked up at Emmett. "My lips are sealed."

Emmett watched his fiancée from the edge of the party, choosing to sandwich roasted turkey breast on a roll rather than sit down for dinner. The police officers who were working the event deserved to enjoy their meals.

Stef didn't sit much, either, hopping up to give a waiter direction or hustle off to the kitchen. He watched her stop at least six times in front of one of the Christmas trees to rearrange the donated presents, or fuss over bow or ribbon placement. She was ridiculously adorable. It was the first time he was able to watch her with unabashed admiration, no other eyes on him caring that he did, so he watched. Watched her with equal parts pride and wonder.

He'd known Stefanie in relation to Chase. He knew she was wild, quick-witted, sharp—and from observing her cry happy tears at Zach and Penelope's wedding, a romantic sap.

He smiled to himself at the thought. She was tender and open alongside headstrong and determined, and those combined traits made her even more attractive to him.

He could do a lot worse in the wife department. She could do a hell of a lot better in the husband one.

Even dressed down in black pants and a white sweater with sparkling gold thread woven into it, Stefanie Ferguson looked like royalty. Or at the very least a celebrity.

He couldn't believe no one had recognized her, but then he guessed she was mostly of interest to the city's elite. The good people of Harlington, Texas, had bigger priorities than a Dallas it girl. Working hard to provide for their families, putting food on the table and shopping for school clothes for their kids took a lot of focus and effort. He could relate.

After his mother and brother died, Emmett had taken on the role of parent. Van stopped caring, damn near stopped breathing. He mostly sat in front of the television, oxygen tank at his side and a glazed expression on his face courtesy of the prescription medication.

At age ten, Emmett had been as responsible as an adult. He'd mowed lawns, picked up groceries for his elderly neighbors and had let some of the smaller kids in school pay him to play bodyguard. Anything to bring in cash so he could put food in his belly and his father's.

A little girl approached Stefanie, a battered stuffed teddy bear in her arms, and Stef knelt to give her a hug. Her face was so genuine and her touch so light, his chest give a tug. She wasn't doing this for the publicity but for the people. He was beginning to see why she'd kept her secret, too. Chase talked to her as if he were in charge of her. As if she were a princess locked in a tower. Emmett could understand her desire to escape home and make her own way. He'd felt like that a lot growing up.

The remnants of dinner and dessert cleared, they moved on to the gift portion of the evening. A dressed Santa in red-and-white velvet was stationed at each tree handing out gifts to the kids.

Emmett watched from afar, sipping on a cup of cocoa delivered to him by Lakesha with another wink, a squeeze of his biceps and a "Congratulations, again!" And then something remarkable happened. He began to feel comfortable at the last place he should—at a charity dinner for the financially challenged…and as Stefanie's fiancé with only a few hours to go until they were husband and wife.

Ten

"That's new." Stefanie let out an uncomfortable laugh when she spotted what was hanging over the entrance of the B and B.

"What's new?" Emmett asked as he turned into the driveway.

"Mistletoe. Yikes."

"Thought you loved Christmas. Isn't mistletoe a holiday staple?"

"No." She had firm feelings about it and none of them were positive.

"No?" His tone was bemused. He parked, but let the engine idle, turning to face her in the dark cab of the SUV. "You're a romantic who loves Christmas and you don't put stock in the tradition of kissing beneath the mistletoe?"

"Well…neither do you, Scrooge. What's the big deal?"

"The *big deal* is that it makes sense for me because I hate Christmas, but you… It makes no sense."

They had a narrow-eyed standoff. "O Holy Night" played quietly on the radio alongside the gentle blow of heat from the vents.

"I told you my story. Tell me yours."

He had her there. On a sigh, she began the sordid tale.

"I was at a Christmas party with my parents when I was thirteen. This kid in my class—a piggish oaf named Reggie Meeks—grabbed me and kissed me underneath the mistletoe. Then he bragged to his stupid friends that I made out with him. Like, hot and heavy *made out*. Meanwhile, I ran into the nearest bathroom and swished with mouthwash until my teeth hurt."

Emmett chuckled.

"It's not funny!"

"You're right." He sobered some but his lips quirked as if he was hiding a smile. "He has an unfortunate name and it's not his fault."

She balled up her fist and punched Emmett's arm, which was like hitting a steel beam. She shook her hand out and frowned.

"I'm kidding." He took her hand and rubbed her knuckles, his palm warm and his eyes warmer. "It's *not* funny that a kid bullied you into a kiss. But holding a grudge against an innocent plant is criminal. You didn't make any new memories under the mistletoe after that?"

"Nope. One kiss from Reggie and I was scarred for life." She shuddered and this time Emmett's soft laughter didn't rankle her. "Thank you. For coming with me to the dinner. I could tell you didn't want to be there. I'm sure there was enough Christmas cheer in there to make you want to hide in a cave."

"It wasn't so bad." He let go of her hand and watched out the windshield, the attractive planes of his face highlighted in the dashboard lights.

He'd been through hell on Christmas Day, and he'd sworn off the happiest holiday because of it. He of all people should understand her grudge against kissing under mistletoe.

How about that? They had something in common.

Outside, the cold wind bit through her clothes and chilled her skin. Emmett walked beside her, head down, hands in his pockets.

"The big moment is fast approaching." He stopped at the bottom of three steps leading to the door. "You sure you want to do this?"

"Positive. I don't like being bullied. By Reggie Meeks *or* Blake Eastwood. I refuse to let Blake push me around like…" She trailed off, considering she might be doing the same to Emmett. Meeting his dark stare, she proceeded carefully. "Are you sure *you* want to do this? Are you feeling pressured? I'd never want to put you in a position—"

He cut off her words with a kiss before she knew what had hit her. His arm lashed against her lower back, he hauled her against the hard wall of his body and laid his lips on hers. The touch of his mouth to hers ignited sparks between them and suddenly the cold air didn't feel so cold.

Her gloveless fingers curled into the lapels of his coat and she dragged him closer, the scrape of the scruff on his chin chafing her sensitive skin. He finished the kiss with one brief stroke of his tongue before reverently kissing her top lip, then her bottom lip. He held her close as she inhaled a ragged breath and blew it out on a puff of steam. He cocked an eyebrow as if waiting for her reaction, but she couldn't muster up one save clinging to him like garland around a Christmas tree.

His eyes turned up and hers followed, to the mistletoe dangling overhead. When their gazes met again, he said, "Time for both of us to make better Christmas memories."

"Oh my heavens! I knew that mistletoe was a bad idea." Margaret stood at the B and B's front door, having flung it open. Their hostess's eyes danced merrily. "I'm teasing. If I were getting married at the stroke of midnight on Christmas Day I'd feel romantic, too."

Stef slipped away from him, sending him a flirty little smile before wrapping her arm in Margaret's. They walked inside, Stef and Margaret chattering about the ceremony, Emmett hanging back. Margaret's son, the officiant of the wedding, stood in the foyer eating a piece of pie. He put his fork down to shake Emmett's hand.

Emmett listened with half an ear as Lyle discussed the

upcoming ceremony, but his attention was on Stefanie. She was wringing her fingers like she was the one with a case of the nerves. He could understand why. She'd probably been planning her future wedding day since she was a young girl, and he hazarded the very safe guess that it didn't involve marrying a man like him. She'd been stoic about their nuptials so far. This was the first time he'd seen her jittery.

A cocky part of him wanted to believe that it wasn't their wedding that had knocked her off-kilter, but the kiss. It sure as hell had short-circuited his brain.

Sliding a stray lock of blond hair behind her ear, she stole a quick look at him, her lashes dipping almost demurely. They'd share another kiss like that soon enough, this time in front of an audience since Margaret had arranged for a few of the B and B guests to be in attendance for the ceremony.

"I also made a cake." Margaret waved when Stefanie protested that she didn't have to do that, and argued, "It was my pleasure. Now, you two go upstairs and change. When you hear the music, you come on in and we'll start... Unless you had a more formal entrance in mind?"

"No..." Stefanie's eyes flashed to Emmett's like she was checking in with him. He agreed with a subtle head shake. "We want to keep it simple."

At the stairs, she gripped the banister, and he took her other hand, gently weaving his fingers with hers as they ascended the staircase. He only let her go to unlock their room and usher her in.

"Do you want to change in here or the bathroom?" she asked, taking the bagged dress from the closet and tossing it onto the bed. "Or should we adhere to the notion that it's bad luck if you see me in the dress before the wedding?"

She wasn't asking for reassurance. The expression on

her face was sheer determination. No longer jittery, she was a woman on a mission.

"I think the concept of bad luck is bullshit."

"Doesn't buy into the concepts of Christmas miracles or true love or bad luck. Got it."

"I didn't say anything about love." He might be incomplete, his heart less than whole, but he'd seen plenty of evidence that true love exists. Chase and Miriam. Zach and Penelope. Even Stef's parents, Rider and Elle. Just because it wasn't in the cards for Emmett didn't mean it wasn't real. "But you're right on the other two."

She unzipped the garment bag, revealing a sheath of white. He fought the urge to turn his back. To give her privacy or to keep himself in suspense, he wasn't sure which.

"I find it hard to believe you'd agree to marry me out of obligation if you thought your Mrs. Right was out there."

"I agreed to marry you because you made a good case for me to do so. Also, it's terrifying to think of some poor woman tied to me for life."

"That's an awful thing to say to your fiancée!" Her tone was teasing, and so was the feisty twinkle in her eyes.

"My *fiancée* was smart enough to include an escape hatch. You'll be done with me in a few months' time."

Which was best for all parties involved. He could give her what she needed in this moment—a husband—but couldn't give her the forever kind of love she deserved.

He tipped her chin, tempted to kiss her again to feel her lips soften beneath his. He liked the way she'd melted against him earlier; liked the heated way she looked at him now.

"I'll change first and meet you downstairs. Do you need help with the dress?"

"I've got it."

"Is it bad luck to kiss my bride before the wedding if she's not in her wedding dress?"

"I don't think so." She gripped his coat with both hands and tugged him closer. "Kisses are usually good luck."

"Good luck," he said as he lowered his mouth to hers, "I believe in."

Eleven

Her husband-to-be was ready in minutes, dressed in dark slacks and a white shirt, with a tie he'd purchased in town. At her request, he'd tried on a few suits at the store, but after unsuccessfully wedging his wide shoulders into three ill-fitting jackets, she'd given him a pass.

Even so, he looked *really* good in the cheery red tie that arrowed down his torso and pointed at the thick leather belt. Good enough that she'd given that tie a yank and brought his lips to hers for another kiss.

How they'd return to this room as husband and wife and keep their hands off each other was beyond her. It was also a prospect that was becoming less and less desirable. They hadn't talked about how they'd proceed, but a loveless *and* celibate marriage seemed unfair, unpleasant at best.

She had no doubt Emmett would be able to compartmentalize sex apart from love and marriage, but could she? In theory it sounded easy, but in practice…

Sex muddied the mind and blurred lines. And whenever a past relationship inevitably met its demise, love had been unmasked to reveal its true identity: infatuation.

Love had been an elusive beast for Stef so far. It was one of the reasons she was sure that an arranged marriage with Emmett would work. How could two people who hated each other fall for each other? But the kisses they'd shared so far were proof that he had a bigger effect on her than she'd previously acknowledged.

A *physical* effect.

While she didn't have a problem with attraction, being attracted to him was foreign. And like any other unfamiliar circumstance, she was both excited and nervous to explore. Could they proceed without getting carried away? She wasn't sure. Even the most carefully managed campfire had the potential to spread.

A soft rap on her door brought her out of her ponderings. Margaret's muffled voice announced, "Do you need help with anything, dear?"

When Stefanie opened the door Margaret cupped her mouth with her hands, the older woman's eyes welling with tears.

"Oh, you're a vision!"

"Thank you." Stef turned to admire her dress in the full-length mirror standing in the corner of the room. The sheath dress featured a lacy pattern over the bodice and slim skirt. The halter neckline was supported by thin spaghetti straps that ran over her shoulder blades, fastening at the middle of her back. There was a cutout showing a slice of her lower back. It was sexy but simple—exactly her taste.

"I brought you this, but you don't have to wear it if you don't want to." From behind her back, Margaret produced a hair clip studded with white baby's breath, green leaves and poinsettia petals. "Is it too much?"

"Not at all." Stefanie stroked the petals of the delicate live bouquet. "It's beautiful."

"I made it." Margaret pointed at the greenery. "That's mistletoe. We had extra."

Stef chuckled. To new Christmas memories indeed.

She turned around and Margaret fastened the flowers in place at the back of Stefanie's updo.

"I have your bouquet downstairs waiting for you. My, does your man look handsome."

"Yes, he has that way about him. Does he also look nervous?"

"My son poured him a few inches of bourbon and joined him in a prewedding toast. Lyle says that it's common practice whenever he officiates a ceremony. But to answer your question, no. Emmett doesn't seem nervous. More…excited. Like he's anticipating seeing you. You're going to knock him out cold."

"Maybe I overshot it." Stefanie swept her hands down her sleek skirt. "My goal was simply to keep him at the ceremony until the end."

"Don't worry about that. I'll lock the front door." Margaret elbowed Stef's arm playfully. "Want me to walk down with you? I'll situate the train of your dress and then run downstairs and out of the way."

At the staircase, Margaret took up a length of the dress's skirt and spread it behind her. Stef rested her hand on the railing to keep from tumbling face-first into her own wedding. Her heart pounded mercilessly with each step she took, her mind on her family and how they were going to absolutely freak out when they learned she'd done this without them.

"Miles!" Margaret called from the top of the stairs. "Your photographer," she whispered to Stefanie. "I'll step out of your shot."

Margaret fluffed Stefanie's dress once more before a thin man with a thick dark mustache stepped around the corner. He lifted his camera, and Stef did her best to hide her thoughts about her family and focus on the present. She smiled as she had for years of family portraits and interviews and a zillion Ferguson Oil events. She was schooled in how to smile with her eyes and position her face for the most flattering angle. As a flash lit the room, she carefully walked down the stairs as classic Christmas carols played in the living room.

Five steps from the bottom, though, her smile faltered, the photographer and guests and background music forgotten. Emmett had been en route to the living room but didn't make it all the way in. He stopped, frozen solid, his mouth dropped open in a gentle gape. Blue-gray eyes scanned her from head to toe, heating when they returned to meet hers.

Margaret tutted and took his arm, practically dragging him into the living room, but not before Emmett's lips curved and he threw Stefanie a sexy, devil-may-care wink over his shoulder.

From his position next to the minister, Emmett swallowed past a dry throat and rubbed together sweaty palms. He'd fooled himself into believing that standing in as a groom would be the same as serving as a groomsman...not that he'd done that before, either. But he'd *attended* weddings before, so he knew the routine.

Watching Stefanie walk toward him in a long white dress was nothing like watching another bride make her way to her groom—mostly because this time, the groom was *him*.

"You've got this," Margaret's son, Lyle, assured him under his breath. He dipped his chin and opened his Bible, and Emmett felt a wobble in his knees that made him wonder how many grooms bit the dust before the vows started.

If what he was feeling were nerves, that'd be not only normal, but expected. But it wasn't nerves that he was struggling with. It was responsibility.

Emmett didn't take his responsibility for others lightly, including this trip with Stefanie. He'd mistakenly assumed that his responsibility was untangling her from Blake by marrying him herself. That the act of saying "I do" would be the end of it.

Wrong.

Stefanie, a red smile on her mouth, her blond hair wound softly at the back of her head, a bouquet of red poinsettias offsetting the stark white of her dress, had made him feel another sort of responsibility for her. He was overcome with the notion of becoming a husband.

Her husband.

Right here. Right now. In front of God and witnesses. And there was nothing mild about that commitment.

In the same way he worked hard to assure himself he earned every dollar he was paid, he wasn't going to marry Stefanie halfway. No matter how they'd originally thought this would go, for him, the ceremony was real. In every way.

Stefanie came to a stop in front of him and sureness rang through him, resonating like a church bell. He wouldn't enter into this commitment lightly. He would give himself to her—as much as he was able—for as long as this marriage lasted.

Margaret stepped in to take Stefanie's bouquet and Lyle instructed Emmett to hold Stefanie's hands.

He did as he was asked, clasping his bride's fingers with his own and meeting her gaze. He nearly sailed off into her aquamarine eyes.

Vows were repeated.

Rings were exchanged.

Her soft "I do" socked him like a punch to the gut.

"What God has joined together, let no one separate." Lyle closed his Bible. "You may now kiss your bride."

Emmett leaned in and pressed his lips to Stefanie's for what was supposed to be a brief kiss. It didn't stay that way. Moving his mouth on hers now that they were married came with a proprietary feeling, giving their union meaning beyond the agreement they'd made. Every pass of his lips over hers was him claiming her as his.

When the kiss ended, their small audience applauded.

His bride's eyes twinkled like the white lights draped over every surface in the room, her beautiful form silhouetted against a white-and-gold Christmas tree. He itched to haul her over his shoulder and take her upstairs, wanting nothing more than to continue their kiss and see how far she'd let him take her.

"I'll pour the champagne!" Margaret announced, snapping him out of the fantasy.

"Champagne?" Emmett asked Stef as the guests stood from their chairs.

"For the toast." She swiped his bottom lip with her thumb and explained, "Lipstick."

"I don't want to have a toast. I want to go to bed." His voice was gravel. His body taut with the desire that felt like a physical presence between them. He let that sentence hang long enough for her eyes to widen. They went wider when he added, "With you."

So, yeah. She needed that champagne.

Unfortunately, one glass of bubbly wasn't going to be enough to erase the X-rated vision of Emmett naked. She didn't know how much longer she could hang out at this party before hauling her husband upstairs and stripping his clothes off.

Alarming, that thought. She'd known Emmett for years and had never once pictured him naked. Pictured him kissing her. Pictured him as her husband. And yet here they were. Kissing. Married. And about to be *very* naked.

"Congratulations, Mrs. Keaton." Anna, a waifish blonde, was one of the guests at the B and B. She and her husband, Clay, had been married a little over a year ago and were here celebrating their first anniversary.

"Thank you."

"The first year is challenging, but in a good way. Don't believe anyone who tells you the honeymoon is over if they overhear you arguing."

"Ha. Well. Emmett and I argue a lot, so nothing new there."

"Even better. The makeup sex is worth it." Anna giggled. Stefanie felt Emmett hovering nearby but wasn't about to turn to find out if he'd overheard.

Anna stepped away from the crowd a few feet and beckoned Stef to follow. In the foyer between the staircase and the living room, the other woman leaned close. "I know who you are," she whispered with a smile. "It took me a while to place you and then I realized where I'd seen your photo. The Dallas Duchess."

"Oh?" Stefanie maintained a neutral expression and tone even as her heart ratcheted up a few notches. That damn blogger.

"What made you decide against a massive wedding in the summer packed with famous guests? Also, I thought you'd be marrying Blake Eastwood. Does your family know you're not?"

Stefanie squirmed at Anna's forwardness and rapid-fire questions.

"I haven't said anything to anyone, and I won't," Anna promised. "But if you don't mind my asking, why are you in Harlington marrying Emmett when that Blake guy said you were his?"

Stef had fielded rumors a million times, but never face-to-face to a nosy woman with zero tact.

"Simple," interrupted a deep, rumbling voice. "Blake's a liar."

Anna started at Emmett's arrival, her mouth gaping. Stef wanted to kiss him for his fantastic timing.

"I need to borrow my bride." He scooped Stefanie into his arms and the small crowd reacted with approving gasps.

"We saved ourselves for the wedding night," he announced. "We're skipping the toast."

Twelve

"Thank you for that," Stefanie said as Emmett set her on her feet in their room. "I have never encountered... What are you doing?"

"Taking off this neck noose." He yanked his tie free and tossed it on the dresser. Then he stalked toward her, standing so close that her dress brushed against his pants. She glanced down and gulped. His *tented* pants. His hand slipped over her back, tickling her bare skin through the cutout in her dress.

"Emmett."

"Tell me to stop. Tell me it doesn't matter that we're married, that you don't want me to touch you."

His words were low and desperate, but his hands never stopped sampling her exposed skin. His fingers trickled up her spine, and his other hand tipped her chin, forcing her to meet his stormy eyes.

"If I kiss your lips again—" he traced her collarbone with the tip of one finger "—then I'll want to kiss you here next." He clasped her waist with one wide hand. "Then I'll want to kiss you here."

That same hand molded her hip and Stefanie's breathing went shallow.

"And then everywhere," he growled. Only a breath separated them. She felt the barest brush of his lips on hers as her name exited his throat like a plea. "Stef."

She closed that minuscule gap and met his mouth with hers. All she'd wanted to do since he'd kissed her under the mistletoe this evening was touch him more. She melted into him, but where her strength faded, his tripled. His fists wound in the delicate material of her dress as he made good on his promise, moving those drugging kisses down her jawline, past her throat and over her collarbone.

A moan sounded—hers. She hadn't counted on shared attraction as part of this bargain, but it was there in spades. And if he thought she would hold up the stop sign now that they were in their shared room, he was crazy.

Crazy for her, apparently.

She couldn't help smiling at the thought as he unzipped the back of her dress, only to swear when he found a second zipper lower on the skirt.

"You find this funny?" Growly and sort of grumpy. Her scrooge.

"I find you impatient." She fingered the top button of his shirt and unfastened it. "What's your hurry?"

"I want to taste you slowly, but I want you naked *now*."

"I want you the same way, cowboy." She flicked open another button, then one more.

He slipped the straps of her dress off her shoulders, the rough pads of his fingers causing goose bumps to crop up on her arms. She pushed his shirt open and reached for the undershirt tucked into his pants. The second his belly, and the line of dark hair pointing to his belt buckle, was revealed she flattened her hand over his abs.

He sucked in a sharp breath, his chest expanding impressively. She ran both hands up his torso and cupped his pectorals, the whorls of hair on his chest tickling her palms.

"Damn," she muttered, overcome by the sheer brawniness of him. "You're so big."

"You ain't seen nothin' yet." He stole her breath with another deep kiss, slipping her dress past her hips and leaving her standing in her bra and panties. "What's this?" A deep laugh transformed his face. He looped a finger in the white lace garter belt and snapped the elastic, lightly stinging her thigh.

"Tradition," she said on the end of a gasp.

"Damn," he concluded before kissing her again.

Her fingers fumbled with his belt, her mind on the way he'd looked the first time she'd laid eyes on him in boxer briefs. *Substantial.* But rather than be intimidating, everything about his size only served to make her feel safe.

"I won't break," she assured him when he loosened his hold on her.

"I won't let you."

He ran the flat of his palm between her breasts and pulled the cups away, freeing her. When he dipped his head to suck a nipple onto his tongue, she grabbed his head both to encourage him and to keep from slipping off the edge of the earth. He repeated the favor on the other breast and then her bra was gone, swept away while sparks shimmered over her sensitized skin.

He dipped one thick finger past the edge of her lace panties and brushed her sex with his knuckle. She gasped, damp and ready for him, and they'd only just begun.

"Merry Christmas to me," he said before tucking both hands into the back of her panties and sliding them down her legs. On his knees in front of her, he took a long look at her. She admired the heat in his eyes, the open white shirt and exposed shoulders. His unbuckled belt.

Him on his knees before her.

"I like you here." She raked her hand through his short hair.

His mouth curved with a devilish tilt. "Worshipping you?"

She nodded.

"Bet you're used to that."

"Hardly." The men she'd shared a bed with in her past hadn't been particularly...noteworthy. She liked sex and pleasure, and didn't mind giving as well as receiving, but she'd never use the word *worship* to describe a past interaction. "I can't say I've experienced that."

"A first. Then allow me to worship you." He leaned closer, his warm breath coasting over the scant stripe of hair on her sex. "My *queen*."

Oh yes. That was working for her. Her face warmed, her thighs pressing together in anticipation of the delicious feel of his tongue on her.

He didn't make her wait, slicking her center so slowly her legs shook.

He encouraged her to sit on the bed. Then he was on his feet, ripping off his shirts and dropping his pants. The bulge in his boxers was as impressive as the rest of him, the thick ridge a promise of the inches to come.

He returned to his task, burying his face between her thighs, and delivering blow after blow of pleasure while she twisted on the comforter. He didn't tell her to come, or command her in any way with his words. Ever the strong, silent type, Emmett let his actions speak for him as he laved her mercilessly.

She let go on a cry that filled the room. The orgasm took its time washing over her and he kept his pace steady until her entire body was sex warmed and sated.

He placed a kiss on each of her inner thighs and then drew a line of kisses up her body as he ascended. Over her, he was more hulking than usual, his turgid cock resting heavily on one of her thighs, his lips glistening, his eyes so lust filled they were almost black.

"I have a condom," she told him. "In my suitcase."

He didn't hesitate to cross the room.

"The zipper pocket."

He pulled out a condom, raised an eyebrow and dropped it back into the pocket. She propped up on her elbows to protest.

"What's wrong?" she asked as he knelt in front of his duffel.

"Too small," was all he said. Then he stood and shucked

his boxers and she got an eyeful of *exactly* why the condoms she'd purchased were "too small."

"Merry Christmas to *me*," she murmured, reciting his words from earlier.

He grinned, his chest puffing with male pride, and rolled on the protection from his bag. Then he came to her in fluid movements that should've belonged to a much slighter man.

"You okay?"

His face pinched like he was concerned about her answer. Like she should demurely ask if he was sure he would fit or maybe remind him not to hurt her. She'd do no such thing.

She could handle every inch of her husband's gorgeous member. *Gladly.*

"I'm better than okay, Em." She grasped his biceps and encouraged him forward. *"Bring it."*

There was something beautiful about him at the brink of making love to her. He was a sculpted specimen, perfectly hewed to pleasure a woman. The twinkle in his eye was merry, but determination set his powerful jaw.

"You got it, honey."

He lowered his body between her legs, his hard abdomen lying against her softer belly. He notched the tip into her entrance and slid in slowly, watching her with an intensity that suggested he was in far more pain than she.

"I'm fine. Really."

Then he slid in deeper and she was better than fine.

She arched her neck and enjoyed the fullness of that first thrust, the feel of him seated deep while her body adjusted to his girth. Then she opened her eyes and met his, holding tight to his shoulders as he drew away inch by excruciating inch.

He made love to her as he promised. Slowly. Seductively. Already sensitive from his earlier pampering, her next release didn't take long to build.

Emmett's face was crimped in concentration as he unerringly sought and found the spot that would crumble her will to hold out. She wanted his release more than her own, having already taken advantage of his mouth.

She wanted *him* to let go.

She wanted to watch every second of him coming and record it in her memory.

Because that was what this would be. A memory. As he tenderly slid in again, she reminded herself that they were pretending—that they might be swept up in each other tonight, but the end would soon come for both of them.

"Gorgeous," he praised. "Every inch of you. You feel incredible."

She palmed his cheek, the rough scrape of his scruff sending chills over her entire body. He was pretty damned incredible, too, but she wasn't capable of forming words at the moment.

"Close?" he asked.

"Don't worry about me," she breathed.

He laughed, a low rumble she felt in her rib cage. "Not worried, Stef."

"I want you to come first."

"No deal." His smile vanished, his eyes dark and his expression raw. He doubled his efforts, slowing the pace but increasing the intensity. He watched her like a bird of prey eyeing his next meal, not so much as blinking as he soaked in her every reaction.

When he hit the spot he was looking for, her high cry gave her away. His grin cocksure and beautiful, he lowered to his elbows and cupped her face. Pistoning his hips, he plunged into her faster and deeper, holding her close as she came apart at the seams.

This orgasm hit her harder than the first, the shuddering aftermath leading to a very disappointing realization.

Emmett had come with her and she'd missed the entire thing!

"Cheater," she huffed. "I was trying to make you do that."

"You did." He kissed the very tip of her nose.

"My eyes were closed!"

"I know. I watched." He kissed her chin.

It wasn't fair that he was the one getting the best show. The next time they did this, she'd be sure not to let him take over.

He slipped free of her warmth and she watched his ass as he padded into the attached bathroom. She considered what a dangerous thought it was to decide she'd have sex with her husband again, but she dismissed the concern just as quickly.

She wouldn't let him have the last word, no way. She was going to weaken his knees and melt his muscles at least once before they wrapped up this marriage.

Thirteen

It wasn't Emmett's first Christmas dinner with the Fergusons—far from it. They'd been taking him in as a stray since he'd become friends with Chase. It was almost humorous that he was as comfortable in Rider and Elle's massive mansion as he was in his own apartment, but he supposed he owed most of the credit to the company.

The Fergusons were billionaires—they made more money than Emmett could fathom even though he'd managed to accrue plenty of wealth for himself—but they were also down-to-earth and, at their core, a family.

So when he walked in with Stefanie fresh off the drive home from Harlington, he knew that the unease he felt had nothing to do with Christmas day with her family and everything to do with the fact that he'd married Zach and Chase's sister—Rider and Elle's daughter—and none of them knew it yet.

During the trip back, Stef had mentioned she wasn't going to share wedding pictures online until she broke the news to her family in person, and Emmett had agreed.

Sort of.

He'd suggested she call her siblings and parents and break it to them one by one. Stef had made the astute observation that one of them could tell the others before she did and then she wouldn't be in control of the spin.

Fair enough.

After a quick stop at her apartment to pack her family's gifts, they'd arrived at the elder Fergusons' estate at six o'clock on the nose. He shut off the engine and eyed the front door.

"We're late."

"It's your fault." She slid him a foxy smile that caused him to shift in his seat.

He remembered exactly why it was his fault. He'd been the one to wake her by dipping his head between her thighs. After exquisite morning sex, he'd gone downstairs and fetched breakfast, turned on the television and refused to leave bed until they'd had at least two cups of coffee and a stack of waffles apiece.

He hadn't wanted the morning to end for fear that reality would creep in like some reverse tale of Cinderella. As if, at the strike of noon, he'd be revealed as a servant rather than a prince.

A fraud, unworthy of her hand.

Stupid. But he'd lingered in that room nonetheless.

"Besides, I sent a text to Chase letting him know we'd be late so if he didn't pass that on, it's his fault." She bit her lip as Emmett shut off the car. "How angry with me do you think they're going to be?"

He couldn't keep from touching her, his thumb stroking her chin with affection. "They'll be pissed at me, not you."

"Don't be so sure. I'm the baby."

"Yes, but you're not *a* baby. You're a grown woman with an incredibly sharp mind and a generous heart. I'll take the brunt of the blame."

She grabbed his hand and tugged him forward, kissing him solidly. He was tempted to pull her into his lap and fog up the windshield before they went in.

It was like the floodgates had opened since that first kiss. Every time he'd touched her since, he couldn't get enough. It awed and amazed him how powerful her pull over him was; how he'd ignored—or maybe *denied* was a better word—that pull until now.

She rested her top teeth on her bottom lip as she took in her parents' house. "Here goes nothing."

They climbed from his SUV, piled his arms and hers with wrapped boxes and then went inside to face the Ferguson firing squad.

"How was she?" Chase pulled Emmett aside to ask.

The presents had been stacked beneath the tree—well, *around*. There wasn't any more room beneath the tree. Dinner had been postponed thirty minutes. As a result, Chase had a few inches of scotch in a glass and had taken it upon himself to check up on Stefanie with his right-hand guy.

Emmett reminded himself that his best friend slash employer had no idea that Emmett was in bed with her that very morning and answered accordingly.

"Smooth sailing."

"Good." Chase's intense glare lessened. "Merry Christmas."

"Merry Christmas." From an inside coat pocket, Emmett extracted an envelope and handed it over. "It's a museum membership for the year. I figured that'd be better than a jam-of-the-month club."

"You didn't have to—" Chase cut himself off. "Thank you, Em."

Emmett nodded his appreciation at Chase's acceptance and then deposited the other envelopes for Zach and Pen, Rider and Elle, and Stefanie under the tree. He knew none of them needed anything Emmett could provide, but he would never crash their Christmas empty-handed.

He kissed Elle's cheek when she walked in, a glass of champagne in hand. "Sorry we're late."

"I like eating late," Miriam, Chase's fiancée, said. She had no problem taking Emmett's side, especially if it meant disagreeing with Elle. Those two had a past patchier than the quilt on the B and B bed that Emmett and Stefanie had shared.

"I alerted the kitchen staff to keep everything warm since my daughter was going to show up whenever she pleased."

Stefanie's eyelids narrowed with determination. When her mouth opened, Emmett interjected.

"It's my fault. I slept in. Late Christmas Eve celebration."

"How was San Antonio?" Elle asked.

"About that... I have an announcement to make before dinner," Stef said, clearly uninterested in exchanging niceties. "Can you grab Daddy?"

"I'm here. I'm here." Rider stepped into the room with a martini in hand. "Emmett, drink?"

"I'd better."

He took one more glance around the room at Rider in a jacket and tie, Elle in a glittery black dress, Stefanie in a pink dress with lace sleeves. Zach and Pen walked in next, a sleeping Olivia on Zach's hip—all of them dressed to the nines, as well. Chase wore his usual suit and tie, and Miriam was in a green velvet dress. Emmett was in his standard security garb: black slacks, white shirt.

One of these doesn't belong.

As soon as Stefanie broke their news, that fact would become more apparent.

Emmett helped himself to scotch from the bar cart and Stefanie crossed the room to stand next to him. He meant to sip, but when she wove her fingers with his, he downed his scotch in one long, burning swallow before setting the glass on the cart.

"Emmett and I didn't go to San Antonio. We were in Harlington, a small town outside San Antonio where I hosted a dinner for families who can't afford their own Christmas celebrations."

Like mine, he thought numbly.

"Harlington?" Elle said, barely above a whisper, her eyes homed in on Stef and Emmett's linked hands.

"Also, while we were there, Emmett and I were married."

"Oh my God." That was Penelope. She'd been the one to suggest Stefanie get married to extract herself from the Blake situation. Emmett could tell by her reaction that she hadn't meant for Stef to take her suggestion to heart… and she sure as hell hadn't expected Emmett to take Stef up on it.

"Married." Chase spoke next, his tone lethal with disapproval. Miriam stood at his side, her lips pursed as if she was deciding how to process the news herself.

Other than those two comments, no one said a word. Though Zach's hardened jaw suggested he might have reacted if his two-year-old daughter weren't sleeping in his arms.

"We've been in denial about our attraction for quite some time," Stef started.

"This is about Blake," Chase said, not buying it for a second. "You did this to distract from the rumors about you and Blake. And Emmett agreed because you railroaded him into it."

"I did not!" But to Emmett, his wife's tone sounded like an admission of guilt.

"Stefanie." Pen stepped closer, shaking her head. "I didn't mean for—"

"It's not true," Stefanie continued lying. "That may seem like a convenient explanation, but Emmett and I are in love. It's Christmas and we were swept away and—"

"You were married without your family." Elle's voice was both hurt and hard at the same time. "You married Emmett without the approval of your father? Without any of us in attendance?" Her burning gaze hit Emmett next. "We invited you into this family years ago, believing we could trust you, and this is how you repay us?"

"That's on me," Chase said. "I was the one who trusted him to watch over my sister. Which is it, Emmett? Are you in love with her or are you helping her through this Blake debacle to repair the damage done to her reputation and my campaign?"

Stefanie opened her mouth to speak, but Chase held up a hand to stave her off.

"Emmett?" Chase pressed, daring him to lie. Which he wouldn't do.

"We're not in love, but we are attracted to each other," Emmett said. He wouldn't lie to this family. And he wouldn't lie to Stefanie. "The marriage works on both fronts. We can explore our attraction, and Blake no longer has a leg to stand on."

Rider was a wall of displeasure, his face creased, his martini glass empty. He glared at Emmett for a long beat before jerking his eyes to his daughter.

"How long are you planning to carry on with this farce?" Rider asked her.

"It's not a farce, Daddy. We're *really* married. I have the license in the car. I have photos. I'm sharing them on social media later. I wanted to tell you all in person." She let go of Emmett's hand to pull out her phone. She handed it to Penelope, who swiped through the pictures while Zach and Chase looked over her shoulder.

"You continue to embroil this family in scandal," Elle said, her chin trembling with anger. "First you slept with Chase's opponent, and then you marry Emmett without so much as one second's notice to us? And what's with your running off to feed the poor?"

How Elle had said that and made it sound like Stef had run off to join an escort service Emmett couldn't understand.

"It's a noble cause," Stef said. "Some families can't afford presents or a family dinner. I was able to provide a filling meal, a beautiful venue and wrapped gifts for their children."

"Did you vet these people? What if they were addicted to drugs or alcohol? What if they were lying or simply over-budgeted themselves?"

"They were families in need of kindness during a difficult holiday season," Emmett said, unable to keep silent any longer. It was as close as he had ever come to snapping at the matriarch of the Ferguson clan. "Your daughter has a beautiful, giving heart. I saw the tears in the eyes of parents in attendance. She provided a service they needed badly."

He glanced down to see his wife's brows bent with gratitude. She stepped closer and he wrapped a protective arm around her while he spoke.

"Not everyone has the luxury of silver spoons," he continued. "It's a testament to Stefanie's character—and yours—that she would think of people who don't have what she's always had. Your daughter's also a grown woman and you should respect her choices, even if you don't approve of our marriage."

Or me, he mentally added.

Elle had probably pictured her daughter marrying someone well-bred and brought up in the same kind of luxury as Stef was accustomed. Not a man who was an underling to her eldest son.

"I know what I'm doing." Stefanie rested her hand on Emmett's waist as she snuggled closer to him. "Emmett wasn't railroaded." She sent a scathing glare over her shoulder at Chase. Next, she pegged Pen with a gaze, though it was a softer one than the one she reserved for her brother. "And your suggestion may have planted the seed, but it was my idea to propose to Emmett. I know he'd never hurt me. And our attraction is real."

Zach's mouth turned down like he'd tasted sour milk.

"You married some random woman in Vegas and told no one," Stefanie pointed out to him. "And then you two—"

her gesture included both Pen and Zach "—pretended to be engaged when you weren't." She went after Chase next. "And you and Miriam were splashed all over the Dallas Duchess blog before any of us knew you were reunited."

She let go of Emmett to stand in the circle of her family and address them.

"I'm my own person, like Zach. Like Chase. Like Emmett. Just because I'm your youngest child," she said, spinning to peg her father with a stern glare, "doesn't mean I'm incapable of making decisions without your approval."

She took her parents' hands with her own. "I love you both, but this had nothing to do with you."

"Marriage is about love," Elle argued. "Not arrangement."

Penelope regarded her shoes. Zach even managed to look sheepish.

"I think it's wonderful." Every head snapped around to Miriam, who'd linked her arm around Chase's. The mayor looked like an emotionless Easter Island statue, but at least he wasn't fuming any longer.

"And married on Christmas?" Miriam smiled. "It's romantic. This calls for a celebration."

Stef smiled back at her future sister-in-law and mouthed the words *thank you*.

"Sometimes things happen out of order and that's okay. That's life." Miriam shrugged before peering up at Chase. "Right, honey?"

Then and only then did Chase's rock-hard facade chip. He gazed down at his fiancée both tenderly and lovingly. "Right."

Stef faced Zach and Pen next. "Right?"

Zach, his daughter a physical reminder that things definitely had happened out of order for Penelope and him, managed a reluctant "Right."

"Okay then. Now that we have that out of the way, let's eat."

Stefanie took Emmett's hand and pulled him toward the dining room. He followed, feeling the entire Ferguson clan's eyes on his back.

Fourteen

The silence at the dinner table was deafening and would lead to a gift exchange that would likely be less merry and bright than it was awkward and stilted.

But Stefanie refused to shoulder the woe of "ruining Christmas." She'd meant what she said about being her own person—about making her own decisions.

She was certain she'd won over Penelope and Miriam, and Zach had seemed less concerned when he'd learned his wife was indirectly responsible.

Chase was another matter.

Stef had always been closest with her oldest brother. She'd been gung ho about her plan originally, but sitting across from him had her doubting herself a little.

The place cards had been rearranged to seat Emmett next to Stefanie per her mother's request—the woman was nothing if not formal. *A husband and wife always sit together*, she'd declared primly.

"Will you change your name?" Pen asked.

"No need for that," Elle interjected, aghast.

"No," Stef answered. She'd rather not agree with her mother, but Elle was right. If Stefanie changed her name legally, she'd only have to change it back.

To her left, Emmett dug into his dinner, uninterested, or unwilling, to participate in this conversation.

"You should." Pen spooned a bite of food into Olivia's mouth.

"Hyphenating is popular. It's what I'm planning on doing," said Miriam.

"Mimi." That was Chase, who sounded equal parts shocked and perturbed.

Miriam patted his arm and promised they'd discuss it later.

"When I announce your marriage to family and friends, I'll simply explain you don't have the same last name as your husband." Elle hadn't touched her dinner, but instead lifted her martini glass. "It's a modern marriage, after all."

"She's not a Keaton," Emmett said. "She's nothing like a Keaton."

"She's a Keaton now," Rider boomed, startling the table into silence. "You took my daughter's hand. You won't shirk your responsibilities as her husband. No matter what you believed when you said 'I do,' you said it. You will honor it."

Adrenaline prickled her fingers as Stef watched the stare down between her father and her husband. Emmett's jaw was granite, and her father's eyes two lumps of black coal. They broke their staring contest when Emmett spoke.

"Yes, sir."

"Will you move in together?" Pen asked. Stef could practically hear the gears turning about how to spin this announcement to the public. "Your place or his?"

"Mine," Emmett and Stefanie answered simultaneously.

"I'm not moving into your apartment," he stated.

"I have everything I need at my apartment," Stef said. "Your belongings fit into a gym bag. Plus, my home is decorated and my Christmas tree is up and my kitchen is stocked. It makes more sense to live there."

"Why don't you try staying with Emmett tonight? You might like it there," Pen suggested. Stef knew her sister-in-law was only being practical, and possibly trying to end the argument before it started, but Rider and Chase both shifted in their seats, uncomfortable with the idea of Stef going home with Emmett, whether they were married or not.

"I have an idea," Stefanie announced. "Why don't we

table this discussion for, oh, *eternity*? And then we can eat Christmas dinner and open gifts in peace."

"What is it about family that is particularly exhausting over the holidays?" Stefanie asked rhetorically as she sagged in the passenger seat of Emmett's SUV. Realizing belatedly that he didn't have a family to deal with over the holidays, she added, "Sorry about that."

"Don't be." He drove in silence, the dashboard's blue lights glowing against his firm mouth. "I understand."

After a gap of silence, she asked, "Do you feel like I roped you into marrying me?"

"Yes."

She winced.

"And I'd do it again." He grasped her hand, giving it a brief squeeze before returning his palm to the steering wheel. "We have something here. It might not be till death do us part, but it's something."

She didn't know what to say to that so instead she said, "It was kind of you to buy for me."

"I buy for you every year."

"Yes, but this year felt…weirder." He'd given her tickets to the fanciest New Year's Eve ball in Dallas, and she had no idea how he'd scored them. Even as Dallas's youngest female billionaire, she hadn't yet managed a coveted invite. "How'd you land two tickets to Sonia Osborne's Sparkle & Shine gala? I've wanted to go for years."

"I know." Those two words were the most touching of the evening.

Who knew Emmett had paid attention to what she wanted or cared about?

He turned into a complex with modern, cozy town houses. Gray siding, white windowsills, charcoal-black roofs. When he turned right onto a street charmingly named Lamplight, she noticed Christmas lights strung on every house but one. And that was the driveway he pulled into and waited patiently for the garage door to raise.

The garage was tidy and organized. One set of metal shelves stood on the right side by an entry door, and on it were rows of black milk crates where he stashed his garage-wares.

"This is it." He shut off the engine. "I'll grab the bags. Go on in."

Since it was cold outside and he offered, she let him do his husbandly duty and entered in through the kitchen. The light was already on, so no there was need to find the switch.

The interior was as manly as the man she'd married with its dark floors, polished wood, a white ceiling striped with thick exposed beams. Edison lights dangled over a stainless steel countertop, flanked by black cabinetry. She stepped down three stairs that led to a sunken room and flipped on one switch, then another, illuminating a wide-open living room and tall windows, leading to a slatted staircase and a second floor.

If not for the warm lights, Emmett's brown-and-gray town house would closely resemble a nuclear bunker.

"He's all set up in the—oh... Hello."

Stefanie spun around to face the stairs and met eyes with a tall, curvy brunette. Her medium-length hair was straight and sassy, her breasts bursting from a plum-colored V-neck sweater. Her heeled boots and tight leather leggings made her legs look ten miles long and her wide mouth was painted with berry-colored lipstick. Each detail became more apparent as she glided down the steps and into the living room.

"I was expecting Emmett," the beautiful Amazon purred. "I'm Sunday."

Stefanie blinked, not understanding...well, much of anything at the moment.

She folded her arms, unsure who this strange woman was or why she was in Emmett's house. She didn't recall a tale about him having a sister but found herself silently hoping for a pop-up sibling at the moment.

"And you are?" the other woman asked.

"My wife." Emmett joined them and looped his arm around Stefanie's back. "Stefanie Ferguson, this is Sunday Webber."

"Wife. Wow." A sharp glint lit Sunday's brown eyes. She was surprised, and not in an oh-I'm-so-happy-for-you way.

"And Sunday is your…" Stef started.

"Friend," the other woman supplied, her smile snapping into place. She then addressed Emmett, which Stefanie didn't like at all. "Oscar's set up in your spare bedroom. Litter box, food and a few toys. He's grouchy from having to travel, but he'll come out eventually." She waved a hand. "You know what he's like."

Stef didn't like the familiarity in that statement, either. Or the fact that his "friend" Sunday had a key. At least the mention of a litter box stalled any assumption that there was a child named Oscar upstairs.

"This is still okay, right?" Sunday's gaze flickered from Emmett to Stefanie.

"Yeah. It's been a busy weekend. I forgot about the cat, but it's fine."

Stef had a million questions, but she wasn't going to dispense them with Sunday as an audience.

"I'm off to Denver. Thanks again. I'll pick him up next weekend." She moved to Emmett like she would have normally kissed or hugged him goodbye, when Stefanie wrapped both her arms around his waist. She stopped short of hissing.

Emmett's arm tightened around Stefanie's shoulders as if reassuring her. He nodded his goodbye to Sunday. "Have a safe trip."

"I'll let myself out. Nice to meet you, Emmett's wife."

"Stefanie."

"Ferguson. I know." Sunday let that comment hang and wiggled her perfect heart-shaped ass across the living room and out the front door.

Once she'd left, Stefanie let go of Emmett and lifted her arms in exasperation. "What was that about?"

"I'm going to have a drink," Emmett had the nerve to say. "Can I pour you one?"

"Um. Hello?" She chased him into the kitchen. "Who was that? What's going on?"

"That was Sunday Web—"

"Yes. I know her name. Who is she?"

"She's my ex-girlfriend," he stated simply. "Drink?"

"What's your ex-girlfriend doing in your apartment? Why does she have a key?"

With a sigh, he pulled open a cabinet and extracted two wineglasses. He slid a wine bottle from a curved metal hanger on the wall and showed her the label.

Stefanie shrugged. *That's fine.*

"I gave her a key when we were dating," he said as he worked the corkscrew.

"And were you dating when you married me?"

"No." He spared her a glance after he filled his glass, hovering the neck of the bottle over hers.

Stef nodded. She most definitely needed a glass of wine.

"And you watch her cat?"

"He's funny with strangers."

Her brow scrunched—she could *feel* herself scowling.

"Sunday and I are friends and I promised I'd cat-sit. The end." Emmett handed Stefanie her wineglass. She took a sip, the bright red berry flavors bursting on her tongue. Unfortunately, the color of the wine reminded her of both Sunday's lipstick and her low-cut sweater, so Stef found herself frowning anew.

"As you might recall, I had no plans to marry or date you three days ago."

She crossed her arms, knowing she was being unfair but not caring. He rounded the stainless counter and set his glass next to hers, tipping her chin to address her.

"How do you think I felt when you were photographed coming out of a hotel room with Blake Eastwood?"

She blinked, stunned. "I don't know," she answered honestly.

A handful of seconds passed in silence, as if he was debating whether to continue. Finally, he did.

"If you had any idea what I wanted to do to him after I found out he'd touched you… After I found out he'd *used* you… If I didn't value Chase's reputation, or staying out of prison, I'd have torn Blake to pieces with my bare hands."

It was wrong for her to luxuriate in the notion that Emmett was jealous, but she didn't care. She let it surround her like a security blanket. All of her grew warm, starting with her cheeks.

"You didn't like that I was with Blake," she said, wrapping her head around his admission.

"No."

"And you wanted to hurt him because he hurt me?"

"I wanted to erase him from this planet because he hurt you."

She reached up and fingered the open placket of his shirt, his chest hot to the touch. "I feel the same way about Sunday Webber. Did you love her?"

"Did you love Blake?"

"Of course not. But you already know that. Answer me."

"Sunday was… That was a long time ago."

"She's very pretty." Stefanie unbuttoned another of his shirt buttons, then one more. "And *very* busty." She pressed a kiss to his chest and he sucked in a deep breath, palming the back of her head. "Say something." Stef rested her chin on his chest and peered up at him.

"What do you want me to say?" He looked down at her.

"What would've made you feel better after you found out about me and Blake?"

"If you'd never done it." Emmett's chest rose and fell, his hand in her hair.

"What if I told you that I was lonely, and he was falsely charming. Would that make it better?"

"No."

"What if I told you that if I'd known you were in my future—" she undid his remaining shirt buttons and parted the fabric, sweeping her hands along his broad chest "—I never would have given Blake the time of day."

Emmett struck like a snake, lifting her and depositing her on the countertop. She yipped in surprise, parting her legs for his big body a moment later when he stepped between them. "I'd say I liked that a lot."

"Your turn." She linked her fingers at the back of his neck and waited.

His granite-colored eyes warmed as he cupped her rib cage with both hands. "If I had any clue I'd earn my way into Stefanie Ferguson's bed, I'd have remained celibate until my wedding night."

She gulped. He'd rendered her speechless.

"Even if the wedding night was our only night together, waiting would've been worth it."

She tipped her chin and he didn't hesitate to kiss her. She wrapped her legs around the firm globes of his butt, rubbing her center against the hard-on that now pressed against the fly of his slacks.

"Lucky you," she whispered against his panting mouth. "It's not just one night."

Fifteen

Emmett knew it was exactly what Stefanie had wanted to hear, but at the same time, it hadn't been a line. He'd have forsaken all others and waited for her if it would have guaranteed him even one night with her.

It was a realization that shocked the hell out of him. He was coming to terms with the amount of pent-up attraction for Stef that he'd apparently been disregarding over the years, but he didn't suspect there'd been more to it. And maybe there wasn't. Maybe this was the responsibility he'd promised when he'd said "I do" combined with a hell of a lot of attraction. Maybe the core of what he was realizing was about vows and honor—*loyalty*. Loyalty, he understood.

Stef had nothing to be jealous of where Sunday was concerned. The relationship with his ex-girlfriend had been about companionship. Someone to share dinner or watch movies with. He'd mostly gone to her house, though there at the end, she'd talked him into giving her his key. That'd been the beginning of the end. Sunday asking for the "more" that he knew he was incapable of giving. Yet he'd found a way to give that "more" to Stefanie.

He'd told himself that marrying her was to save Chase's campaign and keep Stefanie safe, but if he were forced to admit the truth, he'd been attracted to her for years. Attraction had been dressed up as concern, but it'd been there all the same. He'd shrouded what he now recognized as jealousy with a cloak of anger.

Now with his lips sealed over hers and the tip of her tongue dancing with his, he knew he'd been both attracted to her and burning with jealousy that she'd been in anyone else's bed but his.

He hadn't understood when she turned an envious shade of green over Sunday. Him being jealous of whomever Stefanie touched was understandable. But Stefanie jealous of another woman who'd touched him?

It was *heady*.

Made him feel powerful.

Made him want to strip her bare and take her right on this countertop.

"My queen," he muttered against her throat when he grazed her pulse point with his lips.

"Mmm, I really do like that," she sighed sweetly in his ear.

"Is it too lowly to screw you here and now?" He slid one palm up her skirt and along one thick, honey-sweet thigh.

"You can screw me wherever you like, Keaton," she said, raising her butt off the counter so he could shimmy her panties down her legs. His sly vixen. "I'm your wife. Not your ruler."

"From what I've come to understand, those are one and the same."

She snatched each side of his shirt and tugged him closer, her breath hot against his parted mouth. "Is that so?"

But she didn't let him answer.

"Your mission this time—" she flicked her tongue out to lick his upper lip, and his balls tightened "—is to come before I do."

He grinned, teeth and all. A low laugh rumbled in his gut. "Sorry, toots. You deliver first. Those are the rules."

"We'll see." She grabbed his crotch and stroked his erection through his pants.

Up. Down. Hard. Fast. Then slow again.

He palmed her hand before he lost his mind. "What the hell do you think you're doing?"

His wife smiled up at him. *"Winning."*

Not on his watch.

He knotted his fraying self-control, snatching her hand and bracing it on the counter behind her back. He mimicked the move with her other hand so that her pert breasts were high and lifted with every breath she took.

Her pupils darkened with want, and his body protested not being touched.

"Is this how you want me? Under your control?" She hoisted one fair eyebrow in challenge. "I prefer things the other way around."

"You deserve the royal treatment."

Her expression softened, some of the determination seeping away. Stefanie wanted to be treated well. Deserved to be treated well.

And he was the man for the job.

He left her on the counter and grabbed a stool, sliding it across the gray-tiled floor and positioning it in front of her. When he sat, his mouth was perfectly at the junction of her thighs. A wily smile on her lips, she spread her legs and showed him a glimpse of the promised land.

"Keep those hands behind you or else," he warned as he rested first one of her knees and then the other on his shoulders.

"You have five minutes. If you fail, then it's my turn."

"I won't fail." It was a vow he took as seriously as any other. Serving her was at the top of his priority list.

"We'll see," she said, and then he went to work.

"Dammit!" Stefanie breathed through her release, cheeks warm and mouth parted.

Emmett's head rose from her thighs and he swiped his mouth before a smirk plastered itself there and stayed.

"So, you won this time. So what?"

He moved the stool aside while she pushed off the counter. When he turned to find her on her feet, he spun her around and smoothed his hands over her bare ass before pulling her dress up to her waist.

"Not done yet, wife." His voice was gravel filled and her response was a whimper of capitulation.

A drawer to her left was slid open and he extracted a condom.

"Why do you have those in there?" she asked, though she wasn't sure she wanted to know.

He rolled on the protection and stayed silent.

"For Sunday?" Stef peeked over her shoulder.

"Shut up." His breath was hot in her ear as he pressed his erection against her. "Do you want this or not?"

"Yes." She did. More than anything.

"Then *behave*."

A moment later he was filling her, taking his sweet time stroking them both to oblivion. Her challenge, and the searching question about why he kept condoms in the kitchen drawer, was forgotten.

"Together." She reached behind her and wrapped a hand around the back of his neck. "Emmett."

"Yes." He nipped her earlobe and gripped her hips, plunging deep. Pleasure ricocheted through her body as he worked hard to match her pace.

"Now. Now!" She tightened her grip on his neck, vaguely aware of her nails digging into his flesh. And then…

They brought down the house.

Her cries mingled with his, their shouts competing for space in the kitchen. His grip loosened on her hips as his ragged breaths tickled her ear.

"That… Amazing." Those broken words were the only two she was capable of.

"Better" came his argument.

She turned, stood on her toes and pressed a kiss to the center of his lips. "Merry Christmas, Emmett."

A blip of what might be memory shadowed his eyes, but only for a moment. In a blink it was gone and replaced with a tentative smile. "Merry Christmas, Stefanie."

His wife excused herself for a bath. He assured Stefanie the tub was clean—he was a borderline neat freak with a lot of free time on his hands. Once he showed her where the towels were and changed into jogging pants and a loose gray tee, he went back downstairs and refilled his wineglass.

His phone showed texts from employees who were part of Chase's security team—no emergencies, just updates—and from a few friends wishing him a merry Christmas. They didn't know not to. Stef knew not to, but she'd wished him a merry Christmas, anyway. He'd returned her sentiment, the barbs of his past not digging into his skin as deeply as before.

Could've been the world-class sex that helped with that endeavor.

He sat on the brown leather couch in front of a trunk that served as a coffee table, the exposed brick wall punctuated by a simple gas fireplace. He pressed a button to start it and for the first time considered what his place might look like to Stefanie Ferguson. She loved Christmas and twinkly lights and fluffy, fuzzy decorative pillows. He imagined she equated his place with a morgue for all the personality it had.

"Mowr."

Emmett turned his head to find Oscar, Sunday's twenty-two-pound cat, swaggering into the room after almost tripping down the bottom two steps. Graceful, that cat was not. He was good-looking, though, his bright, round green eyes and uniquely patterned brown and darker brown fur making up for the clumsiness.

"Mowr," Oscar repeated, too masculine to manage a dainty sound like "meow."

"I know," he told the cat. "You're stuck with me for about a week. It sucks, but I promise I won't let you die."

Oscar slowly blinked, sitting at the foot of the stairs and curling his tail around his feet. A tail the cat forgot was there a few seconds later when he stepped on it, yowled and sprinted into the next room.

From his seat on the sofa, Emmett shook his head. How he'd ended up with his ex-girlfriend's cat for the week was simple. She'd asked and he couldn't think of a single reason to say no. He'd spent time with Oscar before and noticed he and the feline had a few things in common. They were both supersize, neither of them into frills, both single and both enjoyed chicken salad.

It wasn't Sunday's or Oscar's fault that Emmett had returned home from his trip *married,* so he couldn't very well kick Oscar out.

The water upstairs shut off and he wondered how long his wife would soak. Wondered if he should join her. He smiled at the rim of his glass at the idea of climbing into the water with her and overflowing the tub. He decided to give her a moment to herself. She deserved a break. He'd been in her space, and then inside her, since they arrived at his house.

His phone rang. He answered it without looking. That ringtone belonged to only one individual in his contact list.

"Hey, boss."

"Give me one good reason why I shouldn't fire your ass," Chase said in greeting.

"I'm better at watching your six than anyone on the planet."

A long beat of silence and then, "You hurt her, Em, you'll hear from me. Decorum, my position as mayor of this city and our friendship won't stop me from beating the shit out of you."

"Understood." He'd never roughhoused with Chase, but Chase was no weakling. He worked out, and while the mayor wasn't as wide as Emmett, he had reach. Emmett imagined if he did hurt Stef, he'd deserve whatever justice her brother doled out.

"Is any of it real? I need to know if she's…serving a purpose for you or if you care about her." Chase's voice was steel, his tone the dangerous hum of a transformer about to blow.

"She's an adult. And I'm not Blake. Give me some credit."

"That wasn't an answer."

"I answer to you at work, not about my personal life."

"Emmett."

"Chase. I've been in your life for a long time. I care about everyone in your family. You shouldn't have any worries as to whether I'd hurt her or not. I value your family more than my own life."

Chase's sigh was weighty. He had to know Emmett was telling the truth. Emmett placed loyalty above all else.

"If the scales start tipping," Chase said, "if you notice that she's beginning to care for you more than you will ever care for her, don't drag her along. Let her go."

Chase didn't need to say more. He was talking about love. He meant if Stef started falling and Emmett wasn't falling for her, that Emmett should let her go.

There was no fairer request than that.

"Promise me." Chase's voice was low. "Or it'll be more than your career on the line. I'll cut you out of my family so fast it'll be like we never knew each other."

Even issuing the threat, Emmett could hear in his friend's voice that it was the last thing Chase wanted to do.

"If it comes to choosing between you and my family—"

"Your family comes first," Emmett said, his heart cracking under the pressure of that realization.

He wasn't family. He wasn't blood. Blood in the Ferguson line mattered more than a friendship that spanned a decade. Hell, he'd been surprised Rider and Elle let him walk out of their home with their only daughter since he'd sullied the Ferguson family tree with a Keaton leaf.

Even though it killed him to say it, Emmett couldn't blame Chase for defending his sister.

"I understand."

Sixteen

Movement drew his attention to the staircase. Stef, wrapped in a thick gray bathrobe that she must have found in the back of his closet, held up the yards of extra material and came down the steps like royalty holding her robes.

My queen.

Her frown was evident, the ends of her blond hair dark and wet.

"I heard the phone ring earlier. Which one of my over-protective family members was it?" She clomped over and sat on the couch next to him; the robe balled up and she tucked her legs under her. "Let me guess. The one you serve like he knighted you."

He didn't respond since she'd guessed right.

"That fire feels nice."

Taking advantage of her nearness, he wrapped an arm around her. He wasn't much of a cuddler, but where Stefanie was involved he was coming to realize the only place she belonged was in the protection of his arms.

"You don't have a single string of tinsel," she pointed out.

He looked around with her at his utilitarian style, the palette of earthy browns and concrete grays, exposed earth-toned brick walls. The decor was a complete antithesis of her style. It was like she'd been sent from a castle to live in a cave with the dragon.

His fingers brushed her shoulder, the thick terry cloth keeping him from her bath-warmed skin.

"You don't have to stay here."

"I didn't mean that." She gave him a playful shove, not

picking up on the shadow that'd stretched over his soul. "I understand why you didn't deck the halls."

He felt the weight of her ocean-blue stare on his profile. He turned to meet her eyes.

"Where is your dad now?"

"Probably at home. Or at a bar."

"Do you see him much?"

Emmett shook his head.

"Do you want to?"

Another head shake.

"I'm sorry." He could hear the sincerity in her voice.

"Don't be. It is what it is." He touched one of her cheeks with his knuckle.

"Well, you have to admit this is the most unique Christmas you've ever had." She smiled, pleased with her joke. Damn if he couldn't help a small smile of his own.

"Unforgettable," he agreed.

He would never forget her. In the event Stefanie started feeling too much for him—more than he could return— then he would let her go home to her family and exile himself in the process.

Part of him howled in protest, the reverberation of that silent cry shaking him to the core. When it came to letting her go, he didn't have a choice.

He'd do it to protect her. He'd do it *for* her.

He'd do it…even though he didn't want to.

The Dallas Duchess. That slimy wench.

The gossipy blogger had swiped the Tweet Stefanie posted this morning, but rather than offer her congratulations, she'd slapped the wedding picture of Emmett and Stefanie on her website alongside a saucy, tawdry headline.

"Stefanie Ferguson Stoops to Marry the Help."

And lookee here, there was even a comment from Blake the Snake. That flaming pile of dog—

"Refill?" Emmett extended his arm, a cardboard box filled with doughnuts balanced in one big hand.

"One is my limit."

"Wimp." He lifted a perfect sugary ring and ate most of it in one bite, a moan echoing in that barrel chest of his.

"Oh, for goodness' sake." She set aside her iPad and stood to take a doughnut, but he tugged the box away and shoved the rest of his into his mouth. He offered her the box again and she snatched a chocolate-covered one and took a sinful bite. After a few swallows of coffee to chase her sugar buzz, she tried to sag on Emmett's couch. Impossible. The back and sides were hard and flat, not a couch meant for sagging.

"I don't typically indulge in something so decadent," she called out as he carried the box into the kitchen. He returned with a mug of coffee in hand.

"Neither do I." He crossed the room and lifted his wallet off the mantel before shoving it into his black slacks. "To be clear, I'm talking about waking up and making love to you."

Damn. Now that was sweet. She had no idea Emmett could be sweet until she'd married him. She'd convinced herself they hated each other—had told herself for years that he only tolerated her because she was Chase's sister. But that couldn't have been true, could it? He'd slipped into her life—into her *bed*—almost seamlessly.

He bent to kiss her. She tipped her chin to catch that kiss and the meaning behind it.

"Ready?"

"Yes." She stood and grabbed her coat while he fetched his own. "Even though I don't think anyone in the free world should have to go to work until New Year's Day."

But she had an appointment with Penelope that couldn't be missed. She hadn't left herself much of a choice.

Emmett pulled to a stop at Zach and Penelope's home. Pen used to have a shingle hung downtown, but since her daughter was born she'd moved her office to the house and employed a nanny to watch over Olivia during work hours.

Zach stepped outside, on his way to his own office no doubt. He wore a suit and a scowl that was meant for either her husband or Stef herself. Maybe it was meant for both of them.

Emmett put down his window when Zach approached.

"Hey, big brother," she chirped. "Before you dole out any overblown speeches and squarely place yourself in the pot-calling-the-kettle-black category, you should know that Chase beat you to it and I don't care what either of you think."

She blew her brother a kiss, and then grabbed Emmett's shirt collar, pulling him close for a real kiss—one he returned, albeit stiffly. He was glaring when she pulled away, and she was flushed, and suddenly wishing she'd started that smooch at his house instead, where they could continue it in privacy.

Anyway.

Stefanie left Zach and Emmett in the driveway and announced her arrival to Pen quietly in case Olivia was sleeping.

"In here. She's upstairs playing." Penelope appeared in the entryway wearing a slimming white dress and waved Stef into her office. It used to be a formal dining room, but they'd converted it into a modern office with French doors and curtains for privacy. Pen shut the door behind her.

"I'm assuming you saw the blog." Stef sat on the white leather couch.

"Oh yes. I check her site regularly." Pen rolled her eyes. "Tea?"

"Please."

Pen poured two cups from a kettle from a small table behind her desk and rested the delicate china on saucers before joining Stef on the couch.

"How's it going?" Pen sipped her tea.

"Fine."

"How real is this marriage?" Pen tilted her head. "Did you consummate it yet?"

"Penelope!"

"Did you?"

Stefanie lifted her tea both to buy time and to wet her parched throat before admitting, "A few times."

"I am going to say something very unpopular."

"Chase and Zach beat you to it," Stef grumbled.

"I like you two together."

Not what Stef was expecting to hear. Pen drew a hard line when it came to her clients, and she could be as bull-headed as Zach when it came to doing things her way.

"He's always watched you. I didn't think of it before, but now that I'm in the family and I've seen him at a few family functions…" Pen nodded as if envisioning one such function now. "Emmett stays in your orbit."

She sent Penelope an unsure smile. The idea that Stef was newly attracted to Emmett made sense—they'd never spent time together unchaperoned until recently. But what about those times he'd lurked in her periphery, or stepped into her line of vision to scowl…

"I guess I always assumed he was in Chase's orbit."

"Yes, but I think that has to do with you. He knows that staying close to the Fergusons comes with the perk of being close to you."

He'd certainly stayed close by lately. They'd slept in the same bed, had slept together, had shared meals and break-fast and had even given Oscar, the cat, a bath after he darted out the front door and straight into a slushy mud puddle.

But for how long? She'd married him with the stipula-tion that he could walk away. She doubted he would re-main in a marriage that was for show. If he couldn't make it work with the buxom brunette *Sunday*, who he easily stayed friends with, Stef wasn't sure she and Emmett had a chance. They'd never been friends.

"I doubt he's the forever type, so don't get your hopes up," she told her sister-in-law.

Pen let out a *pfft* sound of disagreement and rested her cup and saucer on the glass coffee table.

"What was that for?"

"You are the one who personally pulled Zach's head out of his ass when he and I split. How can you say Emmett has no hope?"

"That's different. Zach's so obviously in love with you."

"And I'm in love with him." Pen's smile was gooey before vanishing altogether. "Are you in love with Emmett?"

"What? No! How?" Penelope wisely remained silent but Stefanie kept protesting. "I can't be in love with him. We've only been married for thirty-two hours."

"Yes, but you've known him for *years*."

"You're making no sense." Stef swept aside the conversation with one hand. For one, it was making her uncomfortable, and two, it was…making her uncomfortable. "Advise me how to behave in public with him. That's what I want to know. That's *all* I want to know."

She didn't want to entertain an idea that her heart might follow where her body led—that she might stumble and fall into a big pile of "I love you." She knew how this ended—Emmett and Stef had constructed the end from the beginning.

But Pen wasn't convinced. "Mmm-hmm."

Well, Stefanie didn't need to convince her. She didn't need to convince anyone of anything. And she certainly didn't need to entertain the notion that happily-ever-after was in store for her and Emmett.

It wasn't.

It was as simple as that.

Seventeen

"Try to look like you're not completely miserable."

Stefanie's arm was looped in Emmett's as she stood at his side at the museum fund-raiser. She'd dragged him to the event, being held at the Dallas Museum of Art in the Renaissance room, but attending the private function had been Penelope's bright idea.

His wife wore her for-the-public expression, an amiable twist of her lips suggesting she had a secret no one knew but her. Meanwhile, his frown was frowning. He wasn't good at faking anything. He hadn't had the practice and, frankly, didn't give a damn what anyone thought.

His arms were straight at his sides, his fists wound into twin hammers. His focus jerked around the room in search of a particular lowlife by the name of Blake Eastwood, who was "scheduled to appear," according to Pen. Personally, Emmett would have liked to find and pummel him into paste.

"Or like you're out for blood," Stef whispered as they walked through a pair of velvet ropes. A security guy in a tux asked for their tickets and Emmett handed them over.

Pen had also arranged for a local photographer to be here to snap photos of Emmett and Stef holding each other close. Bonus if it included a seething, flame-red-faced Blake in the background.

"Breathe."

"I'm not as good at this as you," he said between his teeth. Understatement. Given the choice, he'd rather be in the background five hundred percent of the time and in the foreground never. *Ever.*

Stef walked him to a painting, a huge, wall-size painting of angels and demons and people with knives in their guts and dogs snarling, their teeth bared.

He wasn't sure which of the subjects he identified with most at the moment.

Next to him, his wife pressed close, her breast brushing his arm. She was wearing a short black dress, the slit in the side high enough to expose one creamy thigh when she walked. Her boots were the pair he'd taken note of in Chase's office: knee-high with brass buttons running the length and ending in high, spiked heels.

His attention on her helped his temperament stabilize. She'd had a calming effect on him lately—sleeping with her was probably the dominating factor in that effect. Before he'd taken her to bed, whenever she was around he'd been strung as tight as a string on that angel's harp.

"Keep your eyes on me," she told him. "Pretend I'm the only person in the room."

"I can't." He lowered his voice so they wouldn't be overheard. "I'm trained to notice that the old guy standing by the Renoir is checking out your ass, and a blonde lady is snapping pictures of the whole event in the corner by a painting of a well-endowed woman eating grapes."

"That's our planted photographer. She's legit."

He slid a glance over at the woman again and then back to the old guy. To Stef, he said, "Wasn't Renoir an Impressionist? I feel like that painting's in the wrong room."

Stef grinned. "Impressive, Mr. Keaton."

"I have my moments."

He'd always watched over Stef. She was in his sights because he watched over Chase, and she was an extension of Chase. He'd regarded her like he had any of her family members. Although, that wasn't true, was it? He'd felt a pull toward her that eclipsed standard Ferguson concern. And now his desire to protect her was stronger than it'd ever been—and growing. Those wedding vows weren't only for show. He'd taken them to heart.

She towed him over to a different painting, another he didn't recognize, tucked into a quiet corner that was populated only by them.

"How's this?" she asked.

"Perfect. Let's live here." He took a quick look around to make sure they weren't being watched. When her hand brushed innocently over his crotch, he jerked his attention back to her.

"I'm the only person here."

"If that were true—" he lowered his lips to hover just over hers "—you'd pay for that."

She nuzzled his nose and he caught himself smiling down at her, his arm wrapped around her waist. Something about the way she tipped her head told him she was posing.

"Is it happening *now*?"

"Yes. The woman by the grape painting. Kiss me."

He'd intended to give her a chaste kiss, but chastity where he and Stef were concerned always approached inappropriate. By the time her tongue touched his, he was ready to get the hell out of here.

Her attention moved from him to across the room and she gripped his arm, giving it a hard squeeze. "He's here."

Emmett didn't have to ask who "he" was. Blake, with a small-boned, big-eyed woman on his arm, glided into the place like he owned it. Smarmy bastard. He turned and spotted Stefanie, then Emmett and stopped cold.

Emmett pulled his wife closer.

Mine.

Blake, incapable of taking a hint, excused himself from his date and completed the journey over to where they stood.

"Stefanie." Blake ignored Emmett.

"Blake." She rested her hand on Emmett's torso. Anyone looking on might think she was smoothing his tie, but Emmett knew she was attempting to tamp down his ire. Didn't work. The need to punch Blake's face in still simmered.

"I noticed—" Blake started.

"Get the hell away from her." Emmett was off script, but he didn't care.

Blake's face oozed into a smile. "Relax, Keaton. You've clearly won this round. Though I never dreamed she'd sell herself off to you."

Emmett's arm flinched and Stefanie moved both hands to his forearm. Blake jerked away before sending Stefanie a bemused smile.

"Better keep your dog on a leash, Stef. Is he the best you could do on short notice?" Blake asked. "Some wild animal that can't be taken into public?"

"Better a wild animal than a slithering, slimy reptile." Stef loosened her hold—which she was about to regret. Emmett had enough of this conversation. The condition of Blake's nose relied on his own response.

Blake sneered. "That's not what you said when I took you to bed, unless you mean—"

Emmett shook off Stef's hold and slammed a fist into Blake's face.

"You were warned," Emmett growled.

The other guests gasped and backed away as the blonde with the camera ran forward to catch a pic of the action. She'd snap a good one, too, given that Blake was doubled over, streams of blood running between his fingers. His date cooed over him, but Emmett was done.

He took Stefanie's hand and led her from the event, splitting the crowd like well-dressed bowling pins.

"No matter how hard I try, I can't be upset with you." Stefanie moved the plastic bag filled with ice from Emmett's knuckles to inspect his red fingers. "No scrapes, though. Impressive."

"He has a soft face." Emmett smirked at his own joke. "I'm done with the ice."

She went to the kitchen and dumped it into the sink, returning with a beer for him and a glass of wine for herself.

He accepted the bottle, taking a few long swallows. She watched the column of his neck work as he drank, wanting nothing more than to drag her tongue over his Adam's apple. Never before had she thought of Emmett as "sexy" but now that she saw it, it couldn't be unseen. She'd been wondering lately how she'd missed it.

His legs were spread, knees wide as he sat on his couch. She had no idea how he could like that rigid piece of furniture. She took the equally uncomfortable chair nearest him.

"Mowr." Oscar padded into the room and she stroked the cat's back. He responded by arching, his tail flicking into the shape of a question mark.

"I like this cat despite him belonging to your ex-girlfriend."

Emmett sighed, evidently not wanting to return to this discussion.

"I suppose we'll see her sooner or later."

"Later," he said. "She extended her trip."

"And stuck you with her cat?" Stef stroked Oscar again and winked her apology.

He wasn't any trouble, really. Even though the day she'd bathed him he'd looked at her like she was performing torture as she shampooed the mud from his coat. Oscar had claimed the guest bedroom for himself but trotted into Emmett's bedroom to greet his temporary human caretakers each morning. More often than not, the cat approached her side of the bed and she'd murmur her good morning before walking downstairs to feed him. It wasn't lost on her that this entire setup—the cat, the marriage, her living with Emmett—had an expiration date. Soon she'd be in her own bed, cat-less and Emmett-less. The thought bothered her more than it should.

She didn't even know she liked cats.

Or Emmett, she thought with a soft smile.

"What are you wearing to the Sparkle & Shine gala?"

"Sorry?" His face pinched in confusion.

"The tickets you bought me to the New Year's Eve party. You're accompanying me."

He digested that information for a second. "I didn't picture myself as your date when I secured them."

"Who did you picture as my date?"

"Someone…else."

"Not Blake."

"No." His visage darkened. "Not Blake. But someone…" He appeared to roll a few options around in his head before deciding on his answer. "Not like me."

"Someone who…doesn't work for my family?"

His stare was grave. "Yes."

"Someone—" she rose from her seat on the chair and sat with him on the couch "—who knows how to behave in public?"

She crossed one leg over the other. His eyes ran the length of her boots slowly. She'd noticed him admiring them before.

"You like these?" She pointed a toe.

"Immensely." His fiery gaze locked on hers.

"Who knew attraction was hiding under all this…animosity?" She fiddled with the collar of his shirt. "I always thought you hated me."

He didn't deny it, but he was scowling.

"The way you slid me those glares whenever I came to visit Chase at work. Or whenever you came to my parents' house for a party." She pointed at his face. "Like that. I bet no one believes we're in love."

A tiny needle of sadness pricked her, but she ignored it. Obviously, *she* knew they weren't in love, but that didn't mean she couldn't take advantage of his nearness.

"There's a thin line, my queen." He broke eye contact to lean, his elbows on his knees, his beer dangling between thick fingers. He was so easy to admire. She'd never thought to admire him before. She thought she'd disliked him as much as he disliked her.

Now they liked each other in equal measures. When had that happened? She guessed somewhere between convincing him to enter city hall with her and the moment he insisted on buying the ring and sliding it onto her finger. She blinked, coming to the slow realization that what was between them couldn't be categorized as simply physical. He blew her mind in bed, but he also honored her at every turn. Like tonight, when he'd broken Blake's nose.

Gosh. She really hoped he'd broken it.

Stef had never been treated like gold by a man. By her father and brothers, sure, but never in a romantic relationship. She'd always been willing to have fun and made it clear she wasn't interested in being tied down. Yet here she was. Having fun *and* tied down.

Temporarily tied down. She couldn't forget that part.

Even though during these quiet moments with Emmett, she wished she could.

Eighteen

Thankfully, no photos from the museum surfaced. Penelope made a call to the photographer and paid her generously to bury the photos of Emmett hitting Blake in the nose. The story was officially dead. The Dallas Duchess had posted about "whisperings" that Blake had two black eyes, but she'd been "unable to reach him for comment."

Over the span of what amounted to only a couple of days, Stefanie had made her way from the top of the news feed online to somewhere in the middle. She'd never been so happy to not be "trending."

She set her phone on the counter as Emmett stepped into the kitchen, freshly showered and dressed for work, eyeing her with a primal gaze that reminded her of everything she'd done to him last night—and everything he'd done to her this morning.

Sharing his bed each and every night was much better than she'd anticipated. And she barely missed her apartment—well, she missed it a little. Mostly the cheery baubles sitting around that made her apartment feel like a home.

There were no baubles in Emmett's town house. It was stocked with necessities. Utilitarian and simple.

"You need a painting or two."

"Why?" His frown was outlined by the light from the open fridge door.

"What do you like?" she asked rather than answered.

"I like *not* to dust superfluous surfaces."

So much for that idea.

Bottle of half-and-half in hand, he moved to the cabinet for a mug.

"We're off the top-ten list of people to talk about in Dallas," she said. "Blake has retreated into a hole in the ground. For now."

"Good. I'll check in with the staff at the mayor's office and make sure the heat's off Chase." Emmett lifted the coffeepot and filled a mug. "In hindsight, he's the one who should've gotten married to salvage his campaign and take the heat off you."

The comment settled into the air like a foul stench.

"Having regrets?" she asked.

"That's the wrong question."

"That's not an answer."

"No. I'm not having regrets. Regret is as useless as worry." He crossed the kitchen and put a kiss on her forehead. "So stop doing it."

Who knew gruff and sweet could coexist in one big, burly package? He continued to surprise her.

"The gala is tomorrow."

"I know."

"I'm going to have to stop by my apartment to dig through my closet. I've been too preoccupied to shop properly for a dress and now it's too late."

"The tragedy of off-the-rack," he said with a healthy dose of sarcasm.

"It's your fault!" she accused with a grin. "You keep me in bed for longer than I've ever stayed there before."

He set aside his steaming coffee mug to cup her jaw. "That's because there are far more fun things to do with you in my bed than out of it."

See? Sweet.

She savored the feel of his giving and taking mouth, losing herself in the fantasy that this was her life. Their life. That they'd come home each and every day to each other—and to their cat, Oscar—and argue about what to wear to the next social function or what kind of art belonged in their home.

And when he tilted her head to deepen their kiss, she wondered if he wasn't doing the exact same thing—reveling in this moment rather than dealing with reality.

Chase's nod was final but there was an ellipsis in his eyes.

"Spit it out, boss." Emmett shut Chase's office door and crossed to the middle of the room to stand before his best friend, arms folded.

His armor.

"How's it going?" Chase asked, and Emmett lifted an eyebrow at the mild line of questioning.

"Peachy."

"I'm serious."

"The world is my oyster," Emmett responded, his tone flat.

Chase offered a head shake and pinched the bridge of his nose. "God, what a mess."

Whether he was talking about Emmett marrying Stef or about the Blake drama, it was hard to say.

"The heat's off you for the immediate future. Relax in that."

"I assume you're attending the Sparkle & Shine gala with Stefanie tomorrow night?"

There was a segue.

"So I'm told."

"Mimi and I will be there. Sonia Osborne sent me a pair of tickets. Evidently she's a fan of the mayor." He smoothed his tie and lifted his chin. Smugness was a good look on Chase. Emmett preferred it to his best friend threatening to kick him out of the only family he had.

That was the inevitable conclusion, wasn't it? Stefanie poured her entire heart into everything she did—charity

Christmas dinners, dressing for events…*marriages*. She was in deep—he could feel it. And the tragedy was that to keep his word to Chase, Emmett would have to eventually walk away. Because he didn't have an "entire heart" to pour into anything—or anyone.

Dread crawled up his spine at the thought of losing it all. *Again.*

"Don't look so downtrodden. It's a party, not a natural disaster," Chase said. "All you have to do is show up, have a few drinks and deliver a New Year's kiss…to my sister."

He tacked on that last bit as if it'd just occurred to him.

"That's taking some getting used to." Chase slid a glance at Emmett, who dropped his arms. "For both of us, I presume."

Despite the hope in his friend's voice, Emmett couldn't agree.

"Stef and I have it down. We're good."

Chase's eye twitched, but his words were encouraging. "I wouldn't want her to be unhappy. Or you."

"All due respect, boss, but she's the important one." Emmett was trained in the art of being unhappy. He could handle it if he had to be that way again.

"Agreed." Chase's desk phone purred at the same time Emmett's cell phone buzzed. "Work calls."

Emmett gripped the doorknob and checked his phone, pausing to read the message and decide what to do about it. Chase's voice faded into the background.

The text lit both Emmett's phone and his brain on fire.

The photo was Stefanie's tall, sexy boots he'd grown so fond of. Toes pointing, a concrete square of sidewalk in the city beneath her feet, that pair of knee-high boots sent his mind straight to the gutter. The following text message blanked out everything else.

How about I wear these tonight? ONLY these.

"Em." Chase's voice crashed into his psyche.

Emmett tucked the phone into his pocket as guiltily as if Stef had sent him a nude selfie instead of a photo of her shoes.

"What?" he snapped.

Chase frowned, phone still against his ear. Oh, right. Work. Chase briefed him on a potential issue and asked that he relay it to the security team. Emmett listened, his mind slowly descending to earth, where it belonged.

With a "No problem, boss," he yanked open Chase's office door and got to work.

Penelope, a glass of sauvignon blanc in one hand, was all smiles. She'd taken a break from work when Stef called her to catch up. The invite hadn't come because of a PR need, but because Pen was now her sister and Stef hadn't been a very good one. Lately her relationship with her sister-in-law had revolved around Stef screwing up and Pen bailing her out.

Not cool.

"Can I get you ladies anything else?" the waitress, a young brunette, asked.

"Just the check," Penelope said.

"On me," Stefanie interjected. The waitress nodded her understanding and walked away. "I owe you, Penelope. Also…"

She extracted her cell phone, called up the text she'd sent to Emmett before lunch and showed Pen.

Penelope's face was serious for a beat until she figured out that Stef wasn't showing her dirt she'd have to clean up, but a fun little secret she'd told no one about until this very moment.

"I love it." Pen gasped, proud. "I love his response more."

Stef grinned as she reread Emmett's response for the fourteenth time.

Hell yes. That was it. He expressed himself as he normally did: without decorum or silly emoji. Just two words, straight to the point.

"This arrangement is working out between you two."

"It's early. I'm not sure we've passed the will-we-make-it portion of the test yet."

"That's ongoing." Pen waved a hand in dismissal. "Miriam hit the nail on the head the night you announced you two were married. I'm also over everyone trying to do things the 'right' way. Your parents mean well by worrying about you, but you're an adult. You make your own decisions and if they don't accept that, that's on them."

"Right." Stef nodded, feeling vindicated. She'd been trying to prove to them—hell, to everyone—that she was responsible for a while now. "I didn't do this to spite them. I did this for myself. And for Chase."

"What about Emmett's parents? Did they have a kitten when you told them the news?"

"We…didn't tell his dad. And his mother died a long time ago." Sharing any more about his family felt like a betrayal. She trusted Pen implicitly, but it wasn't Stef's story to tell.

"I'm so sorry to hear that. I assumed they weren't close since Emmett shows up at so many Ferguson functions. If you count in years, he's a bigger part of this family than me. Does he plan on reaching out to his father?"

"Not that I know of. It's…complicated." Impossible, really, but who was she to judge?

"Give it time. If it feels like the right move to include his family in your life, you'll know it."

"That's assuming a lot, Pen." Stef reached for her water glass.

"Not too long ago I was on the fast track to building my business into a Fortune 500 company, I'd sworn off men, and I was fairly sure I'd never have children." Pen waggled her wedding band. "Now I'm married to an oil tycoon, raising a daughter and advising the wealthiest family in Dallas."

"Not just advising." Stef reached for Pen's hand and squeezed. "You're family."

Just like Emmett was. Just like he'd always been.

Except where Stefanie was concerned, that bond had taken on a new, more interesting shade. He was at her side, making her see life differently. Helping her see herself differently. She was beginning to wonder if she would've uncovered the stronger side of herself without him.

"I like having you as a sister, Stef." Pen, an only child, smiled, her eyes misting. "It's an honor."

"Same to you. You're the best thing that's ever happened to Zach."

The waitress set the bill on the table, but Pen wasn't finished with her assessment yet.

"I have a feeling Emmett feels the same way about you."

Chills ran the length of Stefanie's arms as she considered that possibility. Could it be that as much as he was unknowingly giving to her, she was also giving to him? Giving him the same sense of family and belonging on a more intimate level than he'd ever experienced? It was heady. It was... scary. Was she ready for something so...life changing?

Pen's smile turned saucy, unaware of Stef's bend of thought. "Have fun in those boots tonight."

"Oh, I will." Stef stabbed her credit card into the black book as she offered the expected response. In truth, Pen's assessment had taken hold. Could there be more to come in Stef's little marriage?

The prospect of more excited her right down to the toes of her sexy boots.

"Hello?" Stef called from Emmett's empty, dark kitchen. "In here."

She stepped into the living room to find him in front of the fireplace, a beer in hand, a frown on his face.

"Everything all right?" She'd expected to come home to a trail of rose petals leading to the bedroom after his response to her text. Well, maybe not rose petals, but she'd expected him to be at least excited to see her.

"Fine."

From a shopping bag in her hand, she pulled out a bottle of champagne. "I thought we could have a sexy evening. Sexy begins with champagne."

She'd actually thought they'd have a *romantic* evening, but the adjective might be too much for Mr. Emotes Not.

"I have a beer, but thanks."

She sighed her disappointment.

"You look beautiful." He stood and came to her, lowering his mouth for a kiss she accepted. "Can I pour you a glass?"

"No, that's okay. We'll save it for brunch." His stony expression sent an ominous shiver up her spine. "What's wrong?"

"I spoke with Chase today."

"Major mood killer." She slid the champagne back into the bag and set it on the trunk coffee table.

"He doesn't want you to be unhappy." Emmett's expression remained severe. "And neither do I."

"I'm not."

"Are you sure?" He studied her as if asking a deeper question. "Because if you're not...you don't have to stay married to me until your brother is reelected."

She blinked, stunned mainly because she'd begun thinking in the opposite direction. That maybe, if he was open to it, they could remain married awhile longer. And here Stef had spent the day imagining that Emmett's feelings were deepening for her.

Raw acceptance reflected in his eyes. "I don't want you to leave, but if you're ready to go…it's okay."

"Emmett." She palmed his face. "I don't want to leave."

He exhaled, and to her it sounded as relieved as she felt.

"Besides…" What if they ended up like Penelope and Zach? What if the pretend became real and a happy life followed? Stranger things had happened. "What if we defied odds and made it? What if we stayed married, had great sex and you continued defending my honor at public gatherings?"

"What are you saying?" His expression was tortured, his jaw set.

"It's working. That's what I'm saying." There had been plenty of prognosticating about this marriage—from the bloggers, from the public and from her family. She'd even caught herself wishing for a crystal ball so that she could see what lay ahead. But no one, no matter how vehemently they stated their opinion knew what the future would bring. Emmett and Stef were in charge of that.

She knew her husband on another level than "her brother's friend." Stef and Emmett might not have been outwardly friendly over the years, but their bond was deeper than surface. If it wasn't, there was no way she would've felt comfortable sharing a bed—sharing a life—with him. Not even for show.

And if she descended into the dark, private depths of her soul, she'd admit to feeling a ripple of wanting more. Since her "I do" at the wedding, she'd done more than pretend to have more. She'd *embraced* it. Now that it was shaping up to have potential, and if Emmett didn't want to leave any more than she did, why not explore what they had?

"You can't know it's going to work. Not after a handful of days." He turned away and scrubbed his jaw. Stef couldn't tell if he was more tormented by the idea that they could last, or by the idea that they wouldn't.

Sure, it was scary, but if they faced it together it somehow seemed doable. Scarily doable.

"Plenty of couples implode after *decades* of being together. You think they knew any better than we do?" She pulled his hand from his face and smiled at up him. "You don't have my gut. I trust my gut."

She trailed a finger over his neck and into the open placket of his shirt. He palmed her back, lust replacing some of the pain in his eyes. Stef had the stray thought that she would do almost anything to keep the pain out of his eyes. Including moving this conversation into the bedroom, where they were always on the same page.

She continued trickling her finger over the buttons on his shirt, stopping short of grabbing his belt buckle and demanding he carry her to bed for some naughty, too-fun-for-words sex.

Turned out she didn't have to.

He bent and scooped her into his arms.

"Champagne can wait," he rumbled as he carried her to the stairs. "I have plans for you and these boots."

Nineteen

When Emmett had gifted the Sparkle & Shine gala tickets to Stefanie for Christmas, he'd been a *million* percent sure she wouldn't ask him to attend as her plus-one.

And he'd been a million percent sure that the man who came with her would be someone who knew how to smile for the camera. A clean-cut, refined guy in a suit who would appear affable to any onlookers.

So. Not. Him.

He knotted the strangling bow tie at his neck, his tension rising.

He was aware that he had a responsibility to her and to her family not to take advantage of Stefanie in any way, shape or form. But he was also staunchly aware that the attraction they had for each other wasn't going to evaporate into the ether. They'd been ignoring it before, and even if they signed annulment papers today, there was no denying the hot snap of awareness every time she stepped into his personal space.

He hadn't been able to escape the words Stefanie had said about their marriage before he took her to bed that night.

It's working. That's what I'm saying.

It was working. As long as no one started confusing great sex for something more. Something…deeper.

She wasn't beholden to him. If she wanted to resume her normal life, he wouldn't stand in her way. However, he was beholden to her. Both Stefanie and the Fergusons as a whole.

Emmett was duty bound to the Fergusons and had sworn

years ago to protect them at all costs. That was what family was supposed to do—a lesson he'd learned from the Fergusons since his own father had done a piss-poor job of setting an example.

Van Keaton had taught him that when the going got tough you looked out for number one. Forget that your brokenhearted six-year-old son was as unmoored as a ship lost at sea. Forget that you had a responsibility to let family and friends know how to contact you rather than hide behind closed curtains in a shabby apartment in a bad part of town.

His parents' extended families had been distant and scattered, so they fell by the wayside after Emmett's mother died. Not helping was that his grandparents on his mother's side never approved of his mother marrying Van. He was bad news, they'd said. Selfish, they'd argued. By the time Emmett had grown up enough to recognize that they were right, his grandfather had passed and his grandmother was in an Alzheimer's disease facility and didn't know her own name, let alone his.

"Whoa, baby." Stefanie entered the living room via the stairs, a vision in a sparkling gold gown. The color made her fair skin shimmer, and her hair fell over her shoulders in matching golden curls. "You look hot."

"Took the words out of my mouth."

Emmett had seen Stefanie in a lot of dresses at a lot of fancy parties, but she'd never been more beautiful than she was in this moment.

Because he was her date? Because she was in his house? *Because she's yours*, his brain argued.

He stuffed that thought to the back of his head, where it belonged.

She swept over to him and he folded her into his arms. It was as natural as breathing. She *fitted* there.

"Sadly, my boots don't match this dress." She poked the toe of a strappy gold sandal from beneath the long skirt.

"Not complaining." He eyed her gold-painted toenails. "Though I have a newfound appreciation for your boots."

That'd been some sex for the books. Stefanie in knee-high black leather boots straddling him. *Riding him.* Her pert breasts had bounced to the rhythm she set while a sheen of sweat coated her skin as she worked them both into a frenzy.

"Dammit." He adjusted the bulge behind his fly and blew out a tormented breath. His wife *beamed.* "Stop looking so satisfied with yourself."

But he liked when she was satisfied with herself. She should be. And not for making him come—that was simple mechanics. The part that was all Stefanie was the way she'd caused his head to detach from his neck and float into the atmosphere. And when he'd finally come back down to earth, he'd been greeted by her draped over his chest, her fingers playing with his chest hair, her sultry sighs of pleasure in his ear.

She'd absolutely *owned* him in that bedroom. And that was a feat no other woman could claim.

An hour later they stepped into the ballroom where the gala was being held. The ritzy, high-end mansion made Chase's mansion look like a cute starter home by comparison. The color palette was übermodern silver and blue, the theme an aquatic one. Glass room dividers with rivulets of water running down them separated the room into sections and ice sculptures accented every corner. One was shaped like a massive merman, another like a conch shell that doubled as service for a buffet of cocktail shrimp, and there were several other smaller frozen vignettes lit with blue or green lights. Music thumped the speakers and guests stood around high-top tables with bases shaped like seahorses.

"Oh! Champagne. We must." Stefanie was a ball of energy, fitting in at the gala like she'd planned it rather than simply attending as a guest.

Emmett had landed the invitation from Sonia herself after having received a call from her assistant that Sonia was in need of a bodyguard for an event last year. He'd phoned one of the key players off his security team and Doug had picked up the gig, happy for the extra money. Sonia had given two tickets to the event to Doug, who had handed them over to Emmett without a second thought.

"I'm not sure I belong in this crowd," Emmett told his wife.

Understatement. He most *definitely* did not belong in this crowd.

"Don't be silly." She handed him a flute filled with bubbly liquid.

"Your net worth has about a hundred more zeroes than mine."

She rolled her eyes. "We didn't sign a prenup, you know. My income is your income."

"No. It's not." He cupped her elbow, making sure he had her attention. "I'd never take your money, Stefanie."

"So serious all the time."

She took a sip of the champagne, her eyes on the near-barren dance floor lit by wavy, undulating lights meant to look like water. He could've guessed what she was about to ask, but before he could argue she'd divested them of both their glasses.

"Dance with me."

"No."

Her husband had turned obstinacy into an art form.

Sliding her hands into the black jacket and over his crisp white shirt, she tipped her chin, taking in every big, grouchy inch of him. The tuxedo had nearly turned her into mush tonight. On the drive over, she was tempted to untie that bow tie and then palm his crotch while murmuring dirty, fun promises in his ear.

She hadn't, though, and now regret was a heaving, growling beast.

"It's time to admit that you've earned me."

He said nothing, but the storm in his blue-gray eyes said plenty.

She could read his pained expression as clearly as if he held a cue card. She didn't like what she saw. He believed he was beneath not only the people at this party, but Stefanie herself.

Suddenly, she wasn't interested in waiting until they arrived home to have her way with him. She was going to teach him an unforgettable lesson *and* collect what she'd wanted from him since their first night together.

Him. Tumbling over the edge of the orgasm cliff *first*.

"Walk with me." She palmed his forearm. When he resisted, she gripped him tighter. "I promise no dancing."

He walked with her as they meandered away from the crowd.

"No one here is better than anyone else no matter how much they'd like you to think so," she leaned close to say. "No one is above gossip and I've heard it all. Monique's third husband, Samantha's Botox addiction. Terrence's calf implants."

Emmett raised an eyebrow.

"You heard me."

She walked arm in arm with Emmett until they reached a curtained-off section at the back of the room. A thick swath of semisheer fabric was lit by a wall of white twinkle lights but she couldn't see what was behind them.

Perfect.

She found an opening in the material and tugged Emmett with her.

"What the hell are you doing?" His voice dominated the small space, where open cardboard boxes with a few remaining champagne glasses were stacked. Evidently they were using this area as storage.

"We should be safe hidden here unless they run out of glassware."

The fabric cast a blue light onto the planes of his angled face. So damn handsome.

"Stefanie."

"You can call me *queen*." She tugged his bow tie free, and seeing that strip of untied silk lying on either side of his collar had lust pooling low in her belly. "Guess what you become when you marry the queen?"

She began unbuttoning his shirt. Three buttons down, he gripped her hand. But he did not stop her. Instead, he brushed his thumb along her skin and then loosened his hold.

Yes. He wanted this as much as she did.

She parted his shirt and exposed his glorious chest, pressing a kiss to his rock-solid pecs.

When she dragged her tongue to his abs, he caught her elbows like he was torn about allowing her to sink to her knees before him.

Tenderly, she laid her lips on his stomach and then teased the tip of her tongue past the waistline of his pants. She brushed his hold aside and worked his belt from its buckle. Emmett's hands hovered uselessly at his sides while his eyes burned twin holes into her.

Stefanie opened his zipper, pleased to find a hard ridge pushing against the seam of his boxer briefs. At least one part of his anatomy had no argument about what she was trying to do.

My accomplice.

She took him in her hand and Emmett's head dropped back on his neck. A moan of pleasure vibrated down his form, low enough that she barely heard it over the bumping bass outside their shrouded hiding place.

"Marrying the queen," she said as she tugged his pants and boxers past his heavy thighs, "makes you—" she flicked her tongue over the head of his erection "—the *king*."

Opening her mouth wide to accommodate him, she took him onto her tongue and laved his soft flesh. He tasted *heavenly*, his masculine fragrance filling her nostrils as he filled her mouth.

His expelled breath was a gruff echo of her own pleasure as she hummed and took him deeper. She uncurled one of his fists and laid his flat palm on the back of her head, letting him know it was okay to encourage her.

He stood stiffly for a few seconds before giving in to the pleasure she was delivering. Then he let her do what she'd wanted to do since their wedding night.

Her husband was going to come *first* tonight.

She sucked the tip of his shaft, refusing to let up even when his knees locked and he growled her name.

"Stef." His voice was a rumble of far-off thunder. *"Stefanie."* That one, too, but closer. *Louder.*

She released him and locked her eyes on his, making the same request he had in the jewelry store when he bought their rings. "Let me."

He sent one concerned look at the curtain behind which they'd hidden, but before the conflict in his brain could ruin their fun, she took him on her tongue again.

Then he was no longer conflicted.

His hands encouraged her, his words praising her with gentle gruffness. "Yes, honey. Like that. Just like that."

He wound his fingers into her hair and tightened his grip pleasantly. She picked up the pace, spurred on by the popping threads of his control.

A moment later, he spilled his release into her mouth. She let him, relishing a moment that was about more than her winning, more than him coming first. She wanted him to know that he was as worthy of her as she was of him.

That they'd found forever in the unlikeliest of circumstances.

In that moment, on her knees behind the Sparkle & Shine gala, Stefanie allowed her heart to have a say.

It was just a whisper, but she recognized the four-letter word. A word that normally preceded marriage rather than following the vows.

She shut it out and rose to her feet, focusing on the here and now and the dazed look in her husband's eyes. But the blissful afterglow was short-lived when a familiar voice spoke from directly outside the curtain.

"Have you seen Stef and Emmett yet?" the voice asked.

"Not yet," a woman answered.

Emmett wrestled with his pants as Stefanie bit her lip to hide a laugh. He palmed her mouth to stifle that giggle, his brow a thundercloud of displeasure.

Evidently, Mayor Chase Ferguson was looking for them.

Twenty

Mimi assessed Emmett from one seahorse table away, her long lashes dipping to conceal the color of her eyes. Stefanie had been talking with her over champagne while Emmett and Chase found glasses of liquid that were *not* bubbly or French.

"What do you think they're talking about?" Chase asked. *Hopefully not Stef going down on me at this very party.*

"No idea," Emmett answered. Chase appreciated honesty but he wouldn't appreciate *that* much honesty.

"How does Mimi make a simple red dress look so damn tempting? Is it midnight yet?" Chase's irritated tone made Emmett smile.

A decade back, Emmett had witnessed Chase fall over himself for Miriam Andrix. Neither Emmett nor Chase had been looking for anything permanent that summer. Emmett had indulged in a few very *im*permanent hookups, but not his best friend. No, Chase had followed Mimi around like a puppy. Then he'd let her go when she hadn't successfully fitted into the Ferguson family fold.

Emmett bristled as he considered how much he had in common with Chase's fiancée.

"...toast at midnight and then I'm getting the hell out of here," Chase was saying. He shot an elbow into Emmett's ribs. "Hey. What's up with you?"

"Never thought I'd see the day where you and Miriam were reunited," he said to conceal the deeper truth.

Chase's irritation faded in a blink. He was a man in love and it encompassed him and anyone around him whenever his future bride was near.

"You never thought I'd pull my head out of my ass, you mean?" Chase chuffed at his own expense before taking a drink of his whiskey. "I'm better with her in my life. Great, actually."

Miriam's attention was on Stefanie, who lifted her hand and gestured as she told a story. Her wedding ring caught the light and winked like a lighthouse warning Emmett away from the rocks.

Warnings he'd ignored since he placed that ring on her finger.

It's working. That's what I'm saying.

Stef tossed her head and laughed, and a ribbon of longing tied itself into a knot in his gut. She'd called him a king before lowering herself to her knees in front of him this evening. Every part of him had wanted to lift her into his arms and haul her very fine ass out of here. To finish what they'd started. To take her over the edge the way she had him.

His best friend's muttered curse brought him back to the present. Chase's expression was a mask of acceptance.

"I thought your attention to Stefanie over the years was about loyalty to our family. Or to me," he added with a grunt.

"It was," Emmett said before correcting with, "Is."

"What's in it for her?"

He knew what Chase was asking. What did Stefanie have to gain from this marriage? The way Chase saw it, the decks were unevenly stacked—in Emmett's favor.

"She can decide that for herself. You know where my loyalty lies."

"I know where it used to lie." Chase raised a sardonic eyebrow. "I've been usurped."

"She is the queen," Emmett murmured against the rim of his glass, unable to conceal a knowing smile. Chase didn't hear him. The countdown had started at the fifteen-second mark and the crowd had joined in.

Miriam rushed over to take Chase's hand and dragged him into the sea of partygoers. That left Stefanie and Emmett standing at separate tables eyeing each other through the melee.

She lifted her flute of champagne in silent cheers as the countdown raged on.

Five...

Four...

Emmett set aside his rocks glass and walked toward her, breaching the gap by half. She could meet him halfway if she wanted to. He wouldn't force her.

Three...

She started toward him, confidence making her eyes sparkle like her shimmery dress.

Two...

One!

With shouts of "Happy New Year" on the air, he scooped his wife into his arms and kissed her long and hard. The same way he would make love to her in his bed tonight.

In *their* bed tonight.

When they parted, her eyes glazed with lust as the gala's guests warbled along to "Auld Lang Syne."

His wife opened her mouth to join in, and her eyes never left his.

What he saw in their depths shook him to the core. Her aquamarine gaze revealed nothing short of adoration. Lust darkened her pupils, too, but beneath that there was more.

Much more than he'd anticipated.

She climbed to her toes, her warm breath brushing over his cheek. His balls tightened. He wanted this woman again already. When she whispered in his ear, he prayed that it'd be a request he could accommodate and not the three-word phrase she'd expect him to return.

But instead of that three-word bomb, she dropped a different one—one that sizzled his nerve endings and had him bolting for the door a nanosecond later. Three words shaped by the promise of her capable mouth.

"Take me home."

"I'm falling in love with him and I have no idea what to do." Stef barged into Penelope's office, the words exiting her mouth before she could register what she was seeing.

"Oh my God!" She slapped her hand over her eyes.

"Get the hell out!" Zach shouted before taking the Lord's name in vain in a more colorful way than she had. Unfortunately, the hand that covered her eyes had been the slightest bit delayed, so she'd gotten an eyeful of her brother's naked rear.

"I had an appointment!" Stef yelled, hand still protecting her retinas as she backed from the office. She shut the door as Penelope laughed, apparently finding this very unfunny situation hilarious.

"I'm sorry, Stef!" Pen called out around another laugh. "I lost track of the time."

Zach was still swearing. He also muttered something about how they needed to move farther away from his family, but Stefanie didn't think he meant that part.

Pen soothed him with words Stef couldn't make out, and when those words gave way to the telltale slurping sound of long kisses, Stef decided to help herself to something from the kitchen.

Conveniently, the kitchen was on the opposite side of the house, far away from her canoodling brother and sister-in-law.

More minutes than she would've liked to acknowledge later, her brother entered his kitchen, his nostrils flared and his hair a wreck. There was no sign of his always present "good ole boy" smile and dimple.

"I had an appointment," Stef insisted before munching another potato chip.

"She did." Penelope walked in behind Zach and pinched his butt. He spun around and kissed her, his smile and dimple returning.

Stef let out a wistful sigh.

"All right, all right. Let's give Stef a break." Pen patted his face and smiled.

"I have to go back to the office. See you tonight." His murmur was low and, yes, seductive. Stef hadn't missed that.

"As for you…" He turned to Stef, serious again. "I'm going to pretend I didn't hear what you said when you barged in there. I can't handle that right now."

"You! I'm the one who got a look at your full moon while you were in a very tender position with your wife. All you had to hear was my feelings for Emmett."

"No." Zach put his hands out in front of him as if that could keep her from saying any more offending words. "I have to go."

Once he was gone, she shook her head at Pen. "And you love him."

"As much as hot cocoa at Christmastime."

Stef had to agree that her favorite beverage during her favorite holiday was fabulous. "That's the best."

She munched another chip, but her sudden craving for cocoa ruined the salty bite.

Pen filled a water glass from a pitcher in the fridge and sat down at the breakfast bar beside her. "You're falling for your husband."

"I think so. Why are you shaking your head?"

Had Stefanie lost her one and only confidant? Did Pen think Stef was too young, too caught up, too *whatever* to know what love was?

"I've seen this happen before. This isn't my first time helping clients navigate a marriage of convenience, you know."

Hope flared in Stefanie's chest. "You mean…couples who started out like Emmett and me ended up staying together?"

She nodded. "I'm not saying I have the success rate of eHarmony or anything, but I have been invited to a *lot* of anniversary parties."

"Your shirt's buttoned wrong." Stef grinned.

"Brat." Pen winked to let Stef know she was kidding before rebuttoning her shirt. "Talk to me."

Stefanie did talk to her, and it came out in one long stream of consciousness diatribe.

"I'm falling in love with Emmett and I don't want to tell him because I'm afraid he'll freak out since we've been married for about thirty seconds. But how long is long enough to admit you're in love with someone? Am I supposed to draw up an agreement or contract about that, too? Is no one allowed to share their *feels* until we're sure Chase is reelected?"

"Oh my heavens. All right." Pen gripped Stefanie's shoulders. "Listen. You were sitting in this kitchen when Zach was considering buying me an island when he and I were on the rocks."

"True. He was racking his brain about how to win you back." Stef remembered it well. Her blockhead brother had no idea he was in love with Pen when it was obvious to anyone watching that he'd fallen for her so hard he was sick over it.

"That's partially my fault," Pen said.

"I could never blame you. Not when it's so much easier to blame my idiot brother." Stef smiled affectionately.

"I didn't tell Zach how I felt. He didn't know I loved him. We could've saved some heartbreak if I'd been honest."

"But it worked out in the end." At the time Pen had been pregnant with Olivia and was juggling her entire life around a pretend engagement to Zach. Who could blame her for clamming up?

"How does Emmett feel?"

"Well, he loves going to bed with me."

"God in heaven" came a gruff, pained voice. "Forgot my keys," Zach called from the foyer. "I'm leaving now."

The door opened and shut and Stefanie shook her head. "He's so screwed when Olivia is old enough to date."

"Luckily, we have many, *many* years before that possibility." Pen smiled. "You and Emmett are compatible physically...but is there more?"

"For me there is, but it's probably best to wait to tell him how I feel. Just a little while. Until I'm sure that it's real."

Pen nodded. "In your circumstances, I think that's very smart. You don't want to go off half-cocked and then realize you were wrapped up in the moment."

"Right. Okay." Stef felt better already. "So...how long should I wait?"

"Not too long. Follow your heart."

"My gut's more reliable."

"Then follow your gut. You've got this."

Twenty-One

"I miss Oscar." Stefanie looked cute slumped in a padded chair at the classy downtown restaurant.

Sunday had stopped to pick up her beloved cat this morning, which also happened to be Sunday. The second his ex left his town house, Stefanie had thrown her arms around him and announced they were going to brunch.

He couldn't argue. Not after his wife had dealt with his ex-girlfriend and was forced to say goodbye to her temporary cat.

The first sip of coffee hit his tongue like battery acid. "What the hell?"

"It's vanilla cinnamon. Their house specialty," Stef chirped.

"It's repulsive."

She tsk-tsked and reached over to touch the corner of his frown. He waved the waitress over while Stef accused him of being a "spoilsport" and requested coffee that *didn't* taste like a Christmas tree was sitting in his mug.

"Salmon Benedict. How yummy does that sound?" Stef asked as she perused the one-sheet menu.

He was ordering *off* the menu. He didn't want foie gras with baby greens or savory pancakes with chives. He wanted coffee—unflavored, thank you very much—two eggs over easy and three slices of whole-wheat toast.

He still didn't understand the concept of "brunch." A first meal was *breakfast*. Period. No matter what time it was eaten.

About twenty minutes later, Emmett was in the midst of changing his mind.

He dug into his eggs over easy and found himself enjoying "brunch" with his wife.

Her stack of waffles resembled the Leaning Tower of Pisa, and he begrudgingly admired her technique of syrup and butter application. He polished off his plate, finished hers when she said she was full and leaned back to palm his very satisfied stomach as the waitress refilled his coffee mug.

"How's Chase's campaign going?" Stef asked, hands wrapped around her Christmas potion.

"You didn't ruin his chances, if that's what you're asking," Emmett said after a furtive look around.

They weren't news any longer. Two weeks of wedded bliss later and everyone was bored of them. According to Penelope, the Dallas Duchess was too busy reporting on dating Blake Eastwood *herself*, if that could be believed.

Who knew what was real anymore?

Except Emmett was beginning to suspect his own marriage was realer than anyone knew. As such, there was something he needed to tell Stefanie that he hadn't come clean about yet.

"I told him, by the way," he said.

"Told... Chase? Told him what?"

"No. I told my dad."

Her eyes widened. He went quiet while the waitress cleared their table and dropped off the check. Once she'd gone, Emmett rested his hands on his thighs and watched Stefanie carefully.

"You talked to your dad?"

"He called the mayor's office and left a message. He'd heard about the wedding and wanted to know if it was true. I don't tell him much. I never confide in him. But this... You're important."

He could see on her face what that meant to her—that he'd march into territories unknown for her. That he'd put himself in a position of discomfort for her. He would. *Repeatedly*, and for as long as she asked him to.

"I wanted Dad to hear the truth and I wanted him to hear it from me."

"That must've been hard for you." Her brow crimped. Concerned for him still. She was amazing.

"I know I haven't had many nice things to say about him but I don't think he's interested in your money. Even if he was, I'd never let him touch a red cent."

"Emmett." Stef's expression broadcast sincerity. "I don't think that. But if he needed it—"

"He doesn't." Emmett reclaimed his mug. "He said he hoped we were happy."

He took a drink, aware that the conversation was on hold. A glance at his wife's unreadable expression proved him right.

"Are you…?" He paused, not sure he wanted an answer. "Happy?"

She leaned forward and put her hand on his arm. "Yes."

So trusting. So beautiful. And all his.

For now.

"You okay?" he asked when Stefanie's eyes filled with concern.

"No. I mean, yes." She pulled her hand away and folded her hands in her lap. She blew out a breath, her eyes on the crumbs on the table in front of her.

"Stef?"

She met his eyes and blurted out, "I'm in love with you."

His world stopped on a dime, the restaurant fading into the background, the world canting to one side like an earthquake had opened the ground beneath them.

"My feelings for you tipped into L-word territory a while ago. I was waiting to tell you until the right moment. I guess that's now," she mumbled at the edge of her mug. "It's not like it's going away."

"Stefanie."

"I know." She closed her eyes. *"I know."*

At the idea of this being more—of having more—every part of him bristled. He couldn't love her the way she needed to be loved—the way she *deserved* to be loved. His past was dark, the cracks filled in with loss and distance. He couldn't ask her to be a permanent part of his life.

Stefanie *was* life. Life and verve and wealth. She was Ferguson royalty. Emmett...wasn't.

Even as he resisted, his mind played a motion picture of what it could mean to love his wife—a wife who loved him.

Them living in his town house or a house that they bought together. A daughter with blond ringlets, a son who would never know the meaning of neglect. Making love to Stefanie in the morning. Making love to Stefanie in the evening. Showering her with affection and gifts and serving at her pleasure...

But then he considered the rest of her family. Chase had warned Emmett not to let her get too close. How far would he take it when he learned how Stef felt? Would the mayor fire his head of security? And if Emmett lost his job, then what would he do? He wouldn't let Stefanie support both of them.

The idea of being a husband who didn't live up to his responsibilities, who was unable to provide for his wife—was abhorrent.

Even if he acknowledged his dormant feelings—even if he uncovered that he felt a dangerous combination of love and respect for her alongside the terror of losing her—he would ignore those feelings.

He'd ignore what he felt for her because she deserved better than the pittance he could offer.

He'd made a habit of living in the present. He didn't look back. He didn't look forward. And *presently*, they had a marriage based on convenience and a hell of a lot of attraction.

That was it.

His big heart suffered another fissure knowing he'd have to let her go. Knowing that for him, goodbye would leave another permanent scar of loss in his soul. But he had plenty of memories. He'd forever be grateful for the time he'd spent with her.

That, as much as it ached him to the bone, would have to be enough.

Her husband had turned to stone at her announcement. Emmett glared at his cooling coffee as if attempting to heat it with laser vision.

She'd considered keeping the fact that she loved him to herself, but she was tired of keeping things to herself. She was *tired* of playing it safe where he was concerned. She'd let her brother's election hold her back—let it keep her from doing what she really wanted for long enough.

Emmett had stepped *way* out of his comfort zone to contact his dad about her. And then he'd told her that she was important, and by the time he'd made vows to protect the Ferguson fortune and her well-being… Well, she'd been swept up.

Clarity blew in like a fierce storm. She finally knew what she wanted. And what she wanted was to stay married.

Emmett didn't mention her "I love you" on the drive home from the restaurant. She hadn't expected him to, but she'd be lying if she said she wouldn't have leaped for joy if he had offered up an "I love you, too."

In his kitchen, she dropped her purse on the counter and watched as Emmett hung his keys on the hook by the door. He barely glanced her way when he walked by.

"Hey." She touched his arm.

He turned, his eyes slowly climbing from her hand to her face.

"You probably have to sit with this for a while. *I've* been sitting with it for a while," she said. "I know it seems fast, but we've done something remarkable. We were married. We're living as husband and wife after knowing each other for a decade. This is something worth exploring and I don't want you to talk yourself out of it." She ran her fingers down his arm and squeezed his hand. "You can take your time deciding how you feel about me. I won't force it, and I won't pout because you didn't say it back."

"That's enough." His voice was gruff. "That's enough talk about how you feel and how I feel and how this is going to work out. This is temporary. This has always been temporary."

"Things change."

"You couldn't possibly know that you love me after only—"

"Do *not* finish that sentence. I'm sick to death of people questioning my heart and my will—both of which are *mine*. Both of which I am the authority on. I, of all people, know how I feel about *you*."

On a deep sigh, he came to her, but not out of anger and not to argue with her. Instead he pulled her close and dropped his forehead on hers. His eyes sank closed and she wrapped her arms around his waist, holding on to him as well as to the hope that this meant he accepted how she felt about him.

He didn't have to say it back—she'd meant that—but she wouldn't stand for him, for anyone, contesting how she felt. Not ever again.

"I need a nap." He put a kiss on her forehead.

"Okay."

He walked into the living room and she stood in the

center of the kitchen wondering what the hell to do with herself now.

"I'm going out...to do a little shopping."

"Okay," he called as he stretched out on the sofa.

Retail therapy had always cleared her head in the past, and right now her head couldn't be foggier.

Twenty-Two

In the week since I-Love-You-gate, Stefanie had gone shopping...a lot.

Since she'd been raiding every boutique within a thirty-mile radius, she decided to put a few of her new things—furniture, dress, champagne glasses—to good use and have a girls' night in.

She'd been practically buried in Emmett's world and had started missing her own. Namely, her apartment decor, which she might have taken to the extreme. She'd spotted a shimmery throw pillow and decided to redecorate everything in gold and white. Clean, comfy lines and crisp, bright, clean colors.

Hence the new white leather sofa, gold-and-white leopard-print ottoman, gilt-framed mirror, gold candles and sheer white curtains.

Yes, she'd done *plenty* of shopping.

Champagne poured, Stefanie glided into the living room with a tray of stemmed glasses. Pen sat on the ottoman, her white pantsuit pristine and fitting in nicely with Stef's new living room, and Mimi was dressed as per her usual in bright jewel tones. She sat on the sofa in a no-muss-no-fuss pair of slim dark denim jeans and ruby-red sweater.

"You do know how to entertain," she praised, taking a flute from the tray and pushing a lock of her wavy dark hair behind her ear.

"Is this new?" Pen patted the ottoman with one hand before taking her own flute.

"Yes. The couch, too." Stef set the tray on the coffee

table, a clear acrylic one she'd bought last year. See? She'd kept a few things!

"Hmm." Pen tapped the glass with her fingernail and looked around.

"*Hmm*, what?" But Stef was pretty sure she knew.

"It's interesting that you're buying new furniture for your place. I was under the impression you were staying with Emmett."

"I am." Stef smoothed her hand over the middle cushion and sat, aware of Mimi's raised brow of interest. "I had to have this sofa, and white isn't exactly in Emmett's color scheme at his place."

"I like it," Mimi said. Kindly. "Thank you for inviting me out. I don't spend enough time with you two."

"Sorry about that," Pen said with a wince. "I'm so busy with work and Olivia. I haven't been prioritizing my friends—or my family."

"Totally understandable." Mimi, ever the laid-back one, brushed the topic aside with a hand. "It's nice to do something girlie that doesn't require hiking boots."

Miriam worked in Dallas at the Conservation Society. She had a history of protesting the oil industry, which had caused some bumps in the road between her and Chase— *and a certain pain-in-the-keister Dallas blogger*, Stef thought with an eye roll. But Miriam wasn't only tough and opinionated, she was also lovely and had added the perfect bevel to Chase's straightedge.

"That said..." Mimi eased back onto the sofa, crossing an arm over her waist and propping the hand holding her champagne flute. "What's *really* going on with your marriage to Emmett, Stef?"

"I not only suspect you have formed your own opinions," Stefanie answered, "I also assume that my marriage is a frequent topic of discussion in the Chase Ferguson mansion."

Mimi had relocated from Montana and moved in with

Chase almost instantaneously. Stef had always been amazed by that—the way her future sister-in-law had turned away from her life in Montana for him. Although Chase owned a drop-dead gorgeous Montana lake house, so it wasn't as if they'd never go back. They'd decided to have their wedding in the mansion, but the date was on hold due to—what else?—Chase's campaign.

"Chase might've brought up your names a few times." Mimi gave her a coy smile. "I understand what it's like to leave everything behind and move into a man's house." She nodded as she took in the living room. "I *also* understand the desire to have your own space."

"As do I." Pen's tone could only be described as droll. "When Zach bought me out of my lease, I felt evicted from my own life. Good thing I love that man." But her smile warmed at the memory. At the time Pen hadn't felt *warmly* about Zach's heavy hand, but it'd been his way of showing he loved her.

"You two are meant to be, and Olivia is a princess," Miriam said approvingly. "I love Chase. I have always loved Chase." Her gaze softened on a distant point in the room before snapping back to Stef. "When you're in love it makes the compromise worth it."

"Only when you are *both* in love. With each other," Stef murmured into her delicate flute. She swallowed the rest of her champagne before grabbing the bottle and pouring herself a refill. When she offered her guests the same, she found both women eyeing her with interest.

"You're in love with him," Mimi said matter-of-factly.

"She has been for a while," Pen confirmed. "She busted into my office, and caught Zach on top of me with his pants down, to announce how much she loved Emmett."

"Scarred for life," Stef said, and everyone giggled, including her.

"Have you told him?" Miriam asked.

With a deep sigh of acceptance, Stef confirmed that she had. "He didn't react. We finished our brunch and drove home and then he took a nap."

"A nap!" Mimi's outrage satisfied a part of Stefanie that felt the same way.

"*Yes.* And then he told me that I couldn't be sure how I felt this soon."

"Oh *hell* no." Pen helped herself to more champagne. "He has no right to tell you what you feel. No one does. Only you can know that."

"Exactly what I keep telling Chase." Mimi held up her glass and Pen emptied the last of the champagne into it. "Your oldest brother is so protective of you, Stef. Too protective. But… I understand why."

"Traitor!" Stef playfully accused.

"Ugh. I know. I hate that I understand him, but, hon, I do." At least Miriam had the decency to sound apologetic. "Emmett and Chase have been friends for a long time. Emmett has been at your brother's side—at your *family's* side—for years. For him to take advantage of you after—"

"*I* was the one who proposed!" Stef didn't mean to shout, but she was fed up with everyone thinking she was a helpless little girl in need of coddling. "*I* was the one who asked him to marry me. *I* was the one who dragged him to city hall. Emmett slept on the floor of that B and B until our wedding night. Even then he approached me carefully. He's been nothing but careful," she said, her voice softening. "He's been gentle and giving and protective. I thought he was feeling more for me than the physical, but if he is, he's keeping it to himself."

"He probably doesn't know," Pen said, then added an eye roll and an explanation. "Zach."

"Great point." Zach had had no idea he was head over heels for Penelope until Stef had sat in front of him and forced him to admit it.

"Chase left me. *Left!* He flew back to Texas and left me crying in my apartment," Mimi said, joining in to air her own grievances. "On the plane ride home Emmett helped him understand that Chase was as in love with me as I was with him."

"Emmett did that?" Stef had never heard this story. She tried to picture Emmett convincing practical Chase to fight for something as impractical as true love and failed.

"It's easier to see it in others than in yourself. He probably has no idea how he feels."

Then someone should make him see it.

Maybe *Stef* should make him see it.

There was more to them than sex and a shared bedroom. Emmett was in denial for reasons she hadn't figured out yet, but it was high time he fessed up to what he was thinking.

If he hadn't realized how he felt yet, then she'd provide an opportunity for him to do just that.

"My mother has an art show at her house on Saturday," Stef said, a light bulb clicking on over her head.

"Don't remind me." Miriam wrinkled her nose. "I'm sorry. I didn't mean for that to sound disrespectful. Your mother and I have only recently mastered 'cordial' when we're side by side. An evening spent with her and the Dallas elite brings forth a serious case of the don't-wannas for me."

"Believe me, I get it." Stef had to laugh. "Just be yourself, Mimi. That's the secret with a crowd like that. When you don't put on airs they know you don't care and respect you more."

"She's right," Penelope, who'd had her own experience in the limelight, said. "It wasn't so long ago I was at your fiancé's birthday party and every pair of eyes were on me when Zach announced to everyone that we were *engaged*. Know what I did? I ate pear-gorgonzola salad and lamb and then I danced with Zach. We caused quite the scandal, but I was content to let the crowd think whatever they wanted."

While Mimi and Pen chatted, Stef was busy thinking whatever *she* wanted. Like how she planned on proving to Emmett that what he felt for her was love and nothing short of it.

Elle Ferguson's art show was in full swing. The massive house was filled with women dripping with jewelry, and men drinking enough scotch to dull the pain when it came time to surrender their wallets.

Emmett wasn't bankrolling tonight, but he was drinking scotch.

Zach ambled over, his own lowball glass filled with brown liquid, his assessing gaze taking in Emmett's position in the corner.

"Is it your security background that has you holding up a wall and keeping an eye on the crowd, or is it that you don't want to mingle with any of these stiffs?"

"Bit of both."

Zach positioned himself next to Emmett and scanned the crowd. Zach's wife was among them, admiring a painting with Stefanie by her side. Emmett had always thought Penelope was a beautiful woman, but even in a white floor-length gown with her pale blond hair in a twist, Penelope couldn't hold a candle to the beauty Emmett's wife possessed.

Stefanie's blue dress reminded him of the color of her eyes. Shimmering with secrets he wanted to uncover. Since the afternoon brunch where she'd mentioned she was in love with him, Emmett had been playing it cool. He acted on the outside like he hadn't thought another thing about it when, in reality, it was *all* he'd been able to think about.

Earning the heart of a woman you'd never imagined being this close to was humbling. And terrifying when what he had to give back was so little.

"Think she'll buy it?" Emmett nodded toward the painting where their wives stood.

God, that was still weird to think about. Emmett had a *wife*. Even an impermanent one.

An impermanent one who loves you.

"Given that a majority of the proceeds go to charity, I'm positive Penelope is going to buy something. Hell if I know what she's going to do with it. The last time we came to one of these I had no idea what she'd purchased until it was delivered and hung in our living room." Zach shrugged, embodying affable charm and laid-back ease. He definitely had that side to him, and since he'd slid a ring onto Penelope's finger and vowed to be hers forever, that side of him had expanded.

The right woman could make a man better.

Before Emmett could chew on that thought for too long, Zach spoke again.

"Anything new with you and my sister?"

"Why do I have the feeling you know something?" Emmett shot Zach a raised eyebrow.

Miriam, Penelope and Stef had spent an evening together not too long ago. No doubt Emmett's name had come up.

"If you think Pen would come home and tell me what they talked about, you don't know her. Pen and Stef were thick before Pen and I were." His smirk turned cunning. "Well. *Almost* before Pen and I were."

"There's nothing new to report." Emmett sipped his scotch and forgave himself for the lie.

To his surprise, Zach didn't try to pry information out of him or threaten him like Chase had. They talked about football, about how much money their wives would spend tonight and then about getting together for dinner soon. It was the most reasonable, and possibly the longest, conversation Emmett had ever had with Zach. He could get used to having another Ferguson in his corner.

Penelope moved on to another painting and waved Zach over for his opinion. Stef caught Emmett's eye and smiled before becoming tied up in a conversation with an older woman in front of a sculpture in the corner.

A *hideous* sculpture. One Emmett hoped to hell didn't end up in his house.

Moving across the room to refill his scotch, he imagined Stefanie buying it and what she might say when she brought it home.

"You are not storing that thing here," he'd tell her.

"It's not a thing. It's a work of art."

"It's horrifying and it'll give me nightmares."

"You'll love it because you love me."

The imaginary conversation made him smile at first but as he pictured the end of it, him agreeing that he did love her and telling her as much, the cord stringing his heart to the center of his chest snapped.

Like a shot, he realized he was in too deep.

After brunch he hadn't been any closer to throwing out an "I love you, too" in spite of Stef's profession. He'd thought that had spoken volumes. Hell, he didn't know if he was *capable* of love—not of the long-lasting variety.

But he loved her. Of that he was sure. It rang in his gut, tuning fork true, and caused a falling sensation that sent his stomach into his throat.

Chase had warned him about Stefanie having feelings for him. That if it was unequal in any way, Emmett was to walk away.

But what if it was equal? What if he was in love with her and wanted a life with her? What would Chase say then? And how would Stefanie's parents react? Already they'd expressed their displeasure that she'd married Emmett Keaton. No doubt they'd prefer someone with blue blood to enter into the Ferguson family rather than someone with a blue collar.

He was embarrassed to admit that until just now, he'd been thinking of what he could lose—of all he could lose—but he hadn't considered what Stef might lose.

If she dug in her heels and decided to be stubborn, if she was as in love with him as she'd claimed—she'd never walk away no matter how her parents or her brothers felt about the permanent union.

"Sir, may I get you a refill?" a passing waiter asked.

Emmett blinked out of his epiphany and handed over his empty glass. "Scotch. Neat. You know what? Make it a double."

Because the conclusion that Emmett had just drawn was not a pretty one.

Stefanie might choose him.

Over her family.

Losing the Fergusons pained him more than he could fathom, but he refused to let Stefanie lose them, too.

How far would Chase take his threats? If Emmett defied him—defied Stef's entire family—would they cut her out? Would she be left on the outside, like his mother was by her family when she'd married Van?

He couldn't imagine any of them drawing that line, but *Stefanie* might.

For him.

Because she loved him.

No. He would never allow her to know a life of loss and heartache. He'd never maroon Stefanie on an island with himself as her only refuge.

Even though he loved her. *Especially* because he loved her.

That thought filled him with both hope and devastation. Evidently he was far more capable of loving than he'd ever imagined… And yet he couldn't allow himself to stay. Not when Stefanie could lose everything.

The waiter brought over a double scotch, and with a

shaking hand, Emmett downed most of it in one burning swallow. He'd never ask Stefanie to live without her family. To sacrifice her stakes in Ferguson Oil; to give up the life she knew to slum it with a guy from the wrong side of town. No matter how much wealth he'd gained or how hard he'd worked to get to where he was, it didn't change where he was from.

With that realization came a healthy dose of sad acceptance. As much as he loved her, he wouldn't ask her to choose—or risk her losing her family for him. This room of richies was a timely reminder of how he didn't fit in here or at brunch or beside any of them. And Stef didn't belong with him, either.

She'd see the truth of it after a month or a year. She'd grow tired of his quiet nature and flat sense of style. She'd want someone as vibrant and lively as her and he would never measure up.

She'd miss her family.

She'd told him that marrying a queen made him king, but what if it was the opposite? What if him marrying a queen made her a commoner?

Stefanie was too vibrant to ever be common.

He wouldn't let her stay and try to change his mind.

But he would minimize her suffering.

He would end this farce with her family around so she'd have shoulders to cry on—people who loved her and could take care of her while the man who loved her the most did what was best for her.

He'd walk away.

She deserved no less and he'd be selfish to expect more.

A flash of blue sparkled toward him and Emmett's stomach made a quick trip to his toes. There was no better time than the present—and her entire family was already here.

Twenty-Three

Her husband looked foxy in black pants, a pressed white shirt and the patterned black-and-turquoise tie she'd bought to match her dress. He looked *so* good, in fact, Stefanie was considering dragging him into one of the bedrooms of her mother's massive home.

But her steps faltered as she grew closer and noticed that Emmett's face was a mask of hard lines.

"Yikes. What happened to you? Did Mrs. Morrison ask you for a donation for the city statue? She's been hitting up everyone this evening. Dad had to tell her to stop twice."

Emmett watched her darkly, his jaw sawing back and forth before he opened his mouth and said something she never thought she'd hear. "I love that you love me."

His words were gravel laden and accompanied by a pained expression that didn't match what she felt upon hearing them. She was…*elated*. Cloud nine wasn't high enough. All the complicated feelings that arose whenever she was in bed with him or next to him in the car or at his side converged into one indelible fact: she was married and in love with her husband…and he was on the cusp of admitting he was in love with her, too.

Her smile emerged, filling her with warmth, but his next words were ice-cold.

"I want an annulment."

"An…annulment?"

"Or a dissolution." He gulped the scant bit of remaining liquid in his glass. "Whichever one means I want nothing from you."

"What are you talking about?" She was tempted to pinch

herself to find out if she'd slipped into a dream. No, a *night-mare*. But this was real. As real as the guests at the party, who were carrying on their conversations and refilling their drinks as if Stefanie's world wasn't crumbling around her.

Emmett had just told her he wanted *nothing* from her. How could that be when she wanted *everything* from him?

"I don't understand," she tried again. "You don't want to stay married to me?"

She was missing something. Unless...

"Did Zach threaten you? Did he—"

"This is my decision, Stefanie." Emmett's tone was dry, his face set in stone. "I can't let you continue in a marriage where you feel more for me than I'm capable of returning."

"I'm the one who decides that." Her voice was thick with grief. Shaking with fear. The pain came next as realization set in.

He was done with her. Done with *them*.

"I agreed to marry you for one reason. It's my job to protect you."

"Your *job* is to protect my brother, the mayor. Your right, your *privilege*, is to love the woman who loves you."

Tears welled in her eyes as the pain pummeled her with rapid-fire punches to the heart. Emmett's expression told her all she needed to know. He didn't love her. Not in the way she wanted—the way she needed. He felt loyalty to her because she was a Ferguson, because he was duty bound, but he was no closer to giving her his heart than before they were married.

His next words eviscerated her.

"It was a privilege to be yours."

The ugly flare of hope fizzled out instantaneously.

Was.

He was saying he wasn't hers any longer.

"You still don't believe you're worthy of me." Tears trembled on the edge of her lashes. "I already told you—"

"You don't know all there is to know about me." His angry tone cut into her. "I grew up as poor as the families in attendance at your charity Christmas dinners. My family wasn't from a wealthy section of Dallas. Hell, we weren't middle-class. I didn't grow up in a fancy neighborhood with college savings. I lived in a house with a dilapidated roof, a termite problem and a yard the size of a stamp."

"Do you think I care where you came from?"

"No. I don't. And that's the problem. I'm a man who can't possibly be what you need me to be. You're an heiress to the goddamn Ferguson fortune and I *serve* at the pleasure of the mayor of Dallas."

His raised voice carried on the air—no doubt the entire guest list had heard every word.

"I love you for who you are, Emmett. Not for who you were."

He stepped forward and for one fleeting second she saw a dab of hope in his eyes. She sensed that he wanted to let go, lean in and commit to her forever and ever, amen.

But that hope was dashed a second later.

And his words were the final straw.

"I'll never not be the guy who lost half his family on Christmas day. I'll never not be from a broken family and a poor home. I'll never fit in at art shows where you spend tens of thousands of dollars on shit like that—" he gestured to the painting nearest him as a few guests let out astounded gasps "—rather than buy something for someone who needs it." He sent a scathing look down her dress that made her feel self-conscious. "Your heart's in the right place, Stefanie. You are giving and loving and care about people. But I'm not one of your charity cases. And I won't stay in a marriage that never should have happened in the first place."

Witnessing Stefanie's rage was helping him through his speech. He wanted her angry. *Anger*, he could take. *Anger*, he knew what to do with. He'd been empowered by anger years ago. It'd driven him to become a strong man rather than curl up next to his father on the couch and gather dust. Anger was an action. And if Stef needed to be angry to accept what he was telling her, he'd gladly be her target.

He'd warmed up for the felling blow, so he might as well get to it.

"We're nothing alike. You eat at five-hundred-dollars-per-plate charity auctions and buy dresses you wear once and replace all the furniture in your house because you had a bad day."

Stef blanched. Out of the corner of his eye he saw Chase breaking through the crowd and coming at him full steam ahead.

Fine by Emmett; he was almost done.

"We're over. This. Is. Over."

She blinked and tears streamed down her face, but a diamond-hard glint shone in her eyes. His wife. So strong.

"You can't stand here and tell me you don't feel anything."

He was tempted to lie to her but he couldn't. Not even to spare her feelings. He valued her too much—and what she knew in her heart. After she'd worked this hard to be independent and gain confidence in herself, he wouldn't rob her of it.

"I didn't feel enough." His lip curled, his gut somersaulting as the anger faded from Stef's expression and hurt replaced it. "I'll send your things to your apartment."

He turned away before more tears spilled down Stefanie's cheeks, but he heard the gut-wrenching sob that climbed her throat. It was enough to weaken his knees and his resolve—but he couldn't afford to take it back.

He'd done this *for* her.

Grateful for Zach and Chase, Penelope and Miriam, Emmett left comforting Stefanie to her capable family. The Fergusons always tended to their own.

It was a mistake to believe he ever could be one of them.

Twenty-Four

Annulment.

No. *Dissolution.*

That was what Emmett had asked for. Whichever one would leave them both blameless.

Well, *tough.*

Stefanie couldn't stop blaming him. He was the one to blame! Another tear tumbled onto the cardboard box she was unpacking. Her things had arrived today via courier. She hadn't left much at Emmett's place. Only a few toiletries, sleepwear and—oh yeah—her stupid heart. She sifted through the box again, but there was no sign of the necessary organ.

She'd entertained a few scenarios—one involving keying his SUV, another taking a baseball bat to the headlights in true Carrie Underwood fashion, but Stef's rage had been eclipsed by pain.

When they'd entered into a marriage it'd been with an understanding: that they would say "I do" and walk away when it was time. Now that he'd lured her in, made her love him and then took away her choice of staying, she regretted proposing. She couldn't see an ounce of good that could come of his leaving her decimated in a roomful of her family and her family's friends.

She stopped rummaging through the box, reminded by the shards of regret that her heart was right where it should be—eating a hole through her chest like battery acid. She hated herself for falling in love with him.

A dissolution made the most sense. She'd been completely disillusioned by their marriage.

After Emmett had left the party, her brothers and Penelope and Mimi surrounded Stef in a semicircle. Once they were sure she was okay, Chase had started for the door. She'd stopped him with a plea.

"Chase, please don't."

He'd turned to argue, but the anger in his expression quickly faded to concern for her.

"Please," she'd repeated.

She didn't need her brother taking up for her any longer. She didn't need to cause any more problems like, oh, say, Chase punching out Emmett in her mother's driveway. Besides, what good would it have done? It wouldn't have changed Emmett's mind. Just as she hadn't been able to change his mind about loving her. About making their marriage work.

And so Chase had stayed at the party and the Dallas Duchess didn't have the scoop on the dysfunctional billionaire Fergusons stepping in it yet again.

Stef was grateful for one thing—that Chase's reputation was in fine standing. His campaign was in full swing, the polls in his favor. It looked like he would still be mayor come May…which couldn't come soon enough.

She longed to skip forward a few months. To pass over the valley of the shadow of hurt and arrive at a place of peace and acceptance.

That kind of closure was an impossibility in three days' time. It was impossible for three *weeks'* time.

Hopefully it'd be a distant memory in three months. It'd better not take longer than three months. If it did she was going to move to the mountains and live in a yurt.

Emmett believed he didn't belong with her, that he couldn't love her the way she loved him. He'd been raised by a cold, disconnected father and evidently her soon-to-be ex-husband was a chip off the old ice block.

"Can I top you off?" Mimi carried in a thermos of homemade hot cocoa. It was too early in the afternoon for wine, and the warmth and sweetness of the cocoa had set Stefanie's innards at ease, if not her heart and mind. Warm innards would have to do.

Chase and Miriam had stopped by to check on her and Stef was so glad to see them, she'd promptly burst into tears. At least *they* loved her.

Chase carried in a tin of fancy homemade marshmallows. His eyebrows were bent in distress. Stef was the one problem he couldn't seem to fix.

"I'm so sorry, Chase." Her chin wobbled but she refused to cry anymore. Emmett was testing her limits, but she was tougher than this.

"Don't apologize for anything." His voice unyielding, as per his usual. The mayor of Dallas was nothing if not decisive.

"Worry about yourself, babe." That came from Miriam. She popped a marshmallow into her mouth as she sat next to Stefanie on the couch.

"I'm going to his house. Do you have anything I need to drop off to him?"

"Sure. You can give him this." Stef held up her middle finger and Mimi chuckled.

Chase's smile was sad—sad for her.

"I don't have anything to say to the man who feels nothing for me."

"He didn't say that," Mimi said.

"Close enough." Stef slurped a melting marshmallow off the surface of her cocoa.

Chase muttered something that sounded like "That thickheaded prick" before grabbing his coat off the back of a chair.

"I don't want him to love me because my big brother threatened him," Stefanie told Chase.

"He resigned as head of security yesterday," he said.

"I'm discussing that. Not you. I'm not interested in changing his mind if he feels nothing for you."

"You wouldn't want him anywhere near me if he was madly in love with me, either," she half joked.

"That's not true." Chase's eyes were narrowed, serious. "You deserve someone who knows your worth. It's all I've ever wanted for you. An arranged marriage—worse, one for the sake of my campaign—isn't what you deserve." A flicker of guilt colored his handsome features.

"Thank you."

"He's been smarter since he realized he's in love with me." Mimi winked at Stef and then looked up at her fiancé with adoration.

"You love him in equal measure, Mimi," Stef said. "We all see it."

Stefanie's heart ached for her own love lost at the same time it swelled to include the pure joy on her future sister-in-law's face. Enough of this wallowing. Mourning what could've been was a waste of time. There was too much good in the world to celebrate.

"Speaking of 'I do'—" Stef set aside her cocoa and faced Mimi on her sofa "—let's talk about your upcoming wedding. Have you found a dress? Who's your planner? What color bridesmaid dress will I wear?"

Mimi let out a sheepish laugh. "I do have wedding magazines in my purse…just in case."

"Good." Stef smiled through her hurt, determined to feel good instead of lousy for a few minutes. "Let's see them."

"I'll be back to pick you up after…after," Chase tacked on ominously before he kissed his future wife on the lips.

"No fighting," Stef warned him as he dropped a kiss on her forehead.

But his smirk and wink before he walked out the door told her that her warning had fallen on deaf ears.

Twenty-Five

Emmett trudged into the kitchen and opened the fridge, studying the paltry offerings. A box of pizza from two nights ago was wedged onto the shelf, balanced on a carton that used to hold six bottles of beer but now held two. Besides pizza and beer he had some cheese—moldy; lunch meat—scary; and eggs—not expired.

"Eggs for dinner, it is." Carton in hand, he walked to the stovetop, but when he bent to grab a skillet from a low cabinet, the world slipped off its axis. At least his world did.

That'd been happening a lot lately. It was like he was living on a damn Tilt-A-Whirl.

Since he'd called it quits with Stefanie three nights ago, he'd found a new weight to haul around in place of the fear of not being enough for her. A heavy, burdensome load that sat in the pit of his stomach like a cannonball.

Or a wrecking ball. That was how he felt.

Fucking *wrecked.*

All of a sudden his stomach soured at the idea of food. He shoved the carton of eggs back onto their shelf and reached for a beer at the same time his phone vibrated in his pocket.

Chase.

Emmett would finally face him. He'd expected his best friend to come sooner, and come in hot, his temper preceding him. Instead, Chase had accepted Emmett's leaving without fanfare.

It made sense. Chase had promised he'd choose Stefanie, which was what Emmett had wanted him to do. Emmett had emailed his resignation letter yesterday, which had solved another problem for his best friend. Chase wouldn't be forced to fire his head of security.

I'm in your driveway, the text read.

Come in, Emmett typed back. He opened the fridge and pulled out a second bottle of beer, setting it beside the other and popping off the caps.

Seconds later, Chase stepped into the kitchen and took one look at him, and his mouth flattened into a mirthless line.

"I opened you a beer." Emmett gestured, but before he had a chance to lift his own bottle and suck down half its contents, pain bloomed over his left cheekbone in a neon flash.

Blinking, he palmed his face and stared in astonishment at his houseguest. Chase's face was neutral, and if he hadn't been shaking out his hand, Emmett would've sworn he'd imagined the sucker punch.

"Should've expected your head to be that hard after what you pulled with Stef." Chase winced as he flexed his hand.

Emmett blinked, his vision finally clearing. "Expected this three days ago. You're late."

"My baby sister is in tears and it's your fault."

Emmett's chest caved in. "Still?"

He *hated* that she'd cried—that she was still crying. And because of him? Shouldn't she be over him by now, or at the very least shouldn't she accept that she'd dodged a bullet?

Chase came toward him, but Emmett was ready this time. Emmett ducked and Chase's fist swiped the air. Emmett landed a clumsy sock to Chase's gut, but it hit hard enough that Emmett steadied his best friend when it took the wind from his lungs.

Chase recovered quickly, ramming Emmett in the belly with his shoulder and smashing his back against the stainless steel fridge door.

"You son of a bitch." Chase pressed his forearm against

Emmett's throat. "Do you have any idea what you cost her? What you took from her? And for what? So you could fuck her?"

Incensed, Emmett traded their positions, pressing Chase's back to the fridge. He raised his fist, poised to ruin the mayor's perfect nose, but then stopped cold, the taste of blood—or maybe that wrecking ball weight of regret—sobering him.

Chase was his best friend, but Emmett hadn't told him the truth.

Hell, Emmett had only recently admitted the truth to himself.

He lowered his hand and unwound his fist from Chase's shirt.

"Go on. Finish what you came here to do." He backed away a step so Chase could come for him. It'd be no less than what he deserved. "I realized the truth I was in denial about the moment I stepped into this house and she wasn't in it."

Chase, chest heaving and unspent anger simmering in his eyes, paused long enough to ask, "What truth was that?"

"I gave up the best thing that ever happened to me. But I did it because I would never make her choose between her family or me. I've never loved someone the way I love her. Like she's my sun. My reason to wake up. Warmth coming at me from all angles. Without Stefanie I'm in the shadows and so cold... She loves me, too. She told me and then I had to let her go."

"Tell me it's not because of what I said." Chase's shoulders sagged.

"Don't feel bad about that. Your threat that I'd lose your family—that you'd choose Stefanie—was exactly the reminder I needed. My losing you was what I had to do to make sure *she* didn't lose you."

"Emmett." Chase's expression was chagrined.

He raised an arm, but not to deliver another mind-clattering punch. Chase palmed Emmett's shoulder and squeezed, the move almost…brotherly.

"I was angry when I said that. I would never blacklist you from the family any more than I would Stefanie. You could never do anything that would warrant it." He gestured at Emmett's face, where, no doubt, a bruise was forming. "A black eye, sure, but that's different. You *are* family, Em."

He blinked, taking in what Chase had said and trying to wrap his grieving mind and heartbroken soul around it.

He was family.

"Family doesn't run out on each other," Chase said.

"Mine does." The words were rusty, but no less true.

"Mine *doesn't*. Especially when my sister's heart is on the line. I came here to knock some sense into you. About the resignation from my team, and about the way I know you feel about Stef. Once I stopped seeing red, I realized why you were doing this. You were always loyal to a fault. You're the guy who dives in front of bullets and keeps everyone around him safe. But no one is firing at you, Emmett. You're safe." Chase shrugged like it was a simple realization. Like he hadn't just brought Emmett's world back to center. "You're home."

Since he was a little boy, Emmett had wanted a home. Not only the physical place to lay his head but also a family who would live in service to one another—who would stand by one another no matter the rift. He'd found that in the Fergusons, accepting that if he couldn't have it for himself, at the very least he could be in proximity to it.

"When are you planning on delivering this big speech of love to my sister?" Chase asked.

Then a dash of blond caught the corner of Emmett's eye and he turned to find Stefanie standing in his kitchen, arms folded.

"How about now?"

Miriam stepped in behind her, arms folded as well, her expression speaking for her. *Make it good, buddy.*

"Mimi. Stef." Chase turned, clearly surprised to find his fiancée and his sister here.

A second look at Stefanie told Emmett that his wife was as sad as he felt. Her arms might be crossed, her voice might be strong, but her cheeks and nose were pink, her eyes red and tired like she hadn't slept well outside the circle of his arms.

"What are you two doing here?" Chase asked.

"I suggested we stop by and see how the intervention was going." Miriam snapped her head over to Emmett. "Nice shiner."

"Well?" Stefanie asked, her heat-seeking gaze landing on Emmett. He was aware of Chase and Mimi stepping off to the side.

"How much did you hear?"

"Oh, something about how I was your *sun* and your reason to wake up in the morning."

He swallowed past a thick throat, not sure how she felt about his admission. She'd heard it all.

"We'll be outside." Chase took Miriam's elbow but before they left, he gripped Stef's shoulder. "If you need me—"

"I can handle him."

She wasn't wrong. And now that Emmett had a second chance staring him in the face, he'd be more cooperative. Once Chase and Miriam were gone, Stefanie strolled to the center of the wide kitchen, leaving several feet between them.

"How did you go from wanting nothing from me to feeling everything?"

"Those two can coexist."

"Not in my book."

"I love you so damn much I can hardly breathe without

you," he admitted. "But I'd never ask you to choose between me and your family. I'd never ask you to live without them when I knew firsthand how hard that is to do."

"Chase just made it clear there was no escape for you from this family."

"I know."

"I'm not the only one who deserves better. So do you." She took another step in his direction.

The relief he felt when Chase told Emmett he was home was unparalleled. Like his best friend had voiced what Emmett had been searching for since he was a very small boy. In that same way, Emmett had known what it was like to be half of a whole with Stefanie—to earn her heart and her love when she'd asked for nothing in return.

Emmett was a good husband, and with some work, he knew he could be a great one.

"I'm learning." He swallowed thickly, the faint copper taste of blood on his tongue. "I want it back. Our marriage. Our promise." He lifted her hand, where the wedding band still sat. "Us."

Certainty filled his chest. *This* felt right. Having her here, him admitting that he'd been wrong.

"I want you back. And not just back in my bed. Back in my arms. Back in my life. Next to me every step of the way. I will always protect you, Stef. It's in my nature. It's the way I'm built. But I want to do that because I love you. No other reason."

"I hear you resigned from the protection business," she said, holding his fingers with hers. "What were you planning on doing?"

"I hadn't figured it out yet." A sharp laugh left his chest. "My priority was—always has been—you. I thought it'd be easier if I was out of your life completely. If we didn't accidentally cross paths."

Stef shook her head, tears welling fresh in her eyes.

He swiped them away with his thumb. "Don't cry over me, Stef."

"I'm not." She sniffed. "I'm crying because you're so dumb."

A laugh shook his shoulders. Laughing felt so damn *good* after feeling so damn miserable.

"You were going to leave us behind."

He hadn't thought of it that way.

"Your mom and baby brother left not of their choice. But your dad *chose*. How did it feel to love someone as much as you loved him and not have him around?"

He pushed the truth from his tight throat. "Awful."

"Exactly. *Awful.* You let all of us love you, but you kept your love to yourself."

"I thought… I thought you'd be better off."

She rested her hands on his chest and looked up at him. "Dumb."

He'd missed her warm touch so much that he didn't move a muscle for fear of scaring her off.

"I love you," he said, and it was easy to say to her. Like breathing.

"How much?"

"Enough to marry you. Again."

Her smile broke forth. "We're already married."

"We'll do it better this time. We'll do it right. With your family present. On a beach. In Europe. Whatever you want."

"Whatever, huh?" A mischievous smile curved her lips.

If he had a prayer of getting this woman to forgive him—to make her happy, he'd give her whatever her heart desired. As long as she desired him above all else.

"Whatever," he confirmed, his lips dangerously close to hers. "Can you forgive me?"

She *hmm*ed, but in her shining bright blue eyes, he saw he was already forgiven. It was enough to send his confidence through the roof. His strength returned like Samson with a full head of hair. He was enough for this woman. He was the only man who could fill her heart and make her body sing. She was the only woman for him—the only one who could crack through the wall he'd been trapped behind for years.

"You're for me, honey," he said before he placed a tender kiss on the center of her lips.

"You're for me," she confirmed, gripping his neck tight.

"One favor?" he asked.

"Just one?"

"For now."

"What's that?"

"Don't make me wait until our second wedding night to take you to bed again."

Her warm laugh tickled his lips as he folded her into his arms. "I'd never put myself through that kind of torture *twice*."

She melted into him, her body softening against his as she twined her arms around his neck.

"Is that a yes?" he asked when she gave him a chance to catch his breath.

"Yes."

He bent and scooped her into his arms. "To the wedding or the sex?"

"Yes to both."

He wasted no time carrying her upstairs to his bedroom and showing her exactly how much he missed her. Exactly how much she meant to him and exactly how much he loved her.

On the cusp of her orgasm, he proposed again, vowing to love her forever. On his own release he repeated the word.

Forever.

It sounded like the perfect place to start.

Epilogue

Chase's Dallas mansion had been turned into a virtual winter wonderland. Every room Emmett walked through was draped in silver shimmery something.

Garland.

Ornaments.

Sheer material of some sort hanging on the back wall of the ballroom with curtains of twinkle lights that reminded him of the Sparkle & Shine gala.

He smiled to himself. That was one of his favorite memories.

Two tall Christmas trees stood at either side of a white altar, where their officiant, Reverend James Woods—yes, really—stood with a leather Bible in hand. James was a good friend of the Ferguson family, and Rider and Elle had been overjoyed that Stefanie and Emmett agreed to allow him to perform the ceremony.

Emmett, strangling bow tie be damned, wore a tux. So did Rider and both of Stefanie's brothers. Chase and Zach were standing to Emmett's left, both groomsmen fighting not to sweat through their black jackets.

Stefanie's dream "Christmas" wedding was happening in Texas in *May*.

When he'd won Stefanie back, Emmett had promised her anything and he'd meant it. She whipped together a plan to renew their vows, employing both Miriam and Penelope to help. After Chase was reelected the mayor of Dallas for another term, Stef pulled the trigger on her own wedding plans.

To get it out of the way so Mimi and Chase can have a wedding, she'd told him.

He loved her giving heart. He loved her passion for other people and her desire to do things big. There were no small celebrations in Stefanie's world, and that Emmett was a part of her world was a gift.

A gift he deserved.

Miriam and Penelope made their ascent up a runner littered with fake snow, both waving at little Olivia, who waved back from her grandmother's lap. Elle smiled and sent Emmett an approving nod. It meant more to him than she could possibly know. He'd tell her later, but for now he simply nodded back.

This was a fairly small affair for the Fergusons; fewer than fifty chairs had butts in them. In one of those chairs sat Emmett's father, who smiled proudly from his seat next to Miriam's mother, Emmett noticed. He suspected his wife was responsible for seating the only two single people in attendance side by side. Another subject to broach later.

His relationship with his father was a work in progress, but when Emmett finally met with him a few months ago, he'd been able to progress past some of the hurt that had haunted them both for years.

The formal music bled into Stefanie's favorite Christmas song: Mariah Carey's "All I Want for Christmas Is You." And then his bride appeared around the corner, arm in arm with her father, her smile as bright and contagious as it had been the day Emmett met her.

Like the first time she strolled to him in a wedding gown, his gut clenched with what he now knew was certainty. That feeling of *rightness*. The expression on his face was no longer the stunned shock of a man who didn't deserve her but the confident acceptance that this woman belonged with him.

She'd told him just last night that she'd decided to legally

change her name to Stefanie Keaton. That, and the fact that
Chase had claimed Emmett as an honorary brother, was
enough to cause Emmett to blink suspiciously scratchy
eyes. He'd never accepted the good that'd come his way,
but it was hard to resist when it came in tsunami form.

Stefanie stood in front of him now, having been given
away by her father, her white dress the same one she'd worn
during their original wedding. She claimed it was "lucky."

He couldn't agree more. He was the luckiest man alive.

They joined hands as the reverend began the ceremony.
Emmett thumbed the wedding ring that had been at home
on her hand for five months. He recalled the story about
the widow who wanted the rings to have another life—to
be a part of another union that would stand the test of time.

Emmett and Stefanie planned on doing her proud.

"You may kiss your bride," James, the reverend, said,
inspiring quiet chuckles from the crowd when he added,
"Again."

Stefanie threw her arms around Emmett's neck and laid
one on him. He caught her, lifting her off the floor to hold
her close. Applause rippled around them as he lost himself in her mouth.

Never had he imagined he could live a life overflowing
with love and happiness, but he'd accepted his fate. And
he had this woman in his arms to thank for it.

And thanking her was exactly what he intended to do.

Starting with today, and every day thereafter that he
walked this good earth.

* * * * *

LET'S TALK
Romance

For exclusive extracts, competitions
and special offers, find us online:

facebook.com/millsandboon

@MillsandBoon

@MillsandBoonUK

Get in touch on 01413 063232

For all the latest titles coming soon, visit
millsandboon.co.uk/nextmonth